THE
DEATH
INSTINCT

By Jed Rubenfeld and available from Headline Review

The Interpretation of Murder
The Death Instinct

THE DEATH INSTINCT

JED RUBENFELD

headline
review

First published in Great Britain in 2010 by
HEADLINE REVIEW
An imprint of HEADLINE PUBLISHING GROUP

1

Cataloguing in Publication Data is available from the British Library

Hardback ISBN 978 0 7553 4399 7
Trade paperback ISBN 978 0 7553 4400 0

Typeset in Bembo by Palimpsest Book Production Limited, Falkirk, Stirlingshire
Printed and bound in Great Britain by
Clays Ltd, St Ives plc

Headline's policy is to use papers that are natural, renewable and recyclable products and
made from wood grown in sustainable forests. The logging and manufacturing processes are
expected to conform to the environmental regulations of the country of origin.

HEADLINE PUBLISHING GROUP
An Hachette UK Company
338 Euston Road
London NW1 3BH

www.headline.co.uk
www.hachette.co.uk

To my brilliant daughters, Sophia and Louisa

On a clear September day in lower Manhattan, the financial center of the United States became the site of the most massive terrorist attack that had ever occurred on American soil. It was 1920. Despite the then-largest criminal investigation in United States history, the identity of the perpetrators remains a mystery.

PART 1

CHAPTER ONE

D<small>EATH IS ONLY</small> the beginning; afterward comes the hard part. There are three ways to live with the knowledge of death – to keep its terror at bay. The first is suppression: forget it's coming; act as if it isn't. That's what most of us do most of the time. The second is the opposite: *memento mori*. Remember death. Keep it constantly in mind, for surely life can have no greater savor than when a man believes today is his last. The third is acceptance. A man who accepts death – really accepts it – fears nothing and hence achieves a transcendent equanimity in the face of all loss. All three of these strategies have something in common. They're lies. Terror, at least, would be honest.

But there is another way, a fourth way. This is the inadmissible option, the path no man can speak of, not even to himself, not even in the quiet of his own inward conversation. This way requires no forgetting, no lying, no groveling at the altar of the inevitable. All it takes is instinct.

At the stroke of noon on September 16, 1920, the bells of Trinity Church began to boom, and as if motivated by a single spring, doors flew open up and down Wall Street, releasing clerks and message boys, secretaries and stenographers, for their precious hour of lunch. They poured into the streets, streaming around cars, lining up at favorite vendors, filling in an instant the busy intersection of Wall, Nassau, and Broad, an intersection known in the financial world as the Corner – just that, the Corner. There stood the United States Treasury, with its Greek temple facade, guarded by a regal bronze George Washington.

3

There stood the white-columned New York Stock Exchange. There, J. P. Morgan's domed fortress of a bank.

In front of that bank, an old bay mare pawed at the cobblestones, hitched to an overloaded, burlap-covered cart – pilotless and blocking traffic. Horns sounded angrily behind it. A stout cab driver exited his vehicle, arms upraised in righteous appeal. Attempting to berate the cartman, who wasn't there, the taxi driver was surprised by an odd, muffled noise coming from inside the wagon. He put his ear to the burlap and heard an unmistakable sound: ticking.

The church bells struck twelve. With the final, sonorous note still echoing, a curious taxi driver drew back one corner of moth-eaten burlap and saw what lay beneath. At that moment, among the jostling thousands, four people knew that death was pregnant in Wall Street: the cab driver; a redheaded woman close by him; the missing pilot of the horse-drawn wagon; and Stratham Younger, who, one hundred fifty feet away, pulled to their knees a police detective and a French girl.

The taxi driver whispered, 'Lord have mercy.'

Wall Street exploded.

Two women, once upon a time the best of friends, meeting again after years apart, will cry out in disbelief, embrace, protest, and immediately take up the missing pieces of their lives, painting them in for one another with all the tint and vividness they can. Two men, under the same conditions, have nothing to say at all.

At eleven that morning, one hour before the explosion, Younger and Jimmy Littlemore shook hands in Madison Square, two miles north of Wall Street. The day was unseasonably fine, the sky a crystal blue. Younger took out a cigarette.

'Been a while, Doc,' said Littlemore.

Younger struck, lit, nodded.

Both men were in their thirties, but of different physical types. Littlemore, a detective with the New York Police Department, was the kind of man who mixed easily into his surroundings. His height was average, his weight average, the color of his hair average; even his features were average, a composite of American openness and good health. Younger, by contrast, was arresting. He was tall; he moved well; his skin was a little weathered; he had the kind of imperfections in a handsome face that women like. In short, the doctor's appearance was more demanding than the detective's, but less amiable.

'How's the job?' asked Younger.

'Job's good,' said Littlemore, a toothpick wagging between his lips.

'Family?'

'Family's good.'

Another difference between them was visible as well. Younger had fought in the war; Littlemore had not. Younger, walking away from his medical practice in Boston and his scientific research at Harvard, had enlisted immediately after war was declared in 1917. Littlemore would have too – if he hadn't had a wife and so many children to provide for.

'That's good,' said Younger.

'So are you going to tell me,' asked Littlemore, 'or do I have to pry it out of you with a crowbar?'

Younger smoked. 'Crowbar.'

'You call me after all this time, tell me you got something to tell me, and now you're not going to tell me?'

'This is where they had the big victory parade, isn't it?' asked Younger, looking around at Madison Square Park, with its greenery, monuments, and ornamental fountain. 'What happened to the arch?'

'Tore it down.'

'Why were men so willing to die?'

'Who was?' asked Littlemore.

'It doesn't make sense. From an evolutionary point of view.' Younger looked back at Littlemore. 'I'm not the one who needs to talk to you. It's Colette.'

'The girl you brought back from France?' said Littlemore.

'She should be here any minute. If she's not lost.'

'What's she look like?'

Younger thought about it: 'Pretty.' A moment later, he added, 'Here she is.'

A double-decker bus had pulled up nearby on Fifth Avenue. Littlemore turned to look; the toothpick nearly fell out of his mouth. A girl in a slim trench coat was coming down the outdoor spiral staircase. The two men met her as she stepped off.

Colette Rousseau kissed Younger once on either cheek and extended a slender arm to Littlemore. She had green eyes, graceful movements, and long dark hair.

'Glad to meet you, Miss,' said the detective, recovering gamely.

She eyed him. 'So you're Jimmy,' she replied, taking him in. 'The best and bravest man Stratham has ever known.'

Littlemore blinked. 'He said that?'

'I also told her your jokes aren't funny,' added Younger.

Colette turned to Younger: 'You should have come to the radium clinic. They've cured a sarcoma. And a rhinoscleroma. How can a little hospital in America have two whole grams of radium when there isn't one in all of France?'

'I didn't know rhinos had an aroma,' said Littlemore.

'Shall we go to lunch?' asked Younger.

Where Colette alighted from the bus, a monumental triple arch had only a few months earlier spanned the entirety of Fifth Avenue. In March of 1919, vast throngs cheered as homecoming soldiers paraded beneath the triumphal Roman arch, erected to celebrate the nation's victory in the Great War. Ribbons swirled, balloons flew, cannons saluted, and – because Prohibition had not yet arrived – corks popped.

But the soldiers who received this hero's welcome woke the next morning to discover a city with no jobs for them. Wartime boom had succumbed to postwar collapse. The churning factories boarded up their windows. Stores closed. Buying and selling ground to a halt. Families were put out on the streets with nowhere to go.

The Victory Arch was supposed to have been solid marble. Such extravagance having become unaffordable, it had been built of wood and plaster instead. When the weather came, the paint peeled, and the arch began to crumble. It was demolished before winter was out – about the same time the country went dry.

The colossal, dazzlingly white and vanished arch lent a tremor of ghostliness to Madison Square. Colette felt it. She even turned to see if someone might be watching her. But she turned the wrong way. She didn't look across Fifth Avenue, where, beyond the speeding cars and rattling omnibuses, a pair of eyes was in fact fixed upon her.

These belonged to a female figure, solitary, still, her cheeks gaunt and pallid, so skeletal in stature that, to judge by appearance, she couldn't have threatened a child. A kerchief hid most of her dry red hair, and a worn-out dress from the previous century hung to her ankles. It was impossible to tell her age: she might have been an innocent fourteen or a bony fifty-five. There was, however, a peculiarity about her eyes. The irises, of the palest blue, were flecked with brownish-yellow impurities like corpses floating in a tranquil sea.

Among the vehicles blocking this woman's way across Fifth Avenue was an approaching delivery truck, drawn by a horse. She cast her composed gaze on it. The trotting animal saw her out of the corner of an eye. It balked and reared. The truck driver shouted; vehicles swerved, tires screeched. There were no collisions, but a clear path opened up through the traffic. She crossed Fifth Avenue unmolested.

Littlemore led them to a street cart next to the subway steps, proposing that they have 'dogs' for lunch, which required the men to explain to an appalled French girl the ingredients of that recent culinary sensation, the hot dog. 'You'll like it, Miss, I promise,' said Littlemore.

'I will?' she replied dubiously.

Reaching the near side of Fifth Avenue, the kerchiefed woman placed a blue-veined hand on her abdomen. This was evidently a sign or command. Not far away, the park's flowing fountain ceased to spray, and as the last jets of water fell to the basin, another redheaded woman came into view, so like the first as almost to be a reflection, but less pale, less skeletal, her hair flowing unhindered. She too put a hand on her abdomen. In her other hand was a pair of scissors with strong, curving blades. She set off toward Colette.

'Ketchup, Miss?' asked Littlemore. 'Most take mustard, but I say ketchup. There you go.'

Colette accepted the hot dog awkwardly. 'All right, I'll try.'

Using both hands, she took a bite. The two men watched. So did the two red-haired woman, approaching from different directions. And so did a third redheaded figure next to a flagpole near Broadway, who wore, in addition to a kerchief over her head, a gray wool scarf wrapped more than once around her neck.

'But it's good!' said Colette. 'What did you put on yours?'

'Sauerkraut, Miss,' replied Littlemore. 'It's kind of a sour, kraut-y—'

'She knows what sauerkraut is,' said Younger.

'You want some?' asked Littlemore.

'Yes, please.'

The woman under the flagpole licked her lips. Hurrying New Yorkers passed on either side, taking no notice of her – or of her scarf, which the weather didn't justify, and which seemed to bulge out strangely from her throat. She raised a hand to her mouth; emaciated fingertips touched parted lips. She began walking toward the French girl.

'How about downtown?' said Littlemore. 'Would you like to see the Brooklyn Bridge, Miss?'

'Very much,' said Colette.

'Follow me,' said the detective, throwing the vendor two bits for a tip and walking to the top of the subway stairs. He checked his pockets: 'Shoot – we need another nickel.'

The street vendor, overhearing the detective, began to rummage through his change box when he caught sight of three strangely similar figures approaching his cart. The first two had joined together, fingers touching as they walked. The third advanced by herself from the opposite direction, holding her thick wool scarf to her throat. The vendor's long fork slipped from his hand and disappeared into a pot of simmering water. He stopped looking for nickels.

'I have one,' said Younger.

'Let's go,' replied Littlemore. He trotted down the stairs. Colette and Younger followed. They were lucky: a downtown train was entering the station; they just made it. Halfway out of the station, the train lurched to a halt. Its doors creaked ajar, snapped shut, then jerked open again. Evidently some latecomers had induced the conductor to let them on.

In the narrow arteries of lower Manhattan – they had emerged at City Hall – Younger, Colette, and Littlemore were swept up in the capillary crush of humanity. Younger inhaled deeply. He loved the city's teemingness, its purposiveness, its belligerence. He was a confident man; he always had been. By American standards, Younger was very wellborn: a Schermerhorn on his mother's side, a close cousin to the Fishes of New York and, through his father, the Cabots of Boston. This exalted genealogy, a matter of indifference to him now, had disgusted him as a youth. The sense of superiority his class enjoyed struck him as so patently undeserved that he'd resolved to do the opposite of everything expected of him – until the night his father died, when necessity descended, the world became real, and the whole issue of social class ceased to be of interest.

But those days were long past, scoured away by years of unstinting work, accomplishment, and war, and on this New York morning, Younger experienced a feeling almost of invulnerability. This was, however, he reflected, probably only the knowledge that no snipers lay hidden with your head in their sights, no shells were screaming through the air to relieve you of your legs. Unless perhaps it was the opposite: that the pulse of violence was so atmospheric in New York that a man who had fought in the war could breathe here, could be at home, could flex muscles still pricked by the feral after-charge of uninhibited killing – without making himself a misfit or a monster.

'Shall I tell him?' he asked Colette. To their right rose up incomprehensibly tall skyscrapers. To their left, the Brooklyn Bridge soared over the Hudson.

'No, I will,' said Colette. 'I'm sorry to take so much of your time, Jimmy. I should have told you already.'

'I got all the time in the world, Miss,' said Littlemore.

'Well, it's probably nothing, but last night a girl came to our hotel looking for me. We were out, so she left a note. Here it is.' Colette produced a crumpled scrap of paper from her purse. The paper bore a hand-written message, hastily scrawled:

Please I need to see you. They know you're right. I'll come back tomorrow morning at seven-thirty. Please can you help me.

Amelia

'She never came back,' added Colette.

'You know this Amelia?' asked Littlemore, turning the note over, but finding nothing on its opposite side.

'No.'

'"They know you're right"?' said Littlemore. 'About what?'

'I can't imagine,' said Colette.

'There's something else,' said Younger.

'Yes, it's what she put inside the note that worries us,' said Colette, fishing through her purse. She handed the detective a wad of white cotton.

Littlemore pulled the threads apart. Buried within the cotton ball was a tooth – a small, shiny human molar.

A fusillade of obscenities interrupted them. The cause was a parade on Liberty Street, which had halted traffic. All of the marchers were black. The men wore their Sunday best – a tattered best, their sleeves too short – although it was midweek. Skinny children tripped barefoot among their parents. Most were singing; their hymnal rose above the bystanders' taunts and motorists' ire.

'Hold your horses,' said a uniformed officer, barely more than a boy, to one fulminating driver.

Littlemore, excusing himself, approached the officer. 'What are you doing here, Boyle?'

'Captain Hamilton sent us, sir,' said Boyle, 'because of the nigger parade.'

'Who's patrolling the Exchange?' asked Littlemore.

'Nobody. We're all up here. Shall I break up this march, sir? Looks like there's going to be trouble.'

'Let me think,' said Littlemore, scratching his head. 'What would you do on St. Paddy's Day if some blacks were causing trouble? Break up the parade?'

'I'd break up the blacks, sir. Break 'em up good.'

'That's a boy. You do the same here.'

'Yes, sir. All right, you lot,' Officer Boyle yelled to the marchers in front of him, pulling out his nightstick, 'get off the streets, all of you.'

'*Boyle!*' said Littlemore.

'Sir?'

'Not the blacks.'

'But you said—'

'You break up the troublemakers, not the marchers. Let cars through every two minutes. These people have a right to parade just like anybody else.'

'Yes sir.'

Littlemore returned to Younger and Colette. 'Okay, the tooth is a little strange,' he said. 'Why would someone leave you a tooth?'

'I have no idea.'

They continued downtown. Littlemore held the tooth up in the sunlight, rotated it. 'Clean. Good condition. Why?' He looked at the slip of paper again. 'The note doesn't have your name on it, Miss. Maybe it wasn't meant for you.'

'The clerk said the girl asked for Miss Colette Rousseau,' replied Younger.

'Could be somebody with a similar last name,' suggested Littlemore. 'The Commodore's a big hotel. Any dentists there?'

'In the hotel?' said Colette.

'How did you know we were at the Commodore?' asked Younger.

'Hotel matches. You lit your cigarette with them.'

'Those awful matches,' replied Colette. 'Luc is sure to be playing with them right now. Luc is my little brother. He's ten. Stratham gives him matches as toys.'

'The boy took apart hand grenades in the war,' Younger said to Colette. 'He'll be fine.'

'My oldest is ten – Jimmy Junior, we call him,' said Littlemore. 'Are your parents here too?'

'No, we're by ourselves,' she answered. 'We lost our family in the war.'

They were entering the Financial District, with its granite facades and dizzying towers. Curbside traders in three-piece suits auctioned securities outside in the September sun.

'I'm sorry, Miss,' said Littlemore. 'About your family.'

'It's nothing special,' she said. 'Many families were lost. My brother and I were lucky to survive.'

Littlemore glanced at Younger, who felt the glance but didn't acknowledge it. Younger knew what Littlemore was wondering – how losing your family could be nothing special – but Littlemore hadn't seen the war. They walked on in silence, each pursuing his or her own reflections, as a result of which none of them heard the creature coming up from behind. Even Colette was unaware until she felt the hot breath on her neck. She recoiled and cried out in alarm.

It was a horse, an old bay mare, snorting hard from the weight of a dilapidated, overloaded wooden cart she towed behind her. Colette, relieved and contrite, reached out and crumpled one of the horse's ears. The mare flapped her nostrils appreciatively. Her driver hissed, stinging the horse's flank with a crop. Colette yanked her hand away. The burlap-covered wagon clacked past them on the cobblestones of Nassau Street.

'May I ask you a question?' asked Littlemore.

'Of course,' said Colette.

'Who in New York knows where you're staying?'

'No one.'

'What about the old lady you two visited this morning? The one with all the cats, who likes to hug people?'

'Mrs Meloney?' said Colette. 'No, I didn't tell her which hotel—'

'How could you possibly have known that?' interrupted Younger, adding to Colette: 'I never told him about Mrs Meloney.'

They were approaching the intersection of Nassau, Broad, and Wall Streets – the financial center of New York City, arguably of the world.

'Kind of obvious, actually,' said Littlemore. 'You both have cat fur on your shoes, and in your case, Doc, on your pant cuffs. Different kinds of cat fur. So right away I know you both went some place this morning with a lot of cats. But the Miss also has two long, gray hairs on her shoulder – human hair. So I'm figuring the cats belonged to an old lady, and you two paid a call on her this morning, and the lady must be the hugging kind, because that's how—'

'All right, all right,' said Younger.

In front of the Morgan Bank, the horse-drawn wagon came to a halt. The bells of Trinity Church began to boom, and the streets began to fill with thousands of office workers released from confinement for their precious hour of lunch.

'Anyway,' Littlemore resumed, 'I'd say the strong odds are that Amelia was looking for somebody else, and the clerk mixed it up.'

Horns began honking angrily behind the parked horse cart, the pilot of which had disappeared. On the steps of the Treasury, a redheaded woman stood alone, head wrapped in a kerchief, surveying the crowd with a keen but composed gaze.

'Sounds like she might be in some trouble though,' Littlemore went on. 'Mind if I keep the tooth?'

'Please,' said Colette.

Littlemore dropped the cotton wad into his breast pocket. On Wall

Street, behind the horse-drawn wagon, a stout cab driver exited his vehicle, arms upraised in righteous appeal.

'Amazing,' said Younger, 'how nothing's changed here. Europe returned to the Dark Ages, but in America time went on holiday.'

The bells of Trinity Church continued to peal. A hundred and fifty feet in front of Younger, the cab driver heard an odd noise coming from the burlap-covered wagon, and a cold light came to the eyes of the redheaded woman on the steps of the Treasury. She had seen Colette; she descended the stairs. People unconsciously made way for her.

'I'd say the opposite,' replied Littlemore. 'Everything's different. The whole city's on edge.'

'Why?' asked Colette.

Younger no longer heard them. He was suddenly in France, not New York, trying to save the life of a one-armed soldier in a trench filled knee-high with freezing water, as the piercing, rising, fatal cry of incoming shells filled the air.

'You know,' said Littlemore, 'no jobs, everybody's broke, people getting evicted, strikes, riots – then they throw in Prohibition.'

Younger looked at Colette and Littlemore; they didn't hear the shriek of artillery. No one heard it.

'Prohibition,' repeated Littlemore. 'That's got to be the worst thing anybody ever did to this country.'

In front of the Morgan Bank, a curious taxi driver drew back one corner of moth-eaten burlap. The redheaded woman, who had just strode past him, stopped, puzzled. The pupils of her pale blue irises dilated as she looked back at the cab driver, who whispered, 'Lord have mercy.'

'Down,' said Younger as he pulled an uncomprehending Littlemore and Colette to their knees.

Wall Street exploded.

CHAPTER TWO

Younger, a man who had witnessed the bombardment at Château-Thierry, had never heard a detonation like it. It was literally deafening: immediately after the concussion, there was no sound in the world.

A blue-black cloud of iron and smoke, ominous and pulsing, filled the plaza. Nothing else was visible. There was no way to know what had happened to the human beings within.

From this heavy cloud burst an automobile – a taxicab. Not, however, on the street. The vehicle was airborne.

Younger, from his knees, saw the cab shoot from the cloud of smoke like a shell from a howitzer – and freeze, impossibly, in midair. For a single instant, in perfect silence, the vehicle was suspended twenty feet above the earth, immobile. Then its flight resumed, but slowly now, impossibly slowly, as if the explosion had drained not only sound from the world but speed as well. Everything Younger saw, he saw moving at a fraction of its true velocity. Overhead, the taxi tumbled end over end, gently, silently, aimed directly at Younger, Littlemore, and Colette, growing increasingly huge as it came.

Just then Littlemore and Colette were blown onto their backs by the concussive pressure from the blast. Only Younger, between them, who knew the burst of air pressure was coming and had braced himself for it, remained upright, watching the devastation unfold and the tumbling taxi descend upon them. Somewhere, as if from a distance, he heard Littlemore's voice yelling at him to get down, but Younger only cocked his head as the vehicle passed no more than a few inches above him. Behind him the taxi – without haste or sound – made a gentle landfall, skidding, flipping, embracing a metal lamppost, and bursting into flame.

Next, shrapnel. Iron fragments tore slowly through the air, leaving turbulent currents visible behind them, as if underwater. Younger saw the metal projectiles, red hot, softly destroying push carts, rippling human bodies with infinite patience. Knowing such things cannot be seen by the human eye, he saw them all.

The dark smoke cloud in the plaza was rising now, the color of thunder. It rose and rose, a hundred feet high, blooming and mushrooming as it ascended, blocking the sun. Fires burned inside it and at its edges.

Beneath the smoke, the street reappeared. Engulfed in darkness, though it was noon. And snowing. How snowing? The month, Younger asked himself, what month again?

Not snow: glass. Every window in every building was shattering up to twenty-five stories above, precipitating a snow shower of glass, in tiny bits and jagged shards. Falling softly on overturned cars. On little bundles of clay and flame, which had been men and women seconds before. On people still standing, whose clothing or hair was on fire, and on others, hundreds of others, struggling to get away, colliding, bleeding. Mouths open. Trying to scream, but mute. And barely moving: in the dream-like decelerated world that Younger saw, human motion was excruciating, as if shoes were glued to molten pavement.

All at once, the dense burning cloud overhead blew apart like an enormous firework. Dust and debris still occluded the air, but the glass storm ended. Sound and movement returned to the world.

As they got to their feet, Littlemore spat a broken toothpick out of his mouth, surveying the chaos. 'Can you help me, Doc?'

Younger nodded. He turned to Colette, a question in his eyes. She nodded as well. To Littlemore, Younger said, 'Let's go.'

The three thrust themselves into the stupefied crowd.

* * *

At the heart of the carnage, bodies lay everywhere, this way and that, without order or logic. Gritty dust and bits of smoldering paper wafted everywhere. People were streaming and stumbling out from the buildings, coughing, badly burned. From every direction came screams, cries for help and a strange hissing – super-heated metal beginning to cool.

'Jesus mother of Mary,' said Littlemore.

Younger crouched beside what looked like a young woman kneeling in prayer; a pair of scissors lay beside her. Younger tried to speak with her but failed. Colette cried out: the woman had no head.

Littlemore battled farther into the crowd, searching for something. Younger and Colette followed. Suddenly they came upon an open space, a vacant circle of pavement so hot that no one entered it. At their feet was a crater-like depression, fifteen feet in diameter, blackened, shiny, smoking, without crack or fissure. Part of a horse's torn-off cloven hoof was visible, its red-glowing shoe fused between two stones.

Doctor and detective looked at one another. Colette gripped Younger's arm. A pair of wild eyes stared up at her from the pavement: it was the severed head of the decapitated woman, lying in a pool not of blood but of red hair.

Far too many people were now packed into the plaza. Thousands were trying to flee, but thousands more were converging on Wall Street to see what had happened. Rumors of another explosion momentarily gripped a corner of the crowd on Nassau Street, causing a panic that trampled dead and wounded alike.

Littlemore climbed onto an overturned motorcar at the corner of Wall and Broad. This gave him a good four or five feet above the crowd surrounding the vehicle. He called out, asking for attention. He said the words *police* and *captain* over and over. The strength and clarity of his voice surprised Younger, but it was to no avail.

Littlemore fired his gun above his head. By the fifth shot, he had the crowd's attention. To Younger's eyes, the people looked more frightened than anything else. 'Listen to me,' shouted Littlemore after identifying himself once again, his voice reassuring in the midst of havoc. 'It's all over now. Do you hear me? It's all over. There's nothing to be afraid of. If you or someone you're with needs a doctor, stay put. I've got a doctor with me. We'll get you taken care of. Now, I want all the policemen here to come forward.'

There was no response.

Under his breath, Littlemore berated Captain Hamilton for ordering his officers on parade duty. 'All right,' he said out loud, 'what about soldiers? Any veterans here?'

'I served, Captain,' a youngster piped out.

'Good lad,' said Littlemore. 'Anybody else? If you served in the war, step forward.'

On all sides of Littlemore, the crowd rippled as men came forward.

'Give 'em room – step back if you didn't serve,' shouted Littlemore, atop his car. Then he added quietly, 'Well, I'll be.'

More than four hundred veterans were mustering to attention.

Littlemore called out to Younger: 'Could you use some men, Doc?'

'Twenty,' returned Younger. 'Thirty if you can spare them.'

Littlemore, commanding his companies, quickly restored order. He cleared the plaza and secured the perimeter, forming a wall of men with instructions to let people out but no gawkers in. Within minutes fire trucks and wagons from the Water Department began to arrive. Littlemore cleared a path for them. Flames were shooting out of windows fourteen stories overhead.

Next came the ambulances and police divisions – fifteen hundred officers in all. Littlemore stationed men at the entrances of every building. From an alleyway next to the Treasury Building, too narrow for the fire trucks, dark smoke poured out, together with the smell of burning wood and something fouler. Littlemore fought his way in, past a blown-out wrought-iron gate, ignoring the shouts of the firemen, looking for survivors. He didn't find any. Instead, in the thick smoke, he saw a great fiery mound of crackling wood. Everything metal pulsed scarlet: the iron gate, ripped from its hinges; a manhole cover; and the copper badge pinned to a corpse lying among the burning timber.

The corpse was a man's. Its right side was utterly unharmed. Its left was charred black, skinless, eyeless, smoldering.

Littlemore looked at the half-man's half-face. The one good eye and half a mouth were peaceful; they reminded him unaccountably of himself. The man's glowing badge indicated that he had been a Treasury officer. Something glinted and steamed in his incinerated hand: it was an ingot of gold, clutched by blackened and smoking fingers.

Younger used his squadron to take charge of the casualties, dead and alive. The walls of the Morgan Bank became his morgue. Younger had to tell the ex-soldiers not to pile the dead in a shapeless heap, but to line them up in even rows, dozen after dozen.

With supplies from a local pharmacy, Colette threw together a temporary dressing station and surgery inside Trinity Church. Shirtsleeves rolled, Younger did what he could, assisted both by Colette and a volunteer Red Cross nurse. He cleaned and stitched; set a bone or two; extracted metal – from one man's thigh, another's stomach.

'Look,' Colette said to Younger at one point, while helping him operate on a man whose bleeding the nurse had not been able to stop. She was referring to an indistinct motion beneath Younger's operating table. 'He's hurt.'

Younger glanced down. A bedraggled terrier, with a little gray beard, was wandering at their feet.

'Tell him to wait his turn like anybody else,' said Younger.

When Colette's silence became conspicuous, Younger looked up from his work: she was dressing the terrier's foreleg.

'What are you doing?' he asked.

Several hundred people sat or lay on the pews of Trinity Church, with blackened faces or bleeding limbs, waiting for an ambulance or medical attention. 'It will only take a minute,' said Colette.

It took five.

'There,' she said, turning the terrier loose. 'All done.'

In mid-afternoon, Littlemore sat at a long table erected in the middle of the plaza, the air still thick with dust and smoke, taking statements from eyewitnesses. Two of his uniformed officers – Stankiewicz and Roederheusen – interrupted him. 'Hey, Cap,' said the former, 'they won't let us into the Treasury.'

Littlemore had instructed his men to inspect the surrounding buildings for people too injured or too dead to get out. 'Who won't?' asked Littlemore.

'Army, sir,' answered Roederheusen, pointing to the Treasury Building, on the steps of which some two hundred armed United States infantrymen had taken up positions. Another company was advancing from the south with fixed bayonets, boots trooping rhythmically on the pavement of Wall Street.

The detective whistled. 'Where'd they come from?'

'Can they order us around, Cap?' asked Stankiewicz, demonstrating a grievance by tipping back the shiny visor of his cap and sticking his chin out.

'Stanky got in a fight, sir,' said Roederheusen.

'It wasn't my fault,' protested Stankiewicz. 'I told the colonel we had to inspect the buildings, and he says, "Step back, civilian," so I says, "Who you calling civilian – I'm NYPD," and he says, "I said step back, civilian, or I'll make you step back," and then this soldier pokes his bayonet right in my chest, so I go for my gun—'

'You did not,' said Littlemore. 'Tell me you didn't draw on a colonel in the United States army.'

'I didn't draw, Cap. I just kinda showed 'em the heater – pulled back my jacket, like you taught us to. Next thing I know, a half-dozen of them are all around me with their bayonets.'

20

'What happened?' asked Littlemore.

'They made Stanky get on his knees and put his hands behind his head, sir,' said Roederheusen. 'They took his gun.'

'For Pete's sake, Stanky,' said Littlemore. 'How about you, Lederhosen? They take your gun too?'

'It's Roederheusen, sir,' said Roederheusen.

'They took his too,' said Stankiewicz.

'And I didn't even do anything,' said Roederheusen.

Littlemore shook his head. He handed them a stack of blank index cards. 'I'll get your guns back later. Meantime here's what you do. We need a casualty list. I want a separate card for every person. Get names, ages, occupations, addresses, whatever you—'

'Littlemore?' shouted a man's authoritative voice from across the street. 'Come over here, Captain. I need to speak with you.'

The voice belonged to Richard Enright, Commissioner of the New York Police Department. Littlemore trotted across the street, joining a group of four older gentlemen on the sidewalk.

'Captain Littlemore, you know the Mayor, of course,' said Commissioner Enright, introducing Littlemore to John F. Hylan, Mayor of New York City. Hylan's straggly, oily hair was parted in the middle; his small eyes bespoke considerable distress but no great intellectual ability. The Commissioner presented Littlemore to the other two men as well: 'This is Mr McAdoo, who will be reporting to President Wilson in Washington, and this is Mr Lamont, of J. P. Morgan and Company. Are you sure you're all right, Lamont?'

'The window shattered right in front of us,' answered that gentleman, a diminutive well-dressed man with a nasty cut on one arm and a staggered, uncomprehending expression on his otherwise bland face. 'We might have been killed. How could this happen?'

'What *did* happen?' Mayor Hylan asked Littlemore.

'Don't know yet, sir,' said Littlemore. 'Working on it.'

'What are we going to do about Constitution Day?' whispered the Mayor anxiously.

'Tomorrow is September seventeenth, Littlemore – Constitution Day,' said Commissioner Enright. The Commissioner was a man of imposing and appealing girth, with abundant waves of gray hair and unexpectedly sensitive eyes. 'The celebrations were to take place right here tomorrow morning, in front of the Exchange. Mayor Hylan wants to know if the plaza will be ready by then.'

'She'll be clear by eight this evening,' said Littlemore.

'There you are, Hylan,' replied Enright. 'I told you Littlemore would get the job done. You can hold the celebration or not, just as you wish.'

'Will it be safe – safe for a large gathering?' asked the Mayor.

'I can't guarantee that, sir,' said Littlemore. 'You can never guarantee safety with a big crowd.'

'I just don't know,' replied Mayor Hylan, wringing his hands. 'Will we look foolish if we cancel? Or more foolish if we proceed?'

McAdoo answered: 'I haven't reached the President yet, but I've spoken at length with Attorney General Palmer, and he urges you to carry on. Speeches should be given, citizens should assemble – the larger the assembly, the better. Palmer says we must show no fear.'

'Fear?' asked Hylan fearfully. 'Of what?'

'Anarchists, obviously,' said McAdoo. 'But which anarchists? That's the question.'

'Let's not jump to conclusions,' said Enright.

'Palmer will give a speech himself,' said McAdoo, a handsome, slender, tight-lipped man with a fine strong nose and hair still black despite his age, 'if he arrives in time.'

'General Palmer's coming to New York?' asked Littlemore.

'I expect he'll want to head the investigation,' said McAdoo.

'Not my investigation,' said Commissioner Enright.

'There can be only one investigation,' said McAdoo.

'If we're having a big event here tomorrow morning, Mr Enright,' said Littlemore, 'we'll need extra men on the street. Three or four hundred.'

'Why – is there going to be another explosion?' exclaimed the alarmed Mayor.

'Calm down, Hylan,' said Enright. 'Someone will hear you.'

'Just a precaution, Mr Mayor,' said Littlemore. 'We don't want a riot.'

'Four hundred extra men?' said Mayor Hylan incredulously. 'At time and a half for overtime? Where's the money going to come from?'

'Don't worry about the money,' said Lamont, pulling himself to his full diminutive height. 'The J. P. Morgan Company will pay for it. We must all go about our business. We can't have the world thinking Wall Street isn't safe. It would be a disaster.'

'What do you call *this*?' asked Hylan, gesturing around them.

'How are your people, Lamont?' said Enright. 'How many did you lose?'

'I don't know yet,' said Lamont grimly. 'Junius – J.P. Jr's son – was right in the way of it.'

'He wasn't killed, was he?' asked Enright.

'No, but his face was a bleeding mess. There's only one thing I know for certain: the Morgan Bank will open for business as usual tomorrow morning at eight o'clock sharp.'

Commissioner Enright nodded. 'There we are then,' he said. 'Business as usual. That will be all, Captain Littlemore.'

When Littlemore returned to the table where his men were interviewing witnesses, Stankiewicz was waiting for him with a businessman who was sweating profusely. 'Hey, Cap,' said Stankiewicz, 'you better talk to this guy. He says he has evidence.'

'I swear to you I didn't know,' said the businessman anxiously. 'I thought it was a joke.'

'What's he talking about, Stanky?' Littlemore asked.

'This, sir,' said Stankiewicz, handing Littlemore a postcard bearing a Toronto postmark, dated September 11, 1920, and addressed to George

F. Ketledge at 2 Broadway, New York, New York. The postcard bore a short message:

> *Greetings:*
>
> *Get out of Wall Street as soon as the gong strikes at 3 o'clock Wednesday, the fifteenth. Good luck,*
>
> > *Ed*

'You're Ketledge?' Littlemore asked the businessman.

'That's right.'

'When'd you get this?' asked Littlemore.

'Yesterday morning, the fifteenth. I never imagined it was serious.'

'Who's Ed?'

'Edwin Fischer,' said Ketledge. 'Old friend. Employee of the French High Commission.'

'What's that?'

'I'm not entirely certain. It's at 65 Broadway, just a block from my offices. Have I committed a crime?'

'No,' answered Littlemore. 'But you're staying here to give these officers a full statement. Boys, I'm taking a quick trip to 65 Broadway. Say, Ketledge, they speak English at this French Commission?'

'I'm sure I don't know,' said Ketledge.

Several hours having passed, Colette announced to Younger that they were almost out of bandages. 'We're running out of antiseptic too. I'll go to the pharmacy.'

'You don't know the way,' said Younger.

'We're not in the trenches anymore, Stratham. I can ask. I have to find a telephone anyway to call Luc. He'll be worried.'

'All right – take my wallet,' Younger replied.

She kissed him on the cheek, then stopped: 'You remember what you said?'

He did: 'That there was no war in America.'

At the foot of the steps she ran into Littlemore. The detective called up to Younger, 'Mind if I borrow the Miss for a half-hour, Doc?'

'Go ahead. But come up here, would you?' said Younger, bent over a patient.

'What is it?' asked the detective, ascending the steps.

'I think I saw something, Littlemore,' said Younger without interrupting his work. 'Nurse, my forehead.'

The nurse wiped Younger's brow; her cloth came off soaked and red.

'That your blood, Doc?' asked Littlemore.

'No,' said Younger untruthfully. Apparently he'd been grazed by a piece of shrapnel when the bomb went off. 'It was just after the blast. Something out of place.'

'What?'

'I don't know. But I think it's important.'

Littlemore waited for Younger to elaborate, but nothing followed. 'That's real helpful, Doc,' said the detective. 'Keep it coming.'

Littlemore trotted back down the stairs, shaking his head, and led Colette away. Younger shook his too, but for a different reason. He could not rid himself of the sensation of being unable to recall something. It was almost there, at the edges of his memory: a fog or storm, a blackboard – a blackboard? – and someone standing in front of it, writing on it, but not with chalk. With a rifle?

'Shouldn't you take a rest, Doctor?' the nurse asked. 'You haven't stopped for even a sip of water.'

'If there's water to spare,' said Younger, 'use it to wash this floor.'

The bells of Trinity Church had tolled seven when Younger finished. The wounded were gone, his nurse gone, the terrier with the little gray beard gone, the dead gone.

The summer evening was incongruously pleasant. A few policemen still collected debris, placing it in numbered canvas bags, but Wall Street was nearly empty. Younger saw Littlemore approaching, covered in dust. Younger's own shirt and trousers were soaked with blood, browned and caked. He patted his pockets for a cigarette and touched his head above the right ear; his fingertips came away red.

'You don't look so good,' said Littlemore, looking in through the doorway.

'I'm fine,' Younger replied. 'Might have been finer if you hadn't deprived me of my assistant medical officer. You said you only needed her for half an hour.'

'Colette?' asked Littlemore. 'I did.'

'You did what?'

'I brought her back after half an hour. She was going to a drugstore.'

Neither man spoke.

'Where's a telephone?' Younger asked. 'I'll try the hotel.'

Inside the Stock Exchange, Younger called the Commodore Hotel. Miss Rousseau, he was informed, had not been back since the early morning. Younger asked to be put through to her room, to speak with her brother.

'I'm sorry, Dr Younger,' said the receptionist, 'but he hasn't come back either.'

'The boy went out?' asked Younger. 'By himself?'

'By himself?' said the receptionist in a peculiar voice.

'Yes – did he go out by himself?' asked Younger, irritation rising along with concern.

'No, sir. You were with him.'

CHAPTER THREE

THE ATTACK ON Wall Street of September 16, 1920, was not only the deadliest bombing in the nation's hundred-fifty-year history. It was the most incomprehensible. Who would detonate a six-hundred-pound explosive in one of New York's busiest plazas at the most crowded time of day?

Only one word, according to the *New York Times*, could describe the perpetrators of such an act: *terrorists*. The *Washington Post* opined that the attack was 'an act of war,' demanding an immediate counterattack from the United States Army. But war with what country, what foreign nation, what enemy? There was no answer. In this respect the attack on Wall Street was not only appalling, but appallingly familiar.

Fifteen million souls had perished in the Great War – a number almost beyond human compass. Yet despite this staggering toll, the war had been fathomable. Armies mobilized and demobilized. Countries were invaded and invaders repelled. Men went to the front and, much of the time, returned. War had limits. War came to an end.

But by 1920 the world had become used to a new kind of war. It had started a quarter-century earlier, with a wave of assassinations. In 1894, the President of France was murdered; in 1898, the Empress of Austria; in 1900, the King of Italy; in 1901, President McKinley of the United States; in 1912, the Prime Minister of Spain; and of course in 1914, a Hapsburg archduke, launching the great conflagration. Assassination as such was nothing new, but these killings were different.

Most of them lacked any clear, concrete objective. They lacked even the erratic rationality of a festering grudge.

All, however, were somehow the same. All were committed by poor young men, usually foreign, linked by shadowy international networks and sharing in a death-dealing ideology that made them seem almost to welcome their own demise. The assassinations appeared to be an attack on all Western nations, on civilization itself. The perpetrators were called by many names: anarchists, socialists, nationalists, fanatics, extremists, communists. But in the newspapers and in public oratory, one name joined them all: *terrorist*.

In 1919, the bombings on American soil began. On April 28, a small brown package was delivered to the Mayor of Seattle, who had recently broken up a general strike. The return address said 'Gimbel Brothers'; a handwritten label promised 'Novelty – a sample.' Inside lay a wooden tube that was indeed a novelty. It contained an acid detonator and a stick of dynamite. The crude bomb failed to explode. But the next day an identical novelty, delivered to the home of a former United States senator, blew off the hands of the unlucky housemaid who opened it.

The following evening, riding home from work in a New York subway, a mail clerk reading the newspaper realized that he had seen over a dozen similar packages that very day. Rushing back to the post office, he found these parcels still undelivered – for insufficient postage. Eventually, thirty-six 'novelty' package bombs were discovered, targeting an eclectic roster of personages including John D. Rockefeller and J. P. Morgan.

A month later, synchronized explosions lit up the night in eight different American cities at the same hour. The targets were houses – of an Ohio mayor, a Massachusetts legislator, a New York judge. By far the boldest of these attacks was the blast at the home of the nation's Attorney General, A. Mitchell Palmer, in Washington, DC. Here the bomber blundered. As he mounted Palmer's front steps, his explosive detonated while still in his hands, leaving only scattered body fragments for the police to pick through.

Palmer responded with sweeping raids, his G-men breaking down doors all over America, whether by day or under cover of night. Thousands were rounded up, detained, or deported, with or without charge. Telephones were tapped. Mail was intercepted. Suspects were 'forcefully interrogated.' The perpetrators, however, were never identified.

Yet however monstrous, all this murder was directed at public men. Ordinary people felt no personal danger. They felt no need to alter the way they lived. That skin of felt security was burned away when Wall Street went up in flames on September 16, 1920.

Crossing the police barricade, Younger and Littlemore were immediately set upon. A large crowd – much larger than Younger had realized – pressed in at the roadblocks around the blast area. Women with infants in their arms tugged at Younger's sleeves, begging for news of their husbands. Anxious voices called out in the dusk, wanting to know what had happened.

Littlemore tried to answer every entreaty. He reassured one woman that no children had been killed. To others he explained where they could go to see a list of the casualties. All the rest he advised firmly but without temper to go back home and wait for more news tomorrow.

Even the officers on duty, keeping the crowd at bay, were not immune from the general anxiety. One of them whispered to Littlemore as they passed: 'Say, Lieutenant, was it Bolsheviks? They say it was Bolsheviks.'

'Naw, it was a gas pipe, is all,' another officer chimed in, holding up a newspaper as evidence. 'Mayor Hylan says so. Ain't that right, Lieutenant?'

'Give me that,' answered Littlemore.

The detective took the paper, which an on-duty policeman should not have been carrying. It was the *Sun*'s four-page extra edition. 'Can you believe this?' asked Littlemore, reading from the inner pages. 'Hylan's telling everybody it was a busted gas main.'

As both Younger and Littlemore knew, the most important fact about the blackened crater they had seen in the plaza was something that wasn't there. There was no fissure, no rupture in the pavement, as there would have been had a gas pipe broken and sent a geyser of flame into the street.

'That was a bomb crater,' said Younger.

'That's sure what it looked like,' replied Littlemore, still reading as they walked.

'That's what it was,' said Younger. 'Will you put the goddamned paper away?'

'Geez,' said the detective, throwing the paper into the backseat.

'Where's the crank?' asked Younger, in front of the vehicle, eager to get it running.

'You *have* been away. There's no crank; they have starter pedals now,' said Littlemore. He saw the worry in Younger's eyes. 'Come on, Doc, she's fine. She went back to the hotel, took the kid out for dinner, left a message for you at the desk, and they bollixed up the message – that's all.'

At the corner of Forty-fourth Street and Lexington Avenue, one block from the Commodore Hotel, stood a public establishment called the Bat and Table. Alongside it lay a narrow, unlit alley, which, used primarily for the collection of garbage, was typically empty of an evening. Atypically, it was occupied on the evening of September 16, 1920, by a motorcar with four doors, a closed roof, and an idling engine.

The driver of this vehicle was not a genteel man. He had a fat, round, hairless face shiny with perspiration. His shoulders were so massed up within his threadbare jacket that they left no neck at all. His hat was at least one size too small, so that his ears bulged out beneath it. Although the car was stationary, he kept his hands glued to the steering wheel, and the woman next to him could see thick short thick hairs protruding from his knuckles. That woman was Colette Rousseau, whose hands were tied behind her.

In the backseat was another individual who conveyed an air of uncongeniality less by his musculature, of which he possessed little, than by a pistol, which he pointed at Colette. His small, wiry torso was housed in an overlarge checked suit, rank with stale beer. His breath was equally aromatic; it smelled of raw onion.

These two men exchanged words in a language Colette could neither understand nor identify. The driver was evidently named Zelko; the man in the backseat, Miljan. Colette said nothing. A slight bruise showed over her left eye.

A rear door opened. Into the backseat a boy was flung headlong, followed quickly by another man, taller than the other two, dressed not well, but better, in a striped suit that was once a decent piece of gentlemen's apparel. He had so much facial hair, copious and black, that his mouth was invisible; his eyes peered out from a thicket of eyebrow and whisker. He slammed the door behind him and barked orders in the same unidentifiable language; the other two men called him Drobac.

Evidently Drobac's orders were to tie up the boy and get the car moving. At least that's what the other two began to do. In French, Colette asked Luc if he was hurt. He shook his head. She went on quietly but quickly, 'It's all a mistake. Soon they will realize and let us go.'

Miljan spat a few incomprehensible sentences that stank of onion. Drobac silenced him with a curt shout.

'They can't understand us in French,' Colette whispered rapidly to Luc. 'He didn't find the box, did he? Just nod, yes or no.'

Drobac barked unintelligibly; the driver, Zelko, jerked the car to a halt. '*Quelle boîte?*' said Drobac, in French. 'What box?'

Colette, who had been facing her brother in the rear seat, now swung back around, her eyes fixed on the street ahead.

'What box?' Drobac repeated.

'It's nothing – only my brother's toy box,' said Colette too quickly. 'His precious toys, he is always worried about them.'

'Toy box. Yes. Toy box.' Drobac grabbed Luc by the shirt collar and placed the barrel of a gun to the boy's head. Colette screamed. One of Zelko's hairy-knuckled hands flew to her face, slapping her. 'You lie again,' said Drobac, keeping his pistol in contact with the temple of the struggling boy, 'I kill him.'

'Please − I beg you − it's something for sick people,' entreated Colette. 'It's extremely valuable − I mean, valuable for curing people. It won't be valuable to you. You'll never be able to sell it. Everyone will know it's stolen.'

Drobac gave a command to Zelko, who swung the vehicle into reverse. They headed back to the unlit alley beside the Bat and Table. Drobac smiled. So, inwardly and imperceptibly, did Colette.

Younger, at the front desk of the Commodore Hotel, learned from the reception clerk that no one was in Miss Rousseau's room. Neither the lady nor her brother had returned. 'My key,' said Younger, wondering if they might have gone to his room.

'And you are?' asked the clerk.

'Dr Stratham Younger,' said Younger.

'Certainly, sir,' said the clerk. 'Might I ask for some identification?'

Younger reached for his wallet before remembering that he had given it to Colette. 'I don't have any.'

'I see,' said the clerk. 'Perhaps you'd like to speak with the house manager?'

'Get him,' said Younger.

The clerk's information − that no one was in Miss Rousseau's room − was incorrect. Twelve stories overhead, a man with black whiskers all around his face and black gloves on his hands stood before Colette's open closet, looking with irritation at a leather-lined case, the size of a small trunk. The case, Drobac had discovered, was too heavy for him to carry inconspicuously through the lobby and out of the hotel. Laboring, he worked the unwieldy box off the shelf and lowered it to the floor.

★　★　★

The ornate hotel lobby was strangely hushed. People huddled in anxious knots, below palm trees and between marble columns, whispering, disbelieving, each describing where they had been when they heard or heard about the catastrophic explosion on Wall Street. It was the same everywhere, Younger had noticed as he and Littlemore drove uptown: people were paralyzed, as if the reverberations of the blast were still propagating up and down the city, shaking the ground, confusing the air.

He felt perversely like shouting at them. This was not death, he wanted to say. They had no idea what death looked like.

'You are the man claiming to be Dr Younger?' asked the hotel manager, a tall, bespectacled man in white gloves and evening attire.

'No,' said Younger evenly. 'I *am* Dr Younger.'

The manager, eyeing distastefully Younger's blood-spattered suit, removed the conical receiver from the front desk telephone and held it in suspense as if it were a weapon. 'On the contrary,' he said. 'I personally gave Dr Younger his key two hours ago, after receiving incontestable proofs of identity.' Into the receiver, he added primly to the hotel operator, 'Get me the police.'

'They're already here,' answered a voice behind Younger. Littlemore, having parked his car, now joined Younger at the front desk. He displayed his badge. 'Dr Younger's wallet's been stolen. You gave his key to an impostor.'

The manager regarded the disheveled and dust-covered Littlemore with undiminished suspicion. He scrutinized Littlemore's badge through his spectacles and, still holding the telephone receiver to his ear, declared his intention to speak with the police to 'confirm the detective's identity.'

Cigarette protruding dangerously close to his jungle of beard, Drobac rifled the contents of Colette's laboratory case. He found two flasks, a half-dozen rubber-stoppered test tubes filled with bright green and yellow powders, and several jagged-edged pieces of ore. These rocks, as large as sirloin steaks, were jet-black, but they glistened as if made of congealed oil, and they were marbled with rich veins of gleaming gold and silver. Drobac stuffed his pockets, leaving nothing behind.

'Any dental offices in the hotel?' Littlemore asked the manager while the latter waited for his telephone call to be answered.

'Certainly not,' said the manager. 'The lines are engaged, I'm afraid. Perhaps you'd like to take a seat?'

'I got a better idea,' said Littlemore, dangling a set of handcuffs over the counter. 'You hand over the key or I take you downtown for obstructing a police investigation. That way you can confirm my identity in person.'

The manager handed over the key.

Inside a plush elevator car, the detective and doctor ascended in silence. When the doors finally opened, Younger exited so precipitously he knocked the hat off a man who had been waiting for the car. Younger noticed the man's profuse beard and teeming mustache. But he didn't notice the peculiar way the man's dingy striped jacket tugged down at his shoulders − as if his pockets were loaded with shot.

Younger apologized, reaching for the hat on the carpet. Drobac got to it first.

'Going down,' said the elevator operator.

Whatever Younger hoped or feared to find in Colette's hotel room, he didn't find it. Instead, at the end of an endless corridor, he and Littlemore found − a hotel room. The bed was made. The cot was made. The suitcases were undisturbed. On a coffee table, sprays of burnt matchsticks fanned out in tidy semicircles: the boy's handiwork.

Only Colette's lead-lined laboratory case, lying open and empty in front of her closet, testified to a trespass. Cigarette odor hung in the stifled air.

'That's what they came for,' said Younger grimly. 'That case.'

'Nope,' said the detective, opening closets and checking behind curtains. 'They left the case.'

Younger looked at Littlemore with incredulity and vexation. He took a step toward the open laboratory box.

'Don't touch it, Doc,' the detective added, glancing into the bathroom. 'We'll want to dust it for prints. What was inside?'

'Rare elements,' said Younger. 'For a lecture she was supposed to give. The radium alone was worth ten thousand dollars.'

The detective whistled: 'Who knew?'

'Besides a professor in New Haven, I can think of only one person, and she's no kidnapper.'

Littlemore, checking under the bed, replied: 'The old lady you and Colette visited this morning?'

'That's right.'

With his magnifying glass and a tweezer, the detective began examining, on hands and knees, the carpet surrounding Colette's laboratory case. 'Wait a second. Wait a second.'

'What?' asked Younger.

Littlemore, having pried a bit of cigarette ash from the thick pile of the carpet, was rubbing it between thumb and forefinger. 'This is still warm,' he said. 'Somebody just left.'

Littlemore bolted back into the hall, heading for the elevators. Younger didn't follow. Instead he went to Colette's balcony door and stepped out into the night. Far below, in the light flooding out of the hotel's front doors, Younger saw the man he somehow knew he would see, standing by the curb in his striped suit.

Younger called out: 'You!'

No one heard. Younger was too high up, and the street noise was too great. A car skidded up next to the striped suit, its rear door opening from within. The sudden, swerving halt threw a small body – a little boy's body – half out of the car. A moment later, the boy was snatched back inside by invisible hands.

'No,' said Younger. Then he called out at the top of his lungs: 'Stop that car!'

This time Drobac hesitated. He looked up, searching but not finding the source of the cry. No one else took notice. Younger shouted the same futile words again as the man climbed into the backseat, and again as the car sped down Park Avenue, its headlamps and taillamps going suddenly dark, disappearing into the night. Two drops of Younger's blood, flung from his hair as he cried out, drifted downward and broke on the sidewalk not far from where the man had stood.

By the time the echo of Younger's voice had died, Littlemore was back in the room, having heard the doctor's shouts.

'It was the man at the elevator,' said Younger.

'The guy with the hair,' replied Littlemore, 'and the bulging pockets? Are you sure?'

Younger looked at the detective. Then he slowly lifted the coffee table – the one with Luc's matches on it – off the floor and hurled it into a mirrored closet door. There was no satisfying explosion of glass. The mirror only cracked, as did the coffee table. Burnt matchsticks spun in the air, like maple seedpods spiraling down in autumn.

'Jesus, Doc,' said Littlemore.

'You saw something in his pockets,' Younger replied quietly. 'Why didn't you stop him?'

'For having something in his pockets?'

'If you had stationed a single man in front of the hotel,' said Younger, 'we could have caught him.'

'I doubt it,' said Littlemore. 'You know you're bleeding pretty good.'

'What do you mean you doubt it?'

'If I put a uniform outside the front door,' the detective explained, 'the guy doesn't use the front door. He goes out a side door. Or a back door. We would have needed six men minimum.'

'Then why didn't you bring six men?' asked Younger, advancing toward Littlemore.

'Easy, Doc.'

'Why didn't you?'

'You want to know why? Besides the fact that I had no reason to,

I couldn't have gotten six men if I had tried. I couldn't have gotten one. The force is a little busy tonight, in case you hadn't noticed. I'm not even supposed to be here.'

Instead of responding, Younger shoved Littlemore in the chest. 'Go back then.'

'What's the matter with you?' asked Littlemore.

'I'll tell you why you didn't stop him. You weren't paying any goddamned attention.'

'Me? Who waited four hours before noticing that his girlfriend had disappeared when she was supposed to be gone for half an hour?'

'Because *you* took her,' shouted Younger, taking a straight left jab at Littlemore's head. The detective ducked this blow, but Younger, who knew how to fight, had thrown a punch designed to make Littlemore do just that. Younger followed it with a clean right, putting Littlemore on the carpet and taking a lamp down with him.

'Son of a gun,' said Littlemore from the floor, his lip bloody.

He sprang toward Younger, charging low and driving him backward all the way across the room. Younger's head snapped back against the wall. When they came to a standstill, Littlemore had his right fist raised and ready, but Younger was staring blankly over his shoulder.

'How many died today?' asked Younger. 'Thirty?'

'Thirty-six,' said Littlemore, fist still raised.

'Thirty-six,' repeated Younger contemptuously. 'And the whole city's paralyzed. I hate the dead.'

Neither man spoke. Younger sank to a sitting position on the floor. Littlemore sat down near him.

'I'm taking you to a hospital,' said Littlemore.

'Try it.'

'You know I outrank you,' said the detective.

Younger raised an eyebrow.

'Captain beats lieutenant,' added Littlemore.

'A police captain doesn't outrank a doughboy in boot camp.'

'Captain beats lieutenant,' repeated Littlemore.

A silence.

'What do you mean you hate the dead?' asked Littlemore.

'Luc wrote that to me – Colette's brother. He doesn't talk. I was – what was I doing? I was reading a book he'd given me. Then he handed me a note that said, "I hate the dead."' Younger looked at the detective. 'Sorry about – about—'

'Slugging me in the jaw?'

'Blaming you,' said Younger. 'It's my fault. My fault they're in America. My fault she went off by herself.'

'We'll get them back,' said Littlemore.

Younger described what he'd witnessed from the balcony. Littlemore asked him what kind of car he had seen. Younger couldn't say. He'd been too far overhead. He couldn't even be sure of the color.

'We'll get them back,' Littlemore repeated.

'How?' asked Younger.

'Here's what we do. I go to headquarters and put out a bulletin. We'll have the whole force looking for this guy by tomorrow. You wait here in case they send a ransom note. Meantime I question the old lady you met with. What's her name?'

'Mrs William B. Meloney. Thirty-one West Twelfth.'

'Maybe she told some other people about the samples Colette brought with her.'

'It's possible,' said Younger.

'So maybe the wrong kind of person found out.' At the doorway, Littlemore added: 'Do me a favor. Patch up your head.'

CHAPTER FOUR

L IBERTY, EQUALITY, FRATERNITY — *terrorist*: the word comes from
the French Revolution.

The Reign of Terror was the name given to Robespierre's ferocious
rule. Hundreds of thousands of men and women were branded 'enemies
of the state,' jailed, starved, deported, tortured. Forty thousand were
executed. 'Virtue and terror,' proclaimed Robespierre, were the two
imperatives of the revolution, for 'terror is nothing other than justice
– prompt, severe, inflexible justice.' Those who supported him were
called *Terroristes*.

A century later, another revolutionary took a similar stand. 'We
cannot reject terror,' wrote a man calling himself Lenin; 'it is the one
form of military action that may be absolutely essential.' His disciples
became the new century's 'terrorists.'

But with a difference. In France, terror had been an instrument of
the state. Now terror was directed against the state. Originally, the
terrorist was a well-bred French despot, haughtily claiming the authority
of law and government. Now the terrorist became a seedy, bearded,
furtive murderer – a Slav, a Jew, an Italian planting his crude bomb
or hiding a pistol inside his shabby coat. It was one such terrorist, a
Serb, who in 1914 assassinated Archduke Hans Ferdinand of Austria,
launching the Great War.

The Germans wanted war, undoubtedly, but it would never have
materialized without a keenness for battle on the part of ordinary
young men all across Europe. Soon enough, their readiness to die for

their countries would be rewarded in a hell they had not foreseen, where sulfuric gases ate the flesh off living men crouched ankle-deep in freezing, stagnant water. But in the hot summer of 1914, European men of every class and station wanted nothing more than an opportunity to meet and mete out death on the battlefield.

Comparable feelings grew in the United States, especially when German submarines attacked American merchant ships on the high seas. Even as President Wilson steadfastly maintained neutrality, the drumbeat of war grew ever more incessant.

In the end, a German blunder forced America's hand. In January 1917, Germany telegraphed an encrypted message to the President of Mexico, proposing a joint invasion of the United States. Mexico would regain territories that America had seized from her; Germany would gain the diversion of America's forces. Great Britain intercepted the telegram, decoded it, and delivered it to Wilson. The United States at last declared war. Before long, America would be sending ten thousand men a day to the killing fields of Europe.

Dr Stratham Younger was among the first to arrive, posted as surgeon and, with the rank of lieutenant, as medical officer in a British field hospital in northwest France.

After Littlemore left the hotel room, a wartime recollection visited Younger: Colette bending over a bathtub in a blown-out building, clad in two white towels, one around her torso, the other around her hair, as the steam of hot water filled the air. But he had never seen her that way. In this memory that wasn't a memory, Colette turned toward him with fear in her eyes. She backed away as if he might attack her, asking him if he had forgotten. Forgotten what?

Younger went to the bathroom sink, forcing this pseudo-memory down, only to find in its place a grainy image of a blackboard in a fog or rainstorm, with someone drawing on it, although not with chalk. This memory too, if it was a memory, he suppressed with irritation. He was suddenly sure he was in fact forgetting something – something more immediate.

He rinsed his face. The moment the cold water struck his eyelids, it came to him.

Younger rushed out once more to the darkness of the balcony. He saw Littlemore far below, waiting for his car, just as he'd seen the man in the striped suit waiting before. This time his shouting had effect. Waving his arms, he signaled Littlemore to wait.

Younger burst through the front doors of the hotel onto Forty-second Street. Piled in his arms was an unwieldy collection of hastily gathered items: a curtain rod, stripped from a window; a metal box with dials and switches on it; a pair of long electrical wires; a roll of black tape; and an eight-inch sealed glass tube. He crouched at the sidewalk, where he deposited this load. 'I need your car,' he said to Littlemore, attaching the wires to the glass tube. 'How could I be such a fool?'

'Um – what are you doing?' said the detective.

'This is a radiation detector,' said Younger, connecting the other end of the wires to the metal box. 'Colette was going to use it at her lecture.'

'That's swell. Couple of things I could be taking care of right now, Doc.'

'Every sample in Colette's case is radioactive,' said Younger, connecting the other end of the wires to the metal box. 'Their car is leaving a trail of radioactive particles like bread crumbs. We can't see them. But this thing can – if we hurry.'

Younger flipped a switch on the box. A flash of yellow ignited in the glass tube, accompanied by an explosive blast of static from the box. Just as suddenly, the tube went dark and the box fell quiet.

'Was that supposed to happen?' asked Littlemore.

'Not exactly,' said Younger. 'Radioactivity should produce a blue current. I think.'

Younger picked up the box in one arm and extended the curtain rod out in front of him, with the glass tube taped to its end, as if it were the tip of a divining rod. Nothing happened. He stepped into Park Avenue, probing along the pavement and in the air. A single blue spark flashed inside the glass. 'Got them,' he said.

Younger took a step to his right. Nothing. He took a step the other way: another single blue flash lit the tube, and then another. He followed these sparks – until he was face-to-face with Littlemore, his wand pointing directly into the detective's chest.

'Hello?' said Littlemore.

'It must be because you got so close to the open case,' said Younger. He returned to the street, cars veering to avoid him. He was looking for a signal much stronger than the individual sparks that led him to Littlemore. In the middle of the avenue, a miniature blue firework burst within the glass tube. As he advanced down the avenue, the firework became a steady blue current, and audible clicks emanated from the metal box.

'Well, I'll be,' replied Littlemore for the second time that day.

Moments later they were driving down Park Avenue at full throttle, Littlemore behind the wheel, Younger standing on the running board. Younger held the curtain rod out in front of him, the glass tube at its tip sparkling electric blue in the warm Manhattan night.

In Times Square, the current went dead. 'They turned,' said Younger.

He jumped from the running board, carrying his apparatus, while Littlemore wheeled the car around. Younger searched for a signal. To the north, he found nothing. But when he went to the downtown side of the square, a blue current flickered back to life inside the glass. Soon they were heading south on Broadway. For more than two miles they hurtled down the avenue, the device flashing and clicking steadily.

'Why?' Younger shouted over the car's din.

Littlemore interpreted: 'Why kidnap her?'

Younger nodded.

'They take girls for two reasons,' shouted the detective. 'Money is one.'

★ ★ ★

What Colette would have done, had she been on her own, she didn't know. When the car finally came to a halt and they pulled her out into an unlit street, the two stupid underlings, Miljan and Zelko, fought with each other constantly. She might have made a run for it – if she had been on her own. But they had her brother too, so any thought of wrenching loose and running was out of the question.

Miljan – the small one, who smelled of onion – was apparently competing with Zelko to be keeper of their female prisoner. Each tried to yank her away from the other, coming to the point of blows until Drobac forced Miljan to take Luc, while Zelko got Colette.

In the warrens of the Lower East Side, Younger had to get down at almost every intersection, hunting for radioactivity through a series of twists and turns in the labyrinthine byways. A few minutes later, on a dark street, the chatter from Younger's device grew so loud he had to dampen it.

'We're close,' said Younger.

Luc was thrown to the floor of an apartment in a decrepit old house, where peeling paint revealed a green mold. Rats scurried behind the walls. Miljan tied the boy to a rusting radiator.

Colette stood in the middle of the room. The beefy, no-necked Zelko had her by the hair, waiting for his orders. Drobac went to a table and wound the hand crank on a phonograph. The cylinder began to turn, and Al Jolson's playful voice, backed by a swing orchestra, came scratchily out of the amplification horn, singing that he had his captain working for him now. Drobac nodded with the beat.

'Is good,' he said. 'American music is good.' He turned the volume as high as it would go.

Suddenly the clicking in Younger's device abated. 'Back,' he said. 'We passed them.'

A few moments later, Younger identified the locus of the radiation: a black sedan, parked in the middle of the block. No one was inside it. The street was lined mostly with warehouses, dark and lifeless. Only one structure showed signs of habitation: an old brick two-story, flat-roofed house. It might once have been a decent family residence, but now it hulked in disrepair. A dingy light shone in several large but dirty windows. Music came from somewhere within.

Younger picked up a faint signal leading from the sedan to the front door of this house. Neither man said a word. Littlemore produced what looked like a ruler from his jacket, along with a small metal pick.

Drobac drew from his pockets a series of objects that Colette knew well: brass flasks, stoppered tubes with colored powders, coruscating pieces of ore. He deposited them on the table next to the blaring phonograph. Then he issued commands to the other two in their unintelligible language, went to the door, and held it open.

Miljan, in his checked suit, smiled nastily. Evidently Drobac had ordered Zelko out of the room. The latter cursed and spat on the floor; despite these indications of complaint, he picked up a chair, carried it out into the corridor, and sat down heavily upon it, his burly arms crossed. Drobac left the room as well and shut the door behind him.

Colette felt a warm, rank breath on her neck.

Gun drawn, Littlemore preceded Younger into a tiled, grimy vestibule. The first floor was devoid of life. Swing music played overhead. Younger picked up a signal going upstairs. Littlemore drew a line across his neck; Younger turned off his clicking device. The stairs were filthy but solid, making little noise as they ascended.

On the second floor, a bare electric bulb dangled from the ceiling, its filaments visible. The big band music romped unnaturally. Human sounds filtered out of the rooms – kitchen clatter, the flush of a toilet. Littlemore, advancing down the hallway, crouched low, peered around a corner, and saw Zelko on a chair, arms folded, at the far end of the corridor. The detective immediately withdrew and led Younger back to the stairwell.

'A lookout,' Littlemore whispered. 'On a chair. End of the hall.'

'Can you take him?' Younger whispered back.

'Sure, I can take him, but then what? The guys inside the room hear the noise. Colette and the kid become hostages – or dead.'

A girl's voice cried out, muffled by the walls. Only one word was intelligible – 'No.' It was a female voice, with a French accent. Then something substantial, perhaps a body, fell to the floor.

Littlemore had to restrain Younger: 'You'll get her shot,' whispered the detective. 'Listen to me. I need a distraction. Noise out in the street. Throw something at their window. Break it. Something loud enough to pull that guy from the chair back inside the room.'

'I'll give you a distraction,' said Younger. But instead of returning down to the street, he went up, mounting a narrow stairway that led to the roof.

Colette had been forced to her knees, half on and half off a thin, soiled mattress. She lay cheek-first against the hard wood floor, hands tied at the small of her back. Miljan, in his oversized checked suit, was behind her, gun in hand.

She smelled his reeking breath and felt one of his hands groping at her waist. Blindly, she kicked out and made satisfying contact with the man's knee. Miljan stifled a cry and hopped in pain on one leg. Rolling over, Colette kicked his other leg. He fell to his knees, and she kicked the gun right out of his hand. Surprised and furious, he chased the pistol, which clattered to the floor near Luc. Just as Miljan reached for it, Luc – still tied to a radiator pipe – kicked it away from him, so that it slid along the floor back toward Colette.

She had worked her tied wrists to the side of her body. Guided by fortune or providence, the sliding gun found its way right into her hands. She had already closed her fingers around it when Miljan stepped on her knuckles as he might have stepped on a cockroach.

She cried out. Even as Miljan ground her hands with the sole of his shoe, still she tried to get a finger onto the pistol's trigger. It was in vain. He ripped the gun away and put it to her temple.

At the top of the stairs, Younger pushed open a rickety door and emerged in the moonlight. He could make out a clothesline hung with sheets; a tipped-over table; a brick chimney at the far end. He went to the edge of the roof overlooking the street. There was no parapet, no rail. The chimney was right next to him. He was, he judged, directly above the room in which Colette and Luc were being held. He tore the curtain rod free from his radiation device, broke the glass tube, and used the jagged glass to hack down the clothesline.

Colette felt a jerk at the back of her dress, followed by a skittering sound: a button, bouncing on the wood floor. Miljan was behind her again. He tore open the top of her dress; more buttons flew loose. Miljan caressed the white skin between her shoulder blades with the muzzle of his pistol. A little clear button twirled like a spinning coin next to Luc. Whatever the boy felt, he didn't show.

Younger stood at the edge of the rooftop, his back to the open air, directly above the window he wanted. He had tied one end of the clothesline to the chimney. Tucked beneath one of his arms was the curtain rod, which, with its broken glass end, had turned into a weapon quite familiar to him: a bayonet. He gave the rope a good tug as a test; it held.

Younger took a deep breath and jumped backward and outward. For a split second he let the rope slip through his fingers. Then he gripped again, the rope went taut, and he swung toward the window. He smashed through it, feet first, in a splintering of dingy glass and brittle pine.

Littlemore, waiting inside, heard the crash and saw Zelko leap from his chair at the end of the corridor. Zelko lumbered into the room. Littlemore ran down the now-empty hall.

Younger hit the floor rolling and came to his feet, bayonet in hand, spitting paint and wood chips. What he saw surprised him: a frail old man in a nightgown, gap-toothed and gape-mouthed, wisps of gray about his head. Younger had broken into the wrong apartment.

Littlemore broke into the right one. The detective, counting on Younger's distraction, had hoped to surprise the men in the room with their backs to him, looking out the window. Instead, as he charged through the door, Miljan and Zelko were staring straight at him. It took them only a second before they opened fire, but that second was enough for Littlemore. Barreling into the room, he dropped to his knees: their shots missed high while he skidded forward on the hard-wood floor.

Littlemore knew better than to try for both men, which would have had him wagging his gun back and forth, probably missing both. He had immediately sized up Zelko as the one to worry about, and the detective sent three bullets into that man's chest, driving him backward into the fireplace.

Miljan kept shooting as Littlemore slid toward him, but he was too frantic. He pulled the trigger too quickly, failing each time to compensate for the gun's recoil. The result was that he missed repeatedly over the detective's head until Littlemore slammed into him, the two of them tumbling down over Zelko's corpse. There was no tussle: Littlemore brought his gun down on Miljan's head, knocking him unconscious, and handcuffed him to an iron ring that jutted out from the fireplace.

Younger sprang into the room, pine chips embedded in his hair, fiercely brandishing his bayonet – which sadly was no longer a bayonet, but only a curtain rod, having been denuded of its glass spike at some point during his crash through the window. Colette and Luc looked up at him. The phonograph filled the room with a swing tune.

'Nice distraction, Doc,' said Littlemore, keeping his eyes off Colette, whose dress had fallen off her shoulders, and going instead to Luc to untie him.

Younger went to Colette. A little shake of her head and a tiny smile told him she was all right. He pulled her dress over her shoulders, saw the bruise above her eye, and wanted, inappropriately, to embrace her.

'Do you think you could untie me?' she asked.

'Right.'

'The other man, the one with the beard,' she added. 'Did you catch him?'

Younger and Littlemore looked at each other; then they sensed that someone else was watching them from the doorway. Littlemore moved first. He jumped to his feet, trying to turn and draw his gun in one motion, but he never had a chance. From the open door, Drobac fired a single shot, which sent Littlemore spinning, blood spattering, banging into the table, his gun sailing across the room.

Younger rose much more slowly, back to the door, hands raised to indicate that he had no firearm – although his right hand held the curtain rod. Littlemore lay on the floor, clutching a bloody left shoulder. The gramophone had gone dead when Littlemore crashed into the table. The only sound in the room now was that of a large test tube, on its side, rolling slowly along the tabletop.

Drobac barked something unintelligible at Miljan, who, still hand-cuffed in the fireplace, gave an answer, equally unintelligible. 'You turn round,' Drobac ordered Younger, in a thick Eastern European accent Younger couldn't identify. 'Before I kill you.'

Younger noticed Luc gesturing solemnly toward the table. The boy's eyes were fixed on the gently rolling, stoppered test tube, which was filled with a crystalline black powder and would in a moment fall off the table right at the feet of the prostrate Littlemore. That black powder was, as Luc evidently knew, uranium dioxide, a substance not only radioactive but pyrophoric, meaning it spontaneously combusts on contact with air.

'Catch that,' Younger said quietly to Littlemore.

'What?' asked the detective.

'Catch that tube.'

Littlemore looked at the table just as the glass test tube rolled off its edge. Reaching out his good right hand, he caught it in midair.

'Now feed me a nice fat one,' Younger continued in a low voice to Littlemore, 'right down Broadway.'

'Shut mouth!' ordered Drobac. 'Where are they? I said turn round. I shoot you in back.'

'All right − I'm turning around,' Younger called out. As he turned to face Drobac, very slowly, he met Littlemore's eyes and nodded. The detective understood what Younger wanted him to do: a 'fat one down Broadway' is baseball slang for a pitch easy to hit. What he didn't understand was why. Nevertheless, shrugging, Littlemore lobbed the test tube into the air a couple of feet in front of Younger. Using the curtain rod as a baseball bat, Younger swung hard and shattered the tube, shooting at Drobac a black cloud of uranium dioxide, which ignited immediately into a fireball.

Drobac was suddenly aflame from the shoulders up, a pillar of particolored fire, blue and green and yellow and crimson. Arms reaching out blindly before him, he staggered into the center of the room, dropping his pistol, clutching at his burning facial hair. Younger seized the man's gun from the floor. Littlemore scrambled across the room and retrieved his own pistol.

Not a moment later, the powder had burned itself out, like flash paper. The fire was gone, leaving only curls of smoke and a charred, striped-suited man standing stock-still in the middle of the room, patting at his face as if to confirm that he still had one. His eyes went from wild to calm to sheepish. No one moved; Younger and Littlemore kept their guns trained on Drobac. The smell of singed hair was every-where.

Drobac tensed. Slowly he drew a long knife from his jacket.

'You've got to be kidding,' said Littlemore.

Drobac ran straight at the large window, flicking his wrist just before crashing through the very panes that Younger had meant to use as a point of entry minutes before. Littlemore didn't fire on him. Younger did, repeatedly, but his gun, the fugitive's own weapon, had jammed – its mechanism apparently fouled by the flaming uranium dioxide. Littlemore and Younger rushed to the windowsill, where in the shadows they saw a man pick himself off the pavement and run, limping, into the darkness.

'Look!' Colette called out, pointing toward the fireplace.

Miljan was staring into space, eyes wide, transfixed. Drobac, it turned out, had left his knife behind, planted in his associate's heart.

It was a long time before other policemen arrived along with an ambulance to take the bodies. Eventually Littlemore agreed to go to the hospital for his shoulder. After that, the question was where to install Colette and Luc for the night. Littlemore said they couldn't go back to the Commodore Hotel. Betty Littlemore, the detective's wife, who had rushed to the hospital upon learning that her husband had been shot – and then appeared half-annoyed because his wound was so superficial – persuaded everyone to come home to the Littlemores' apartment on Fourteenth Street.

'We'll stop by headquarters on the way,' said Littlemore. 'Statements. Paperwork. Sorry.'

Two hours later, the last police reports were signed. A squad car, empty, engine running, awaited them in the midnight darkness outside the magisterial police headquarters on Centre Street.

In two pairs they descended the steps in darkness: in front the women; behind them, Littlemore and Younger, the latter carrying Luc over his shoulder. Littlemore's jacket hung loosely over his left shoulder, which was trussed in a sling.

An officer called out to Littlemore from the doorway, asking for instructions. Younger and Littlemore turned around to face him. As a result, Luc was looking toward the street, where his sister and Betty were climbing into the police car. What he saw, no one else saw: two female forms, lit up in the glare of the squad car's headlamps. One had red hair fluttering in the midnight breeze; the other wore a kerchief. The first slowly approached the car; her feet were below the beam of light, creating the impression that she was floating. The second remained standing in the headlights; she had a scarf coiled around her neck, which she began to unwrap.

The first woman reached for the handle of Colette's door. Betty saw her, cried out, then looked in front of the car and pointed. Colette, startled by the alarm in Betty's voice, tried to lock her door, but was too late. The catch gave way; the door cracked open. At the same moment, the woman in the headlights finished unwinding her scarf and exposed what lay beneath.

Betty screamed in terror.

Littlemore called out; he and Younger ran down the steps. The red-haired women saw them coming, turned, and disappeared into the darkness. Littlemore gave chase. So did the officer who had asked Littlemore for instructions, and so did a half-dozen other officers, who came rushing from various directions at the sound of Betty's scream. They fanned out, went up and down the block, banged on doors, shined flashlights into parked cars, but found no trace of either woman.

When Littlemore returned to the squad car, Betty's hands were still covering her mouth. 'You saw it?' Betty asked Colette.

'Saw what?' said Colette.

Betty looked stricken, aghast. 'She was a monster, Jimmy.'

'Easy,' said Littlemore.

'It was — growing.'

'What was?' asked Littlemore.

'I don't know,' said Betty. 'It was alive. Like a head, like a baby's head.'

'She was carrying a baby?'

'She wasn't carrying anything!' exclaimed Betty. 'It was attached to her. Like a baby's head, but growing out of her neck.'

A silence followed.

'Let's get out of here,' said Littlemore, helping Betty into the car. He threw the keys to Younger. 'You drive, Doc.'

At two that morning, Younger and Littlemore were drinking bourbon at the detective's kitchen table, a half-empty bottle between them. Everyone else in the apartment was fast asleep.

Littlemore appeared to be counting in his head. 'When you shipped out,' he asked, 'how many kids did Betty and I have?'

Younger didn't reply.

'Whatever it was, it's three more now,' added Littlemore.

'That would make seventy-two.'

'Okay, I'm going to sum up what we've got. We got a tooth, we got a bomb, we got a kidnapping, and we got two women outside my squad car, one of them with a spare head growing out of her neck. You're wondering how it's all connected, right?'

'Maybe.'

'Well, don't think of it like that. Never assume connections. Take things one at a time. So let me sum up what we got again, one thing at a time: a bunch of crazy stuff that doesn't make any kind of sense.' Littlemore cocked his head. 'You knew that bomb was about to go off. How'd you know that?'

Younger shook his head.

Littlemore swirled the whiskey in his glass. 'A baby can't grow out of a woman's neck, can it?'

Younger shook his head again.

'You don't say much anymore, do you?' asked Littlemore.

Younger considered shaking his head, but decided against it.

'So let me get this straight,' replied Littlemore. 'You haven't asked for your professor job back. You're not doing your scientist thing. You haven't started doctoring again. What *are* you doing?'

'Tempting fate.'

'Not much of a job.'

'I just got back.'

'Yeah, but the war ended two years ago. Where have you been?'

Several minutes went by. The men drank.

'Nobody I know's so willing to die,' said Littlemore.

'What's that?'

'This morning you said it didn't make sense that men are so willing to die.'

Younger knew Littlemore was trying to draw him out; that was all right with him. 'You should have seen France in 1918,' said Younger. He got up and lit a cigarette with one of the Littlemores' long stove matches. 'The Brits, the French – they were sick of it by then. Just wanted to survive. Couldn't believe their eyes when the Americans came. Like we'd lived our whole lives starved of the chance to die.'

'I would've been there,' said Littlemore. 'If not for Betty and the kids.'

'It's not just war either,' said Younger. 'Give people a taste of terror, and they lap it up. Why are there roller coasters on Coney Island?'

'Not so people can die,' answered Littlemore.

'So they can feel the terror of death. Rich men, with comfortable lives, kill themselves climbing mountains. Flying aircraft for sport. Do you know what happens when newspapers report that someone died on a Coney Island roller coaster? *More* people come out to ride the next day.'

'Well, I don't ride coasters.' Littlemore refilled their glasses. 'Why would somebody bomb a street corner? It doesn't figure.'

'Because you're thinking like a policeman. Looking for a motive.'

'Sure am,' said Littlemore.

'What if they just wanted to kill people?'

'Why?'

'Whom do you assassinate,' replied Younger, 'if you hate a whole country? In the old days, it would have been the king. Attack the King of England, you attack England itself. But a president? A president's just a politician who will be gone in a few years anyway. With a democracy, you have to take assassination out of the palace. You have to assassinate the people.'

Littlemore thought about that. 'Why would they hate us?'

'The whole world hates us.'

'Nobody hates us. Everybody loves America.'

'Germany hates us because we beat them. England and France hate us because we saved them. Russia hates us because we're capitalist. The rest of the world hates us because we're imperialist.'

'That's not a motive,' said Littlemore. 'Say, you never asked me why I needed Colette today.'

'Why did you?'

'There's this guy, Fischer, okay? Couple a days ago, he sends a warning to a banker pal of his telling him to stay out of Wall Street after the fifteenth. Fischer works at some French outfit a few blocks from Wall. So I went there. Took Colette to translate. Now get this: the French got a letter from Fischer yesterday too, warning them to get everybody out because something was going to happen on Wall Street.'

Younger whistled: 'Who is he?'

'Question is *where* is he. Seems he went AWOL from the French about a month ago. Looks like he's in Canada somewhere. We'll find him: I told the press. A million people will be looking for this guy in a few hours. Know what's funny? Fischer's French boss tore his letter up and threw it away. We had to pull the pieces out of a wastepaper basket. Nobody took this guy seriously.' Littlemore corked the whiskey bottle, laid it on one side, and spun it on the table. 'They're trying to cut us out.'

'The French?'

'The Feds. They're trying to take over the investigation. Big Bill Flynn's here already. Palmer's coming up too.'

A. Mitchell Palmer was the Attorney General of the United States, William J. Flynn the director of the Federal Bureau of Investigation.

'The whole Bureau's coming up to New York,' Littlemore went on, looking like he had a bad taste in his mouth. 'Plus Treasury guys, Secret Service guys – dozens of them. The investigation is "in the hands of the federal government": that's what Big Bill told the boys last night. Flynn. Tell you what – he's no Teddy Roosevelt. Big Bill used to be chief of detectives here a couple years back. Nobody liked him. You know, when I was a kid, all I wanted was to become a federal agent. My dad and I used to talk about how it would be. Still do. I'd work my way up in the Department, then go to DC and work for Roosevelt. Guess it's a good thing I didn't make it. With Palmer and Flynn running the show down there, and the Congress passing Prohibition, I don't know what they're doing in Washington anymore.'

'Too bad about Roosevelt,' said Younger. Unlike the detective, who said *Roos-velt*, Younger pronounced it *Rose-a-velt*, as did the Roosevelts.

'What killed T.R. – the bullet they never got out of his chest?'

'No,' said Younger. 'It was his malaria.'

'You ever meet him?' asked Littlemore.

'Once or twice,' said Younger. 'He was a cousin.'

'Everybody's your cousin.'

'Not by blood. And very distant. I'm better acquainted with his daughter Alice. That is, I was – briefly – acquainted with her.'

'Don't tell me.'

Younger said nothing.

'Darn it, Doc – Roosevelt's daughter?' cried Littlemore. 'And a beauty girl? Why didn't you marry her?'

'For one thing she had a husband.'

'Doc, Doc, Doc,' said Littlemore. 'T.R.'s daughter. Was this before or after you and Nora?'

'A notorious philanderer,' added Younger.

'You're no philanderer.'

'I meant Alice's husband. But thank you.'

'You're more of a womanizer.'

'Ah. A fine distinction,' said Younger. 'I'm not a womanizer. I don't sleep with them. Unless I like them. Which is rarely. You don't – stray?'

'Me?' Littlemore laughed. 'I always ask what my dad would do. He would never have done something like that, so I don't.'

'How is he – your dad?'

'Good. I still visit with him most every weekend.' Littlemore drummed his fingers on the table. 'What kind of name is Drobac anyway?' Colette had told the police that the kidnapper who escaped – the leader of the three men – had been called Drobac by his confederates. 'And why'd he ask us, "Where are they"? Where are what?'

'Why did he kill his own man?' rejoined Younger.

'That's easy – to keep him from talking.' Littlemore put his heels up on the table, and his voice changed tone. 'But you know what I really don't get?'

'What exactly I'm doing with Colette,' said Younger.

'You bring her back from France,' said Littlemore, warming to the theme, 'but you got her living in Connecticut. You go crazy when she disappears, but you act, I don't know, all proper when she's around.'

'You're wondering when I plan to propose.'

'Why'd you bring her across the Atlantic otherwise? Unless you plan to ruin her.'

'You seem anxious about my marital prospects tonight.'

'Well, are you or aren't you?' asked Littlemore.

'Planning to ruin her? Tried that already,' said Younger. He took a long drink. 'Want to hear about it?'

'Sure.'

CHAPTER FIVE

IN OCTOBER 1917, Lieutenant Dr Stratham Younger was transferred to the American field hospital in Einville, not far from Nancy, where US Army troops had finally been deployed in the front lines. At that time American soldiers served under French command; Younger ended up treating more Frenchmen than Americans. Throughout the harsh winter and the following spring, attached to the First Division and later to the Second, Younger traversed the Western Front, assigned wherever the need was greatest: the Saint-Mihiel salient, Seicheprey, Chaumont-en-Vexin, Cantigny, the Bois de Belleau.

It was there, near the woods of Belleau, on the outskirts of Château-Thierry, that he met Colette.

Dawn was breaking. With a reddening sky came a lull in the savage bombardments of the night. Younger, on foot, emerged from the woods into an open field, dragging a wounded old French corporal to the medical compound. The compound was intact – white tents, tables, and instrument chests all in place – but not a doctor or orderly was in sight. The medical staff had obviously decamped in a hurry.

Noises came from across the field. French infantrymen had gathered at a Red Cross truck. They reminded Younger of children crowding around an ice-cream van, except for an air of male wildness about them.

With the corporal's arm draped over his shoulder, Younger crossed the field through pockets of mist clinging to the rutted soil. A young woman stood outside the truck, hemmed in by a semicircle of boisterous men. Her back to them, she leaned through a window into the cab of the truck. The men called out – in French, which Younger understood – invented maladies and mock pleas for treatment. One of them, with a particularly raucous voice, begged the girl to reach inside his shirt; his heart, he said, was pounding and swelling dangerously.

The girl emerged from the cab, a brown bag in her hands. She was slim, graceful, dark-haired, about twenty years old, chin held high, eyes unnaturally green. Dressed in a plain wool skirt and light blue sweater, she was evidently not a nurse.

She spoke to the men. Younger couldn't hear what she said, but he saw her toss her bag to the loudmouthed one, who caught it, dropping his rifle in order to do so, which provoked laughter from the others. The girl spoke again. One by one the men fell silent and, abashed, began skulking away. She had no air of triumph. She looked – weary. Beautiful, distracted, and weary. As the infantrymen dispersed, only Younger was left standing, the wounded corporal resting heavily on a shoulder of his filthy uniform. The girl saw Younger, staring at her. She brushed a lock of hair from her face.

Laying the corporal on the grass – an ancient-looking fellow, with a leather face and grizzled hair, one hand clutching his stomach – Younger strode toward the girl, who drew back a step instinctively. He passed her without a glance and opened the truck's door. Inside he saw two things that surprised him. The first was a boy, no more than eight, sitting in the rear of the cabin, reading a book in the shadows. The second was a complex radiological apparatus, complete with a large glass plate, heavy curtains, and gas ampoules.

Younger turned to the girl. 'Where's your boyfriend?' he asked in French.

'What?'

'Where's the man who operates this X-ray machine?'

'I operate it,' she answered in English.

He looked her up and down: 'You're one of Madame Curie's girls.'

'Yes.'

'Well, get to work. Unless you want this corporal to die.'

'It's pointless,' she said. 'There's no surgeon. They're all gone.'

'Just make him ready by nightfall.' Younger went to the corporal, said a few low words in the man's ear, and disappeared into the woods the way he had come.

The moon had risen when Younger returned. He found the encampment as it had been that morning: intact but deserted. One of the tents was illuminated by electric light. The truck was parked next to it, engine on, a set of cables running from the vehicle along the ground into the tent. The girl was using the truck's motor for power.

Younger lifted the tent's flap and walked in. All was prepared. The old corporal, whose name was Dubeney, lay asleep on an operating table, face washed, hair combed. Instruments were neatly laid out. Basins of water were at hand. The girl rose from a chair. The little boy was at her feet, still reading. Without a word, she retrieved a set of radiograms and mathematical computations, which she handed to Younger.

He held up the plates to one of the bare electric bulbs. Against a background of white bones and grayish viscera, small black dots and balls stood out with remarkable clarity. When a man took shot in the gut, the greatest danger was not organ damage; it was blood poisoning. In the old days, recovering every fragment of shot was virtually hopeless, and the man was likely to die. With a good set of radiograms, properly computed, any competent surgeon could save him.

Younger washed his hands, wrists, face, and forearms. He took a long time at it, rinsing the dirt and blood from his mind as well as his skin. Meanwhile the girl applied more chloroform to Corporal Dubeney, who pushed at her hands ineffectually until slipping off again. Younger set to work, the silence broken only by his requests for instruments and, a short time after his incision was made, the occasional *plank* of a metal fragment dropping into a ceramic bowl.

Sweat began to form on Younger's brow.

'Wait,' said the girl in English. It was the first word she had spoken.

While he held his knife aloft, she mopped his brow, then applied the cloth to his cheeks, his jaw, his neck. Younger gazed down at her delicate but serious features. She didn't once look into his eyes.

'What was in the bag?' asked Younger.

'I beg your pardon?'

'You threw the soldiers a bag.'

'Oh. Just groceries. Cheese, mostly. They don't get enough food; they're all hungry. Like a band of mice.'

'What did you tell them?'

'That they should be killing Germans instead of bothering a French girl.'

Younger, nodding, returned to his patient. 'We say mischief.'

The girl frowned as she rinsed the soiled cloth.

'In English,' he said, 'it's a "mischief" of mice. Was it Madame Curie herself who trained you?'

'Yes,' said the girl.

'What did you think of her?'

Her reply was immediate: 'She's the noblest woman alive.'

'Ah, an admirer. Personally, I'm surprised they allow it.'

'What do you mean?'

'An adultress, after all, training young girls—'

'She did not commit adultery,' said the girl sharply. '*He* did. Monsieur Langevin is the one who was married, yet he is not blamed. They do not call for *him* to leave the country. They do not stone *his* house. Now he has another mistress. Einstein has an illegitimate child – everyone knows it. Why should Madame Curie lose her chair, why should she be threatened with death, when they do the same or worse?'

'Because she is a woman,' said Younger complacently. 'Women should be pure.'

'Men should be pure.'

'And because she's a Jew. Scalpel.'

'What?'

'Scalpel. And a Pole.'

'What does that have to do with it?'

'And her worst crime of all – she won the Nobel Prize not once, but twice.'

She frowned again. 'I can't tell when you mean what you say.'

'If you want the truth,' said Younger, 'I'm only honest with men. With women I can't be trusted.'

She looked at him.

'Women teach men to lie,' he went on. 'But we're never as good at it as they want us to be. How did you meet Madame Curie?'

After a while, the girl answered: 'I walked into the Sorbonne and told them I wanted to apply in chemistry. I was seventeen. They all laughed at me, because I had no baccalaureate. By chance – or providence, who knows? – Madame came in at that moment. She had overheard. How she terrified them. She looks so old, but very kind. I don't know why, but she took an interest in me when she heard that my father had tutored me in math and science. She asked me questions, so I was able to show her what I knew. She arranged for me to take an entrance exam.'

'Which you passed?' asked Younger.

'I received the highest marks of the year.'

'You should be in class then, not taking X-rays of wounded soldiers.'

'I did go to classes, for two years. But then I found out what Madame was doing for the soldiers. These trucks, they were her idea. She was the first to see how many lives could be saved if we had radioscopes in the field. Everyone said it was impossible, so she designed a unit that could work inside a truck. The government, because they are so stupid, refused to pay, so Madame raised all the money herself. Then the army said it could not spare any men to operate the trucks, so Madame trained girls to do it. Then the government announced that women could not be permitted to drive, so Madame operated the first one herself, daring the government to stop her. She learned to drive; she changed tires; she took the X-rays. When they saw she was saving lives, they finally relented. Now there are over a hundred fifty of us – and our only problem is with the men.'

'The men?'

'Some of them become very – aggressive – in the presence of a woman.'

'They're at war.'

'That's no excuse. We're not the same as the filthy Germans.'

Younger looked at the girl from the corner of his eye. A hardness had come to her face; he had seen a glimmer of it before, when she was speaking to the soldiers, but now it was impenetrable. He went on with his laborious work.

After a long while, she spoke again: 'He is very sweet, this corporal. How did he come to be in your care?'

'Not by my doing,' replied Younger. 'He got lost in the night. Crossed to our line by mistake. Threw himself on me, the poor blighter.'

'Don't listen to him, Mademoiselle,' murmured Corporal Dubeney.

'What – are you awake?' said Younger. 'Nurse, the chloroform.'

'He came into no-man's-land and pulled me out,' said Dubeney. 'In the thick of it.'

'Hallucination,' said Younger.

'He sleeps at the front,' said Dubeney.

'Where's the blasted chloroform?' asked Younger.

'No need, no need, I can't feel a thing,' said Dubeney.

Younger made a sound of annoyance through closed lips. No one spoke.

'I could hardly let my best experiment go to waste,' said Younger. 'Look at his right knee.'

The girl, curious, asked Corporal Dubeney if he minded. When he shook his head, she rolled up one of his trouser legs and saw a nasty wound. 'This needs antiseptic,' she said.

'I've put antiseptic on it,' said Younger. 'Every day. Now look at the other knee.'

When the girl got Dubeney's other pant leg over his knee, she let out a gasp. This knee too was wounded, but there was a seething movement on it. 'What are they?' she asked.

'Maggots. What else do you observe?' asked Younger.

'The wound is clean,' she said.

'Identical wounds, inflicted at the same time on the same man by the same causes. Yet one has healed, while the other has festered. And the wound that has healed has been treated only with maggots. It's not my idea. Men in the field have been using them for years. And this old buzzard, knowing how important his knees are to science, goes and gets himself shot in the stomach. No sense of duty whatever.'

Younger noticed that the little boy had silently taken up a position beside the girl, eyeing raptly Corporal Dubeney's maggoty knee.

'My brother,' she said to Younger. 'His name is Luc.'

The boy had dirty blond hair, quite unlike his sister's, unkempt, and for a boy quite a lot of it, down to his shoulders. His skin was much less white than hers – or perhaps simply much dirtier – but his brown eyes shared a similar severity, equally intelligent but more watchful than the girl's, less distracted. Younger had the feeling the boy saw everything. 'And how old are you, young man?' he asked.

The boy neither looked at Younger nor answered.

'Luc, you are very poorly mannered,' said the girl. 'He doesn't like to speak. So you are the one.'

'I beg your pardon,' said Younger.

'The men have been telling stories of an American doctor who refuses to leave the front lines. Who treats wounded men on the field.'

'I'm not treating them. I'm conducting experiments on them.'

'And who fights, they say.'

'Rubbish.'

'Like the devil,' said Dubeney.

The boy looked up at Younger with interest.

'Can't feel a thing, eh?' said Younger to Dubeney, repositioning his knife and prompting a howl from the old corporal.

★　　★　　★

Hours later, under the stars, they repacked the girl's truck. She was surprisingly strong for her size. An explosion shook the earth gently beneath them, its firestorm erupting far away, deep in the woods. 'You're not afraid?' asked Younger.

'Of the war?'

'Of being alone with a stranger.'

'No,' she said.

'You're trusting.'

'I never trust men,' she answered. 'That's why I'm not afraid of them.'

'Sound policy,' said Younger. He looked up at the twinkling canopy above. 'I saw something today I'll never forget. An American marine sergeant was ordering his platoon out of a trench. They were outgunned, outmanned, but the sergeant decided to attack. His marines were too afraid to come out. The sergeant said to them – well, it involves a term that shouldn't be used in polite company. Shall I say it?'

'Are you joking?' asked Colette.

'The sergeant yelled, "Come on, you sons of bitches, do you want to live forever?" His men came out. It was a bloodbath.'

'Did he live, the sergeant?'

'Yes, he did.'

A sound like a banshee's scream was followed by another explosion. This time the blast was closer. The ground shook, and they could see fires burning perhaps a thousand yards away.

'You should get out,' said Younger. 'Tonight. If the Germans break through, they'll be here before morning. They may do worse to a French girl than your soldiers did.'

She said nothing. Younger reshouldered his gear and set off for the woods again – in the direction of the explosions.

It was July, 1918, before he saw her again. Germany had commenced a series of ferocious offensives in France, determined to seize victory before the United States could fully mobilize. Hundreds of thousands of seasoned German troops were pouring in from the east, where Russia's new Bolshevik rulers had surrendered, releasing the Kaiser's armies from the Eastern Front. By the end of May, Germany had pressed the French forces back to the Marne, only fifty miles from Paris.

But there, at Belleau, at Vaux, at Château-Thierry, Americans blocked the German advance, charging to their deaths with an abandon unseen in Allied troops since 1914. United States newspapers trumpeted the Yankee victories, wildly exaggerating their importance. The question was whether the new line would hold.

For forty days, the two sides threw wave after wave of firepower and young men into brutal, indecisive combat. Slowly the fighting ground to a halt, reduced to the exchange of blistering shell attacks from well-fortified entrenchments. The pause was ominous. The Germans appeared to be reinforcing again, massing yet more divisions.

In this quiet before the storm, a produce market of dubious legality had sprung up in the village of Crézancy, overlooked by the huge, glinting American guns planted high up on the Moulin Ruiné. Bent and wizened French farmers sold whatever goods they had managed to keep back from government requisitioners.

It was Luc whom Younger saw first. He recognized at once the little boy buying cheese and milk, wordlessly shaking his head at some exorbitant demand and consenting to pay only after receiving an acceptable price. Younger greeted the boy warmly. In a burst of inspiration, he pulled from his pocket a sealed jar crawling with maggots. Luc's eyes opened wide.

'They're larvae,' said Younger in French. 'In a short time, each of these fellows will wrap himself up in a cocoon. A week or two later, the cocoon will break open, and out will crawl – do you know what will crawl out?'

The boy shook his head.

'A fly. A common, bluebottle blowfly.'

This information appeared to boost the boy's already high estimation of the seething mass inside the jar.

'Would you like to know why they're such good friends to wounded men? Because they eat only dead tissue. Living cells have no appeal to them. Here, take the jar. I have more. Very few young men have pet maggots.'

The boy accepted the present and drew something from his own pocket, offering it in exchange.

Younger raised an eyebrow. 'A grenade.'

Luc nodded.

'It's not live, is it?' asked Younger.

Setting down the grubs, Luc engaged the grenade's pin, unscrewed its cap, withdrew the spring, removed the pin, unhinged the nozzle, and held it up in the air.

Younger leaned down, smelled the dry powder within. 'I see. Excellent. Live indeed.'

The boy reversed the process, deftly reassembling the grenade, and offered it again to Younger, who accepted the gift quite carefully. He was thanking Luc when a girl's voice spoke sternly behind him.

'Did you let him touch that?' she asked.

Younger turned to see the boy's sister.

'You want him to think grenades are toys?' she went on angrily. 'So the next time he sees one on the ground, he'll pick it up and play with it?'

Younger glanced at Luc, who plainly didn't want his sister to know he'd been carrying a live grenade around. 'Quite right, Mademoiselle,' said Younger, pocketing the weapon. 'I don't know what I was thinking. Luc, a grenade is not a toy, do you hear me? Only someone completely familiar with how they work should ever touch one.'

'I'm sorry,' she said to Younger, mollified. 'He likes to play with guns and ammunition. He's forever scaring me.'

'I heard you went back to Paris,' Younger answered.

She frowned. Luc tugged her skirt. The girl excused herself, bent toward him, and the boy made hand gestures between their faces – some kind of sign language. Her answer to him was strict: 'Absolutely not. What's the matter with you?' To Younger she explained, 'Now he wants to go to the front with you.'

'I'm afraid that's impossible, given your age, young man,' said Younger. 'Although the way this war is going, you may yet have your chance. But perhaps you'd like to see an American base?'

The boy nodded.

Younger spoke to the girl: 'It would be a great service to us if you came to our base with your truck. We have an X-ray machine, but compared to yours it's primitive. There are many men I could help.'

'All right,' she said. 'I can come this afternoon. But I still – I don't know your name.'

For the next several days, Colette's truck pulled into Younger's field hospital every evening, rumbling up the dirt road in a cloud of dust. With Younger seated beside her, they would set off to various encampments as far away as Lucy-le-Bocage. Dozens of men, wounded but reinserted into their platoons, had not regained their health as they should have. Younger wanted to reexamine them all. Usually the X-rays uncovered nothing, but every now and then, as Younger suspected, the ghostly skeletons showed a minuscule fragment of shell previously missed.

The first time this happened, Colette cried out in triumph. Younger smiled. As they worked at close quarters in the back of the truck, her fingers would frequently touch his when exchanging an instrument. Or her body would brush against him. On every such occasion, she would quickly separate herself, yet Younger had the notion that the contact might have been deliberate.

With the wounded or sickly, Colette was kind, but not particularly gentle or compassionate. With the healthy, she was flint. In part, Younger could see, this brusqueness was self-protection; she was too pretty to interact with soldiers on other terms. But there was more to it. Younger wondered what it would take to soften her.

★   ★   ★

One evening when Colette was busy with her computations, Younger took advantage of the lull to work by flashlight on some equations of his own. He became conscious after a while that Luc was standing by his side.

The boy handed Younger a book. It was in English, published the previous year. The author was one Toynbee; the title was *The German Terror in France*. The short volume had been well-thumbed; was it possible the boy could read English?

Younger began paging through the book. It was then that the boy handed him a note saying he hated the dead – the first time Luc had ever communicated to him in this fashion. After that the boy sat down against a tire of the truck, playing with an old toy.

'Where did you get that?' asked Colette suddenly, seeing the book in Younger's hands.

'Your brother gave it to me.'

'Oh.' Her body relaxed. 'He wants me to tell you what happened to our family.'

'You needn't.'

She looked at Luc, who kept playing his game. 'You can read about it if you want,' she said, indicating a place in the book where a page had been dog-eared and a passage underlined. Younger read it:

> *Sommeilles was completely burnt on Sept. 6th. 'When the incendiarism started,' states the Mayor, 'M. and Mme Adnot (the latter about sixty years old), Mme X (thirty-five or thirty-six years old), whose husband is with the colours, and Mme X's four children all took refuge in the Adnots' cellars. They were there assassinated under atrocious circumstances. The two women were violated. When the children shrieked, one of them had its head cut off, and two others one arm, while everyone in the cellar was massacred. The children were respectively eleven, five, four and one and a half years old.'*

'Great God,' said Younger. 'I pray this wasn't your family.'

'No, but that was our village — Sommeilles,' she said. 'We moved there when I was little — Mother, Father, Grandmother, and I. Luc was born there. When the war started, all our young men went off to the army. The village was defenseless. The night the Germans came, Luc and I were sent to the carpenter's, because he had a hidden basement. That's the reason we lived. The Germans killed everyone, but they never found us. All night long we heard gunshots and screaming. The next day, they were gone. Our house was burned, but still standing. Mother and Father were dead on the floor. Father had put up a heroic fight, you could see that. Grandmother was still alive, but not for long. Mother was naked. There was a lot of blood.'

Luc had stopped his game while his sister spoke. When it was clear that she had finished, the boy started playing again.

'Everyone assumes you have to be sad,' said Colette, 'for the rest of your life.'

CHAPTER SIX

WITH THE GREAT War came great disease – unheard-of illness on an unprecedented scale.

The last was the worst: the flu of 1918–19, spreading with the continent-crossing armies, hiding in the warm but broken lungs of homeward-bound soldiers, ultimately killing millions in every corner of the earth. Before the Spanish flu, there had been the agonies of phosgene and mustard gas, which could burn away a man's eyes and his flesh down to the bone. Before the poison gas, there had been the repulsive incapacitations of fungi and parasites attacking men's feet, gangrenes propagating in undrained, rat-infested trenches. But before all this, there was shell shock.

The initial reports of the strange condition were baffling. Seemingly unhurt men presented a congeries of contradictory symptoms: rapidity of breath and inability to breathe, silence and raving, excessive motion and catatonia, refusal to let go their weapons and refusal to touch their weapons. But always nightmares – in case after case, night terrors that woke and alarmed their comrades-in-arms.

Then came symptoms more peculiar still. Deafness, muteness, and blindness; paralyzed fists and legs. All without apparent organic injury.

The French had a name for these men: *simulateurs*. The British too: malingerers. In fact the earliest treatment prescribed by the English was the firing squad, cowardice being an offense punishable by death in the British army. German doctors, by contrast, used electricity. The avowed theory behind the Germans' electrocution therapy was not that it cured, but that at a sufficiently high voltage it made returning to the front a preferable alternative. The German doctors had, however, overlooked a third option, of which quite a few of their patients took advantage: suicide.

Yet even these compelling disincentives failed to stem the tide. The numbers of afflicted men rose to staggering proportions. Eighty thousand soldiers in Great Britain would eventually be diagnosed with the mysterious ailment. Many of these were officers of high character and, from the British viewpoint, of unimpeachable blood and breeding. As a result, the malingering thesis came finally to be doubted.

The first doctors to take the condition seriously announced that exploding missiles were to blame. The concussive detonations set off by the mighty shells of modern warfare were said to produce micro-hemorrhaging in cerebral blood vessels, causing a neurological paralysis or shock in the brain. Thus was coined the term 'shell shock.'

The name stuck, but not the diagnosis behind it. Too many shell-shocked men had lived through no bombardment at all. It soon became apparent that psychology was more important to their condition than physiology. It became equally apparent that only one psychiatrist on the planet had advanced a theory of mental illness that could explain their symptoms: Sigmund Freud.

Gradually but in growing numbers, physicians the world over – men who had previously regarded psychoanalysis with the deepest distaste and suspicion – began to acknowledge that the Freudian concept of the unconscious alone made sense of shell shock and its treatment. 'Fate would seem to have presented us,' wrote a British physician in 1917, 'with an unexampled opportunity to test the truth of Freud's theory of the unconscious.' The test proved positive.

English, Australian, French, and German doctors reported stunning success treating shell shock victims with psychotherapy. In Britain, military authorities called on Dr Ernest Jones, one of Freud's earliest disciples – who was still barred from hospital practice because of his penchant for discussing improprieties with twelve-year-old girls – to treat what was coming to be called 'war neurosis.' Germany sent a delegation to an international psychoanalytic congress, begging for assistance in dealing with overcrowded shell-shock wards. Freud himself – so long calumniated and ostracized – was asked by the Austrian government to lead an investigation concerning the proper treatment of shell shock. By 1918, there may have been only one man alive who both accepted the truth of psychoanalysis and yet felt that Freudian theory could *not* explain war neurosis. That man was Sigmund Freud.

'He should be in school,' Colette said of her brother a few days later. She was behind the wheel of her truck, guiding it over badly rutted roads. She had no qualms about discussing Luc in the boy's hearing. 'But he is too – uncooperative. The teachers in Paris thought he was deaf. They also thought he couldn't talk. But he can. I know it.'

In the back of the truck, Luc was playing with his favorite toy again – an old fishing reel – mouthing unintelligible sounds as he did so.

'How long has he been like this?' asked Younger.

'There was smoke everywhere after they burned Sommeilles. It got into the carpenter's cellar, but Luc wouldn't come out. That whole day he lay there. Then he caught cold, and that night he started coughing – badly. I thought I might lose him too. He got better, but he's been this way ever since.'

'Does he ever have trouble breathing – when he runs, for example?'

'Never,' said Colette. 'Everyone says he must have had a pneumonia, but I think it's something else. Something psychological. A "neurosis," perhaps. Have you ever heard of Dr Freud of Vienna?'

'Left at that signpost,' said Younger.

'He's a psychologist, very famous. Everyone says he is the only one to understand war neuroses. And he treats children.'

'Dr Freud of Vienna,' said Younger. 'He has a peculiar theory of what causes neurosis.'

'You've read his work? I couldn't find anything in French.'

'I've read him, and I know him. Personally.'

'But that's wonderful!' cried Colette. 'When the war is over, I am going to write to him. We have no money, but I was hoping he might agree to see Luc. Will you help me?'

'No.'

'You won't? Why not?'

'I don't believe in Freud's psychology,' he said. 'As a matter of fact, I don't believe in psychology at all. Shrapnel, bacteria, sulfur – get them out of a man's system, and you stand a fair chance of making him better. But "neurosis"? Neurosis means "no-diagnosis." How do you know Luc doesn't have a problem in his larynx?'

'I know he can talk. I know it. He just won't.'

'Well, if you're right, then he's shy. I was shy at his age.'

'He's not shy,' said Colette. 'It's as if he is – how to say it? – refusing the world.'

'Perfectly rational, given what he has seen of the world. Pull up over there.'

Colette did so, bringing the truck to a grinding halt. 'Dr Freud's patients get better,' she replied. 'Everyone says so.'

'That doesn't prove his theories are valid.'

'What does it matter, if his patients get better?' she asked.

'In that case, why not give the boy snake oil?'

'I would if it made him better. I would do anything to make him better.'

Younger opened his door. 'There's nothing wrong with your brother's mind,' he said. 'He just needs this – this bloody war to end.'

On July 13, Younger was kept busy overnight at the front, working on some badly wounded men; he wasn't able to return to base until late the next evening. Despite the hour, he commandeered a transport wagon and drove it to the French position where Colette could usually be found. When he got there, she was laundering clothes in the glare of her truck's headlamps.

She ran to him: they stood face-to-face, but didn't touch. 'Where were you?' she asked. 'At the front?'

At a certain point, men in wartime either stop thinking about death or become paralyzed by it. Younger had stopped thinking about it. 'At the moment I'm absent without leave,' he replied. 'Court-martialable offense.'

'Not really?'

'It's all right. My orderly knows where I am. Couldn't let Bastille Day go uncelebrated.' From the rear of his wagon, he pulled out a bottle of dessert wine, two glasses, a tin of foie gras, a blue cheese, a jar of strawberry preserves, fresh butter, and an assortment of English biscuits. 'Not exactly revolutionary,' he observed, 'but the best I could do.'

'Where did you get all this?' she said in wonder.

'Will you allow me, Mademoiselle?'

'With pleasure.'

She laid a blanket on the grass and arranged the articles he had brought. The night was warm. He threw his leather jacket to the ground, put his cap and pistol belt on top of it, and began corkscrewing the wine – but stopped when blood drizzled down his fingers onto the bottle. 'Do you sew by any chance?' he asked.

She lifted his sleeve and gasped at the deep laceration in his forearm. 'Wait here,' she said. When she came back a moment later with suturing thread and a disinfectant alcohol, she added, 'I don't have any anaesthetic.'

'For this?' he replied.

She poured the clear alcohol onto his wound, where it hissed and effervesced, ran a needle through one piece of his bubbling, bleeding skin and then through another, pulling the thread tight thereafter. 'How can you bear it?' she asked.

'I don't feel it,' he said.

'Of course you do,' she replied, continuing to suture.

'I'm indifferent to it.'

'A man who doesn't feel pain can feel no pleasure.'

'I'm indifferent to pleasure too.'

'That's not what the nurses say.'

'I beg your pardon?'

'How long since you've slept?' she asked.

'There's something about you I don't follow, Miss Rousseau. Specifically, your leaving Paris to live in a truck. And don't tell me it was your duty to France.'

'Why not?' she asked, piercing the last lip of open skin. 'Hold still.'

'Because women don't act out of duty to country. There's always a man in it somewhere.'

'You're unforgivable.' She cut the thread, tied it off. 'Done.'

He flexed his hand, nodded, opened the wine, poured her a glass, and offered a toast to womankind. She returned it with a toast to France. They settled down to their meal; she served him. 'You were following a boy, obviously,' Younger resumed. 'He was called to the front, and this was the only way you could go with him. The only question is whether you lost him or he lost you.'

'I wasn't following a boy.'

'My apologies — a man.'

'Not a man either.'

'A girl?'

She threw a cracker at him.

'Sorry, but it doesn't add up,' he said. 'You left the Sorbonne, which must have been the most important thing in your life. You know they won't reenroll you after the war. There will be too many men whose education was interrupted.'

'Yes.' She swept crumbs from the blanket, barely betraying her deep disappointment: 'Even Madame warned me she wouldn't be able to get me back in.'

'Then why did you leave?' asked Younger.

'I couldn't stand the charity any longer.'

He was unable to read the expression in her eyes.

'There are people,' she went on, 'willing to house those of us who have lost our families, willing to feed us. But charity comes at a price. Out here we have a roof over our heads, and I don't have to ask anyone for bread.'

'What was the price?' asked Younger.

'Dependence.'

'We're all dependent when young. On family, if no one else.'

'To be dependent on your family is a joy,' she said. 'To be dependent on someone else is – different.'

Again she wore her indecipherable expression, but this time Younger deciphered it.

'So,' he said. 'You weren't lying, but I was still right.'

'What do you mean?'

'You weren't following a man when you left Paris. You were escaping one. A man who wanted a return on his charitable investments.'

She looked at him over the rim of her glass.

'You had a – an intimate relationship with him,' said Younger. 'No one can blame you.'

'You are very curious about my relationships.'

'Any girl would have done the same in your place.'

'Maybe an American girl would have. I didn't. You will believe me when I tell you who it was: Monsieur Langevin.'

Paul Langevin was the great French physicist notoriously coupled with Marie Curie in newspaper reports all over the world several years earlier.

'I should have known,' declared Younger. 'You said his name to me once before, with more venom than any word I've heard you speak except "German." What did the rascal do?'

'He tried to undress me in the laboratory.'

'Scoundrel. Where should he have done it?'

'You think it's funny? This is the man Madame loved. The man she lost everything for. And he makes love to me almost under her nose.'

'At least he has good taste.'

'I think you are trying to provoke me,' she said. 'It was dreadful. He had put Luc and me up in his house. I thought he was being kind. But then came the laboratory, and then there was more, at night, in his house.'

'By force?'

'No – when I resisted, he would let me go. But he would make me push him away. It was unbearable. If I had left his home without leaving Paris, Madame would have understood everything immediately, no matter what I told her. It would have been agony for her. And she would have hated me.'

'So you learned to drive this truck,' said Younger.

'I couldn't think of any other way. I had to leave the university. He was always finding ways to be near me. Madame would have seen how it was, sooner or later.'

Younger paused to take it in. 'You gave up the Sorbonne to spare her.'

There was a longer silence. 'There are three things I'm going to do in my life,' she said. 'The first is to make Luc better. The second is to graduate from the Sorbonne, for my father. If they don't take me back right after the war, I'll apply and apply again until they do.'

'And the third?'

She smoothed her skirt. Then she studied him. 'Of course it's different for you. You're a man – you've had many girls, and you are applauded for it.'

'Me? I'm as celibate as a Capuchin.'

She laughed mockingly.

'If you're listening to the nurses again,' said Younger, 'they're just jealous because I spend all my time with you.'

'You never married?' she asked.

'I don't believe in marriage.'

'Let me guess why not,' she said. 'Because you think it's against man's nature to be monogamous.'

'Marriage looks to the future. Not practical, when you're at war.'

'I have another explanation.' She put her glass down and picked up Younger's leather jacket and military cap. 'It's because you're American.'

'Well?'

'Well, if you were a Frenchman and you got married, you could have as many affairs as you liked. You would consider it your right. But as an American, you would have to be faithful.'

'Would I?'

'American married men are much more faithful. That's what Monsieur de Tocqueville says.' She stood up, trying on the jacket and cap. 'How do I look?'

He didn't answer.

'You don't like me to wear your uniform? All right.' She took the cap from her head and set it on his, tilting it to her liking. 'It suits you better anyway.'

As she adjusted the cap on his head, bent at the waist before him, the lapels of his leather jacket, oversized on her, fell open at her neck, allowing a small silver and mother-of-pearl locket to hang down from her white blouse. He took her wrists and slowly lowered her to the grass.

'What are you doing?' she asked.

He undid the top button of her blouse.

'Don't,' she said.

He kissed her neck.

'No,' she whispered.

He stopped, looked at her. Her fiercely green eyes stared up at him, breathtakingly. The locket rose and fell with her chest. He reached for her shirt. She scrambled away like an animal. When she sat up, on her knees, his pistol was in her hands. But it was also in its holster, which she couldn't shake loose. She flapped the gun furiously, making the gun belt wag like a dog's tail. Finally she thrashed the pistol free and pointed it at him.

'Don't move,' she said.

He raised an eyebrow. 'For the record,' he said, 'I was about to rebutton you.'

'I don't need your help buttoning,' she answered, standing and making good on that claim. He began to get up as well. 'I said don't move.'

He rose, ignoring her command.

'Just get in your car and go,' she said, wriggling out of his leather jacket and throwing it at his feet. 'If you take one step toward me, I'll shoot.'

'Go ahead.' He stepped forward to pick up the jacket. 'Better to die at your hands than in a number of other ways I can think of.'

She never had a chance to reply. The motor of a military vehicle roared nearby, and an open two-seater swung its headlights directly onto them. The vehicle pulled up not ten feet away. Younger's orderly hopped out, leaving the engine running; in the glare of the headlights, Colette was still pointing a pistol at Younger.

'Sorry, sir,' said the orderly. 'Everything all right, sir?'

'What is it, Franklin?'

'They want you back, sir. On the double.'

'Why?' asked Younger.

'Two Jerry runners got captured up near Reems,' said Franklin, referring to the city of Rheims. 'They found messages on them. The attack's coming tonight, sir. The big one.'

'Forgive me, Mademoiselle, but my country requires me,' said Younger, picking up his gun belt from the grass and strapping it on.

She frowned. 'Will they send you to the front?'

He smiled. 'I've never heard such solicitude from someone aiming a deadly weapon at me.' He extended his palm for the pistol. She gave it to him.

'Sir?' asked the private anxiously.

'I'm coming, Franklin,' said Younger. He gazed ruefully at the unfinished repast. 'Maybe the boy can have the rest of this tomorrow. Not the wine.'

At 11:45 p.m. that night, as American and French generals in Paris enjoyed a dress-uniform dinner at the former home of Baron Charles

Rothschild, the Allied forces at Château-Thierry opened fire with everything they had on the invisible German divisions believed to be assembling on the north bank of the Marne. For four hours the Germans took the bombardment, unmoved and unmoving. At 3.30 in the morning, their attack began.

Under cover of a furious counter-barrage – 17,500 rounds of gas shells; thirty-five tons of explosives – unseen German hands began filling the Marne with pontoon bridges. Over these bridges came the storm troopers, in wave after wave. The French 125th was instantly overpowered and fell back pell-mell. By contrast, the naive American forward companies held their ground and were soon wiped out to a man.

The German advance was steady, irresistible, overrunning everything in its path. After two miles, the Germans were funneled between the two ridges rising up on either side of the Surmelin valley. This was an eventuality for which the Americans had prepared. Defying orders from French commanders who refused to acknowledge the possibility of a wholesale Allied retreat, the American Third Division had installed heavy artillery, well fortified, on the Bois d'Aigremont on one side of the valley and the Moulin Ruiné on the other, in the rear of the Allied positions. Now these guns rained down on the exposed German infantry. On and on came the German regiments through the enfilade; they died in such great number the soil went red to a depth of six inches.

Younger's dressing station was deluged with casualties. Wagons, both motorized and horse-drawn, shuttled in and out, carrying the wounded, the dead, the dying. In the dark, early hours of July 16, a German officer with shattered ribs was brought in, but Younger, who had barely slept in seventy-two hours, refused to give the officer priority over wounded Allied infantrymen.

'American savages,' the officer remarked, in German.

'Let me think,' replied Younger in the same language as he withdrew a surprisingly long stretch of barbed wire, dripping, from a man's leg. 'Who was it that torpedoed a British hospital ship two weeks ago, then killed the surviving nurses by firing on them in the water? Oh yes, that's right – the Germans.'

The officer spat blood into a handkerchief. 'You Americans are firing on fallen men out there. You are not giving us a chance to surrender. You are killing everybody.'

'Good,' said Younger.

Although the fighting went on for another twenty-four hours, it was clear by the morning of the sixteenth that the German offensive had failed. On the eighteenth, the Allies launched a stunning counterattack, bolstered by an American fighting force now a million strong. Suddenly the Germans, who only days before had Paris in their sights, were reeling, backpedaling, desperately trying to regroup north of the Marne to avoid a complete rout.

The next dawn, Younger's medical corps was redeployed to Soissons. The encampments of Château-Thierry were deserted now. All that remained was rubble, a blown-out church, and the burnt wreckage of a shot-down German Friedrichshafen bomber. The only sounds were those of military transport and the booming of ordnance in the north.

As his company rolled out, Younger looked back at the dirt road on which, for several days, he and Colette had driven, with the silent boy in the rear of the truck. Then he put the thought from his mind. If a man doesn't look ahead, neither should he look back.

He didn't see her for the remainder of the war.

By August, the Germans were beaten. They knew it; everyone knew it. Yet the war churned on. In early November, Younger was in a bombed-out barracks near Verdun, stooped over an English gunner who had been pinned under a half-ton cannon. The gunner's leg was broken; Younger was trying to reset the fibula. Despite his pain, the man kept looking at his watch.

'Begging your pardon, sir,' said the wounded man at last, 'but will you be much longer?'

'I could just chop it off,' answered Younger. 'That would be faster.'

'The Boches, sir,' whispered the man. 'They're going to shell here in ten minutes.'

'How would you know that, soldier?' asked Younger.

The wounded man glanced about to ensure they were alone. 'It's a – a sort of arrangement, sir.'

'Is it?' Younger looked at the man's eyes to see if he was raving. He did not appear to be.

'They bomb us here for forty minutes, and then we got a spot where we bomb them for forty minutes. Same time, same place, every day. That way nobody's the worse for it.'

Younger stopped what he was doing: 'Your officers consent to this?'

'*They* don't know,' said the soldier. 'We gunners worked it out amongst ourselves, so to speak. You won't tell, will you, sir?'

Younger considered it: 'No, I won't.'

Two days later, at 5.45 a.m., radiomen scattered throughout France picked up an all-channels signal broadcasting from the Eiffel Tower. It was a message from Marshal Foch, the supreme Allied commander, announcing the war's end. An armistice had been signed. All hostilities were to cease at eleven hundred hours, French time.

By nine that morning, the cease-fire order had been formally transmitted to Allied commanders and communicated to the men in the trenches. Paradoxically, the soldiers with the most to gain from the news were the ones made most anxious by it. Men who had learned to throw themselves month after month headlong into machine-gun fire, numb to personal risk, suddenly feared they might die in the last two hours of the war.

At 10.30, the regiment with which Younger was serving began ferociously shelling German positions across no-man's-land. In an officer's dugout, Younger shouted to a second lieutenant he knew, asking what on earth was happening.

'We're attacking,' said the second lieutenant.

'What?' yelled Younger, refusing to believe he had heard correctly. Then he saw infantrymen filing through the network of intersecting trenches, faces taut, armed and packed for assault. From the direction of the front, he heard commands shouted and machine guns firing – from the German side, meaning that Allied soldiers were already scrambling out over the top.

'This is madness,' said Younger.

The lieutenant shrugged: 'Orders,' he replied.

At 10.56, the command went out to halt the Allied attack. It took approximately two minutes for that order to disseminate from field headquarters to radio command posts to captains in the field. At 10.58, the last Allied guns fell silent. At 10.59, the rain of German artillery let up. An ethereal, fragile silence hung in the air.

Twelve seconds later, Younger heard the whistle of one last incoming shell – by the sound of it, a volley from a long-range 75-millimeter gun. The shot hit close by; the ground shook beneath him, and plugs of dirt fell from the walls. Possibly the shell had found a dugout, perhaps even an inhabited one. All waited with suspended breath. Then they heard the eruption of three Allied howitzers, presumably aimed at the German gun that had launched the last shell.

'No,' whispered Younger.

Naturally the Germans reciprocated. Soon the air was screaming and shaking again with a full-scale bombardment. The onslaught went on uninhibited for hours. It even featured the explosion of signal flares in the sky, pointless in daytime and harmless in effect. Neither side appeared to have an objective, unless it was to expend every last piece of ammunition in its arsenal.

Eleven thousand men were killed or wounded on November 11, 1918, in fighting that took place after all their commanding officers knew the war was over.

Younger was attached after the armistice to the Allied army of occupation. The border crossing into Germany was a revelation: in enemy country, there were green fields well tended, roofs and chimneys undamaged, cattle fat with sweet grass, farmers' wives round with plentiful harvests. The Allied soldiers – the French especially, but not only they – looked on in disgust, after the ruination of France.

In Bitburg, Younger had hospital duty. He didn't like it. The work was too regular and, if he had to be frank, too safe. One lunchtime in January of the new year, Younger was taken by surprise when an orderly tapped him on the shoulder, told him he had a visitor, and gestured to the refectory doorway, where he saw Colette in her usual wool sweater and long skirt.

He wiped his mouth, went to her. They neither shook hands nor embraced. Soldiers pushed by Younger to enter the huge, raucous mess hall.

'You're alive,' she said.

'So it seems. You're causing a commotion, Miss Rousseau.'

Several of the soldiers rushing through the doorway had skidded to an abrupt stop, causing the ones behind to trip over them, with a chaotic pileup the result, all because of the improbably lovely French girl standing in the doorway.

'On your way, you men – on your way,' said Younger, helping one up from the floor and giving him a shove. 'What brings you to Bitburg?'

'I'm trying to find the German army liaison office. I recognized your company colors outside. I thought I would—' She looked down. 'I wanted to apologize for that night. It was my fault.'

'Your fault?' he said.

She frowned. 'I flirted with you.'

'Yes. My happiest recollection from the war. I know what kind of man you're looking for.'

Her frown grew severer. 'You do?'

'One you can trust,' said Younger. 'You trusted me, and I failed you. I believe I may regret it for the rest of my life. Come on – I'll take you to the liaison office.'

'No. It's all right.'

'Let me,' said Younger. 'They'll treat you better if you're with an American.'

The exterior of the hospital was silent and gray, as were the streets of Bitburg, as was its sky, which seemed perpetually to announce a snowfall that never came. He led her to a squat brick building where a small staff of Germans operated a kind of lost-and-found – not for objects, but for soldiers. A queue of at least a hundred civilians stretched from its front door down the street. Colette, seeing the line, told Younger he should go back. Then someone at the door called out and waved them to the front. The line was for civilians, not army officers.

At the counter, with Younger translating, Colette said she was looking for a soldier named Gruber – Hans Gruber.

The stolid, thick-set German woman behind the counter eyed the French girl without sympathy. 'Reason?' she asked.

Colette explained that she had served in a hospital for flu victims near Paris in the last months of the war. Among the dying was a German prisoner – Hans Gruber. 'He was very sad and very devout. He said his company didn't even know what had happened to him. I promised to try to return his dog tag and belongings to his parents after the war.'

'Give me the tag,' said the woman. 'It is the property of the German state.'

'I didn't bring it,' Colette replied. 'I'm sorry.'

The woman made an expression of contempt. 'Regimental information?'

Colette provided it. She was instructed to come back in seven days. 'But I can't,' she said. 'I have a job and – a little brother.'

The woman shrugged and called for the next in line.

'I'll come back, Miss Nightingale,' Younger said to Colette when they were outside.

The reference made no impression on her: 'No, I'll find a way,' she replied.

A sort of mush began to fall – not snow; more like clumps of congealed rain. 'You have a new job?' he asked.

'Yes,' she said more brightly. 'It starts in March. You were right: the Sorbonne turned me down. But it doesn't matter. I'll get in next year. Anyway, God took pity on me. Madame has offered me a position as a technician at the Radium Institute. I'll learn more there than I would have even at university.'

'God works in mysterious ways.'

She looked at him: 'You don't believe?'

'Why wouldn't I believe? What an outrage – these people who hold up the deaths of a hundred thousand children from the flu and blame it on God. It's not His fault.'

'It's not.' She turned away. Her voice fell: 'They've taken Luc. To a school for recalcitrant children. He was living with me in the basement of the institute. Madame is letting me stay there until my position opens up. It's perfectly nice. There are bathrooms, and books, and hot plates I cook on. But someone reported us to the authorities.'

'Fools,' said Younger. 'What is recalcitrant supposed to mean?'

'The other children are thieves and imbeciles. It's criminal. Luc learns nothing and receives no treatment.'

'He doesn't need treatment. He needs to live.'

'How do you know?' she asked. 'Are you a psychologist?'

He didn't answer.

'You could have helped him get the best treatment in the world,' she said. 'You remember how he used to write notes sometimes? He doesn't even do that anymore. He hasn't communicated with anyone for two months. Oh, why am I telling you this? Why am I here? I hate this country. I have to go – my train is coming.'

She ran away.

He expected to see her the following week. After ten days, he went to the liaison office to find out if she had come back. She hadn't. Younger lit a cigarette and gazed up at Bitburg's perpetually gray sky.

★　★　★

In the spring, when his discharge orders finally came through, he took a train to Paris. At the Radium Institute, he asked for Miss Rousseau. The receptionist told him that Colette was out, but expected back shortly. He waited outside.

The streets of Paris were admirable. Always a tree in the right place. The buildings handsome and large, but never too large. The smell of clean water on pavement. He wondered whether he should move there.

Colette was halfway up the steps before she recognized him. She stopped in astonishment and broke into her most radiant smile, which as quickly disappeared. She was even thinner than she had been. Her cheeks had a pretty pointing of red, but the cause, it seemed to him, might be hunger.

'Come inside,' she said.

He shook his head. They went walking instead. 'Did you find your Hans Gruber?' he asked.

'Not yet.'

'You didn't go back to Bitburg, did you?'

'No, but I will.'

'Because you didn't have money for the train. Have you been eating?'

'I'll be fine in ten days. That's when my job starts. For now I have to save everything for Luc. They don't feed him enough in school. Do I look awful?'

'More beautiful than ever,' said Younger, 'if that's possible. I found your soldier. Hans was Austrian. He volunteered with the Germans when the war broke out. They gave me an address in Vienna. Here.'

He handed her a piece of paper. She stared at it: 'Thank you.'

'How is Luc?' he asked.

'Terrible.'

'Do they ever let him out?'

'Of course. In fact his school goes on holiday at the end of this week. How long will you be in Paris? I know he'd like to see you.'

'I'm leaving this Friday.'

'Oh,' she said. 'Do come and see the institute. We have American soldiers visiting, learning Madame's radiography techniques.'

'I know. That's why I won't go in. I've had enough of the army for a while.'

'But I could introduce you to Madame.'

'No.' They had come to a street with trolley cars rambling on it. 'Well, Miss Rousseau, I don't want to keep you.'

She looked up at him: 'Why did you come?'

'I almost forgot. There was something else I meant to give you.'

He handed her an envelope from his pocket. It contained a short telegram, which read:

I WILL ACCEPT BOY WITH PLEASURE AS NEW PATIENT. ADVISE
SISTER TO CALL ON ME DIRECTLY SHE ARRIVES VIENNA.

FREUD

She was speechless.

'You can kill two birds with one stone,' said Younger. 'Take Luc to Freud, and pay a visit to your soldier's family.'

'But I can't. I don't speak German. Where would I stay? I can't even afford the tickets.'

'I speak German,' he replied.

'You would come?'

'Not if you're going to shoot me.'

To his surprise, she threw her arms around his neck. He had the impression she was crying.

Jimmy Littlemore unburdened the kitchen table of his feet. He stretched his good arm, poured two more whiskeys. 'I don't get you, Doc. First you practically rape her—'

'Completely false.'

'You unbuttoned her shirt. What kind of girl did you think she was?'

Younger scrutinized the autumnal color of the bourbon. 'The rules are different in war.'

'She didn't think so,' said Littlemore. 'What I like is how she knows what she's going to do with herself. She wants her sore bun, and she's going to get it.'

'I beg your pardon?'

'That school, the sore bun. Wants it for her dad. That's how I feel about making it to Washington. My dad missed his only shot with the Feds. When Teddy Roosevelt went to DC, my dad could've gone with him. He was the best cop in New York, but he had family, kids – you know. I'll probably never get the shot myself, but if I do, let me tell you, that would make him proud. So when did you find out her soldier boy wasn't dead?'

Younger's glass stopped midway to his mouth. 'How did you know that?'

'The dog tags,' said Littlemore. 'She goes to a German army office to locate a dead soldier, and she leaves the guy's tags back in France? I don't think so. I don't think she has the guy's tags. Why would that be? Because he's not dead.'

'I always said you should have been a detective.'

'She's sweet on the guy, huh? Didn't want you to know?'

Younger took a moment before answering: 'She's in love with him – her Hans. Want to know what happened in Austria?'

'I'm all ears.'

CHAPTER SEVEN

NO CITY IN the world was more altered by the Great War than Vienna.

Not physically. Vienna was never invaded during the war, nor shelled, as Paris had been. Not one stone was nicked. What the war had shattered was merely Vienna's soul and its place in the world.

In the spring of 1914, Vienna had been the sun around which revolved a galaxy of fifty million subjects speaking dozens of languages, all bound in fealty to Emperor Franz Josef and the House of Hapsburg. Vienna was rich, and its affairs mattered to the world. Five years later, it was a city of no consequence in a country of no consequence – starving, freezing, its factories shuttered, its emperor a fugitive, its empire abolished, its children deformed by years of malnutrition.

The result was a host of contradictory impressions for travelers arriving there in March of 1919. Riding their cab from the railway station – an elegant, two-horse, tandem carriage – Younger, Colette, and Luc saw under a rising sun a Vienna superficially every bit as grand as it had formerly been. The majestic Ringstrasse, that wide-avenue parade of monumentality encircling the old inner city, presented the same invincible visage that it had before the war. The Ring borrowed liberally, and without nice regard for consistency, from the entire Western architectural canon. After trotting by an oversized, blazing white Greek Parthenon, their carriage passed a darkly Gothic cathedral, and after that a many-winged neo-Renaissance palazzo. The first was the parliament, the second city hall, the third the world-famous university. Even the inferior buildings of the Ring would have been palaces elsewhere.

But the figures out for a morning stroll on the Ring, though fashionably dressed, did not display the same imperial bearing. Many of the men were maimed; crutches, dangling sleeves, and eye patches were ubiquitous. Even the able-bodied had a vacantness about them. Off the Ring, in smaller streets, children lined up by the hundreds for food packages. At one point Colette and Younger saw a clutch of these children break into a mad rush; the stampede was followed by angry shouting from adults, then by blows, then by trampling.

Colette wanted the cab to drop her off at Hans Gruber's address.

Younger pointed out that, because of the lateness of their train, which was supposed to have arrived the night before, they were in danger of missing their appointment with Freud.

'Can you ask the driver how far away the address is?' she replied. 'Perhaps it's close.'

It wasn't. Colette relented. After she had settled back, disappointed, their driver spoke to her in excellent French: 'Excuse me, Mademoiselle, but if I may: Does France's hatred of the Germans extend to the Viennese?'

'No,' she answered. 'We know you've suffered as much as the rest of us.'

'We do have our troubles,' agreed the driver. 'Have you noticed, sir, what is so disturbing about the dogs in Vienna?'

'I haven't seen any dogs,' replied Younger.

'That's what's so disturbing. The people are eating their dogs. And you must have heard of the sobbing sickness? People begin to sob for no explicable reason – men as well as women – and can't stop. They sob in their sleep; it goes on so long it ends in epileptic fits. When they wake, they have no memory of it. It's our nerves. We've always been nervous, we Viennese – gay but nervous.'

Colette complimented his French.

'Mademoiselle is as generous as she is charming,' replied the coachman. 'I had a Parisian governess as a boy. Here is my card. If you require a cab again, perhaps you will send for me.'

The name engraved on the card was Oktavian Ferdinand Graf Kinsky von Wchinitz und Tettau.

'You're a nobleman,' said Younger. The word *Graf* is a title of nobility in German; the *von* in his last name carried a similar meaning.

'A count, yes, and a most fortunate count at that. I held on to my very last carriage, and it has given me a living. A baron friend of mine sweeps floors in a restaurant. And consider my livery.'

Younger for the first time noticed the driver's once-dignified but now-threadbare uniform.

'It belonged to one of my servants. I was lucky there too: I had a man as short and round as his master. Here we are – the Hotel Bristol.'

'But this – this is much too grand,' said Colette when she saw her room. Luc's eyes fixed on a table dressed in white linen, where a silver tray was piled high with pastries along with two steaming pots – one of coffee, the other of hot chocolate. He wasn't starving like some of Vienna's children, but he wasn't too far from that condition either. His sister added, 'I've never been in a room like this in all my life.'

'And they dare to charge three English pennies for it,' replied Younger. 'Robbery.'

Less than an hour later, in a small but comfortably middle-class apartment house on Berggasse – a narrow, cobbled lane gently sloping down to the Danube canal – a maid let Younger and Colette into Sigmund Freud's empty consultation room. 'I'm so nervous,' Colette whispered.

Younger nodded. Well she might be, he thought: Colette would be both worried and excited about the prospect that Dr Freud might actually be able to help her brother; and she would be eager to make a good impression on the world-famous Viennese physician. But she, Younger reflected, was not the one who had disappointed him.

Freud's consulting room was like a bath into which civilization itself had been poured. Leather-bound volumes lined the walls, and every inch not occupied by books was filled with antiquities and miniature statuary: Greek vases intermixed with Chinese terracottas, Roman intagli with South American figurines and Egyptian bronzes. The room pulsed with a rich fume of cigar and the deep crimson of Oriental carpets, which not only lay thick on the parquet floor, but also draped the end tables and even covered a long couch.

A door opened. A dog, a miniature chow, trotted through it, yapping. The animal was followed by Freud himself, who paused in the doorway ordering the dog away from Younger's and Colette's shoes. The chow obeyed.

'So my boy,' said Sigmund Freud to Younger without introduction, 'you are no longer a psychoanalyst?'

Freud wore a suit and necktie and vest. In his left hand, half-raised, was a cigar between two fingers. He had grown older since Younger last saw him. His gray hair had thinned and receded; his short, pointed beard was now starkly white. Nevertheless, for a man of sixty-three, he remained handsome, fit and robust, with eyes exactly as Younger remembered them – both piercing and sympathetic, scowling and amused.

'Miss Rousseau,' said Younger, 'may I present to you Dr Sigmund Freud? Dr Freud, I thought you might wish to speak with Miss Rousseau before meeting her brother.'

'Delighted, Fräulein,' said Freud. He turned back to Younger: 'But you didn't answer my question.'

'I no longer practice psychology at all, sir.'

'You were a psychoanalyst?' Colette asked Younger.

'Didn't I mention it?' he replied.

'He never told you he was once my most promising follower in America?' asked Freud.

'No,' said Colette.

'Certainly,' said Freud. 'The first time we met, Younger conducted an analysis under my supervision – of the girl who became his wife.'

'Oh yes,' said Colette. 'Of course.'

Younger said nothing.

'He didn't tell you he was married?' asked Freud.

Colette colored. 'He doesn't tell me anything about himself.'

'I see. Well, he isn't married anymore, in case the subject is of interest. But he's told you what analysis consists of, surely?'

'No, not that either.'

'I'd better explain then – take a seat, please,' said Freud, glancing at Younger. Then he called out to his maid, instructed her to bring tea, and eased himself into a comfortable chair. 'You're a scientist, Miss Rousseau?'

'I'm studying to be one. A radiochemist. I'll be working in Madame Curie's institute. My post begins next week.'

'I see. Good. As a scientist, you will easily follow what I'm about to say. When a child is to be analyzed, we've found it necessary for the parent – or guardian, in your case – to be informed in advance of what we analysts do. That's why Younger has given me an opportunity to speak with you first.'

Younger and Colette had left Luc at the hotel. Paula, the Freuds' maid, came in with a tea service.

'All neuroses,' Freud went on as the maid poured tea, 'are caused by memories, typically a memory from long ago, involving a forbidden wish. The wishes from which neurotics suffer are not unique to them. We all had them in our childhood, but with neurotics, something prevents these recollections from being forgotten and disposed of in the ordinary way. They linger in the recesses of the individual's mind – so well hidden that my patients initially are not even conscious of them. The aim of analysis is to make the patient conscious of these repressed memories.'

'In order to forget them?' asked Colette.

'In order to be free of them,' replied Freud. 'But the process is seldom an easy one, because the truth can be difficult to accept. Invariably the patient – and the patient's family – will resist our interpretations, resist them quite forcefully. There can be good reason. Once the truth is out, the family may be changed unalterably.'

Colette frowned. 'The family?'

'Yes. In fact that's often how we know we've arrived at the truth: the patient's family suddenly demands that the analysis come to an end. Although occasionally there are other, stronger proofs. I'll give you an example. I have a patient – like you, French by birth – from a family of considerable rank and wealth. Her complaint is frigidity.'

Younger shifted. The carnal explicitness of psychoanalysis was chief among the reasons Younger didn't like discussing it with Colette.

'In one of her first sessions,' Freud continued, 'this patient, an attractive woman of about forty, described a dream she'd had the night before. She was in the Bois de Boulogne. A couple she knew lay down on a double bed right there in the park, on the green grass by a lake. That was all – nothing more. What would you say that dream meant, Miss Rousseau?'

'I don't know,' answered Colette. 'Do dreams have meaning?'

'Most assuredly. I informed her that she had witnessed a scene of sexual intercourse that she was not supposed to have seen – perhaps more than one – when she was a small child, probably between the ages of three and five. She replied that such a thing was impossible, because she grew up with no mother. But of course she'd had nurses. Suddenly she remembered that her first nurse had left the family abruptly when she was five. She had never known why. I said it was likely this nurse was involved in her dream. So she made inquiries back home.

'She asked everyone, including the longtime servants. They all denied anything untoward in the nurse's departure, and she reported back to me that I must be mistaken. Then she had another dream, in which this very nurse appeared, but with a horse-like face. I told her that this represented – but, Younger, perhaps you know what the second dream represented?'

'No,' answered Younger.

'No? In that case,' replied Freud, 'why don't you tell Miss Rousseau what *I* said it meant?'

'I'm not sure the subject matter is appropriate.'

'For me?' asked Colette sharply.

'If Miss Rousseau is going to consent to her brother's treatment,' said Freud, 'don't you think she should know what she's consenting to?'

'Very well,' said Younger. 'To begin with, Dr Freud would probably have said that the nurse's horse-like face was an example of condensation: it represented both the nurse herself and the man she slept with.'

'Good,' said Freud, looking genuinely pleased. 'And who was that man?'

'The patient's father was a horseman, I suppose?'

'No,' Freud replied, giving nothing else away.

'Did she associate him with horses?'

'Not to my knowledge.'

Younger paused. 'But horses were kept on the property?'

'They had a stable,' said Freud. 'For their carriages.'

'In that case,' Younger reflected, 'I suspect you would have said that the man the nurse slept with was someone involved with those horses – but associated as well in some way with the patient's father.'

'Excellent!' cried Freud. 'I told her that her nurse was in all probability involved with their groomsman, who was in fact related to her father. She answered that she had already questioned the groomsman – he was one of the servants who had told her the nurse had done nothing illicit. I said she might wish to question him again.'

'Did she?' asked Colette.

'She did indeed,' replied Freud. 'She went to the man and told him she knew all about his affair with her nurse. Whereupon he confessed everything. Their tryst was the stable. The nurse would feed my patient a syrup that made her very drowsy. They would lay her down on a bed of hay and proceed to their business. The groomsman added, by the way, that the maid was quite hot-blooded – he was afraid sometimes she might die of pleasure. The affair began when my patient was three and continued until she was five, when the lovers were discovered and the maid was dismissed.'

'But that's incredible,' cried Colette. '*Vraiment incroyable.*'

'Well done, my boy,' Freud said to Younger, as if he deserved the credit, and rose to indicate that the interview was over. 'You must join us for dinner this evening, both of you. Martha, my wife, especially invites you. Bring your brother, Fräulein. It will give me a better sense of how to proceed.'

Colette said she would be honored.

'Dr Freud,' said Younger, 'might I have a word with you?'

'I was about to ask the same of you. Will you excuse us for five minutes, Miss Rousseau? Younger, come to my study.'

'And how exactly,' asked Freud, seated behind the desk in his private study, which was populated by even more antiquities, 'do you expect me to analyze a boy who can't talk?'

'But you—'

'It's like the beginning of a joke: Did you hear about the mute who went to see Sigmund Freud? Your behavior, my boy, wants analyzing.'

'My behavior?'

Freud raised the lid of a wooden box. 'Cigar?'

'Thank you.'

Freud cut the cigar with fine, delicate scissors. 'Well, you have something to say to me, and I to you. Let's start with what you want to tell me.'

Younger considered how to put it.

'Will you permit me?' asked Freud. 'You want to say, first of all, that bringing the boy to me wasn't your idea.'

Younger didn't reply.

'If it had been your idea,' said Freud, 'you would have explained psychoanalysis to Miss Rousseau, told her you'd practiced it, described its benefits, and so on. You did none of these things. The idea was therefore hers. Moreover, the reason you were reluctant to have the boy analyzed is what you expect me to say about his condition. Miss Rousseau has obviously been the boy's substitute-mother for some time. You expect me to conclude that he therefore wants to sleep with her, and you want me to keep that information from her.'

Younger was astounded. 'There's only one other man alive,' he said, 'whom I constantly ask how he knows what he knows, and he happens to be listening to this story right now.'

'You didn't say that,' said Littlemore, his badly scuffed black shoes once again crossed on top of the kitchen table. 'Don't interrupt like that. It spoils the – uh—'

'Dramatic effect?'

'Yeah. You know, this Freud guy, *he* should have been a detective. But you mixed things up pretty good there, Doc. You made it sound like, according to your man Freud, Luc wants to sleep with Colette. And he wants to sleep with her because she's been his *mom* all these years!'

Littlemore broke into a loud laugh. He stopped when he saw Younger's unchanged expression. 'He doesn't think *that*,' said Littlemore.

Younger nodded.

'No, he doesn't,' said Littlemore.

'That's why I stopped practicing psychoanalysis,' answered Younger. 'I told Freud ten years ago I didn't believe in it. That's how he knew what I was thinking.'

'So what did you say?'

'Yes, I'd appreciate it if you didn't tell her that, Dr Freud,' answered Younger. 'She'll believe it's true.'

'Whereas you don't.'

'No, sir.'

Freud smoked his cigar, nodding.

'I'm sorry,' Younger added, 'but I can't persuade myself that Luc's difficulties have anything to do with a desire to sleep with his sister, his mother, or any member of his family. If he has a neurosis at all, it's a sort of war neurosis. Not sexual at all.'

'Not sexual – a diagnosis you base on what evidence? You remind me of the government physicians who attended our conference in Budapest. "Yes, we have to hand it to Freud. Yes, the old man was right about the unconscious after all. Yes, the war neuroses are caused by unconscious memories, just as Freud always said. But that disgusting sexual business? Thank God it has nothing to do with shell shock." In fact not one case of war neurosis has yet been analyzed all the way down to its roots. We don't know what connection it has to childhood wishes. That's why I'm so interested in Miss Rousseau's brother.'

'To see if you can find Oedipus beneath his symptoms?'

'If he's there, why not find him? But don't be so sure what I expect to find. Something else may be hiding in the boy. I've seen something new, Younger – dimly, but I've seen it. Perhaps another ghost in the cellar.'

'What is it?'

'I can't tell you, because I don't know.' Freud tamped ash from his cigar. 'But we haven't gotten to what I wanted to say to you.'

'You want me to reconsider my rejection of the Oedipus complex.'

'I want you to practice psychoanalysis again. Why are you here?'

'Miss Rousseau—'

'Wanted her brother analyzed,' interrupted Freud, 'and you're in love with her, so you said yes to please her. Obviously. Apart from that.'

'Apart from that?'

'Assuming the boy can be analyzed at all, you could have done it yourself. There was no need to travel to Austria. Indeed coming here was illogical given that Miss Rousseau plans to return to Paris shortly;

an analysis cannot be conducted in a week or two, as you well know. It follows that you had another reason for coming.'

'Which was?' asked Younger.

'You wanted to see me,' said Freud.

Younger reflected. There was a long pause before he finally answered: 'That's true.'

'Why?'

'I think to ask you something.'

Freud waited. There was a longer silence.

'I have no –' said Younger, looking for the right word, – 'no more faith.'

'The loss of religious faith,' replied Freud, 'is the beginning of maturity.'

'Not religious faith,' said Younger.

Freud waited.

'The war,' said Younger. 'Millions of men, millions upon millions of young men, killed for nothing. Meaningless slaughter. Countless more crippled and maimed.'

'Ah,' said Freud. 'Yes. Such destruction as we have lived through is very hard to fathom. Everything I believed I knew about the mind falls short in the face of it. But that's still not why you're here.'

Younger didn't reply.

'The war isn't what you want to ask me about,' added Freud.

'I don't see a point anymore,' said Younger. 'I don't see – the possibility of a point. I have thoughts, I have desires, but I no longer see any purpose.' His right fist clenched; he made it relax. 'Can one live without purpose?'

'The demand that your life have a purpose, my boy, is something you acquired from your parents, probably your father – something to be analyzed.'

'To say that,' replied Younger, 'is to concede that there is no purpose.'

'Then I can't help you.'

Another pause.

'You're not smoking,' said Freud, noticing that Younger's cigar was out and offering him a light. 'I've followed your career from afar. Brill has kept me informed. You've done well.'

'Thank you.'

'You fought?' asked Freud.

'Yes.'

'My sons too. Martin is still a prisoner, in Italy.' Freud drew on his cigar. 'I was very sorry to hear about your wife's death. A terrible thing. Do you treat women badly?'

'I beg your pardon?'

'You never remarried. You have an exaggerated idea of female innocence, to judge by your reluctance to speak about sexuality in front of Miss Rousseau. I'm wondering if you habitually mistreat women.'

'Why would I mistreat women?'

'It's a perfectly common reaction. A man who idealizes women not infrequently maintains a low opinion of them at the same time.'

'I don't have a low opinion of women. I have a high opinion of them.'

'I'm only observing. It was after your wife died that you turned away from psychology. You turned away from the mind.'

'I studied the mind,' replied Younger. 'Biologically.'

'That was *how* you turned away from it – probably a way of striking back.'

'At whom?'

'At your wife. At me, I suppose. At yourself.'

Younger said nothing.

'You abandoned psychoanalysis,' Freud continued, 'and you mistreat women for the same reason: because of a sense of responsibility for your wife's death.'

'That's absurd. I wasn't responsible for her death.'

'Absurdity is an offense to logic,' said Freud, 'but in the mind logic is not master.'

★   ★   ★

Colette was no longer in the consulting room when the two men emerged from Freud's study. Younger went outside, but didn't find her on the street either. He walked down Berggasse toward the canal. He thought she might have taken a walk to see the Danube. She wasn't there. Younger stared at the water a long time.

Back at the Hotel Bristol, Younger asked Luc if his sister had returned. The boy shook his head and showed Younger a picture he had drawn.

'Very accomplished,' said Younger. The boy had drawn a tree with many limbs. On several of those branches animals perched, each of them staring at the viewer with large, hungry eyes. 'Are they dogs?'

Luc shook his head.

'Wolves?'

The boy nodded.

'You realize, little man,' said Younger, 'we don't even know if you can speak. Physically, that is.'

Luc looked interested, but disinterested, simultaneously.

'But *you* know if you can,' said Younger. 'I know you know. And if you can't speak, Luc, there's no reason for you to go to Dr Freud. He's not that kind of doctor.'

The boy remained still.

'But if you *can*,' Younger continued, 'you could get out of all this very easily. By talking. Get out of seeing the doctor. Get out of that school you're in. Make your sister very happy.'

Luc stared at Younger a long while before turning his drawing over and writing a message on the back. It was only the second time he'd done so with Younger. The page bore two words: *You're wrong*.

Watching the boy sit down in a corner with one of his books, Younger wondered on which point he'd been wrong. That Luc knew if he could speak? Or that his talking would make his sister happy?

Colette returned to the hotel an hour later.

'You disappeared,' said Younger.

'I went—' she began.

'To the Grubers'.'

'Yes. I walked. But the address wasn't their house,' she replied. 'It wasn't a residence at all. I couldn't find out anything. I'm not even sure what kind of place it was. A concert hall, maybe. Could you help me?'

Younger accompanied her back to the address to translate. It proved to be a music school. A secretary, kind enough to look in the school records, found that a student by the name of Hans Gruber had attended the school – or at least applied to it – in 1914. She gave them a new address, which, they learned from their cab driver, was in the Hutteldorf district, almost two hours away by horse-drawn, although the trip would be faster and cheaper by train. Colette declared that she would go by herself tomorrow.

'Don't be silly. I'll come with you,' said Younger.

That evening, Martha Freud, her sister Minna, and the Freuds' maid Paula all fawned over Luc, pronouncing him the most adorable *schmächtige Kerlchen* in the world. Martha apologized repeatedly for the meagerness of the dinner fare, which in fact was the opposite of meager, but was extremely simple, as if the Freuds were country farmers. 'The awful war,' said Martha.

'At least the right side won,' declared Freud.

Martha asked how her husband could say such a thing when they had lost everything.

'We didn't lose everything, my dear,' said Freud chidingly.

'Only our life's savings,' replied Martha. 'We had it all in state bonds. The safest possible investment – everyone said so. There were pictures of Emperor Franz Josef on every one.'

'And now they are worth face value,' said Freud.

'They're worth nothing!' said Martha.

'Just what I said, my dear,' answered Freud. 'But our sons are unhurt, and our daughters are happy. True, we don't have Martin home yet, but he's better off where he is. As a prisoner, he's fed every day, while Vienna is starving. My patients pay me in goat's milk and hen's eggs – which has at least kept food on our table. But our movement, Younger, is rich. We received a bequest – a million crowns – from a Hungarian patient. When the money is released, we're going to build free clinics in Berlin and Hungary. Budapest will be our new center. Your old friend Ferenczi has just been appointed professor of psychology there.'

After finishing his meal, Luc was permitted to leave the table. He sat in a corner, absorbed in one of Freud's books.

'Why don't you let the boy stay here a night or two?' Freud asked Colette. 'I can't have proper sessions with him, but if he were under my roof, I could at least observe him.'

Younger found himself inwardly favoring Freud's plan, but not for psychiatric reasons. If the boy stayed with the Freuds, that would leave the two of them – Colette and Younger – alone in the hotel.

'You could stay too, Miss Rousseau,' Freud continued. 'Our nest is empty. Anna is away visiting her sister in Berlin. You could stay in her room.'

Younger spent the night by himself.

Colette was supposed to call at the hotel after breakfast the next morning. She did call after breakfast – but by then it was also after lunch.

'Martha and Minna took Luc to an amusement park,' she said, as if that fact explained the several hours she had been unaccounted for. 'He's so powerful – Dr Freud. Those eyes. He sees everything.'

'I know where you've been,' replied Younger. 'The Hutteldorf.'

'Yes. There was a train station near the Freuds'. I didn't want to trouble you. But—' she raised her eyebrows importuningly.

'You need to go back,' said Younger.

'Could you help me just one more time?' she asked, smiling her prettiest smile. 'I found the building where I think he used to live, but I couldn't understand anyone. I don't think the Grubers live there

anymore, but maybe someone can tell us where they've gone. The
train is quite fast.'

'Where are his things?' Younger asked her as they rode the metropolitan rail to the Hutteldorf. Vienna's winter had evidently been long
and cold: although it was nearly spring, not a tree was yet in bud.

'Things?' answered Colette.

'Your soldier's belongings. Which you were going to return to his
family. Did you forget them?'

'Of course not,' she said. 'I told you – I don't think the Grubers
live where we're going. Why did you hide it from me – that you were
married?'

'I didn't.'

'You never told me.'

'You never asked.'

'Yes I did,' replied Colette. 'You said you didn't believe in marriage.'

'Which was true.'

She looked out the window. 'You tell me nothing. It's just like lying.
It *is* lying.'

'Not speaking isn't lying,' he said.

'It is when it tricks someone. I'd rather you lied. At least if you lied,
I'd know you cared what I thought.'

They sat in silence as the train rumbled along the banks of the
brown, unstirred Danube. Younger watched her profile. He wondered
why or how he saw vulnerability in her, when none showed anywhere
on her face or figure. 'I do care,' he said.

'You don't.'

It was a principle with Younger not to say a word more about
himself, his past, his thoughts, than he had to – at least not to women.
They always asked him to; he never did. Evidently he was losing his
principles. 'It was November of 1909,' he said. 'Her name was Nora.
Would you like to hear about it?'

'If you don't mind telling me.'

105

'She was the most beautiful girl I'd ever met,' he continued, 'to that point. Totally different from you. Blonde. So fragile you thought she might break in your hands. Self-destructive too. I guess I liked that. We had a good six months. In my experience, that's not too bad – a good six months. But there were danger signs even then. I remember taking her shopping for wedding gowns. She got it into her head that the mannequin modeling dresses for us – a girl of about sixteen – was mocking her. I made the mistake of asking Nora what the girl had done. She accused me of defending her. I made the further mistake of laughing. That fight lasted two days. But things really began in earnest after the wedding, when she found some notebooks of mine. Psychoanalytic notebooks; case summaries. My women patients tended to – well – they usually began acting as if they were in love with me, which is exactly what's supposed to happen in psychoanalysis. You can ask Freud if you don't believe me.'

'Of course I believe you,' said Colette.

'The notebooks recorded what happened during each hour of analysis: what my patients said to me, my own inner reactions to them, and so forth.'

'And so forth?'

'Yes.'

'You – you liked your patients? And you said so in your notebooks?'

'One of them. Her name was Rachel.'

'Rachel. Was she pretty?'

'Her figure was like yours,' Younger replied. 'So yes, she was pretty.'

'Did she want to sleep with you?'

'She certainly did,' he said.

'You mean you did to her what you tried to do to me – and she let you.'

Younger only looked at Colette.

'I don't blame you,' she said. 'A pretty girl coming to your office every day and lying down on a couch and telling you her secrets? If I were a man, I would have found that – appealing.'

'Many analysts sleep with their patients. Freud doesn't do it. I didn't either.'

'You did with Nora,' said Colette.

'Not before I'd married her. And she wasn't my patient – not really.'

'I see. You didn't do anything with Rachel; you only said in your notebook that you were attracted to her. So you didn't understand why your wife was upset with you.'

'That's right,' said Younger.

'Well, that was very foolish of you.'

'Really? If women want their men never to have been attracted to another girl in all their lives, it's not the men who are being foolish.'

'What did you say to Nora?' asked Colette.

'I chided her for having read my notes, which were confidential. That was an error. She charged me with trying to hide my "romances" from her. She developed an elaborate theory according to which the entire notion of confidentiality in psychoanalysis was designed to allow doctors to have affairs with their female patients. A point came when not an evening would go by without some reference to my "romances." She said that I disgusted her. That I was unfeeling. That I was weak. She began to throw things. First at the walls, then at me.'

'And you were like a stone – impassive.'

'More or less.'

'That must have made her even angrier,' said Colette.

'Yes. She started to hit me. And kick me. At least she tried to.'

'What did you do?'

'Well, she was very young, and she'd been through some nightmarish events. On top of which she was very slight. I found it almost endearing when she tried to hit me. So I took it, suppressing my temper. Actually, I don't think I knew the extent to which my temper required suppression.

'One evening,' Younger went on, 'I came home to find a cheval glass of ours, an antique, a wedding present from my aunt, lying in pieces on the parlor floor. It turned out that Nora had deliberately broken it. That night she fought more furiously than ever. One of her blows landed, and I finally struck her – with the back of my hand, against her cheek. The force of it was stronger than I intended. She fell to the floor. To my astonishment, she apologized. It was the first time she'd ever apologized. She railed at her own folly, praised me for my kindness, and protested her undying love for me. She threw her arms around me and begged my forgiveness. She began to cry. I thought we had finally come to the end of it.

'Instead a pattern had begun. Our quarreling would start again, swell to its old proportions, and then we'd come to blows. Or rather, she would try to land blows until at last I struck her, at which point she would soften and beg to be forgiven. But the strangest thing of all was that I discovered that I could forestall the worst of our quarreling by – a – by cutting straight to the end of the pattern, in our intimate life.'

'I don't understand,' said Colette.

'No, and I'm not going to explain it,' said Younger. 'But it worked. For a while at least; not for long. When we were out in public – on a street, in a theater, anywhere – Nora began flying into rages, accusing me of being attracted to other women. Which I was, naturally, if they were attractive. At first I didn't deny her accusations, but in the end, just to quiet her down, I told her she was imagining it – that it was all in her head. She knew I was lying, but she seemed to prefer the lie to the truth.

'Then the young wife of a rich old patient asked me to make a house call. Her husband was dying. I was there a long while. Very sad. When I got home that night, I found myself concealing it from Nora. There was nothing to conceal, but the wife was famously charming – she'd been an actress – and I knew if I told Nora, there would have been an endless night of pointless recriminations. It had all become so boring, so monotonous. So I told her a different story; she believed me. At that moment, I realized I no longer loved my wife.

'About two months later, the same woman called me again. Her husband was dead, and she was resuming her career on Broadway. She said she had a painfulness in her lower back from rehearsals. She asked me to come to her house and have a look at it. I did. After that she asked me to make house calls several times a week. I lied about it recklessly to Nora.

'One day a note from the actress came to our apartment, requesting my presence as soon as possible. Of course Nora saw the note, and of course she understood at once all the lies I'd been telling her. She accused me of the affair; I confessed it. We divorced, scandalously, having been married little more than a year – and the most comic fact was that I hadn't had an affair at all. At least it would have been comic if Nora hadn't died shortly afterward. They wired me the news in Boston. She had fallen from a subway platform into a train. They called it an accident, but I doubt it. The one thing they did discover was that she was with child when she died. Freud says I feel responsible for her death.'

'Do you?' asked Colette.

'It's worse than that. I was happy she was dead. I'm still happy about it, to this day.'

Hutteldorf Station was the end of the line. In the town center of an otherwise bucolic and thickly wooded district stood a few low apartment houses. One of these was Gruber's address, but no one by that name lived there now. Younger discovered nothing useful until he approached a matronly woman sweeping the courtyard.

'Hans Gruber?' she said. 'Who all the girls were mad about? The tall young man with the blond hair and beautiful blue eyes?'

Younger translated this description without comment. Precisely by not reacting to it, Colette acknowledged its accuracy. He thought he saw color rising to her face.

'Of course I remember,' said the woman. 'What a lazy, haughty one he was. He had a stipend – his father had died, maybe? – so he didn't have to work. Wouldn't lift a finger. Just took long walks in the woods, playing his violin any old place. And what a temper. Ordered us around when he was sober, and insulted us when he was drunk.'

'It seems you're devoting a lot of effort,' said Younger to Colette after translating these comments, 'to someone who doesn't much deserve it.'

Colette frowned and shook her head, but didn't answer.

Younger explained their errand to the charwoman and asked if any of the Grubers still lived nearby.

'So he's dead,' replied the woman. 'Well, that's another one. No, the family I never knew. He came from one of those river towns in the west, near Bavaria. I don't know where. Ask at the Three Hussars near St. Stephen's. That's where he ate all his dinners. Maybe someone there will know.'

The sun had set when they arrived back in central Vienna. In the taxi, Younger asked the driver if he knew a restaurant called the Three Hussars. The driver said the restaurant was closed, but would be open again Thursday.

'It's just as well,' said Colette to Younger. 'I don't want you to come with me. I've taken up too much of your time already.'

'There's a game your brother plays, Fräulein,' Freud said to Colette that evening, 'with a fishing reel and string. He makes sounds when he plays. A sort of *ohh* and *ahh*. Do you know what he's saying?'

'Just nonsense,' answered Colette. 'Does the game mean something?'

'It means, for one thing, that there's nothing wrong with his vocal cords,' said Freud.

'To play the same game over and over,' asked Colette, 'is it very bad?'

'It's interesting,' said Freud.

Treating his dog to its walk the next morning, as the early sunshine shimmered off damp cobblestones, Sigmund Freud held the hand of a little French boy. Their conversation was distinctly one-sided. Freud chatted amiably, in French, recounting to Luc tales from Greek and Egyptian mythology. The boy was absorbed, but did not respond.

In a small triangular park, they came on a crowd encircling a man convulsing on the grass. His workingman's clothes were clean, if patched and fraying. His cap, evidently thrown to the ground when the fit began, lay next to his writhing body.

'If you were out with my wife and her sister,' Freud said quietly to the boy, 'they would undoubtedly cover your eyes at this point. Shall I cover your eyes?'

Luc shook his head. He exhibited none of the horror that children typically display in the presence of illness. Some in the crowd, taking pity on an epileptic, dropped coins into the man's cap. Eventually Freud led the boy away.

Luc wore a thoughtful expression. Then he tugged at Freud's hand and looked up at him, a question having formed in his eyes.

'What is it?' asked Freud.

The boy tugged again.

'That won't do, little fellow,' said Freud. 'I can't explain anything if I don't know what's troubling you.'

Luc stared, looked away, stared up at Freud again. Then he began pulling his pockets inside out.

Freud watched him, petting his dog's ears. At last he understood: 'You want to know why I didn't give the man any money?'

Luc nodded.

'Because he didn't do it well enough,' answered Freud.

Younger, alone in Vienna's old quarter, happened the next day on an open-air market, large and well stocked. It was clear that Freud wouldn't take money for treating Luc, so Younger decided to have a delivery made to number 19 Berggasse: fresh fruits and flowers; milk, eggs, chickens, ropes of sausage; wine, chocolates, and a few boxes of tinned goods as well.

But he stayed away from the Freuds' the entire day. There were several old, obscure churches he wanted to see. And there was the fact that Colette was hiding something from him.

'By any chance, Miss Rousseau,' asked Freud that night, 'was German spoken in your family?'

Freud had seen his patients that day, finished his correspondence, added notes to the drafts of two different papers he was working on, and apparently found time in addition to interact with Luc. He was standing in the doorway of the kitchen, where Colette was helping the maid clean up.

'We spoke French of course,' she answered.

'No German at all?' asked Freud. 'When you were a child, perhaps?'

'Grandmother was Austrian – she knew German,' said Colette, smiling. 'She used to play a game with us in German when we were very little. She would hide her face behind her hands and say *fort*, then show us her face again and say *da*.'

'*Fort* and *da* – "gone" and "there."'

Colette washed the dishes.

'You're pensive, Fräulein,' he said.

'I'm not,' she replied, looking steadily at her work. 'I was just wishing I could speak German.'

'If what you're concealing,' answered Freud, 'is connected to your brother, Miss Rousseau, I should like to know it. Otherwise, I have no wish to intrude.'

The Three Hussars, located on a quaint, uneven lane in the oldest quarter of Vienna, came alive at eleven-thirty Thursday morning. Shutters parted, windows opened, the front door was unlocked, and an aproned waiter, all black and white, came out to sweep the sidewalk. This man was approached by a very pretty French girl, who smiled shyly and was directed by him into the restaurant.

Younger, installed at a café down the street, watched and waited.

Ten minutes later, the girl emerged, anxiety furrowing her forehead. Younger followed her.

Every street in Vienna's old quarter leads to a single large square – the Stephansplatz – where stands the cathedral of St. Stephen, massive, dark, Gothic, and impregnable, its roof incongruously striped with red and green zigzags, its south tower as absurdly huge as the left claw of a fiddler crab, dwarfing the rest of the body.

Colette passed through the gigantic wooden doors of the cathedral. She lit a candle, dipped two fingers into a stone bowl of water, crossed herself, took a seat on a lonely pew in the cavernous hall near a column three times her width, and bowed her head. A long while later, she got up and hurried out, never seeing Younger in the shadowy recesses of one of the chapels.

She walked more than a mile, stopping several times to ask for directions, showing a piece of paper that evidently bore an address. Having crossed the Ring and then the canal, she entered a large, ungainly building. It was a police station. After perhaps half an hour, she came out again. Younger, smoking, was waiting for her next to the doorway.

'So your Hans is alive,' he said.

She froze as if a spotlight had picked her out of the darkness. 'You followed me?'

He hadn't answered when a kindly-looking, mutton-chopped police officer hurried out of the station. 'Ah, Mademoiselle, I forgot to tell you,' he said in broken French. 'Visiting hours end at two. They are very strict at the prison. If you're not there before two, you won't see your fiancé until tomorrow.'

'Thank you,' said Colette in the awkward silence that ensued.

'Not at all,' replied the officer, beaming genially. He must have taken Younger for a friend or member of the family, because he said to him, 'So touching, two young people falling in love during the war, one from either side. If a single good thing can come from all the death, maybe this will be it.' The officer bid Colette goodbye and returned into the station.

'You should have told me,' said Younger.

'I—'

'I'd still have brought you to Vienna. I'd still have introduced you to Freud. I'd probably have paid for your honeymoon. Whatever you'd asked me, I would have given you.'

She surprised him with her answer: 'You want to kill me.'

'I want to marry you.'

She shook her head: 'I can't.'

They looked at each other. 'I'm too late,' said Younger, 'aren't I?'

Colette looked away – then nodded.

Younger dined, despite himself, at the Three Hussars that evening, a wood-beamed, low-ceilinged restaurant with uneven floors and tables barely large enough to fit the enormous schnitzels served to virtually every customer.

When the waiter was clearing his dishes, Younger placed a substantial number of bank notes on the table and told the man that he was looking for an old friend of his named Hans – Hans Gruber – who was in jail and who used to frequent the Three Hussars. The waiter cheerfully remarked that Hans's fiancée had stopped by the restaurant that very day, at lunchtime, adding for good measure that the girl was French, very good-looking and drooling with affection for him – but then Hans was always lucky with the fairer sex.

Younger drove his meat knife through the wad of bank notes, pinning them to the wood table. He stood, towering over the waiter, and his voice came out barely above a whisper: 'What's Hans in for?'

'He was in the rally,' stammered the waiter, although it wasn't clear whether he was more in fear of physical force or pecuniary loss.

'What rally?'

'The league rally. For the Anschluss – the union with Germany.'

114

'What league?'

'The league.'

Younger left, not because there was no more information to be had, but because he was concerned he might hurt someone if he didn't.

'So,' Freud said to Younger late that night in the splendid lobby of the Hotel Bristol. 'I have a conjecture.'

The statement took a moment to penetrate. Freud was on his feet, hands crossed behind him, coat hanging down from his shoulders, while Younger sat at a low table before an empty snifter of brandy. Freud had been there for more than a minute. Younger hadn't seen him.

'I beg your pardon,' said Younger, coming to his senses.

'My conjecture is that you've discovered what Miss Rousseau has been hiding,' said Freud.

'You knew?' asked Younger.

'Knew what?'

'That she's engaged?'

'Certainly I didn't know. Engaged? Why didn't she tell you?'

Younger shook his head.

'Of the three of you,' said Freud, 'I think I'm analyzing the one who needs it least.'

'Is there a league in Vienna,' asked Younger, 'that marches in favor of union with Germany?'

'The Anti-Semitic League.'

'They call themselves Anti-Semitic?'

'Proudly. In fact most of them are simply anti-Socialist – no more anti-Jewish than anyone else. There was a demonstration a couple of months ago. Several of them were jailed. Why?'

'One of those is Colette's fiancé.'

'I see,' said Freud. 'What are you going to do?'

'Leave Vienna. But I—'

'Yes?

115

'I'll still pay for her brother's treatment. If you think you can treat him.'

'I don't. I intend to tell Miss Rousseau the same thing tomorrow. The truth is I don't understand his condition; I don't understand the war neuroses at all. It would be wrong of me to pretend otherwise. I know just enough to know how much I don't know. I wish I could analyze the boy at length, but under the circumstances, that's impossible.'

Neither spoke.

'Well,' said Freud, 'I came to thank you heartily and to pass on Martha's and Minna's gratitude as well. You gave us enough to provision a small army. Will you join me walking? It's my only exercise. I have something important to tell you. You'll be pleased to hear it, I promise you.'

They strolled toward the city center, leaving the broad and modern Ringstrasse for streets that grew ever more medieval and tortuous, as if they led backward through the centuries. In a small and irregular square, old townhouses faced the back walls of heavier, administrative buildings. The square was empty, dark. 'This is the Judenplatz,' said Freud. 'It's quite historical. There's a plaque somewhere, over four hundred years old. There it is. Come, let's have a look. You see the relief? That's Christ receiving his baptism in the River Jordan. How's your Latin?'

Younger read from the plaque:'"As the waters of the Jordan cleansed the souls of the baptized, so did the flames of 1421 purge the city of the crimes of the − of the − Hebrew dogs"?'

'Yes. In 1421 Vienna tried to force its Jews to convert. A thousand or so took refuge in a synagogue, barricading the doors. For three days they went without food or water. Then the synagogue burned. Jewish accounts say that the chief rabbi himself ordered the fire, preferring death to conversion. About two or three hundred survived. These were rounded up and taken to the banks of the Danube, where they were burned alive. Ever thrifty, the Viennese used the stones from the synagogue's foundations for the university, where, for most of my adult life, I sought to attain a professorship.'

'Great God,' said Younger. 'Don't Jews object to this plaque?'

'Would one have to be a Jew?' replied Freud. They began walking again. 'But the answer is no. Not outwardly. The Jews of Vienna strive with their every fiber to feel, to think, to be Austrian. Or German. I include myself. It's a foolish and quite irrational lie we tell ourselves – that they will accept us if only we outdo them in being what they themselves want to be.'

Passing through an alley barely wide enough for two men to walk abreast, they presently entered the spacious Am Hof, where clothing, much of it secondhand, was in daylight sold from stalls beneath giant umbrellas. Now the stalls were empty, the umbrellas folded and bound.

'Repetition is the key,' added Freud.

'To self-deception?'

'To the war neuroses. Did you treat shell shock in the war?'

'No, but I saw it.'

'Did you encounter any cases in which the patient's symptoms corresponded to a traumatic experience he had undergone?'

'Twice. We had a man with a convulsive wink; it turned out he had bayoneted a German in the eye. There was another whose hand was paralyzed. He'd accidentally thrown a grenade into his own platoon.'

'Yes – such cases are exceptional, of course, but illustrative. They undercut all my previous theories.'

'Undercut?' said Younger. 'They're proof of your theories.'

'That's what everyone says. The whole world suddenly respects psychoanalysts because we alone can explain shell shock. Don't mistake me: I'll take the recognition. But it is certainly ironic – being finally accepted on account of the one thing that disproves you.'

'I don't see it, I'm sorry,' said Younger. 'If shell shock victims are acting out suppressed memories, surely that vindicates your theory of the unconscious.'

'Of course,' answered Freud, 'but I'm talking about what's *in* the unconscious. Shell shock defies my theories because there's no pleasure in it. That's what I wanted to tell you.'

Younger reflected: 'No sexuality?'

'I said you'd be glad to hear it. I don't enjoy acknowledging error, but when the facts don't fit one's theories, one has no choice. The war neurotics behave like masochists – constantly conjuring up their own worst nightmares – except without any corresponding gain in sexual satisfaction. Perhaps they're trying to relieve their fear. Or more likely to find a way to control it. If so, their strategy fails. I suspect there's something else. I sense it in Miss Rousseau's brother. I don't know what it is yet. Pity he doesn't speak. Something dark, almost uncanny. I can't see it, but I can hear it. I hear its voice.'

Jimmy Littlemore bottomed his whiskey glass, but there was nothing in it. He tried to pour himself another; there was nothing left in the bottle either. Daylight had just begun to show in the windowpanes. 'Okay,' he said slowly. 'What happened next?'

'That's all. I left the next day. Went to India.'

'India?'

'Stayed there almost a year.'

Littlemore looked at him: 'Stuck on her, huh?'

Younger didn't answer. India had repelled him – and fascinated him. He kept planning to leave, but stayed on for month after sweltering month, wondering at the snake-headed men of Benares, at the filth of the Ganges where natives washed themselves after bathing their family's corpses, at the harmony of the great palaces and tombs. He knew he remained only because nothing in India reminded him of Colette, whereas in Europe or America everything would have. Eventually, however, Indian girls began reminding him of Colette too.

'Guess it's time to switch to coffee,' said Littlemore. He went to the stove and, with his good arm, set up a percolator. 'What happened to the Miss?'

'She wrote to me. There was a letter waiting when I got back to London. She'd sent it last Christmas. Apparently she'd left Vienna without even going to the prison to see her soldier fiancé. She'd had a conversation with Freud and changed her mind. She returned to Paris, worked at the Radium Institute for six months, and then the Sorbonne finally took her. She was finishing her degree. She asked if I might come down to visit.'

'What did you write back?'

'I didn't write back.'

'Sharp move,' said Littlemore.

Neither spoke.

'Did you ever get to a point with a girl,' asked Younger, 'where you couldn't close your eyes without seeing her? Day and night – awake, asleep? Where you couldn't think of anything without also thinking of her?'

'Nope.'

'I don't advise it,' said Younger.

'Why didn't you write to her?'

'If I were an opium addict, what would you suggest I do – give in to the craving or resist it?'

'Opium's bad for you.'

'So is she.'

'Then what?'

'I came back to America. Last July.'

'But how'd she get here?'

'I recommended her for a position at Yale. A radiochemist named Boltwood was looking for an assistant. She was the best-qualified candidate.'

'You've got to be kidding.'

'She was. By far.'

'Come on – what are you waiting for?' asked Littlemore. 'When are you going to propose?'

The kettle began to rattle.

'What is it with you husbands?' asked Younger. 'You think every man wants to be in your condition. I got stuck on the girl. Now I'm unstuck.'

'You said yourself you wanted to marry her. When you were in Vienna.'

'I was wrong. She's too young. She believes in God.'

'I believe in God.'

'Well, I don't want to marry you either.'

'You're just sore because she lied to you about Hans.'

'I'm sore because I wanted her and never had her,' said Younger. 'Freud was right – I do mistreat women. Once I have them, I don't want them anymore. I use them up. I can't stand the sight of them after three months, and I toss them aside. She's better off with Hans. Much better.'

'She doesn't want Hans. She changed her mind.'

'And she'll change it again,' said Younger. He finished off his glass and spoke more quietly: 'You think she's forgotten him – the man she was engaged to? That's not how women work. I'll tell you what's going to happen. She'll go looking for him. Count on it. Sooner or later, she'll realize she needs to see her Hans again – just once – just to be sure.'

Stirrings came from down the hall, then footsteps. The men glanced at each other. Colette entered the room, squinting, wearing a night-gown too large for her, borrowed from Littlemore's wife. Only youth is beautiful at six in the morning; Colette, despite a confusion of hair, was beautiful. Both men rose.

'Morning, Miss,' said Littlemore. 'Coffee?'

'Yes, please – oh, I'll do it; sit down, you two invalids,' she answered. Bursts of hot water were sputtering in the glass button on the coffee pot's lid. Rubbing her eyes, Colette saw the empty whiskey bottle on the table. 'Isn't that illegal here?'

'You can drink it at home,' said Littlemore; 'you just can't buy it or sell it. Great policy. A lot of folks are making spirits in their bathtubs.

Say, I never complimented you, Miss, on that trick you pulled last night – getting them to steal your radium so we could trace you.'

'Thank you, Jimmy,' said Colette. 'I was lucky.'

'She did that on purpose?' asked Younger.

'Sure,' said Littlemore. 'Kind of obvious, Doc. How many times did the kidnappers go to the Miss's hotel room?'

'I don't know – twice?' asked Younger.

'Twice,' agreed Littlemore. 'The first time, they took Luc. They already had him when you called, remember? But when we got there, Drobac was in the hallway with his pockets stuffed, and the ash next to the Miss's case was still warm. In other words, he went back a second time, and that's when he took the elements. So why didn't he take them the first time if they were worth all that dough? Because he didn't know about them. How'd he find out about them? The Miss must have told him. The only question was whether she let it slip by accident or on purpose. Given how smart the Miss is, I had to figure on purpose.'

Younger nodded. 'I'm impressed – doubly impressed.'

'I have to go back, Stratham,' said Colette.

'To the hotel?' asked Younger.

'To Europe.' Colette unplugged the percolator. She poured coffee.

Littlemore looked at Younger.

'You can't – you're in charge of Boltwood's laboratory,' said Younger. 'Don't judge America because of what happened yesterday. It's safe here.'

'It's not that,' she answered. 'I received a letter. From Austria. It was in the mail that Jimmy's friend Spanky brought back from the hotel.'

'Stanky, Miss,' said Littlemore. 'Not Spanky.'

Younger said nothing.

'Who was the letter from?' asked Littlemore.

'From a policeman who helped me once when I was in Vienna,' she replied. 'Hans is getting out of jail, Stratham. In just a few weeks. I have to go back.'

PART 2

CHAPTER EIGHT

THE MORNING AFTER the attack, a hundred thousand people
gathered on Wall Street.

They came unbidden, drawn by the afterimages of devastation, the
lingering proximity of death. Some were gawkers from out of town.
Others had employment in the financial district. But most drifted in
like wanderers, with no articulate aim, moved by a need they could
not have explained, as if being there might somehow supply a void
they felt without knowing they felt it.

As a result, the Constitution Day celebration was the largest the
country had ever known. Workmen laboring all night erected a wooden
platform in front of George Washington's bronze statue. Bunting had
been hung in red, white, and blue, festooned with American flags.
With a fully armed company of solders still guarding the Treasury
Building, the impression created was halfway between a holiday and
a siege.

Patriotic speeches were made. 'America the Beautiful' was sung, tears
glistening on thousands of faces. While the words 'sea to shining sea'
still echoed in the great canyons of lower Manhattan, a ruddy, white-
whiskered brigadier general took the podium. The crowd quieted.

'September sixteenth,' he proclaimed, his voice echoing off the
skyscrapers. 'A date America will never forget. September sixteenth
– the date on which Americans will say for the rest of time that our
country changed forever. September sixteenth. On this spot where we
now stand, one of the greatest outrages committed in the history of

our country was perpetrated. Are we, as American citizens, going to close our eyes to this infamy? I say no, a thousand times no.'

The word was repeated thousands of times more.

The Brigadier General held up his arms, checking the crowd's cheers: 'The vampires must and will be brought to justice.'

Thunderous applause.

'Ladies and gentlemen, I have spoken this morning with Attorney General A. Mitchell Palmer,' he went on, and the name of Palmer brought fresh cheers and foot stamping. 'General Palmer wished to be here himself this morning, but alas it couldn't be. The General desires me to assure you, however, not only that he is on the way to our city at this very moment but that he already knows the identity of the perpetrators of this outrage. Yes, he has their confession – their boastful confession – in hand. And he has a message both for us and for our enemies. General Palmer says, and I quote, that he "will sweep the nation clean of their alien filth"!'

There was a roar of satisfaction and a thrilling chorus of 'Yes! Yes! Yes!' On the stage a young man stepped forward and began the national anthem. A hundred thousand voices made vigorous harmony.

Younger was writing a letter at a small table in the Littlemores' living room when he sensed, rather than heard, Luc behind him.

In the previous hour, Betty Littlemore had clothed, fed, and packed off to school an endless string of little Littlemores. The apartment was still not wholly peaceful: babies cried, toddlers banged cooking pots, and the detective's wife and mother-in-law were discoursing volubly in the kitchen. Younger couldn't understand their Italian, but the topic was evidently a matter on which both women had strong opinions.

Younger turned to face Luc. The boy stood on the other side of the room, perfectly still, saying as usual nothing. His long dirty blond hair was well brushed, and his large observant eyes conveyed preoccupation with a multitude of thoughts, without giving a single one of them away.

'Your sister has told you,' said Younger in French, 'that she plans to take you back to Europe.'

Luc nodded.

'And you're wondering if I intend to change her mind.'

The boy nodded again.

'The answer is no. She knows what's best.'

Luc shook his head – just once, very slightly.

'Yes, she does,' said Younger. He put down his pen, leaned back, looked out the window. Then he turned back to the boy: 'Well, if you *are* going back to Europe, we shouldn't be wasting time. I'll tell you what: Bring me a newspaper. We'll see when the Yankees are playing. Maybe Ruth will hit his fiftieth today.'

The boy scampered away and returned a moment later, the morning paper in his hands and a disappointed expression on his face.

Younger looked at the page to which Luc had opened the newspaper: the Yankees were on the road and therefore not playing in Yankee Stadium – which the boy apparently understood. 'Can you read English?' asked Younger.

Luc shrugged.

'I see,' said Younger, recalling how, when he was himself a boy, he had once astonished his father by having taught himself to read rudimentary Latin. He also recalled how he used to watch everything that happened in his household, understanding secret expressions on his mother's face that he was not supposed even to have seen. 'Can you speak, Luc? I'm not asking you to talk. I just want to know if you can. Yes or no.'

The boy stared at him, unmoving.

'Right,' said Younger. 'Well, too bad about the Yankees. Let me think – how would you like to go to the roof of the tallest building in the whole world?'

Luc's eyes lit up.

'Go see if your sister will let you,' said Younger. 'And if she'll join us.'

★   ★   ★

Detective Littlemore might have passed for one of the gentlemen of the press packed into uncomfortable chairs in the Astor Hotel, except that the detective's hands were stuffed in his pockets, while the newsmen's were busy scribbling down the remarks of William Flynn, Director of the Federal Bureau of Investigation, who stood at the front of the room next to a chalkboard map of lower Manhattan. Chief Flynn had commandeered several suites of rooms at the Astor, turning them into his personal command center. Littlemore sat in the rear chewing his toothpick, straw hat so far back on his head it looked like he was braving a strong wind.

The pug-nosed, barrel-chested Flynn had massive shoulders, a correspondingly big gut, and surprisingly clean-shaven, fresh-faced cheeks. Dressed in dark suit and tie, his brown hair slicked down, he bore a striking resemblance to a nightclub bouncer. He thought of himself, however, in more militaristic terms. Flynn believed that law enforcement was essentially military in nature and prided himself on knowing how to speak in the argot of the armed forces. 'At approximately oh-twelve-hundred hours yesterday,' said Flynn, tapping the map with a pointer, 'an incendiary device detonated in front of the Morgan Bank at number 23 Wall Street.'

'You mean a bomb?' asked one of the gentlemen of the press.

'That is correct,' said Flynn.

'Captain Carey says it might have been a dynamite truck,' called out another.

'The New York police got zero to do with this investigation,' Flynn shot back. 'The incendiary device was transported to the scene in an animal-powered transport vehicle.'

'A horse and wagon?' called out a newsman.

'Ain't that what I said?' Flynn replied with asperity. 'Now pipe down so's I can deliver myself. I got something important for you boys, and if you'll shut your traps maybe I can get to it. At oh-eleven-thirty yesterday morning, a United States letter carrier opened a mail receptacle here –' he tapped another spot on the chalkboard map – 'at the corner of Cedar and Broadway. The receptacle was empty at that time. At oh-eleven-fifty-eight, the letter carrier made another collection from that same receptacle, at which time he found five circulars' – a word that Chief Flynn pronounced *soyculars* – 'without wrapping of any sort. Three minutes later, the letter carrier heard a loud noise, which was the incendiary device incendiarating. By order of General Palmer, we are making these circulars public, so's the law-abiding people of this country know who their enemies are.'

Flynn handed around five handbills.

'Don't paw at 'em!' Flynn barked. 'Anybody damages one of these, they're going to jail for destruction of evidence. I ain't kidding.'

Each piece of paper was rough and cheap, about seven inches wide by eleven long, and each bore the same red ink-stamped message, the unevenness of which made plain that it had been hand-printed, one letter at a time:

Rimember
We will not tolerate
any longer
Free the political
     prisoner or it will be
sure death for all of you
American Anarchist
Fighters

The newsmen copied furiously.

'Cedar and Broadway,' Flynn resumed, using his pointer again, 'is four minutes by foot from the incendiary location. That leaves no doubt about what happened. The anarchists parked their animal-powered vehicle on Wall Street at approximately oh-eleven-fifty-four. When they reached Cedar and Broadway, they placed these circulars into the mail receptacle, three minutes before the explosion.

'It will be recalled,' Flynn went on, 'that the circulars connected with the bomb outrages of 1919 looked just like these here and were signed by the same enemy organization. If any further cooperation was needed, which it ain't, it will also be recalled that the Chicago Post Office bombing of 1918 occurred on the third Thursday' – pronounced *toyd Toysday* – 'of September, which yesterday was too. The exact anniversary. In other words, these are the same terrorist Bolshevikis who bombed us in 1918 and 1919 – Eye-talians associated with the Galliani organization. There's your story. You print it. I will now read you the names of the wanted.' Reading from what appeared to be an arrest warrant, Flynn continued: 'Carlo Tresca, anarchist leader and known terrorist; Pietro Baldesserotto, anarchist; Serafino Grandi, anarchist and revolutionary; Rugero Bacini, anarchist; Roberto Elia, anarchist.'

The newsmen kept scribbling some time after Flynn had finished his recitation. Then one of them called out, 'Was J. P. Morgan hurt, Chief?'

'What are you – stupid? J. P. Morgan wasn't even in town yesterday,' said Flynn. 'This outrage was not directed at Morgan or any other individual. It was an attack on the American government and the American people and the American way of life. You put that in the papers.'

'What can you tell us about the horse and wagon, Chief?' a newsman asked.

'The witnesses thus far examined,' said Flynn, 'have told us that the horse was facing east, which ain't legal under traffic regulations. But terrorists don't care too much about traffic regulations, do they?' Flynn's torso heaved up and down at the last remark, which he apparently found humorous.

'So you haven't identified the wagon?' asked a reporter.

'They blew it up, you chucklehead,' Flynn shot back, irritated. 'How are we supposed to identify it? It's in a million pieces – and so's the horse. Any more bonehead questions?'

'What about Fischer, Chief?'

'Don't worry about Fischer,' said Flynn.

'Have you caught him yet?'

'Who says I'm looking? NYPD wants Fischer; let them look.'

'But how did he know about the bombing?'

'Who says he knew about it? The postcard never said bomb. And it said the fifteenth, not the sixteenth. I ain't gonna comment on Fischer. If you ask me, he's a mental case who got lucky. Now get out of here, all of you. I got men in the field waiting for orders.'

Under vaulted gold-leaf ceilings, Younger pointed out to Colette and Luc the caricature of old Mr Woolworth himself, carved in stone, counting his fives and dimes. They boarded the express elevator. The boy's eyes fixed in wonder on the winking lights that indicated the breathtaking passage of floors. Only a slight rocking of the car and a whistling of air betrayed the rapidity of their ascent.

Fifty-eight stories up, they emerged through heavy oak doors into a blinding blue sunlight and a wind so fierce Younger had to take Colette around the shoulders and Luc by the hand. The three-sided observation deck was lined with sightseers, coats flapping. At a railing, Younger, Colette, and Luc – on his tiptoes – gazed down on roofs of buildings that were themselves taller than the tallest cathedrals of Europe. Impossibly far below, rivers of mobile humanity – minuscule models of people, cars, buses – flowed and halted en masse to strangely slow rhythms. This was not a bird's-eye view. It was the view of a god witnessing America's breach of the first axiom of divinity, the separation of earth from heaven.

Behind them, the heavy oak doors swung open again, discharging another elevator load of visitors onto the deck. Among the newcomers was a man in a fedora pulled low over his forehead. He walked with a limp, and his clean-shaven face was mottled with scarlet patches – burn marks of some kind.

As the reporters filed out of his office, Big Bill Flynn sat down behind a large oak desk, taking up a fountain pen like a man with important documents to sign, although in fact the only papers on his desk were newspapers. Two dark-suited assistants stood behind him, one on either side of his desk, hands behind their backs, feet apart.

Littlemore remained in his seat, toothpick protruding from his mouth, examining one of the handbills. 'Isn't that funny?' he asked of no one in particular, after the last newsman had left.

Flynn addressed one of his deputies: 'What is this guy, deaf?'

'Hey, buddy, you deaf?' asked the deputy.

'"Or it will be sure death for all of you,"' said Littlemore, quoting the hand-stamped message. 'That's what I call a threat, because it says something's *going* to happen. But how about what *already* happened? I mean, if you were leaving behind a message after you blew up Wall Street, wouldn't you say something about what you just pulled off? You know, maybe ominous, like "Today was just the beginning." Or throw in a little taunt, like maybe, "*We* took down *Wall* Street, next we'll come for *all* streets."'

The detective had sung the last words, to the tune of 'Ring Around the Rosey.'

'Who the hell is this guy?' asked Flynn.

'Who the hell are you?' asked a deputy.

'Captain James Littlemore,' said Littlemore. 'NYPD, Homicide. Commissioner Enright asked me to be the Department's liaison officer with the Bureau. I'm supposed to offer you our services.'

'Oh yeah?' said Flynn. 'Well, there ain't going to be no liaison officer, because there ain't going to be no liaisoning. Now get out of here, will you?'

The second of Flynn's assistants leaned down and spoke softly into his superior's ear.

'You don't say,' said Flynn aloud. He leaned back in his chair. 'So you're the guy who turned up Fischer?'

'That's right,' said Littlemore.

'Think you got something there, do you, Littleboy?'

'Could be,' said Littlemore.

'I'll tell you what you got,' said Flynn. 'A crackpot. You'll be interviewing him inside an asylum.'

'I don't know about that,' said Littlemore.

'I do,' replied Flynn. 'He's in one now.'

'Where?'

'You want him. You find out.'

'How do you know?' asked Littlemore.

'Let's just say I got it out of the air,' said Flynn, his torso shaking again. His deputies seemed to consider this remark a witticism; they joined in his laughter.

'Well, I guess I got to congratulate you, Chief Flynn,' said Littlemore, returning to his scrutiny of the handbill, which he now held up in the light over his head. 'Never seen a case this big broken so fast.'

'That's why they pay us the big bucks,' said Flynn.

'Say, Chief,' said Littlemore, 'did you see all those soldiers outside the Treasury Building? I wonder what they're doing there.'

'They're there because I ordered them there,' said Flynn. 'Somebody's got to protect United States property when the police department's got its heads up its pants. Now scram.'

'Yes, sir,' said Littlemore. He stopped in front of the chalkboard map of lower Manhattan and scratched his head. 'Those anarchists, I'll tell you – how do you catch people who can do the impossible?' asked Littlemore.

'What's impossible?' said Flynn.

'Well, they leave their horse and wagon on Wall Street at 11:54 and walk four minutes to the mailbox at Cedar and Broadway – that's what you said, right? Mail gets picked up at 11:58. Bomb goes off at 12:01. How much time is there between 11:54 and 12:01?'

'Seven minutes, genius,' said Flynn.

'Seven minutes,' said Littlemore, shaking his head. 'Now that surprises me, Chief. You think they'd leave their bomb ticking for seven whole minutes? I wouldn't have. I mean, with the horse blocking traffic and all. If it were me, I'd have set my timer for one or two minutes. Because in seven minutes, somebody might move the horse out of there – maybe even discover the bomb.'

'Well, nobody did, did they?' barked Flynn. 'Nothing impossible about that. Get him out of here.'

'Maybe nobody moved the horse,' said Littlemore as the two deputies approached him, 'because it was only there two minutes.'

Flynn signaled his deputies to wait: 'What are you talking about?'

'My men took statements from a lot of folks who were there yesterday, Chief Flynn. Eyewitnesses. The horse and wagon pulled up on Wall Street only one or two minutes before the bomb exploded. Your anarchists, you got to hand it to them. They leave Wall Street at 11:59 or 12:00, and they get to Cedar and Broadway before 11:58, when the mailman picks up their circulars. How do you catch people who can do that?'

No one answered. Flynn stood up. He slicked back his oiled hair. 'So you're a captain, huh? How many men report to you? Six?'

'Enough,' said Littlemore, thinking of Officers Stankiewicz and Roederheusen.

'I got a thousand. And my men ain't like yours. There are two kinds of cops in the NYPD – the ones on the take, and the ones too stupid to realize that everybody else is on the take. Which kind are you?'

'Too stupid,' said Littlemore.

'You look it,' said Flynn. 'But not stupid enough to get in the way of my investigation. Are you?'

Littlemore went to the doorway. 'I don't know; I'm pretty stupid,' he said, shutting the door behind him.

Flynn turned to his deputies. 'Get me a file on that guy,' he said. 'Get me wife, friends, family – everything. And see if Hoover's got anything on him.'

Luc broke free from Younger and ran to the far side of the deck, which looked out on the water. Nearby, a pack of schoolboys shouted to one another about something they saw below. Luc ran toward them.

'Look at him,' said Younger. 'He understands what those boys are saying.'

'Not their words – how could he?' replied Colette.

'He can read the newspaper,' said Younger.

'In English? Impossible,' answered Colette. They stood side by side at the railing and gazed out onto the vast urban panorama. She put her hand on his. 'I wish I didn't have to go back.'

He removed his hand and took out a cigarette.

'You don't care if I leave?' she asked.

'I recommended you to Boltwood. You're leaving him with no one running his laboratory. Of course I care.'

'Oh. Well, I don't like your Professor Boltwood anyway. Do you know what he called Madame Curie the other day? A "detestable idiot."'

'He's just jealous. Every chemist in the world is jealous of Marie Curie.'

'Men are very cruel when they're jealous.'

'Are they? I wouldn't know.'

No one glancing at the man who had limped into the center of the platform would have seen the dagger in his right hand, tucked invisibly against his inner sleeve. Colette herself might have turned around without recognizing Drobac, whose mass of whiskers was now shaved off. Only his eyes – the small, black, perceptive eyes peering out below his low-cocked hat – could have given him away. He held the knife by its blade, one finger caressing its edge. There was no danger of his being cut: as with all good throwing knives, both of its edges were dull. The point alone was sharp.

An experienced practitioner of the knife-throwing art, if he intends to kill, will throw at the victim's heart. Of those organs whose puncturing is virtually certain to cause death, the heart is the largest – saving of course the brain, which is rendered inaccessible by the hard bone of the cranium. The victim's ribs might be thought a significant obstruction, but it isn't so. Provided that the throw is sidearm, not overhand, there is no real difficulty. Ninety-nine times out of a hundred, the victim's ribs will let the point slip through. Indeed one might almost say they guide it home.

Younger and Colette had their backs to Drobac, as did everyone else on the observation deck, because he stood in the center while they were all at the railings. A good knife-thrower has no compunction about taking aim at his victim's back, which assures, after all, the element of surprise. All that's required is a blade long enough to pass through the soft tissue of the left lung with sufficient metal remaining to pierce the meat of the heart. In the case of a slender victim, a shaft of eight inches will usually do. Colette Rousseau was slender, and the knife in this case was a dagger with a ten-inch steel blade. Drobac's breathing slowed.

'That's good,' shouted Detective Littlemore to a workman operating a pneumatic drill. 'Keep her clear.'

Littlemore was now on Wall Street, in front of the Morgan Bank, where the bomb had exploded the day before. Two uniformed officers – Stankiewicz and Roederheusen – kept pedestrians at bay. Across the street, the Treasury and Assay buildings still looked like an army garrison, with a company of soldiers positioned around them.

The drill bit cracked one cobblestone in the blackened crater, then another. Littlemore signaled the workman to stop. Crouching down, brushing dust and pebbles aside, the detective prized free a horseshoe from the stones. It was a size four shoe; the remains of a shamrock nail were visible. Stankiewicz and Roederheusen peered over his shoulder. Littlemore flipped the shoe over; the letters HSIU were imprinted on it.

'How do you like that?' said Littlemore. 'You boys know what HSIU stands for?'

'No, sir,' said Roederheusen.

'Horse Shoers International Union.'

'Something strange about that, Cap?' asked Stankiewicz.

'Sure is.' Littlemore did not explain what.

On the Woolworth Building observation deck, a clutch of schoolboys erupted with shouts and stampeded at full speed from one side of the deck to the next. Luc chased them, close on their heels; an alarmed schoolteacher trailed after, close on his. Colette cried out her brother's name and broke into a run, certain that Luc was going to trip and tumble over the guard rail.

Drobac smiled. He was still standing, alone and unmoving, in the center of the platform. Colette was running from his right to his left at the far side of the deck. The gusting wind died for an instant, and in that instant he took a single broad step, as a fencer does in a lunge, flinging his knife backhanded. In general, he favored moving targets, which offered more of a challenge. But Colette did not present even that challenge. She had become quite suddenly stationary: Luc had stopped abruptly, bringing the schoolteacher to a halt just behind him, bringing Colette to a similar halt.

The dagger spun in the air exactly three and a half rotations, parallel to the ground, and entered the girl's back. The point slipped through her ribs, puncturing her lung. But it was the right lung, not the left, and as a result the knife point, when it emerged from that lung, never touched her heart.

A knife piercing an individual's back characteristically causes its victim to throw both arms wide and high in the air, to scream, and to fall forward at least a step or two. All that happened here. This was unfortunate, because her forward steps propelled her over the railing. There was still a fair chance her fall might have been arrested by one of the balconies below. It was not to be. Her body, somersaulting, hit a parapet and bounced outward. The collision caused a morsel of concrete to crack loose and fall alongside the girl's body, accompanying her fifty-eight stories to the earth. At exactly the same moment, the girl and the concrete chip hit the sidewalk, which there consisted of a mosaic of colored glass squares. On contact, the concrete chip rebounded several stories high in the air. Considerably heavier, the girl's plummeting body ripped through the colorful glass tiles with a sickening thunderclap, plunging into the subway station below.

Littlemore heard the crash all the way from Wall Street. He listened for an aftermath, for the sounds of riot or terror. Hearing nothing more, he resumed his instructions to his men: 'Stanky, you take this shoe straight to Inspector Lahey.'

'Can I tell the press about it?' asked Stankiewicz.

'Make sure you do,' said Littlemore. 'But the Feds don't touch that shoe, you hear me?'

'Excuse me, Captain,' said Roederheusen. 'Mr O'Neill's still waiting to talk to you.'

Terrified screams rent the rooftop of the Woolworth Building. Schoolboys gaped and yelled in horror. Only Luc was perfectly silent, reaching his hands, with a strange and protective intelligence, to take those of his sister.

The dead girl was the schoolteacher who had stopped short behind Luc. Had Colette taken one more step, Drobac's knife would have found her. But because of the schoolteacher's unexpected halt, the knife had pierced the right lung of the wrong victim – the unlucky schoolteacher – rather than the left lung of its intended target.

The mass of people on the observation deck, not having seen the knife, believed they had witnessed a ghastly accident. A new load of sightseers just then emerging onto the deck added to the confusion. Younger, however, had seen the knife in the schoolteacher's back, and now he saw a man limping toward the heavy oak doors that led to the elevator bank – the only person leaving the platform amid the pandemonium. Drobac glanced back as he passed through the doorway. Younger recognized the small, black eyes at once.

Younger rushed across the deck and through the doorway. Between the closing doors of an elevator car, Younger saw those same black eyes again, peering at him from below a fedora's brim. The narrowing gap between the doors was too small for a man to fit through, but it was large enough for Younger's arm, which he thrust into the car, grabbing Drobac by the lapel. The elevator operator, barking out in surprised protest, reopened the doors. Younger yanked Drobac out and threw him to the floor.

Drobac tried to fight, but it was no contest. Younger beat him and beat him and kept beating him until the bones of his nose, his jaw and even his eye sockets all gave way.

'O'Neill – who's that?' Littlemore asked Officer Roederheusen on a street corner near the Morgan Bank.

'That's him over there, sir. He's been waiting all morning. He says he got a warning about the bomb too.'

'Bring him over. Then go find the mailman who picks up at Cedar and Broadway. And not next week. I want that mailman in my office tomorrow morning, got that?'

'But tomorrow's Saturday,' said Roederheusen.

'What about it?' asked Littlemore.

'Nothing, sir.' Roederheusen crossed the street and returned with a man barely over five feet in height, with a waistline of approximately the same size and whose arms, as he walked, moved like those of a toy soldier. 'Sorry you had to wait, Mr O'Neill,' said Littlemore. 'You have some information for me?'

'Yeah – it was last Thursday, see,' said O'Neill. 'Or else Friday. No, Thursday.'

'Just tell me what happened,' said Littlemore.

'I'm on the train from Jersey, like every morning. This guy, he gets on at Manhattan Transfer and we get to talking. Friendly-like.'

'Describe him,' said Littlemore.

'Nice-looking,' said O'Neill. 'About forty, forty-two, maybe. Never saw him on the train before. Six-footer. Athletic type. Blond. Educated. Tennis racket.'

'Tennis racket?' asked Littlemore.

'Yeah, he was carrying a tennis racket. Anyways, we're in the Hudson Tube, see, and he asks me where I work. I tell him 61 Broadway. He says he works on the same block, at some kind of embassy or something, and we keep talking, this and that, you know, and then he leans over and whispers to me, "Keep away from Wall Street until after the sixteenth."'

'He said the sixteenth?' asked Littlemore. 'You're sure?'

'Oh yeah. He says it a couple of times. I ask him what he's talking about. He says he works on the sly for the Secret Service and his job is to run down anarchists. Then he goes, "They have 60,000 pounds of explosives and they're going to blow it up." He meant it too. You could tell. It was him, wasn't it, detective? It was Fischer?'

'What did you do?'

'I stayed away from Wall Street on the sixteenth, that's what I did.'

Three Woolworth security personnel, when at last they arrived, tore Younger from the bloodied man and put him – Younger – in handcuffs.

They were not impressed by Younger's claim that the victim of his assault had killed the girl who had just fallen to her death. No one else had seen the murder, and Younger conceded that he hadn't actually witnessed the deed. The guards were equally unmoved by Younger's assertion that the man had kidnapped a different girl the night before – a girl who was still standing outside on the observation deck. On the whole, they seemed to think he was raving.

Colette and Luc were brought forward. Without allowing Younger to speak, the guards asked Colette if she recognized the unconscious man whom Younger had beaten almost to death. She said no. Drobac's gashed face was in fact quite unrecognizable.

'Your husband says this man kidnapped you yesterday,' said one of the guards.

'He's not my husband,' said Colette.

'You lying SOB,' the other security officer remarked.

'I didn't say I was her husband,' said Younger.

Luc, tugging sedulously at Colette's sleeve, got her attention and made signs with his hands. She asked if he was certain; he nodded. 'It *is* the man who abducted us,' she said to the guards. 'My brother recognizes him.'

The officers, dubious, asked how the boy knew.

Luc made another sign. 'He just knows,' said Colette.

This assertion somehow failed to allay the security officers' doubts. In the end, they took the bloodied man to a hospital – and Younger into custody.

The Morgan Bank, open for business the day after the explosion, looked more like a hospital infirmary than a temple of high finance. Bandaged heads and patched eyes could be seen at every other desk. Clerks limped. Sling-armed men pecked one-handedly at adding machines. A watchman's face was so heavily wrapped that only his eyes and nose were visible.

'Mr Lamont will be with you in a moment,' said a receptionist to Littlemore.

The J. P. Morgan Company was not an ordinary bank. The House of Morgan was a mover of international relations, a maker of history. It was Morgan that saved the United States from ruin in the gold panic of 1895 and again in the bank panic of 1907. It was Morgan that led a consortium of financiers to float a five-hundred-million-dollar loan to the Allies in the Great War, without which they almost certainly could not have won. The old titan J. Pierpont Morgan had died in 1913; his son Jack Jr, who didn't spend as much time at the bank as his father had, relied on one partner in the firm to manage the company's vast assets and worldwide financial interests. That partner was Thomas Lamont.

Littlemore tipped his hat to the dozen uniformed policemen adding their bulk to the bank's security contingent. He also nodded imperceptibly to the additional half-dozen plainclothesmen scattered about the central atrium. Littlemore looked up at the dome far above, where scaffolding allowed workmen to reach its inner recesses. The resounding echo of hammers filled the air.

Below the dome, Mr Lamont – slight, diminutive, expensively but conservatively dressed – was addressing some twenty other men, answering questions like a tour guide. He was the right sort of man to run the House of Morgan: a graduate of Philips Exeter Academy and of Harvard College, a man chosen by Washington to represent the United States at the Paris peace conference of 1919. He had thinning gray hair, large ears, and risk-averse gray-blue eyes. The twenty men whom he addressed were not tourists; they were a grand jury conducting a physical inspection of the effects of the bombing. Pointing up at the dome overhead, where massive cracks in the plaster could be seen, Lamont explained that a team of engineers had pronounced the dome safe and secure.

'Let me add,' he said to the jurors and newsmen encircling him, 'how proud I am today of this firm. We are J. P. Morgan. We don't panic. We opened today at our usual hour, and rest assured, we will continue to do so.'

Lamont shook hands with the jury foreman and ushered the group into the care of an associate. He approached the detective, introduced himself, and asked how he could help.

'Sorry to take your time, Mr Lamont,' said Littlemore. 'It can't be easy for you.'

'Not easy?' replied Lamont, whose normally bland countenance looked overburdened by responsibility. 'With Mr Morgan overseas, the duty of speaking to the families of the dead and wounded has fallen to me. I feel responsible for every one of them. Do you know that our dome very nearly fell? And the entire Exchange almost came down yesterday as well. We were a hair's breadth from complete catastrophe. Thousands would have died. Wall Street would have been ruined. I can't comprehend how this could have happened. If you could be brief, Captain, I'd appreciate it.'

'Okay,' said Littlemore. 'I'd like to know who your enemies are.'

'I'm sorry?'

'Not yours personally. The company's.'

'I don't think I understand,' said Lamont. 'Mr Flynn of the Bureau of Investigation assured me this morning that the explosion was not directed against the Morgan firm in particular.'

'They left the bomb right outside your door, Mr Lamont. They almost brought your building down.'

'That's not how Mr Flynn sees it.'

'Those are facts, sir,' said Littlemore.

'If I'm not mistaken, Captain, this whole tragedy might yet prove the result of an accident on a dynamite wagon. I will not be party to speculation that J. P. Morgan and Company is under attack.'

'When was the last time you heard of a dynamite wagon loaded with a half ton of shrapnel?'

'But who would attack a bank in such a way?' asked Lamont. 'Where is the profit in it? This firm comes to the assistance of people in need all over the world. Who would want to attack us?'

'Let me put it this way, Mr Lamont. My men deal with murders of loan sharks all the time. Your business isn't too different – just bigger. What I always ask is who the shark's been leaning on to pay up. Or whether there's another shark in the water that might want a piece of the action.'

'I see,' said Lamont.

'If you'll forgive the comparison,' said Littlemore.

'I don't,' said Lamont. 'This firm does not "lean on" its debtors, Captain.'

'Sure you don't. And you don't have any enemies either, right? Only friends?'

Lamont didn't answer.

'You hedge your bets for a living, sir,' said Littlemore. 'Every banker does. I'm offering you a hedge. There's a chance the bombers are after your company. Maybe they were sending you a message. Maybe they'll send you another. Do you want to take that chance?'

Lamont lowered his voice: 'No.'

'I might just catch them if you put in a little time helping me out. That'd be a pretty big return for a small investment, Mr Lamont.'

'It would indeed,' Lamont agreed. 'You are independent of Chief Flynn?'

'I'm with the New York Police Department,' said Littlemore. 'We don't take our orders from Mr Flynn.'

'Give the receptionist your card, Captain. You have a card?'

'I've got a card.'

'I'll consider what you've said.'

Dusk had fallen when Littlemore arrived at Younger's detention cell.

'Geez, Doc, you pulverized him,' said the detective, unlocking the barred door. 'He looks like a bulldozer ran over his face.'

Younger put on his jacket and came out of the cell.

'I bailed you,' said the detective. 'Smoke?'

'Thanks,' said Younger. His shirt collar was loose, knuckles bruised. 'Did he get away?'

'No,' replied Littlemore. 'I sent a couple of boys to the hospital as soon as I heard. When the doctors clear him, we'll put him behind bars. I've got him – for now.'

The detective handed a large brown paper envelope to Younger, from which the latter shook out his necktie, watch, wallet, and other personal effects. 'For now?' he asked.

'How do we prove he's Drobac? Even I can't identify the guy after what you did to his face. We're going to need a lot more before his trial rolls around. But that's okay. Trial won't be for another six months.'

'*I* can identify him,' said Younger, putting on his watch.

'Hate to tell you, but your say-so became a little less weighty when you got yourself charged with attempted murder.'

Younger eyed the detective.

'That's how the DA saw it,' said Littlemore. 'Assault with intent to kill. I was lucky to get you out. The judge wasn't going for it until I mentioned that you were a Harvard man. Harvard man and Harvard professor. And Roosevelt was your cousin. And you slept with Roosevelt's daughter. Okay, I didn't say that.'

'As a matter of fact,' said Younger, looping his tie around his neck, 'I did intend to kill him.'

'No, you didn't.'

'Who does he say he is?'

'Funny thing,' said Littlemore, 'but he's not talking. Seems his mouth is wired shut because somebody broke his jaw in three places. Boy, you better be right.'

'It's Drobac. He was limping. He had marks on his face.'

'Not proof.'

'Can't you take his fingerprints?'

'Did it,' said Littlemore. 'But they have to match something. We got no prints on the knives. No matching prints in the room downtown. No matching prints on the car. No prints at all on Colette's laboratory box. Nothing. He knew what he was doing.'

Neither spoke.

'Why would he come after us?' asked Younger.

'Maybe he wanted to get rid of the people who can finger him.'

'Where is she?' asked Younger, fastening his cufflinks.

'The Miss? Giving her lecture.'

'What?'

'She wouldn't take no for an answer,' said Littlemore. 'Made me get all her samples out of the evidence locker.'

That night A. Mitchell Palmer, the Attorney General of the United States, arrived in Manhattan by special train from the nation's capital.

A long black-and-gold car – a Packard Twin Six Imperial, the kind of car only very rich men could afford – was waiting for him outside Pennsylvania Station. Inside was a dapper gentleman who wore a top hat, with the points of his shirt collar up.

The car took Palmer to the Treasury Building opposite the Morgan Bank on Wall Street. Soldiers, saluting, stepped aside as the two men ascended the marble stairs and passed through the massive portal. A half-hour later, Palmer and the well-dressed gentleman reappeared. The latter led the Attorney General around the colonnade to a narrow alleyway separating the Treasury from the adjacent Assay Building. The alleyway was barred by a tall wrought-iron gate, which had to be unlocked to let the Attorney General through.

The two men walked halfway down that alley, the top-hatted gentleman pointing up to the second floors of the not-quite-abutting buildings. There, one story above the street, what looked strangely like garage doors in midair faced each other across the alley. Attorney General Palmer shook his head grimly, then informed the gentleman that he would be quitting New York the next day. The investigation of the bombing would remain in the hands of Bureau Director Flynn. Palmer himself would travel on to Stroudsburg, Pennsylvania, to visit with family.

The Marie Curie Radium Fund held a special lecture presentation on September 17, 1920, in the Saint Thomas Church on Fifth Avenue. The Fund was the brainchild of Mrs William B. Meloney, a well-upholstered lady of a certain age, well known in New York philanthropic and literary circles. Mrs Meloney was a working woman, a newspaper woman, who by virtue of her tireless reporting on Manhattan high society had eventually taken a place in it. Like many American women, Mrs Meloney had avidly followed – indeed she had reported on – the travails of the great Marie Curie of France.

'How outrageous it is,' declared the bow-tied Mrs Meloney from the opulent but somber church chancel, 'that Madame Curie, the world's most eminent scientist, the discoverer of radium, should for mere want of money be prohibited from continuing her investigations – investigations that have already led to the radium cure for our cancers, the radium face and hand creams that eliminate our unsightly blemishes' – Mrs Meloney was, in addition to her other pursuits, editor of a leading woman's magazine – 'and the radium-infused waters that restore conjugal vitality to our husbands.'

The audience, almost exclusively female, applauded warmly.

Mrs Meloney congratulated her listeners for their fortitude in coming out only one day after the terrible tragedy on Wall Street. 'It has always been woman's lot,' she said, 'to persevere when man's violent passions overwhelm him. And persevere we must. The cost of a gram of radium is appalling – a hundred thousand dollars – but the sum must be raised. The honor of America's women has been pledged. I myself pledged it – to Madame Curie herself, at her home in Paris – and it is now the obligation of every one of us to contribute generously to the Fund, or make our husbands contribute.'

As the ladies applauded once again, the front door of the church creaked noisily.

'Thank heavens,' said Mrs Meloney, 'here is Miss Rousseau at last. We were growing concerned, my dear.'

The audience of fashionable ladies swiveled. Colette walked up the cavernous central aisle in silence, a picture of self-consciousness, lugging with two hands the heavy case of sample ores and radioactive elements. She murmured an apology, but her faint voice failed to carry in the huge, dimly lit Gothic church, with its great columns and vaulted ceiling. Colette had expected a few women in a small lecture room, not two hundred in a place of worship, assembled before a pulpit with a larger-than-life-sized crucifixion on the enormous reredos behind it.

'Over the last several weekends,' Mrs Meloney continued, 'along with Miss Rousseau – who studied with Madame Curie herself in Paris and who will shortly enlighten us on "The Wonders of Radium"

– I have been making a tour of the largest factories in America where radium products are made. We have sought to impress upon the owners of these factories how much they owe to Madame Curie. Our efforts have not been in vain, as I will soon have the pleasure of announcing to you.'

Here Mrs Meloney exchanged a knowing glance with a plump, impeccably dressed gentleman seated to her left, who gestured to the audience munificently. She then turned the pulpit over to Colette, who, smiling to cover her strenuous effort, hoisted the case of elements up the steps to the chancel.

'Thank you, Mrs Meloney,' said Colette. The pallor of her cheeks was attributed by her audience to her foreign birth. 'It is my warm honor and my privilege to give whatever small assistance I can to the Marie Curie Radium Fund.'

Colette paused, somehow expecting that her audience might applaud the name of Marie Curie. Instead there was a noticeable silence.

'Well, I begin,' she resumed, trying to press flat onto the lectern the curling pages on which she had carefully written out her presentation. 'Twenty-four years ago, Henri Becquerel, a French scientist, placed a dish of uranium crystals next to a wrapped photographic plate in a closed drawer and left them there for over a week. Was he conducting an experiment? No – Monsieur Becquerel was only cleaning up his laboratory, and he forgot where he put his uranium!'

Colette waited for laughter; none came.

'But when he unwrapped the photographic plate, he found an image on it – which should have been impossible, because the plate had not been exposed to light. Thus was the mystery of atomic radiation discovered, quite by accident! Two years later, in 1898, Marie Curie and her husband, Pierre, solved this mystery. Madame Curie proved that uranium's atoms emit invisible rays, and she coined a word for this phenomenon – radioactivity. Working in almost complete isolation, Madame Curie discovered two new elements previously unknown to man. The first she called polonium, after her native Poland; the second and by far the more powerful, she called radium. The potential energy of radium is so great it is almost impossible to describe with normal measures. You are familiar with horsepower? A single gram of radium contains an energy equivalent to that of eighty thousand million horses.'

Colette paused again, expecting a gasp at so enormous a figure. The only sound was the rustling of women's skirts and gloves.

'Such power,' Colette went on, speaking now a little too quickly, 'if released at once, would be enough to destroy every building in New York City in one terrible explosion. But science has found a way to harness radioactivity to save lives rather than destroy. Doctors today insert micrograms of radium, encased in tiny glass nodules, directly into a cancer patient's tumor. In weeks, the tumor is gone. All over the world today, because of radium, people are alive and well who would have died from cancer only a few years ago.' Here was a pronouncement the audience was in fact prepared to applaud, but this time, her nervousness growing, Colette failed to pause. 'Now I will demonstrate for you one of the extraordinary by-products of radio-activity: luminescence.'

'Oh, my child,' said Mrs Meloney, 'you're going to experiment – in church? Do you think that appropriate?'

'It will be only a small demonstration,' said Colette.

'All right,' said Mrs Meloney. 'But let's not demonstrate very long, shall we?'

Gathering two vials from her case, Colette stood awkwardly in the pulpit. The awkwardness lay in the absence of a table. Colette needed to combine the two compounds. Smiling nervously, Colette knelt to the floor and set her materials down. This allowed her to work with both hands; unfortunately it also made her invisible to her audience.

Suddenly there was an outburst of clapping. Colette looked up, puzzled. The ladies' attention was fixed on the plump gentleman behind her, who, beaming jovially, had raised his fists high over his head. From each hand dangled a wristwatch, casting a greenish phosphorescent glow.

'There's your luminescence, Miss Rousseau,' announced the gentleman. 'There's the magic of radium.'

More applause.

'Thank you, sir,' cried Mrs Meloney, 'you are a knight in shining armor. And thank *you*, Miss Rousseau, for that most educational lecture.'

'But I –' began Colette, who had only just started.

'And now, my friends,' continued Mrs Meloney, 'for the most gratifying portion of this evening's event. In Connecticut last week, I had the pleasure of meeting one of the titans of American industry, whose kindness and sense of public duty are every bit the equal of his eminence in commerce. He is one of this nation's leaders in oil, in mining, and in radium. Please join me in welcoming Mr Arnold Brighton.'

The plump gentleman came up and bowed in all directions to a long ovation. He was completely bald except for a tuft of wiry brown hair above each ear, but fastidiously attired, with shiny trimmed finger-nails and gold cufflinks that glittered as he raised his arms to quiet the ladies' applause.

'Thank you, thank you – oh my, where did I put my speech?' Brighton patted his pockets with gleaming fingernails. 'Did I give it to you, Mrs Meloney?'

'To me, Mr Brighton?'

'Oh my. Is Samuels here? He would know where I put it. Well, my competitors always say I lose my head with the ladies. They won't employ women, you know, whereas my luminous dial factories are the largest employers of women in their states. My competitors can't understand how I could employ girls in a factory. My answer is simple. The female wage is lower than the male – significantly lower. Oh, I know what you're thinking. With so many men out of work, especially men who served in the war, don't they deserve the jobs? I beg to differ. Men have wives and children they're expected to support. That costs more. Whereas ninety percent of my girls are unmarried. That costs less. And look at their handiwork – look at these lovely watches. Applying radium paint to such tiny surfaces requires feminine dexterity and cleanliness. Mrs Meloney, will you permit a gentleman to offer you a gift? Or would Mr Meloney object?'

Appreciatively scandalized laughter attended this remark.

'For shame, Mr Brighton,' said Mrs Meloney, but she extended her ample arm coyly, allowing Brighton to secure to her wrist the larger of the two watches, in which violet gemstones were embedded. She held up her arm, displaying the object to the ladies of the audience, who clapped most cordially.

'Mrs Meloney can now tell the time in the blackest hour of night,' said Brighton. 'If the police and firemen of this city had been wearing my watches, they would never have been hindered by the great smoke cloud of yesterday's explosion. They would have had a source of light, requiring no batteries, no fuel, no power source at all. That's the wonder of radium. Now for you, Miss Rousseau, we had to make a special item. Our usual products wouldn't fit the delicacy of your wrist. May I?'

The watch Brighton offered to Colette was encircled with round-brilliant diamonds, refracting every color in the rainbow despite the dim illumination of the church. Uncomfortably, Colette lifted her hand. Brighton fastened his gift to her forearm, the green glow of the luminous watch face reflected in his polished fingernails. He expressed the hope that his present was to her liking. Colette didn't know what to say.

'Your generosity leaves us speechless, Mr Brighton,' said Mrs Meloney. 'Pray continue.'

'Continue?'

'Your contribution, Mr Brighton.'

'My contribution? Oh, my contribution, of course.' Brighton patted his pockets again and withdrew a bank draft from his vest – nearly knocking over the lectern in the process. After a lengthy preface, he declared it his great pleasure to present to the Marie Curie Radium

Fund a check in the amount of twenty-five thousand dollars. Gasps came from the audience, together with loud, sustained applause.

Mrs Meloney thanked her benefactor profusely. She then opened the floor to questions, professing her certainty that many in the audience would have questions for Miss Rousseau.

'Excuse me,' said a woman three pews back, 'but I've been using radium soap every day for the last year, and I still have warts on both my elbows. I'm very upset about it.'

'Oh,' said Colette. 'I'm afraid I don't know much about radium's cosmetic uses.'

Mrs Meloney came to Colette's assistance: 'Have you tried Radior night cream, my dear? It's done wonders for me.'

Another hand went up. 'I have a question for Miss Rousseau. What is the proper dosage of radium water for a sixty-year-old man to restore his vitality?'

'I'm sorry?' said Colette. 'His what?'

'His vitality,' repeated the woman.

Mrs Meloney whispered to Colette, whose livid cheeks reddened.

Afterward, during refreshments, Mrs Meloney complimented Mr Brighton on his height. 'You are so very much bigger than one expects, Mr Brighton,' said the gray-haired Mrs Meloney coquettishly. It was true. From a distance, Brighton looked short, and his countenance suggested an absent-minded professor of mathematics. Up close, he proved much taller; one couldn't quite tell where the height came from. The effect was to make his clumsiness considerably more concerning. 'And your gift,' added Mrs Meloney, showing off her sapphire wristwatch, 'I have never received a present so entrancing.'

'While I,' replied Brighton chivalrously, 'have never received so entrancing a visit to my factory as the one you and your assistant paid me two weeks ago.'

'Heavens, Mr Brighton,' protested Mrs Meloney, 'what would my husband say?'

'Why?' asked Brighton in some alarm. 'Did I do something wrong?'

'Would that men always did such wrong,' Mrs Meloney reassured him. 'I must insist you attend our presentation ceremony, Mr Brighton, when we give Madame Curie her radium next May – if only we can raise the rest of the money. I intend to persuade the Mayor to preside.'

'The Mayor?' said Brighton. 'Why not the President? I'll speak with Harding about it; he'll be in the White House by then. Miss Rousseau, have you seen our nation's capital? I'm going down – oh my, when am I going down? Where's my man Samuels? I can't remember a thing without him. There he is now, the dour fellow. What were you saying, Madam?'

'I, Mr Brighton?' said Mrs Meloney. 'I believe you had just made reference to Mr Harding.'

'Oh, yes – I'm going to Washington to meet with Harding. Why don't you ladies accompany me? I have my own train, you know. Quite comfortable. You and Miss Rousseau will find many eleemosynary organizations in the capital – fertile soil for your Fund.'

'We'd be delighted, wouldn't we, dear?' Mrs Meloney asked Colette.

'Look at Samuels,' said Brighton, vexed. 'He wants me, as usual. Will you excuse me, ladies?'

'What a prepossessing man,' declared Mrs Meloney as Brighton went to his secretary, who draped a coat over his employer's shoulders and whispered in his ear. Most of the women in attendance remained in the church, trading information about which radium products they liked best. 'He has his eye on you, my dear,' Mrs Meloney added.

'On me?' said Colette. 'No – on *you*, surely, Mrs Meloney.'

'Tush – what am I? An old lady. Look at the watch he gave you. It's diamond. Have you any idea what such a thing is worth?'

'I can't keep it,' confided Colette.

'Why on earth not?' the excitable Mrs Meloney replied.

'It's very wrong to use radium on a watch face, Mrs Meloney. And please, you mustn't encourage these women to use radium cosmetics.'

'Don't tell me you're a radio-skeptic, dear. My husband is a radio-skeptic of the worst sort, but I assure you my Radior night cream has taken a decade off my face. *I* can see it, even if he can't.'

'It's the cost,' said Colette. 'Companies like Radior have made radium unaffordable to scientists.'

'Tush – my night cream is only ninety-nine cents.'

'Of course, Mrs Meloney, but because so many women pay that ninety-nine cents, a gram of radium now costs over a hundred thousand dollars.'

'I'm afraid you scientists rarely have a firm grasp of economics, dear. The cost of radium determines the price of my Radior night cream, not the reverse.'

'No, Mrs Meloney. Think of all the people buying radium cosmetics and radium watches. The more those products are sold, the less radium there is in the world, and the more precious it becomes.'

'You're making my head spin, Miss Rousseau. All I know is that our Fund is off to a flying start. Let's concentrate on that, shall we?'

'I can't tell you how important this is,' said Colette. 'There's so little radium. Companies like Mr Brighton's consume over ninety percent of it. They leave next to nothing for science and medicine. What they do leave is too expensive to afford. Thousands of people dying from cancer today will never be treated with radium simply because of the cost. These companies are killing people – literally killing people. I tried to explain that to Mr Brighton when we visited his plant, but I don't think he was listening.'

'I certainly hope not,' said Mrs Meloney. 'He'll withdraw his donation. Can't you be a little nicer to the dear man? Why, I daresay he'd fund the entire gram of radium himself if you would just be kind to him.'

A jovial Mr Brighton returned to bid them adieu, bowing this way and that. 'Samuels says I must be off. Don't forget, Miss Rousseau: you've promised me Washington.' He extended his elbow to the older woman. 'Will you escort me to the door, Mrs Meloney?'

'Why, Mr Brighton – people will think we've just been married,' said Mrs Meloney.

'Very well,' said Brighton, 'then both you ladies must escort me.'

Colette tried to decline this invitation, but Mrs Meloney wouldn't hear of it. Descending from the chancel by a short flight of steps, the three made their way down the central aisle of the nave, at the far end of which Brighton's assistant, Samuels, was handing out products to a small crowd of appreciative, departing ladies.

'You uttered the nefarious name of Radior,' Brighton explained to Mrs Meloney. 'I couldn't let the competition be advertised without a response. We've just started our own line of eye shade. Luminous, of course – as you can see.'

A number of ladies had tried on the shadow and mascara they had received, creating paired circles of phosphorescence that turned the dark portal of the church into a kind of grotto from which nocturnal birds or beasts seemed to peer out. Mrs Meloney apologized to Brighton: she'd had no idea that his company had entered the cosmetics line; she would be sure to mention it in the next issue of *The Delineator*. She and Mr Brighton were so engrossed in their affable chat, and Colette so provoked by it, that they didn't notice the solitary figure ahead of them, kneeling among the shadowed pews, head down as if in prayer.

'Mrs Meloney – I left my elements by the lectern,' said Colette. 'I should go back for them.'

'Don't be rude, dear,' replied the older woman, pulling firmly on Brighton's arm, who in turn pulled Colette.

The kneeling figure began to stir as they approached. A hood covered its head.

'Yes, don't desert me, Miss Rousseau,' said Brighton. 'I'll have Samuels collect your things.'

Colette didn't answer. Her tongue had gone dry. The hooded figure had stepped into the aisle, blocking their advance. It was a woman. Wispy red hair emerged from the hood. One bony hand rested on a scarf around her neck – hiding something that seemed to bulge out from beneath it.

'Can we help you, dear?' asked Mrs Meloney.

Colette knew she ought to say something, to cry out in warning. But she found herself transfixed. The gaunt creature's eyes seemed to call out to her. They seemed to take in the connection between her and Mr Brighton and Mrs Meloney – the linking of their arms, their apparent unity – and to condemn it. A hand rose up toward Colette, beckoning her. Colette felt herself surrendering. For reasons opaque to her – perhaps it was simply that she was in a church; perhaps it was the accumulated effect of the harrowing incidents of the last two days, breaking down her resistance – Colette felt she had to meet the creature's outstretched hand with kindness, not horror. Whatever the reason, Colette reached out to the shrouded woman. Their fingers made contact.

The touch was repulsive, damp, communicating illness or contagion as if the creature had emerged from a fouled pool and would soon return there. The hooded figure clenched her fingers around Colette's and took a step backward, pulling Colette with her.

'Stop that at once,' said Mrs Meloney, as if addressing children with bad manners.

'Yes, stop that at once,' said Brighton. The hooded girl turned her eyes on him and pointed an outstretched hand at his face. He fell back, letting Colette go. 'Samuels?' said Brighton weakly.

The shrouded woman drew Colette another step back, always keeping one bony, blue-veined hand on the scarf around her neck. Colette didn't resist. It was the wristwatch – the gift from Brighton, now only a few inches from the hooded girl's face – that broke the spell.

In the greenish luminosity of the watch dial, Colette saw eyes that struck her momentarily as sweet, like a doe's. Then the eyes changed. They seemed to become aware of the glinting diamonds at Colette's wrist, and they filled with fire. With sharp nails, the creature began clawing at the watch and its diamond-studded band, scratching Colette's skin, drawing blood. Colette tried vainly to wrest her hand away.

'It's a thief!' cried Mrs Meloney.

In a fury, the red-haired woman scraped at Colette's flesh and spoke for the first time: 'Give me – give me—

Colette's breath caught in her throat: the woman's voice was guttural, like a man's, only lower in pitch than any man's voice Colette had ever heard. In her thrashing, the woman's scarf fell away from her chin. A pair of thin, colorless lips was the first thing to appear. Then the scarf fell farther down, and Mrs Meloney screamed at the sight, just as Betty Littlemore had.

'My God,' said Colette.

The hooded figure, fixated on the diamond watch, drew from her cloak a shaft of glinting metal – a knife. Colette was now pinioned. Mr Brighton had retreated, but the bold Mrs Meloney had taken his place, evidently believing that she could best render aid to Colette by seizing her free arm and refusing to let go. The redheaded woman, wild-eyed, raised her knife. Colette, with one wrist seized by her assailant, the other by her would-be protector, was helpless.

Mrs Meloney cried out: 'She's going to cut off her arm! Someone help!'

A shot rang out. A bullet ripped into the crucifix behind the pulpit, tearing a shoulder of carved wood off the savior. The hooded woman spun around, holding her knife high above her head. There came another shot, then another. The woman's flashing eyes went still. The knife slipped from her hand. An unnaturally deep groan came from her lips, and blood appeared at the corner of her mouth. Her body collapsed into Colette's arms.

The French girl felt a fleshy, sickening contact as the woman's throat pressed against her own. Shuddering, Colette let the body fall to the floor. In the church vestibule, Brighton's amanuensis, Samuels, stood with a smoking gun in his hand.

For a long moment, no one moved. Then, from behind Mrs Meloney,

Arnold Brighton poked his head out. 'Oh, well done, Samuels,' he said. 'Well done.'

'Mr Brighton,' said Mrs Meloney reprovingly.

'Yes, Mrs Meloney?'

'You hid behind me.'

'Oh, no, I wasn't hiding,' said Brighton. 'Everyone knew where I was. I was taking cover. Most satisfactory cover, I might add. Most ample cover.'

'You held me, Mr Brighton, when the shots were fired. I tried to run, but you held me fast.'

'You mean – oh, I see what you mean. I benefitted from you without compensating you. How can I repay you? Would a thousand dollars be appropriate? Five thousand?'

'My word,' said Mrs Meloney.

'Samuels, don't just stand there,' said Brighton. 'Clean up. One can't leave a dead body on the floor of a church. Could we pay the trash men to take her, do you suppose?'

'She's still alive,' said Colette, kneeling by the fallen woman.

'She is?' asked Brighton, looking as if he might need to take cover behind Mrs Meloney again.

'Police!' shouted Detective Littlemore, bursting through the front door of the church. 'Drop your weapons!'

The woman's body lay crumpled on the cold stone floor, a dark stain of blood spreading out below it. Younger and Littlemore had arrived just in time to hear cries of 'murder' from ladies fleeing the church. As Mrs Meloney explained to the detective how the mad woman had attacked Colette, and how Mr Samuels had saved them, Younger sought a pulse in the fallen woman's wrist. He found one, very faint.

Colette knelt next to him. 'Look at her neck,' she said.

Matted, unhealthy red hair masked the woman's face. Grimly but gingerly, Younger pushed the hair away. He saw vacant eyes, a pretty nose and thin, parted lips. The fraying scarf had regained its place over her neck. Younger pulled it away.

The woman had no chin at all. Where a chin should have been, and where a throat should have been, there was instead an engorged bulbous mass, almost as large as the woman's own head, attached to her neck. It had wrinkles, dimples, lumps, indentations, and many, many veins.

'What in the love of Pete is that?' asked Littlemore.

CHAPTER NINE

A YEAR BEFORE the attack on Wall Street, the President of the United States, sitting on his toilet in the White House, suffered a massive cerebral thrombosis – a clot in the artery feeding his brain. Within moments, the once-visionary Woodrow Wilson became a half-blind invalid, unable to move the left side of his body, including the left side of his mouth.

Wilson's stroke was kept from the public, from his Cabinet, even from his Vice President. It was difficult to say who was supposed to run the country after Wilson's collapse. Indeed it was difficult to say who *was* running the country. Was it Secretary of State Robert Lansing, who secretly convened the Cabinet in the President's absence? Or was it Wilson's wife, Edith, who counted among her ancestors both Plantagenets and Pocahontas, and who alone had access to the presidential sick room, emerging therefrom with orders that Wilson had supposedly dictated? Or perhaps it was Attorney General Palmer, who secured ever more funds for his Bureau of Investigation, and who imprisoned tens of thousands all over the country as suspected enemies of the nation.

Throughout 1920, the country lurched along in this strange, headless condition. In January, Prohibition took effect. In March, the Senate rejected the League of Nations and, with it, Wilson's vision of America joining an international community of peaceful states and taking center stage in world affairs. Wilson had never persuaded his practical countrymen why America would want to entangle itself in Europe's intrigues and ancient enmities. What, after all, had the United States gained from the last war, in which more than 100,000 American young men had perished to save English and French skins?

Uncertain of their direction, deprived of drink, Americans in 1920 were waiting – for a storm to break the gathering tension, for a new president to be elected in November, for their economy to recover. Americans believed they had brought peace to the world. Surely they were entitled to worry about their own problems now.

There was, however, no peace in the world. In the summer of 1920, great armies still ravaged the earth. In August, a Soviet army marched triumphantly into Poland and even entered Warsaw, its sights set on Germany and beyond. Lenin had reason to be ambitious. Armed communists had seized power in Munich and declared Bavaria a Soviet Republic. The same occurred in Hungary. Right next door to the United States, revolutionaries in Mexico overthrew the American-supported regime, promising to reclaim that nation's gigantic petroleum deposits from the companies – in particular the United States com-panies – that owned them.

But most Americans in 1920 neither knew nor cared. Most had had their fill of the world. Most – but not all.

On Saturday morning, September 18, two days after the bombing, one day after Colette's lecture in Saint Thomas Church, Younger and Littlemore met at a subway station a couple of blocks from Bellevue Hospital.

'Any way to identify the girl?' asked Younger as they set off for the hospital.

'Two-Heads?' said Littlemore. 'We'll probably know in a day or two. With girls, somebody usually comes in to report them missing. Unless she's a hooker, in which case nobody reports her.'

'I have a feeling this one isn't a hooker,' said Younger.

The two men looked at each other.

'Did you check her teeth?' asked Younger.

'To see if she lost a molar? Yeah – I had the same idea. But nope. No missing teeth.'

'Why Colette?'

'You mean why are these things happening to her? That's the question all right. But like I said – don't assume everything's connected.'

'What are you assuming – freak coincidence?'

'I'm not assuming anything. I never assume. If I had to guess, I'd say somebody thinks the Miss is somebody she isn't. Maybe a whole lot of people think she's somebody she isn't.'

Bellevue was a publicly funded hospital, required to take all patients delivered to its door, and the catastrophe on Wall Street had added fresh strains upon its already overtaxed resources. Every corridor was an obstacle course of patients slumped over on chairs or stretched out on gurneys. On the third floor, Younger and Littlemore found the woman from the church in a ward she shared with more than a dozen other female patients. She was breathing but unconscious, veins pulsing on the engorged mass bulging out of her neck. A nurse told them the girl had not regained consciousness since being admitted. One bed away, a hospital physician was administering an injection to another patient. Littlemore asked him if he thought the redheaded woman was going to live.

'I wouldn't know,' said the physician helpfully.

'Who would?' asked Littlemore.

'I would,' said the physician. 'I attend on this ward. But I've had no time to examine her.'

'Mind if I examine her?' asked Younger.

'You're a doctor?' asked the doctor.

'He's a Harvard doctor,' said Littlemore.

'I'd like to get a look at what's inside that neoplasm on her neck,' said Younger. 'Do you have an X-ray machine?'

'Of course we have one,' said the doctor, 'but only the hospital's radiology staff is permitted to use it.'

'Okay,' said Littlemore. 'Where can we find the radiology staff?'

'I'm the hospital's radiology staff,' said the doctor.

Littlemore folded his arms. 'And when could you do an X-ray?'

'In two weeks,' said the doctor. 'I perform X-rays on the first Monday of every month.'

'Two weeks?' repeated Littlemore. 'She could be dead in two weeks.'

'So could five hundred other patients in this hospital,' snapped the doctor. 'I'll have to ask you to excuse me. I'm very busy.'

After the physician had left, Littlemore said, 'Maybe I shouldn't have told him you were a Harvard doctor. I don't know why people resent what they ought to admire. What the heck is that thing on her neck?'

'I don't know, but we might find out pretty soon.' Younger pointed to a thin, bluish vertical fissure that was developing on the distended mass. The fissure ran from the girl's chin to her sternum. 'Whatever's inside may be trying to get out.'

'Great,' said Littlemore.

'It could be a teratoma.'

'What's that?'

'Encapsulated hair or teeth, usually,' said Younger.

'Teeth – like a molar?' asked Littlemore.

'Maybe. Or a twin.'

'What?'

'A twin that was never born,' said Younger. 'Not alive. There's never been a case of a live one.'

'First we see a woman with no head on Wall Street, and now we got one with two. That's what I call – wait a minute. She was a redhead too.'

'The woman with no head? Was a redhead?' asked Younger.

'Her head was. We walked right past it. And I'm pretty sure she was wearing a dress like this girl's. I'll go to the morgue. Maybe *she* was missing a molar.'

That same morning, newspapers all over the country reported that Edwin Fischer, the man who knew in advance about the Wall Street bombing, was in custody in Hamilton, Ontario, having been adjudged insane by a panel of Canadian magistrates. Fischer had been taken before the Canadian judges by his own brother-in-law, who had read about the now-famous postcards and motored from New York to Toronto in the company of two agents of the United States Department of Justice.

Younger had a look around Bellevue Hospital after the detective left. It wasn't difficult for a doctor to pose as a personage of authority in a large, overcrowded hospital. At any rate it wasn't difficult for Younger, who had learned in the war how to command obedience from sub-ordinates through the simple artifice of acting as if it went without saying that one's orders would be followed.

He found the roentgen equipment on the second floor. It was as he'd hoped: a modern unit, driven by transformer, not induction, and equipped with Coolidge tubes. The milliamperage was clearly marked. He knew he could operate it.

At police headquarters, Officer Roederheusen knocked on Littlemore's door. 'I've got the mailman, Captain,' said Roederheusen. 'The one who picks up at Cedar and Broadway.'

'What are you waiting for?' asked Littlemore. 'Bring him in.'

'Um, sir, do you think I could have a nickname?'

'A nickname? What for?'

'Stanky has a nickname. And my name's kind of hard for you, sir.'

'Okay. Not a bad idea. I'll call you Spanky.'

'Spanky?'

'As opposed to Stanky. Now bring me that mailman.'

'Yes, sir. Thank you, sir.'

Roederheusen returned in a moment, mailman in tow. Littlemore offered the man a seat, a doughnut, and coffee. The postman, who accepted all these offerings, coughed and sniffled.

'So you're the one who found the circulars,' said Littlemore. 'Did you get a look at the men who mailed them?'

The man shook his head, mouth full.

'Okay, here's what I want to know – when did you first see the circulars? Did you see them when you opened the mailbox or only later, when you got back to the post office?'

The postman blew his nose into a paper napkin. 'Don't know what you're talking about. The box was empty.'

'Empty?' repeated Littlemore. 'The mailbox at Cedar and Broadway? Day of the bombing? Eleven fifty-eight pickup?'

'The eleven fifty-eight? I never made the eleven fifty-eight. Hung my bag up after morning rounds. Too sick. Lucky thing, huh?'

'Did somebody cover for you?'

'Cover for me?' The man laughed into his napkin. 'Fat chance. What's this all about, anyway?'

Littlemore sent the postman away.

Eighty miles away, in a laboratory at Yale University, a human-like creature in a helmet and what looked like an undersea diver's suit was also working on Saturday. The creature was titrating fumaric acid into six tubes of thorium in an attempt to isolate ionium. When this delicate, wearisome task was not quite complete, the creature lumbered out of the laboratory and into the sunshine of a campus courtyard, causing a child to run crying to his perambulating nanny.

The creature took off its gloves and removed its slit-visored helmet. Out shook the long sable hair of Colette Rousseau. She sat on a bench, the brightness of the sun blinding her after the double darkness of the laboratory and her helmet.

Colette and Luc had returned to New Haven early Saturday morning so that she could resume her laboratory duties, from which she had taken two days off. Her experiments were designed to test the existence of ionium, a putative new element that Professor Bertram Boltwood claimed to have discovered – the 'parent of radium,' he called it. Madame Curie did not believe in ionium, judging it to be only a manifestation of thorium. Accordingly, Colette did not believe in ionium either. She had already established that ionium could not be separated from thorium with any of the ordinary precipitants, such as sodium thiosulfate or meta-nitro-benzoic acid. Today she was trying fumaric acid. But her hands had begun to shake within her heavy lead-lined gloves, and she'd had to stop.

She gathered her hair into a long braid, threw it behind one shoulder of her radiation suit, and, using both hands, reached to the nape of her neck. She drew out the chain and locket that always hung at her chest. Turning an ingeniously crafted bezel first one way, then the other, Colette opened the two halves of the locket. Into the palm of her hand fell a thin, tarnished metal oval – like an oblong coin – with two tiny holes punched through it.

One side of this metal oval was bare. Turning it over, Colette let eyes linger on a series of machine-etched letters and numbers: *Hans Gruber, Braunau am Inn, 20. 4. 89., 2. Ers. Masch. Gew. K., 3. A.K. Nr. 1128.*

Although it was a Saturday, Littlemore saw lights in the Commissioner's office. The detective knocked and entered.

'Captain Littlemore – just the man I wanted to see,' said Commissioner Enright from an armchair by a large window, looking up from a report he'd been reading. Enright was revered by his men. He was the only Police Commissioner in the history of New York City to have risen to that position from the rank and file. 'I've been in touch with the Canadians. They're happy to extradite. Send someone to Ontario to collect this Edwin Fischer.'

'Already on their way, Mr Enright,' said Littlemore.

'That's the spirit. You met with Director Flynn of the Bureau yesterday. What were your impressions?'

'Big Bill's not giving us a thing, Commissioner,' said Littlemore. 'Fischer, for example. Flynn knew Fischer was in custody. Wouldn't say where, wouldn't say how he knew. After we turned over all our evidence to them.'

Enright shook his head ruefully. 'It's no more than I expected. That's why I chose you as liaison officer. They have greater resources than we, Littlemore, but not greater brainpower. Keep a step ahead of him. Keep us in it. Flynn found the circulars. Let the next find be ours.'

'I don't like the circulars, sir,' said Littlemore.

'You don't "like" them?'

'Flynn's story doesn't wash. There's no way the bombers got from Wall Street to that mailbox by 11:58. Plus the flyers don't read right. They don't even mention a bombing. If I'm the Wall Street bomber and I want to tell everybody I did it, I'm going to say so. Mr Enright, I'm not even sure the circulars were picked up from a mailbox at all. I just got done with the mailman who would have made the pickup. He went home sick that morning.'

'What are you suggesting, Littlemore?'

'Nothing, sir. All I know is that Flynn's doing everything he can to connect our bombing to the ones from 1918 and 1919. He even said the Chicago Post Office was bombed on the third Thursday of September, so that September 16 was the exact anniversary.'

'Yes, I read that in the *Times*,' said Enright.

'The Chicago bomb went off on September 4, 1918, Mr Enright. I don't know if that was a Thursday, but it definitely wasn't the third Thursday. I just think we should keep looking.'

'Certainly we should keep looking,' said Enright. 'That's why we're going to speak with Mr Fischer. But I should tell you that on this point I quite agree with General Palmer: the bombing on Wall Street was the work of Bolshevik anarchists. Who else would have done such a thing? The Great War did not end in 1918. It was a mistake to withdraw our troops from Russia; we've allowed them to bring the war to our soil. Wilson is useless, but things will change after the election. Harding will take the war to Lenin's doorstep where it belongs. That's all, Captain.'

Younger returned to Bellevue early the next morning. The hospital was much quieter now: it was no less crowded with patients, but because it was Sunday, fewer medical personnel were on hand, and very little treatment was being given or received.

In a bathroom on the second floor, Younger put a white coat over his suit and tie. Striding down the hall, he entered the room where the X-ray machine was kept, wheeled it out, guided it into an elevator, and came out onto a third-floor corridor, where he called out commandingly for a nurse to assist him. A nurse came running at once.

The unconscious redheaded girl lay in the same room in the same condition — alive but comatose. With the nurse's help, Younger laid the girl's body on the wooden X-ray couch, stomach-down, turning her head to one side. Her profile was uncannily angelic save for the monstrosity protruding from her chin and throat, which looked even more distended and unnatural in the electric light of the hospital room than it had in the darkness of the church. Younger prodded the mass with two gloved fingers, which provoked in him a peculiar, highly nonmedical sensation of disgust. The interior of the growth was soft but granular.

Radiographing an unconscious person was considerably easier, Younger discovered, than a conscious one. There was no difficulty with the subject moving during irradiation. The X-ray tube, clamped inside a box running on casters beneath the table, was easily brought directly below the girl's cheek. Protecting himself with a lead panel, Younger turned on the radiation and adjusted the diaphragm until only the growth fluoresced on the test screen over the girl's head. Then he replaced the test screen with an unexposed photographic plate. He let the radiation course through the girl's body for exactly eight seconds and repeated this process several times, from different angles, using a new plate each time.

The same morning, the Littlemore clan was tumbling out of their Fourteenth Street apartment house on their way to church. The children had been scrubbed and soaped until they shone like sprightly mirrors. Littlemore had their toddler, Lily, on his shoulders. Lily always received special treatment; none of the other children objected, because of her condition.

Betty's mother, a half foot shorter than Betty herself, had joined them as she always did on Sunday mornings, wearing her church hat and keeping an emphatic distance from her son-in-law. In deference to Betty's stronger religious feelings, Littlemore had consented to attend Catholic church on Sundays and to raise his children in that faith, but he never got used to all the crossing. Or the kneeling. Or the confessing. He would bow his head, but he just couldn't cross himself. As a result, Betty's mother displayed her piety every Sunday by pretending she didn't know her son-in-law.

One little Littlemore called out to his father that there was mail. He handed Littlemore a small, square, engraved envelope. Littlemore, removing Lily from his shoulders, explained to his son that whatever the envelope was, it wasn't mail, because the mail didn't come on Sundays.

'Is it a bomb?' asked the boy with genuine curiosity.

'No, it's not a bomb, for Pete's sake,' said Littlemore, trying to sound as if the suggestion were absurd. He exchanged a glance with Betty. 'Bombs are bigger.'

The envelope contained a printed card inviting Littlemore to the Bankers and Brokers Club at seven o'clock that evening. The invitation was from Thomas Lamont.

The detective and his family had not progressed half a block when a chunky man in a dark suit crossed the street and tapped Littlemore on his shoulder. It was one of Director Flynn's deputies.

'I got a message for you,' said the deputy.

'Oh yeah?' said Littlemore. 'Spill it.'

'Chief knows you been questioning United States letter carriers.'

'So?'

'He don't like you questioning United States letter carriers.'

'Is that right? Well, I got a message for Big Bill,' replied Littlemore.

'You tell him the word is *mailman*. Just mailman. Going to church today?'

'Think you're pretty smart, don't you?' said Flynn's man. He looked at Littlemore's children and then at their mother in her church dress. 'Nice family. Chief knows all about your family. Eye-talian, ain't they?'

Littlemore walked up close to the man. 'You wouldn't be trying to threaten me, would you?'

'We was just wondering why the son of an Irishman would marry an Eye-talian.'

'Nice investigating,' said Littlemore. 'My father isn't Irish.'

'Oh yeah?'

'Yeah.'

'Then how come he drinks like one?' The deputy, a much larger man than Littlemore, laughed richly at his jest, producing the sounds *har har har*. 'I heard your Pa hasn't been sober since they kicked him off the force.'

Littlemore laughed good-naturedly, shook his head, and turned away. 'Okay, you win round one,' he said before spinning around and leveling the deputy with one punch to his midsection followed by another to his rotund face. The deputy tried to get up, but fell in a stupor back to the sidewalk. 'You might want to work on round two next time.'

Littlemore and his family proceeded to church.

After developing and fixing the exposed plates, Younger thought he must have badly mistaken the machine's milliamperage. There was no image on the plates at all – only a white amorphous cloud, flecked with a seething shadow pattern of a kind Younger had never seen before. On the other hand, the top of the girl's sternum appeared with clarity, suggesting that the film hadn't been overexposed. It was as if the X-rays had simply been unable to pass through whatever was growing inside the girl's neck.

Younger took another set of films. This time he varied the length of irradiation, using both shorter and longer intervals. When the new set of pictures was developed, the results were either useless or identical to the first.

In principle, the fact that a part of the human body was roentgenopaque – impervious to X-rays – wasn't startling. Bones, for example, are roentgenopaque. Nor would it have been unthinkable for the engorgement protruding from the girl's jaw to be composed of solid bone. In advanced rheumatoid arthritis, for example, osseous processes could grow in all sorts of grotesque shapes and at many different places in the afflicted person's body. A bone growth inside the girl's chin and neck would have produced a perfectly white image on Younger's plates.

There were three problems with this theory. First, a bone growth would have shown sharp definition in shape, not the borderless amoeba of white that appeared on this girl's radiograms. Second, bone would not have produced the shadowy, foaming pattern inside the formless white – a pattern that seemed to shift ever so slightly on every plate, as if whatever produced it were constantly altering its position. Finally, Younger had felt the mass with his fingers, pressing on either side of the thin blue fissure. Whatever was inside wasn't bone. It was too pliable – and too evasive, shifting as if to avoid his touch.

Younger considered, swallowing drily, the possibility that something was alive – something impervious to X-rays – inside the girl's neck.

The Bankers and Brokers Club occupied a fine Greco-Roman townhouse downtown. At a quarter past seven that evening, on the fourth floor of the club, Littlemore found Thomas Lamont seated alone in the corner of an otherwise crowded, comfortably appointed room, apparently devoted to whist and cigars. The occupants were all men. Littlemore was surprised at the atmosphere – not the cigar smoke, but the conviviality and enjoyment. Business was apparently still good, notwithstanding the bombing.

Lamont, by contrast, was fidgety. He looked as if he wished he were elsewhere. 'A drink, Captain?' he asked. 'Quite legal, you know. Private club.'

'I'm fine,' said Littlemore.

'Ah, on duty, of course,' said Lamont, waving a waiter away. 'I thought about what you said on Friday. Are you really sure the criminals were attacking my firm?'

'I never said I was sure, Mr Lamont,' said Littlemore. 'I said that if I were you, I'd want to find out.'

'You asked me if the firm had enemies. There is a man who came to mind after you left. But it cannot get out that I named him. Is that understood?'

Littlemore nodded. The hush of Lamont's voice, coupled with the general noise of card-playing, assured that no one would overhear them. Thick smoke curled around the armchairs and wafted into the coffered ceiling.

'He's a banking man,' Lamont went on, almost whispering. 'A foreigner. Before the war, he was the second wealthiest financier in New York – second to J. P. Morgan, Sr, that is. How he hated Morgan for it. Now he's fallen down, and he blames us for his misfortune. It's ludicrous. He's German, a personal friend of the Kaiser's. His house funded the Kaiser's armies. Naturally his lines of credit dried up when our country declared war against his. What did he expect? But he seems to believe there's a conspiracy even now to deny him funds and that we are its masterminds. He threatened me.'

Lamont looked positively fearful.

'What kind of threat?' asked Littlemore.

'It was at our Democratic campaign dinner. No, it was our Republican dinner – for Harding. We do them both, of course. At any rate, he drew me aside and told me to "watch out" – I'm quoting him, Captain – to "watch out" because "there are those who don't like it when one of the houses combines with the others to deny men capital."'

'You say he funded the German army?'

'Unquestionably,' said Lamont. 'Clandestine, of course. You won't find his name on any documents. If you ask him, he'll tell you he loves this country. But he feels no loyalty to us. I doubt he is loyal to any country, even his own. It's in their nature, you know. A Bolshevik, in fact.'

'Wait a minute,' replied Littlemore. 'You're saying the guy's a banker, a friend of the Kaiser—'

'Why, the Kaiser knighted the man. He received the German Cross of the Red Eagle.'

'*And* a Bolshevik?' asked Littlemore.

'He's a Jew,' Lamont explained.

Roars of laughter erupted across the room. A butler approached.

'Oh, a Jew,' said Littlemore. 'Now I get it. What's his name?'

The butler bent toward Lamont and said, 'The gentleman is back, sir.'

'For heaven's sake, tell him I'm not here,' answered Lamont in obvious annoyance.

'I'm afraid he knows you're here, sir,' said the butler.

'Well, tell him to go away. I don't come to my club to do business. Tell him he must see me at my office.' To Littlemore, he added: 'The new financial agent for Mexico. Won't take no for an answer.'

'The man's name, Mr Lamont,' said Littlemore.

'Señor Pesqueira, I believe. Why?'

'Not him. The man who threatened you.'

'Oh. Speyer. Mr James Speyer.'

'Do you know where I can find him?'

'That's why I asked you here. You may be able to converse with Mr Speyer tonight.'

'He's a member?' asked Littlemore.

'At the Bankers and Brokers?' returned Lamont, incredulous. 'Certainly not. Mr Speyer likes to dine at Delmonico's, which is open to the public. I'm told he's there tonight. It may be your last chance.'

'Why?'

'They say he means to leave the country tomorrow.'

★   ★   ★

In New Haven, Connecticut, Colette and Luc Rousseau had also attended church that Sunday, near the stately mansions of Hillhouse Avenue. On their way home, they walked around an old cemetery as overstuffed clouds hung thoughtlessly against a gaudy blue sky. Colette tried to hold her brother's hand, but he wouldn't have it.

After the sun had set, back in their small dormitory room, Colette wrote a letter:

19-9-1920

Dear Stratham:

As I write these words Luc is pretending to be you, swinging an imaginary baseball bat. Then he pretends to be that terrible man, jumping around with his hair on fire.

I don't think he minded being kidnapped. He wasn't afraid at all. In fact he is angry because I want to leave America. I would say he isn't speaking to me, if one could say such a thing of a boy who doesn't talk.

Have you found out who that girl was or examined her neck? I have the strangest feeling whenever I think about her. I wish she had just taken that awful watch and run away.

Stratham, you will not believe me when I tell you how much I don't want to go away. I told the girl who lives upstairs about my trip to New York: one bombing, one kidnapping, one knife throwing, one madwoman in a church. She said she would have died from fright. She said I must want to get out of the country as soon as I can. I don't. I want to stay.

But I made a vow, and I have to go. I know you will not like to hear it, but I've never felt about anyone the way I feel about Hans. Seeing him again is more important than anything in the world for me, even if I only see him once more. I'm sorry. But perhaps you won't care at all; I never know with you.

If you do care, I want to ask you something very foolish – a favor I hardly dare set down, given everything you've already done for me. I am the most ungrateful girl who ever lived. Please come with me to Vienna. That's the favor I ask. I truly expect to see Hans once and never again. Whatever happens, I will wish in my heart that you were there with me. Please say you'll come.

With all my affection,
Colette

The air at Delmonico's was even thicker with smoke, but less crowded and much more subdued. In the main salon overlooking Fifth Avenue, Littlemore noticed that the usual profusion of diamond earrings and glittering crystal was not in evidence. The bombing remained the chief topic of conversation, but the stunned and speechless horror of September 16 was giving way, among some, to vitriol and rage.

'You know what we should do?' asked one man at a table for four. 'Shoot the Italians one by one until they tell us who did it.'

'Not all of them, Henry, surely.'

'Why not?' retorted Henry. 'If they bomb us, we kill them. Simple as that. That's the only way to stop a terrorist. Hit him where it hurts.'

'Why do they hate us so much?' asked a woman next to Henry.

'Who cares?'

'Deport them, I say,' declared the other man. 'Deport all the Italians, and there's the end of this ghastly bombing. They contribute nothing to society in any event.'

'What about the Delmonicos?' asked the other woman. 'Don't they contribute?'

'Deport all Italians except the Delmonicos!' cried the man, raising a glass in a mock toast.

'No, my steak is overcooked – Delmonico must go too!' cried Henry. The table broke out in laughter. The diners were evidently unaware that the Delmonicos no longer owned Delmonico's.

The headwaiter approached Littlemore. Asking for Mr James Speyer, the detective was led to an interior garden, where stained-glass windows ran from floor to ceiling. At a corner table a man sat alone – a man of about sixty, with hair still mostly black and the doleful eyes of a basset hound. The detective approached the table.

'Name's Littlemore,' said Littlemore. 'New York Police Department. Mind if I sit down?'

'Ah,' said Speyer. 'Finally a face to put on the law. Why would I mind? No man likes to dine alone.' Speyer's accent was distinctly German; before him were the plates and glasses of a fully consumed meal. He went on: 'You know what you've done? You've destroyed this establishment.'

Mr Speyer was evidently inebriated.

'I have a joke with the waiter,' he went on. 'I ask if they have any terrapin. I would never eat it, but I ask. He says no, the terrapin's eighty-sixed; you can't cook terrapin without wine. So I order the porterhouse Bordelaise. He says the Bordelaise is eighty-sixed, because that's illegal as well. We go on and on. Finally I ask him what he does have. He says try an eighty-six.'

Littlemore said nothing.

'An eighty-six – the plain grilled rib-eye,' explained Speyer. 'The one they always used to run out of. Now it's the only thing you *can* get. Because everything else is Prohibited.'

'We don't make the laws, mister,' said Littlemore. 'I'd like to ask you a couple of questions.'

'Very well,' said Speyer. 'But not here. If you must, let's go to my car.'

Speyer paid his bill and led the detective out onto Forty-fourth Street. A silver four-seater was parked outside. 'Nice, isn't she?' said Speyer. He opened a rear door; the driver started the engine. 'After you, Officer.'

Littlemore climbed inside. The chauffeur, meeting the detective's eyes in the rearview mirror, turned round and asked him who he was.

'It's all right,' said the detective. 'I'm with Mr Speyer.'

'Speyer? Who's that?' asked the driver.

The door that Speyer had graciously opened for the detective was still ajar.

'You're kidding me,' said Littlemore to no one in particular. The detective got out of the vehicle. There was no sign of James Speyer. Disgusted with himself, Littlemore went back into the restaurant and called his men Stankiewicz and Roederheusen.

On Monday morning, September 20, Edwin Fischer arrived at Grand Central Terminal on a train from Canada, in the custody of two New York City policemen. Reporters from every newspaper in the city were waiting for them, together with a considerable crowd.

The good-looking, tow-headed Fischer did not disappoint. He replied to questions with dauntless good cheer, while admonishing his greeters that he had been forbidden to discuss the bombing. Evidently overheated, Fischer removed his cream-colored suit jacket, folded it neatly, and handed it to a nonplussed policeman – revealing a second jacket below the first, this one navy blue.

'How come the two jackets, Fischer?' one reporter called out. 'Cold up in Canada?'

'I always wear two,' Fischer replied brightly, displaying the waistline of a navy blue pair of pants below his outer pair of cream trousers. 'Two full suits, everywhere I go.'

The newsmen exchanged knowing winks: everyone had heard that Fischer was a lunatic. One of them asked why he wore two suits. Fischer explained that as an American, he liked to sport casual attire, while as a member of the French consular establishment, he had to be prepared for greater formality. With a sparkle in his eye, he then exhibited a third outfit below the first two, which appeared to consist of cotton whites suitable for an outdoor gambol. Asked the reason, he responded that shortly after the last time he won the Open, a pushy fellow had challenged him to a game, which he'd had to decline for lack of appropriate costume. After that, he decided always to be ready for a match.

'The Open?' someone asked. 'What Open was that, Ed?'

'Why, the United States Open, of course,' said Fischer.

Titters greeted this assertion. 'You won the US Open, did you, Eddie?' someone called out.

'Oh, yes,' said Fischer with a broad smile. He had excellent teeth. 'Many times.'

Laughter circulated more broadly.

'How many?'

'Lost count after three,' he answered happily.

'Get going,' said one of the policemen, shoving the cream-colored suit jacket back into Fischer's arms.

From Grand Central, Fischer was taken to police headquarters for questioning by Commissioner Enright, Chief Inspector Lahey, and Assistant District Attorney Talley. Captains from the bomb squad and from Homicide, including Littlemore, sat in an array of hard chairs along a wall. Fischer had sociable words for everyone. With the District Attorney, he was especially effusive, asking after not only Talley's own health but that of Mrs Talley as well.

'You know each other?' Commissioner Enright asked.

'We're old friends,' replied Fischer. 'Isn't that right, Talley?'

'I've never met the man, Commissioner,' Talley replied to Enright.

'Listen to that,' said Fischer, smiling broadly and clapping Talley on the back. 'Always the jokester.'

Commissioner Enright shook his head and ordered the interrogation to commence. 'Mr Fischer,' he said, 'tell us how you knew there would be a bombing on Wall Street on the sixteenth of September.'

'Why, I didn't know, did I?' answered Fischer. 'I only knew it would come after the closing bell on the fifteenth.'

'But how? How did you know that?'

'I got it out of the air.'

'The air?'

'Yes – from a voice,' explained Fischer informatively. 'Out of the air.'

'Whose voice?' asked Inspector Lahey.

'I don't know. Perhaps it was a fellow member of the Secret Service. I'm an agent, you know. Undercover.'

'Wait a second,' said District Attorney Talley. 'Did we meet at the Metropolitan awards dinner a few years ago?'

'Did we *meet*?' repeated Fischer. 'We sat next to each other the whole evening. You were the life of the party.'

'Oh, for heaven's sake,' said Enright. 'Please continue.'

'Who's your contact at the Secret Service?' asked Lahey.

'You're asking for his name?' replied Fischer.

'Yes – his name.'

Fischer threw Talley a look implying that Inspector Lahey was either a little ignorant or a little addle-brained, but that it would be impolite to say so: 'Goodness, Inspector. He doesn't tell me his name. What sort of Secret Serviceman would that be?'

'How did you know about the bombing?' asked Talley yet again.

Fischer sighed: 'I got it out of the air.'

'By wireless?' asked Lahey.

'You mean radio? I shouldn't think so. I'm very close to God, you know. Some people resent that.'

After two and a half hours, Commissioner Enright brought the interrogation to an end, no further results having been produced. Fischer was committed to an asylum.

Littlemore collared District Attorney Talley before the latter left police headquarters and asked him whether it was legal for United States army troops to be stationed on a Manhattan street.

'Why not?' replied Talley.

'I never saw infantry in the city before,' said Littlemore. 'I thought they had to call out the National Guard or something – you know, with the Governor's consent.'

'Beats me,' said Talley. 'That'd be federal law. Why don't you ask Flynn's men? They'd probably know.'

Littlemore returned to his office and paced, irritated. Then he cranked up his telephone. 'Rosie,' he said to the operator, 'get me the Metropolitan Tennis Association.'

As Littlemore rung off, Officer Stankiewicz poked his head through the door, holding a sheaf of papers. 'Final casualty list, Cap,' said Stankiewicz. 'Want to see it before it goes out?'

Littlemore leafed through the unevenly typed document, which gave for every man, woman, and child killed or wounded on September 16 a name, address, age, and place of employment, if any. Page after page, hundreds and hundreds of names. Littlemore closed his eyes – and opened them at a knock on his door. Officer Roederheusen poked his head through.

'I found Speyer's ship, sir,' said Roederheusen, unshaven and red-eyed. 'There's a James Speyer booked on the *Imperator*, leaving tomorrow for Germany at nine-thirty in the morning. I saw the manifest myself.'

'Nice work, Spanky.'

Stankiewicz looked quizzically at Roederheusen.

'I'm Spanky now,' explained Roederheusen proudly.

Littlemore rubbed his eyes and handed the casualty list back to Stankiewicz, whom he waved out of his office. 'What's Speyer been up to?' he asked Roederheusen.

'Nothing, sir,' said Roederheusen. 'He didn't go out all night. This morning at eight he went to work. He's been there all day.'

'Who's on him now?' Littlemore went to his door and shouted, 'Hey, Stanky. Get back in here. Give me that list again.'

The phone rang.

'Two beat officers, sir,' Roederheusen replied as Stankiewicz re-entered the office. 'Should I call them off?'

Littlemore answered the telephone. Rosie, the operator, informed him through the telephone that the vice president of the Metropolitan Tennis Association was on the line.

'Put him through.' Littlemore motioned to Stankiewicz to hand him the list. To Roederheusen, he said, 'No. Make sure somebody keeps an eye on Speyer all day. If he makes a move, I want to know.

If he doesn't, you meet me at his house at five tomorrow morning. Yeah, five. Now go home and get some sleep.' Littlemore cradled the receiver between chin and shoulder as he returned to the page of the casualty list devoted to government officers. 'Where's the Treasury guy, Stanky? There was a Treasury guard who died.'

'Hello?' said a man's crackling voice through the receiver.

'If he ain't on that list, Cap, he ain't dead,' said Stankiewicz.

'Hold the line,' said Littlemore into the telephone. 'Know what, Stanky? Don't argue with me today. Go check the handwritten list.'

'The, um, handwritten list?'

'Hello?' said the telephone.

'Hold the line,' Littlemore repeated. To Stankiewicz, he said, 'What do I have to do, spell it for you? You and Spanky made filing cards for all the casualties. I told you to make me a list from those cards. You wrote me the list. I saw it. Then I told you to have the hand-written list typed up. This is the typed list. I'm asking you to go back and check the handwritten list. Okay? The Treasury guy's name began with R; I saw it on his badge. Maybe you missed some others too.'

'Is anybody there?' said the telephone.

'Um, the handwritten list is gone, sir,' said Stankiewicz.

'Hold the god-busted line, will you?' Littlemore yelled into the receiver. He looked at Stankiewicz: 'What do you mean "gone"?'

Stankiewicz didn't answer.

'Okay, Stanky, you threw away the handwritten list. Nice work. How about the filing cards? Don't tell me you threw those away?'

'I don't think so, sir.'

'You better not have. Or you'll be back on patrol next week. Go through every card. This time make sure you get everybody.'

Alone in his office, Littlemore identified himself to the vice president of the Metropolitan Tennis Association and asked whether an Edwin Fischer had ever won the United States Open.

'Edwin Fischer?' replied the crackling voice. 'The gentleman in all the newspapers?'

'That's the one,' said Littlemore.

'Did he ever win the United States Open?'

'I asked you first,' replied Littlemore.

'Certainly,' said the vice president.

'How many times?' asked Littlemore.

'How many times?'

'Okay, I'll bite,' said the detective. 'More than three.'

'Oh, yes, it was at least four – mixed doubles. A record, I believe. He was number nine in the country back then. Still has one the best overheads in the game. How on earth did he know about the bombing?'

Littlemore hung up. A messenger entered his office and handed the detective a package containing a written report and an envelope. Inside the envelope was a small white tooth, broken cleanly into two pieces.

Littlemore met Younger in a diner that afternoon, reporting to him over acidic coffee that the redhead at Bellevue Hospital was still unconscious.

'She should have woken up,' said Younger. 'She wasn't shot in the head. There's no injury to her skull.'

'What about her voice?' asked Littlemore. 'Colette says she sounded like a man.'

'The growth on her neck must be impinging on her vocal cords. I took X-rays of her yesterday.'

'How'd you do that?' asked Littlemore.

Younger didn't answer that question: 'The X-rays didn't go through. In fact I've never seen anything like it. I'm going to New Haven tomorrow to see what Colette thinks of the films.'

'New Haven?' answered Littlemore. 'You can't leave the state, Doc. You're on bail for a major felony, remember?'

Younger nodded, apparently unimpressed by the argument.

'This is serious,' added Littlemore. 'They can put you away for jumping bail.'

'I'll keep that in mind.'

'Let me put it this way. If you go, I don't want to know about it. And whatever you do, you got to show up for your court date in a couple of months.'

'Why?'

'Because I posted the bail bond, for Pete's sake. If you don't show, they're going to seize my bank account and everything I own to pay the bond. Plus I'll probably get fired, since a law officer isn't supposed to bail his pal out of the joint in the first place – and especially not if the pal ends up on the lam. Okay? When did you stop caring about the law anyway?'

'If you're about to die in a storm,' answered Younger, 'and you see a barn where you could save yourself, do you stay outside and die – or do you break in, even though it's against the law?'

'Of course you break in,' said Littlemore, 'if you're in the middle of nowhere.'

'Everywhere's the middle of nowhere.'

'No wonder the Miss wants to go back to Europe. You're so cheerful. Well, I got some news for you. The headless girl from Wall Street? They never identified her. She disappeared from the morgue – body, head, and all.'

'Why am I not surprised to hear that?' asked Younger.

'The one good thing is that they had already done the autopsy. Guess what: she *was* missing a molar. Couple of molars, actually. It's not proof, but I'd say we found your Amelia. Found her and lost her, that is. Something else too. Look what my dental guys found.' The detective took out his magnifying glass and, in a handkerchief, two tiny halves of a tooth, which he set down on the table. He let Younger examine them through the magnifying glass. 'That's the tooth Amelia left for the Miss at your hotel. See the holes?'

Pockmarking the internal enamel – the inner surface of the tooth, exposed where it had been broken in two – were dozens of almost microscopic vesicles or pores.

'Caries?' said Younger.

'What's that?' replied Littlemore.

'Tooth decay.'

'Nope. The dental guys said it can't be normal decay because the outside of the tooth is too perfect. No discoloration even. It's like the tooth was being eaten away from within.'

Colette's letter arrived in Younger's hotel room the following morning. He read it lying in bed. The letter provoked in him a wave of contradictory feelings. He both wanted to go with Colette to Vienna and found himself contemptible for having that desire.

What kind of man would accompany a girl halfway across the world to find her long-lost lover? He pictured himself smiling as he was introduced to Hans Gruber. The image filled him with disgust. What exactly was he supposed to do in Vienna? And why exactly did she want him there?

It occurred to him at last that she did *not* want him there: that her reason for inviting him was simply that she needed money to pay for the trip. The realization made him stare at the ceiling for a long time. Surely not. Surely Colette would never stoop to using him for his money. Would she?

He wondered how, without his help, she intended to pay for the voyage. And he saw, of course, that she had no means.

CHAPTER TEN

A T THE CORNER of Fifth Avenue and Eighty-seventh Street, a stone's throw from the Metropolitan Museum of Art, stood a grand mansion in the classical style. On Tuesday morning before the sun had risen, Littlemore instructed Roederheusen to cover the back of that mansion while he approached the front door.

There was no activity in the house. Fifth Avenue was quiet at five in the morning; a lone omnibus clattered down the street. One block north, a limousine idled on the park side of the avenue. Littlemore wondered whether it was Speyer's car, waiting to take him to the harbor.

Littlemore rang the front bell – and rang again and again, when no one answered. At last he heard footsteps on stairs. A light went on in the foyer.

'What is it? Who's there?' called a man's voice from behind the door, with the same German accent Littlemore had heard at Delmonico's.

In his best cockney accent, which was fair, Littlemore said, 'Is there a Mr Speyer in the house? Sailing today on the *Imperator*? Message for him from the Captain.' The *Imperator* was a British ship, its crew English.

'The Captain?' asked Speyer, opening the door.

'Yeah,' said Littlemore, pushing through and entering the foyer. 'The Police Captain you played for a sap on Sunday.'

Speyer, in a burgundy satin bathrobe, belted at the waist, fell back a step. 'I wronged you, Officer. I ask your forgiveness.'

'Turn around,' said Littlemore.

Speyer complied, saying, 'I ask you to forgive me.'

Littlemore jangled his handcuffs behind Speyer. 'Give me one good reason not to haul you downtown for absconding from a police officer.'

'I broke faith with you. Please forgive me.'

'Stow the forgiveness thing, will you?' said Littlemore, handcuffing Speyer.

'Sorry,' said Speyer. 'I was required to ask three times today. How much do you want? I'll give you whatever you want.'

'Now you're bribing me? That's five more years in the pen.'

'I beg your pardon. I assumed you were shaking me down.'

'Shaking you down. Pretty good English for a German. What did you do that I'd be shaking you down for?'

'I'm not German,' said Speyer, pronouncing the G in German with a hard *Ch*. 'I was born in this city. I'm as American as you are.'

'Sure you are,' said the detective. 'That's why you bankrolled the German army after we declared war.'

'Not me – my relatives, who live in Frankfurt. I had nothing to do with it.'

'Then why did your pal the Kaiser make you a knight of the Red Eagle?'

'That was in 1912,' protested Speyer. 'And if that makes a man a traitor, you should have arrested J. P. Morgan. He received the Eagle too.'

For the first time, Littlemore was caught off guard: 'Morgan?'

'Yes. He won it the year before I did.'

'If you're such a patriot,' said the detective, 'why are you skipping out of the country?'

'Skipping out? I'm going to Hamburg to have some very important contracts signed. I'll be home the eighth of October.'

'Show me those contracts,' said Littlemore. 'And your return ticket.'

'In my briefcase,' said Speyer. 'On the dinner table.'

Littlemore, pushing Speyer before him, entered a formal dining room, heavily ornamented, with a Michelangelesque fresco splashed on its ceiling. Oil paintings, large and small, adorned the walls. The detective stopped before a small portrait, so dark he could not at first make out its subject; it depicted an old man with a ruddy face and pouches under his eyes. 'This one must be worth a lot, since you can't even see it. How much does a little thing like this go for?'

'Do you know what that "little thing" is, Officer?' asked Speyer.

'A Rembrandt.'

It was Speyer now who was taken by surprise.

'Saw one just like it at the museum,' added Littlemore.

'I paid a quarter of a million dollars for it.'

Littlemore whistled. On a rectangular table long enough to seat twenty lay an open briefcase. Inside was a ream of bond and debenture documents in English, Spanish, and German. Littlemore flipped through them. 'And who did the full-length picture behind me?' asked the detective, without looking up. 'The one of Mr James Speyer.'

'A boy from the Lower East Side,' said Speyer. 'A student at the Eldridge University Settlement. One of the schools I fund.'

The contracts concerned an enormous sum of money, evidently destined for a Mexican bank – whose chief officer was James Speyer. Littlemore also found an American passport and a ticket on the Cunard *White Star* sailing for New York City out of Hamburg on October the first.

'Don't you think this is taking things a little far,' asked Speyer, 'for a bottle of wine?'

'What bottle of wine?'

'The one I had at Delmonico's. Isn't that why you came to my table? Isn't that why you're here?'

'Dry laws aren't my department,' said the detective. 'Let me get this straight. Your story is that you ran out on me at Delmonico's because you were afraid I was going to pinch you for boozing?'

'That's right.'

'And what – you thought I'd just let you go?'

'I didn't realize you knew who I was,' said Speyer. 'But now that you do know, I might as well warn you, Officer. I'm a rich man, and a rich man can make life very unpleasant for a policeman who troubles him.'

'Don't give me that. You're broke, Speyer,' said Littlemore. 'You had to sell off two of your bigger paintings recently. You even let go of your old servants.'

Speyer stared at the detective: 'How do you know so much about me?'

'Just using my eyes.' Littlemore pointed to two spots on the wall where the slightest lightening of the wallpaper indicated that smaller portraits were now on display where two larger frames used to hang. 'You wouldn't be answering your own doorbell if you still had the servants a man who lives in this kind of house ought to have. I'd say you're trying to maintain appearances, Speyer. I'd say things are getting desperate. Why didn't you sell the Rembrandt?'

A long pause followed. 'I couldn't let it go,' said Speyer at last. 'What do you want with me?'

'The NYPD provides security when presidential candidates come to town,' answered Littlemore, not untruthfully. 'We have plain-clothesmen at every dinner. You were overheard at one of those dinners threatening a J. P. Morgan man.'

'Nonsense.'

'You deny telling a Morgan partner to watch out because the Morgan firm was combining with others to deny you credit?'

'What? I wasn't threatening Lamont. I was warning him.'

'You might be surprised, Mr Speyer, but the law doesn't draw too fine a distinction between threats and warnings.'

'You don't understand. I was warning Lamont about the Mexicans – despite everything Morgan's done to me. Mexico's new financial agent, he was the one doing the threatening. Making the wildest claims about what would happen to the House of Morgan — to Morgan himself – if they didn't lift the embargo.'

'What embargo?'

'The Morgan embargo against Mexico. You must know about the default?'

'No.'

Speyer shook his head. 'Where to begin? Twenty years ago, J. P. Morgan – the old man – floated the entire Mexican national debt. A big gamble, unheard of for a United States bank. It was a bold wager. Worked out handsomely for a long time. Made Morgan a fortune. But then Mexico had its revolution, and in 1914, the Mexicans defaulted. They haven't paid a penny since. By now they owe hundreds of millions in interest alone. Morgan pressured all the other houses not to lend Mexico any new money until they've paid what they owe on the old.'

'What's wrong with that?' asked Littlemore.

'Wrong? There's no right and wrong in banking. There are only bets, good ones and bad ones. Morgan didn't see the revolution coming. That's why the Morgan people are so unhinged about me.'

'I don't follow you, Mister.'

Speyer took a deep breath. 'I'm betting on the revolutionaries. I'm breaking the embargo. I'm the only one. Lamont knows I have funds lined up, but he doesn't know where the money is coming from. That's why I ran from you on Sunday. I couldn't afford to be arrested. I can't afford the delay – or the publicity.' Speyer sat down awkwardly, his hands still shackled behind him. 'Lamont knows I'll take my money and lend it straight to the Mexicans. He'd do anything he could to stop me.'

Littlemore took this in. 'If Mexico can't afford to pay Morgan, why would you lend them money?'

'Oh, they can afford to pay. They have railroads. They have silver. Most of all, they have oil. More oil than anybody else on earth. I have to make this trip, Officer. It's my last chance. My wife is very ill. If I'm not on the *Imperator*, I'll lose everything. I promise you I'll be back on the eighth. I can give you collateral.'

'What kind of collateral?'

'Any kind. Name it.'

Littlemore named it. Speyer swallowed hard.

The same morning, Younger sent Colette a reply to her request that he accompany her to Vienna. His letter could not be faulted for excessive length:

September 21, 1920

No.

— Stratham

Back outside on Fifth Avenue, Littlemore let Roederheusen take the driver's seat of their car. The detective's hands were occupied with a rectangular object wrapped in a heavy blanket. When Roederheusen asked what the object was, Littlemore told him it was a quarter-million-dollar bond.

As they drove off, Littlemore noticed the limousine up the street pulling away as well, in the opposite direction.

Because it was still early, Littlemore decided to spend an hour in a law library. The librarian was eager to help, but she knew less about researching the law than did the detective. They found nothing.

The telephone was ringing when Littlemore arrived at his office. Rosie, the operator, informed him that a Mr Thomas Lamont was on the line – and that he'd been calling all morning.

'Did you speak with Mr Speyer?' asked Lamont when the connection was made.

'You know I did, Lamont. Your man was keeping watch.'

'I see. Well, we do like to keep an eye on things. Did you find out anything?'

'Yeah – I found out I was being used by J. P. Morgan. You were hoping I'd arrest Speyer, or at least hold him up a few days. That way he doesn't get his money abroad, and he can't lend it to the Mexicans.'

The line fell silent for a moment. 'Speyer told you about Mexico?' asked Lamont.

'That's right.'

'What did he tell you?'

'Enough,' said Littlemore.

'We are trying to help Mexico, Captain. A nation cannot simply default on her debt. Mexico will destroy her own future if she persists in this shortsightedness. A debt is a sacred obligation. Mr Speyer, like so many of his kind, cannot understand that. For him a debt is only money.'

'Whereas to you it's religion,' said Littlemore. 'I offered to help you, Lamont. You tried to make me a stooge.'

'I swear to you, Captain, that was not my intention. My sole concern is whether my firm is being attacked – and if so, finding out who is behind it.'

'I don't believe Speyer had anything to do with the bombing, and neither do you.'

'But the man threatened me. He practically warned me he was going to resort to violence. Did you ask him about that?'

'It wasn't a threat. He was trying to warn you about a new financial guy from Mexico – maybe the same guy who came to your club the other night.'

'Who – Pesqueira? What about him?'

'I don't know, Lamont. It's your business, not mine.'

'You can't just let Speyer leave the country, Captain. What if he never comes back?'

At that moment, Officer Stankiewicz poked his head through the door. 'Hey, Cap,' he said, out of breath, 'the Bureau –'

Littlemore silenced him with his palm. 'He'll come back,' he said to Lamont, ringing off. 'What is it, Stanky?'

'The G-men found a guy who serviced the bombers' horse and wagon,' said Stankiewicz. 'They say he's fingered Tresca. Flynn's announcing it to the press in ten minutes.'

'Where?' asked Littlemore, putting on straw hat and jacket.

'In front of the Treasury.'

'Go get that horseshoe,' said Littlemore, setting off down the hall. 'Meet me there.'

On the steps of the United States Treasury, with the statue of George Washington behind him and a phalanx of armed soldiers on either side, Big Bill Flynn of the Federal Bureau of Investigation had his arm around a grizzled workman wearing an oil-stained leather apron. To a small crowd of reporters and photographers, Flynn made the following proclamation:

'What we got here is a major break in the investigation. This fine American is Mr John Haggerty, a horseshoer of over forty years' experience, located by agents of the Bureau under my personal command. Get your pens out, boys; here's your story. On or about the first of this month, an individual appeared in Mr Haggerty's stable on New Chambers Street in the company of a horse and wagon, which horse and wagon was in need of new shoes, and which was outfitted with unusual brass turret rings just like the ones we collected from this plaza after the explosion. Mr Haggerty put size-four shoes on that horse, said shoes being united to said horse by means of shamrock nails and Niagara hoof pads – co-operating in every respect with the evidence we collected here.'

'They didn't collect that stuff, Cap,' whispered Stankiewicz to Littlemore. 'We gave it to them.'

Littlemore motioned him to be quiet.

'In other words, the horse and wagon shoed by Mr Haggerty three weeks ago was the exact same horse and wagon employed by the anarchists to transport their incendiary device here on the sixteenth. The individual who brought that horse into Mr Haggerty's stable was approximately five foot seven inches in height, slight of build, poorly shaven, and very dirty and low in appearance. Ain't that right, Haggerty?'

The stableman nodded gravely.

'And this is the kicker, boys,' added Flynn: 'The individual was

Eye-talian and gave his name as something in the nature of Trescati or Trescare. Ain't that right, Haggerty?'

'Could be,' said Haggerty.

'"Could be"?' whispered Stankiewicz.

'Shh,' said Littlemore.

'In other words,' Flynn went on, 'a spitting description of Carlo Tresca, just like I been saying all along. Okay, boys, take your pictures.'

Flynn shook Haggerty's hand. Cameras popped. The reporters asked Haggerty his age (which was sixty-four), what else he remembered about Tresca (which was very little), and so on. Haggerty answered in gruff monosyllables, addressing each reporter as 'sir.' In short order, Flynn brought matters to a close and moved to take the stableman away.

'Mr Haggerty,' called out Littlemore, 'you a union man?'

'Conference over,' shouted Flynn, recognizing the detective. 'No more questions.'

'But Mr Haggerty must be a union man, Big Bill,' said Littlemore innocently. 'Everybody knows an HSIU label was on the horse's shoes. It was in the papers on Saturday, wasn't it, fellas?'

The members of the press agreed that it was.

Flynn cleared his throat. 'An NYPD detective checking up on the Bureau, huh? That's fresh. How's the Fischer investigation going, Policeman? Heard any voices out of the air lately?'

Several of the reporters laughed.

'Okay, Haggerty,' said Flynn, 'the policeman here wants to know if your shop is union. Is it?'

'Yes, sir – HSIU,' answered Haggerty.

'And you put that label on your shoes, right?' asked Flynn.

'Yes, sir – every one.'

Flynn smiled broadly. 'Got any more smart questions, NYPD?'

'Just one,' called Littlemore, stepping forward through the crowd, carrying a numbered canvas evidence bag tied with twine. 'I'd like to show Mr Haggerty the actual shoe – the one we pulled out of the bomb crater. He can tell us if the union label matches the one his shop uses.'

The reporters fell quiet. Flynn hesitated. He obviously wanted to take Haggerty away, but his reluctance to appear doubtful of his own witness's story kept him in place.

Littlemore untied the bag and handed the horseshoe to Haggerty. 'You can see a union label on that shoe, can't you, Mr Haggerty?' asked the detective.

'Yes, sir. HSIU. Same one we use in my shop.'

'There you go!' said Flynn triumphantly, taking the horseshoe from the stableman. 'I'll keep this. Federal evidence. Now let's get going. I'm hungry.'

'Which means, Mr Haggerty,' said Littlemore in a loud voice all could hear, 'the shoe that Chief Flynn is holding, the one from the actual bombing, *isn't* from the horse and wagon you serviced in your shop three weeks ago – am I right?'

'Yes, sir. You're right,' said Haggerty.

The reporters burst into confusion. Flynn shouted above them, 'What's he talking about? The label's a match.'

'The HSIU label on a horseshoe is a surface mark,' said Littlemore. 'Wears away in no time at all. After a few hours, it's barely visible. But the HSIU label on the actual shoe is mint clean. The horse that brought the bomb to Wall Street was new-shod the morning of the attack – the day before at most. Not three weeks ago. Am I right, Mr Haggerty?'

'Yes, sir.'

The following evening, Younger joined Littlemore at a dingy waterfront bar built on a derelict pier near the harbor, where unintimidated rats picked at refuse among the pilings and the detective had to give a password to gain entry. The smoke was so thick, and the lighting so poor, Younger could hardly see the bar counter. 'They got a trapdoor in the back,' said Littlemore as they took a small table in a dark corner. 'Opens right onto the water. When they get raided, they dump all their liquor into a boat and off she goes. Cops never find a thing. If the tide's in, they just dump the liquor into the water. Divers bring it up later.'

'I don't think I've ever seen you break the law before,' said Younger.

'I'm not breaking any laws,' answered Littlemore. 'I'm getting a sassafras.'

'Then why are we here?'

'So *you* can get a drink,' said Littlemore. 'Looks like you could use one.'

Younger considered the proposition and found it accurate. All day long he had kept checking the hotel desk for a letter or wire from Colette. Every time the clerk informed him that there were no messages, Younger was furious at himself for caring about the girl at all.

Littlemore ordered his soft drink; Younger ordered a whiskey. The waiter brought him a fifth – just the unopened bottle – along with a 'setup,' which was a glass of ice and soda.

'You pour yourself the drink,' Littlemore instructed. 'Then you put the bottle in your coat pocket. If the law comes in, they say they only serve sodas. They can't help it if their customers bring liquor in.'

Younger poured himself a double. He and Littlemore toasted silently. Younger felt vaguely louche with the bottle of whiskey in his pocket – if in fact it was whiskey, which Younger doubted, because it tasted more like rubbing alcohol. He finished his glass and poured himself another. 'Boisterous little place,' he said. 'I like the atmosphere.'

At the bar, men hunched over their drinks, speaking in low voices. Even the bartender was taciturn. A solitary woman wearing a boa nursed a cocktail at one end of the counter; no one approached her. Near the door, the man keeping watch handled a pack of cards by himself at a table – not playing, just shuffling and reshuffling.

'It's the same all over town,' said Littlemore. 'Everybody's still spooked from the bombing. Only place they're not spooked is the Bankers and Brokers Club. They were having a ball when I went there a couple nights ago. I think it was relief – that they weren't the ones who got hit. Guess what: a doctor came to Bellevue today for Two-Heads. He heard about the shooting in the church and recognized her description. Her name's Quinta McDonald. I found out what's wrong with her. The doctor said it was confidential, but I got it out of him. She has syphilis. Apparently syphilis can cause a growth on your body?'

'Tertiary syphilis can,' agreed Younger. He thought about it. 'It could have made her demented as well.'

'That's what her doctor said. It got into her brain. Gave her delusions.'

'I did some work on syphilitic dementia a few years ago. If that's what she has, there's no reversing it and no cure for it.'

'So here's what I'm thinking,' said Littlemore. 'There may not be anything left for the Miss to worry about.'

'How's that?'

'Well, let's start with Amelia, the girl who left the tooth at your hotel. Amelia's in some kind of trouble, and she needs to leave a tooth with somebody she knows to get them to help her. But the clerk delivers the tooth to Colette by mistake. Meanwhile, Drobac's following Amelia. He's hunting whoever she's trying to leave the tooth with. When the tooth gets delivered to Colette, Drobac thinks Colette is his target. So he and his two pals kidnap her. After that, Amelia gets killed by the bomb, Drobac's two pals get killed when we rescue Colette, and Drobac himself is behind bars. That leaves only Two-Heads, the McDonald girl. We don't know why she came after Colette – probably she's just crazy from her syphilis – but it doesn't matter because now she's in a coma. So everybody's either dead, jailed, or otherwise out of commission. Case closed.'

'What about the other redhead?' asked Younger. 'There were two of them outside the police station.'

'Friend of the McDonald girl. Maybe her sister. Nothing to worry about.'

'I thought you didn't make assumptions,' said Younger.

'I don't. I was just trying it out to see how it sounded.'

'How did it sound?'

'Didn't make any kind of sense at all,' said Littlemore.

The two men drank for a long while. Younger could feel the cheap alcohol beginning to work on him.

'So the Miss is going back to Europe?' asked Littlemore.

'You can't tell me,' answered Younger, 'that marriage makes men happy. Do you know one married man who's actually happy?'

'I'm happy.'

'Apart from you.'

Littlemore thought about it. 'No. Do you know any unmarried guys who are happy?'

'No.'

'There you go, then,' said Littlemore.

The men drank.

At another table, a man tried to stand, failed, and fell to the floor, knocking his chair over with him. For a moment Younger thought the sound had been a gunshot. Then he heard more gunfire, but he knew it was inside his head. The recurring image that, ever since the bombing, he could neither forget nor interpret sprang into his mind again, this time with greater clarity. 'I know what I saw on the sixteenth,' he said. 'It wasn't a blackboard. It was someone shooting. When everyone else was running around in a panic, in the middle of all the smoke and dust, someone was firing a machine gun.'

'At what?'

'At a wall. Leaving marks on it.'

'Firing a machine gun at a wall?' said Littlemore. 'In the middle of the bombing?'

'Did I mention that I also saw the shrapnel flying through the air so slowly I could make out the individual pieces?'

'No, you didn't tell me that, and don't mention it again. They'll lock you up with Eddie Fischer.'

Detective Littlemore was restive as he paced the cramped offices shared by Homicide and Special Crimes. Overcrowded desks vied for space with overstuffed filing cabinets. Typewriters clacked. Men yelled at one another, their complaints mostly jocular. The joking irritated Littlemore. A week had passed since the Wall Street bombing, and they had made no progress. Loose threads dangled everywhere.

There was Fischer, now confined in a sanitarium, whose prescient warnings remained unaccounted for. There was Big Bill Flynn, determined to hang the crime on Italian anarchists even though each piece of evidence Flynn came up with was thin as cheap typing paper. Then there was Attorney General Palmer – or rather, *where* was Palmer? Everything Littlemore knew about the Attorney General would have predicted Palmer's seizing control of the case, giving press conferences, taking the spotlight. Instead Palmer had passed through town for a night on his way to a family holiday – why? Finally, there was the fact that the attack seemed wholly unmotivated. If there was a target, it appeared to have been the Morgan Bank, yet Littlemore had identified no individual or organization with the right means and motives for attacking Morgan in so blunderbuss a fashion.

'Hey, Spanky,' Littlemore called out.

'Sir?' replied Roederheusen.

'Go over to the Mexican consulate,' said Littlemore, 'and get ahold of a guy named Pesky something or other. *Pesky-air-uh,* I think. I want to talk to him.'

'Say, Cap,' called out Stankiewicz from his desk, 'I found the cards.'

'What cards?'

'The filing cards we made on Wall Street.' Stankiewicz was holding a stack of handwritten note cards made at the scene of the bombing – one card for each of the dead. 'You remember, you thought there was somebody who was killed who should've been on the casualty list, but he wasn't on the list, so you asked me to find the cards.'

'Give me those,' said Littlemore irritably. He flipped through the note cards. 'The guy was a Treasury guard. Name began with *R.*'

Littlemore found what he was looking for. 'Here he is: "Riggs, United States Treasury." Now where's that casualty list?'

Stankiewicz fished through the papers piled haphazardly on his desk. 'I had it a second ago.'

'Tell me you didn't lose the casualty list,' said Littlemore.

Stankiewicz handed the detective the stapled, typed, many-paged document.

Littlemore went through it, checking both the alphabetical listing and the page specifically naming government officers killed in the blast. 'No Riggs,' said the detective. 'What happened to "Riggs, United States Treasury"?'

'Guess they missed him.'

'They?' asked Littlemore. 'Who's they? Didn't you type this list?'

'Not exactly.'

'Who did?'

'Um, the Feds did. A couple of agents came over the day after the bombing and asked if we had a list of the dead and wounded. I said sure and let them have a look – you know, at the handwritten list, which we made from the cards. They volunteered to have it typed up for us over the weekend. They said they had typists who would do a nice job. So I—'

'You gave the Feds our list?' asked Littlemore, incredulous.

'I'm not too good with a typewriter, sir. I figured it would come out better this way.'

'You figured you were too lazy,' said Littlemore. 'What kind of Feds? Flynn's boys?'

'No, sir. They were T-men,' said Stankiewicz, using the shorthand name for Treasury agents.

A second letter from Colette arrived on Thursday, but it turned out she must have sent it before receiving Younger's reply. The letter lay open on Younger's hotel room bed:

21-9-1920

Dearest Stratham,

I am finished with your Professor Boltwood. He is going to prevent Yale University from awarding Madame Curie an honorary degree when she comes. He says she is both academically and morally unfit. He is unfit to tie her shoelaces. My one consolation for running his laboratory is that I am disproving his theories. I can't stay on here, no matter what.

But I also have wonderful news! I dared to wire Dr Freud in Vienna, and he has wired back. He says he will see Luc again, and also that he is very eager to see you as well. He says he has a great deal to tell you.

Please, please come. I need you there with me.

Affectionately,
Colette

Younger returned by himself that night to Littlemore's waterfront clip joint. A woman in red lipstick and an orange dress approached while he drank the foul whiskey. 'What about it, handsome?' she said.

'No thanks,' he replied.

CHAPTER ELEVEN

THE ORDINARILY GENIAL Police Commissioner Enright liked to drop in on the men he wanted to see. Written summonses appeared only in cases of severest displeasure; they struck dread in the Commissioner's subordinates. On Friday morning at police headquarters, Littlemore received such a summons.

'Is it the Rembrandt in the evidence locker, sir?' asked Littlemore as he walked into the Commissioner's office. 'I can explain.'

Enright, behind his mahogany desk, raised his eyebrows: 'You have a Rembrandt in the evidence locker?'

'Was it the horseshoe, Mr Enright? I couldn't let Flynn get away with that story about Haggerty.'

'I didn't ask you here to play horseshoes, Mr Littlemore, or to discuss portraiture.' Enright got up, his gold watch chain glinting on an extensive waistline, his wavy gray hair abundant over a fleshy, good-natured face. A prodigious reader, an eloquent speaker, and largely self-educated, Enright had the eyes of a man who loved reciting poetry from memory. 'You remember Mayor Hylan, I'm sure, and Mr McAdoo, the President's adviser?'

Littlemore turned and saw those two important gentlemen at the other end of the office. McAdoo was seated, cross-legged, in an armchair, staring imperturbably at the detective, taking his measure. Hylan, standing and fidgeting with a glass object he'd picked up from Enright's bookcase, studiously avoided eye contact.

'Mayor Hylan received a visit from an attorney yesterday, Littlemore,' Enright continued. 'You were the subject of that visit.'

'Me, sir?'

'I want him fired, Enright,' declared Mayor Hylan.

'The attorney,' Enright continued, 'is a man of considerable reputation, well connected to the political establishment of this city. A client of his is currently a guest in one of our custodial facilities.'

'I said I want him fired,' repeated the Mayor, who had decidedly less poetry about him than did the Commissioner. Hylan was a short personage, greasy hair falling over his forehead in continual need of a comb, eyes darting like a squirrel's. A favorite occupation of Mayor Hylan's was railing from a podium, which he did often and poorly. He wore an air of perpetual embattlement, as if enemies were constantly casting outrageous aspersions on his good name. Prior to becoming Mayor of New York, he was an engineer with the Brooklyn Elevated Railroad Company, which discharged him after he nearly ran a locomotive over a supervisor. He had ascended to the mayoralty from nowhere, politically speaking, dredged up from obscurity by Tammany Hall, the doyens of which rightly estimated him a man they could trust. 'And I want that man out of jail. Today.'

'Unfortunately, Mr Mayor,' said the Commissioner, 'much as I wish I could execute your orders without question, I am subservient to another master as well – the law.'

'Don't law me,' retorted Hylan. 'I know the law. Don't forget who you're talking to, Enright. I could have you fired too.'

'That's your prerogative,' answered Enright.

'Let's keep our tempers,' said McAdoo mildly, 'and hear the facts, shall we?'

'This is none of Washington's business,' snapped Mayor Hylan. 'It's city business.'

'On September sixteenth,' answered McAdoo without raising his voice, 'New York City's business became Washington's business. I haven't reached the President today, but my wife thinks Wilson would not be pleased if the Captain were fired.'

'His wife?' asked the Mayor, incredulous. 'His *wife*? How about your wife, Enright — does she have an opinion? Excuse me, I'll go ask my wife what the President wants.'

'For heaven's sake, Hylan,' said the Commissioner. 'McAdoo's wife is the President's daughter.'

There was a momentary silence.

'Daughter,' Mayor Hylan humphed and wiped his brow with a soiled handkerchief.

Littlemore cleared his throat: 'Um, would I be the Captain every-body's talking about firing?'

Commissioner Enright answered: 'Is it true, Littlemore, that you took a man out of the hospital last week and jailed him even though he had just received major surgery for compound facial fractures?'

'That guy?' responded Littlemore. 'That guy has a fancy lawyer?'

'Yes. His name, I'm told, is Mr John Smith. I'm also told that Mr Smith's assailant is a very close friend of yours. And that you person-ally secured your friend's release on bail.'

'How'd the lawyer know that?'

'I take it these facts are true.'

'Yes, sir. I think the guy's real name is Drobac, Mr Enright, and I think he may be the Woolworth rooftop killer.'

'*May* be the killer?' repeated Hylan scornfully. 'Anyone *may* be the killer.'

'No, sir, Mr Mayor. There are only about fifty people who could be the Woolworth killer. That's how many were on the observation deck at the time of the murder, and over a dozen of them were kids. This guy was there, and he was recognized by an eyewitness as a wanted kidnapper.'

'Allegedly recognized, Captain,' corrected Enright. 'By the man who assaulted him. Whom you released. Your friend. Who is himself charged with attempted murder.'

'Dr Younger's helped the force before, sir,' said Littlemore. 'He's a Harvard man. And he fought in the war.'

'The war,' repeated Enright darkly. 'You know as well I do, Littlemore, that many men who fought have behaved unaccountably and committed criminal assaults since returning home.'

'Not this man,' said Littlemore.

'Enright, ask your Captain,' interjected Hylan, 'what proof he has that Smith committed the Woolworth murder. I'm told there's no evidence whatsoever.'

'Littlemore?' asked Enright.

The detective shifted uncomfortably: 'Okay, I don't have any proof – for now. But Dr Younger definitely identified him as Drobac, who committed a kidnapping and another killing the night before.'

'Bosh – the kidnapped girl herself doesn't recognize the man,' added Hylan. 'Not to mention the fact that she's left the state.'

'She's only in Connecticut,' said Littlemore.

'Yes, in New Haven, I know,' said the Commissioner. 'Is it true that she failed to recognize the man?'

'Yes, sir.'

'Can *you* identify him, Littlemore?' asked Enright. 'You rescued the kidnapped girl. Could you testify that the man in jail was one of her kidnappers?'

'No, sir,' conceded Littlemore. 'He's a little – uh – banged up at the moment.'

'You see, Enright?' declared Hylan. 'Your own officer can't identify him.'

'Would you say you have probable cause, Littlemore?' asked the Commissioner.

'Probable cause? You're not talking about letting him go, are you, Mr Enright? This guy's dangerous. He's gone after the French girl twice. He might kill her if we let him out.'

Enright sighed: 'You can't presume guilt, Littlemore, and you can't hold a man without probable cause. You know that.'

'We've held plenty of men on a lot less than this, sir,' objected Littlemore. 'We've held them for months.'

'Yes, but in those cases, the men we were holding – well –' Enright did not finish his sentence.

Littlemore did: 'Didn't have a lawyer fancy enough to get a meeting with the Mayor.'

'That's the way of the world,' said the Commissioner.

'Give me a few weeks, sir. I'll nail him.'

'A few weeks?' said Hylan. 'An outrage. I won't tolerate it. I've always stood up for the common man against the interests. There's only one true threat to this Republic – the international bankers, the moneymen, like a giant octopus spreading their slimy legs over all our cities. As long as I'm Mayor, the interests won't rule this city. The common man will have his rights.'

His back to Hylan, Commissioner Enright rolled his eyes. 'I'm sorry to say it, Littlemore,' said Enright, 'but your conduct merits an imme-diate suspension. Releasing from jail a personal friend charged with attempted murder. Imprisoning his victim without probable cause. Really. You should know better.' The Commissioner was one of those men who, when standing, like to bob up and down on the balls of their feet, hands behind the back. 'However, Mr McAdoo happened to be in my office at the very same time Mayor Hylan came in. As fate would have it, McAdoo was also speaking to me about you. He gave me this.' The Commissioner picked up from his desk several pieces of typed stationery. 'It's a copy of a letter delivered today to President Wilson and every member of his Cabinet in Washington, DC. The letter is from Senator Fall of New Mexico. Do you know Senator Fall?'

'No, sir.'

'A very powerful man,' said Enright. 'He sits on the Senate Foreign Relations Committee and will soon be Secretary of State, in all like-lihood, under Mr Harding.'

'What's that got to do with me, sir?' asked Littlemore.

'Can you enlighten Captain Littlemore, McAdoo?' said Enright.

'Certainly,' said McAdoo, putting his fingertips together. His calm demeanor, smooth-backed hair, fine features, and long elegant face contrasted sharply with the uncombed, frowning, and overanxious Mayor. McAdoo spoke with a distinctly Eastern, well-educated accent, with only the occasional twang giving away his Tennessee roots. 'Fall's a fire-breather – and a very effective one. He's been denouncing us – the Wilson Administration, that is – for our failure to respond to the outrage on Wall Street. Fall says that an attack of this magnitude can only have been organized and carried out by a foreign power intent on our destruction – a reference, I assume, to Lenin and his Bolsheviks. He says the bombing was an act of war plainly targeting one of America's most important financial houses, while we in the Administration, far from preparing for war, proclaim that it was the work of a few disorganized Italian malcontents. And then, Captain Littlemore, Senator Fall names you.'

'Me?'

'You. He says that the New York Police Captain closest to the investigation – naming you personally – has in private advised Mr Thomas Lamont of J. P. Morgan and Company that the evidence refutes Flynn's theory of the case and demonstrates a purposeful attack against the Morgan firm.'

'I didn't say demonstrates. I said it was a possibility.'

'You are to be congratulated, Captain Littlemore,' said McAdoo.

'I am?'

'Yes. I share Senator Fall's views in every respect.'

'If you'll excuse me, Mr McAdoo,' said Littlemore, 'I don't get it. I thought Senator Fall was criticizing President Wilson, and I thought you were the President's man.'

'I don't know if I'm his man, Captain,' said McAdoo, 'but I'm certainly in his camp. The President wants this bombing solved. That's all he wants. And he doesn't, to speak frankly, have perfect confidence in Chief Flynn. Flynn works for Attorney General Palmer; together they see a cabal of Italian and Hebrew anarchists lurking everywhere, or at least so they want our citizens to believe. If you, Captain Littlemore, are willing to pursue avenues that Flynn can't or won't, the President is entirely in favor. Many of us agree with Senator Fall that this attack was of a magnitude too great for a handful of impoverished anarchists.'

'Whoever did it wasn't impoverished – I'm pretty sure about that,' said Littlemore.

'Why?' asked Commissioner Enright.

'The horseshoe, sir,' said Littlemore. 'It was brand-new. You could tell from the union mark on it. Shoeing a horse isn't cheap. Nobody poor would ever put brand-new shoes on a horse they're about to blow to pieces. I'd say these guys had plenty of cash behind them.'

'Excellent, Captain,' replied Enright. 'That's how a detective does his job.'

'Making it more likely,' said McAdoo, 'that a foreign power was behind this outrage. If that's true, it must come out, and the enemy must be made to feel the full force of American might. Commissioner, your Captain can't be fired – or suspended. It would look as if we feared war and feared the truth. They would say we'd deliberately eliminated the one man daring to ask what enemy of this country might have massacred our people and attacked our finances. Fall would undoubtedly cast it in that light, and the story would run in every newspaper in the country.'

'I make the decisions in this city,' said the Mayor.

'To be sure, Hylan, to be sure,' replied McAdoo. 'I wouldn't dream of interfering. Nor would I hesitate to urge the Attorney General to revisit your statements in opposition to the late war. The Sedition Act is still in force, I believe.'

Hylan looked stricken. 'I don't care about your Littlemore. Let him stay on. Just give me Smith.'

'And I don't care about your Smith,' said McAdoo. 'Let him go free.'

'I don't know what's wrong with me,' said Enright. 'I seem to be the only one who cares about both Captain Littlemore and Mr Smith. I'm not going to suspend Littlemore —'

'Good,' said McAdoo.

'And I'm not going to release Mr Smith,' said Enright.

'What?' said Hylan.

'You have until Monday, Captain,' replied Enright.

'I'm sorry?' asked Littlemore.

'To obtain probable cause against Smith, if that's in fact his name.'

'But today's Friday, Mr Enright,' said Littlemore.

'And you've had Mr Smith in jail since last Friday, when he should have been in a hospital. By Monday you will have had ten days to collect evidence against him, Littlemore, which is more than adequate. Either you come up with hard evidence by Monday, or you let him go. Will that do, Hylan?'

'That'll do,' grumbled the Mayor.

'That will be all, Captain,' said Enright.

Younger tried to write a letter to Colette, seated at his hotel room desk. How could she love a convicted criminal so devoted to the German cause that he had volunteered to serve in its army? There had to be some reality to love — surely. If a girl loved a man who wasn't the man she thought he was, she didn't really love him — did she?

But perhaps Hans Gruber wasn't the man *Younger* thought he was. Why shouldn't Gruber be the sweet, devout, ailing soul that Colette remembered? Yes, he was in prison for assault on an innocent victim, but his imprisonment might be a mistake. Younger himself had been jailed for assault only last week. Worse, much worse: Didn't Gruber deserve Colette more than Younger did? Gruber had instantly seen what Younger had taken years to grasp — that his life would be void and dull and pointless and black without her.

The letter he was trying to write, offering Colette reasons not to go to Europe, failed to flow trippingly off his pen. He started, stopped, and started again, crumpling sheets of hotel stationery and throwing them into a wastebasket. Eventually he pulled them out and burned them, one by one, in an ashtray. It had come to him that, with Freud having agreed to treat Luc, Colette would never be dissuaded from going to Vienna.

Younger packed his bags.

Littlemore reexamined the evidence seized from Colette's and Luc's kidnappers. He combed through every item, turned inside out every article of clothing. He looked for laundry marks, for threads of hair, for anything that would connect the jailed man, Drobac, to the kidnapping. All to no avail.

Then he went to the police garage, where he personally re-dusted the criminals' car for fingerprints, both exterior and interior, from tailpipes to steering wheel to ashtrays. This painstaking process took many hours. It proved equally futile, revealing a host of prints, none of which matched the ones taken from the man Younger had assaulted. Frustrated but not beaten, Littlemore went home for the night.

Even as the train conductor announced New Haven as the next stop, Younger still had not decided whether to disembark there or continue on to Boston, the city that had been his home most of his life.

The landscape outside the train's windows had grown increasingly New England. Trees blazed with color. Every bridge over every river, every bend of the coastline, was familiar to him. He had taken the Shore Line into or out of Manhattan too many times.

When the train pulled into New Haven, Younger stepped out on the platform. He smelled the autumn air and dropped into a mailbox a letter for Colette. Under his Boston address, the letter said:

September 24, 1920

I'll come to Vienna, but only on one condition: that you renounce any intention of seeing Hans Gruber.

— Stratham

The whistle blew, the conductor called out, and Younger returned to his seat.

Littlemore spent the next day – Saturday – tracking down and interviewing occupants of the building where the criminals had stayed. No one had anything of value to tell him. He found the owner of that building, but the landlord was equally unhelpful. He cut through the police ropes and reentered the room where Colette and Luc had been taken. On hands and knees, he went over every inch of the room with his magnifying glass. This too was in vain.

Younger woke up Saturday morning in his old bedroom in his old house in the Back Bay. It wasn't the house of his parents – the house he'd grown up in – but a townhouse he'd bought after returning to Boston when his marriage broke up in 1911. It was a handsome place, with fine old furniture, high ceilings, and well-proportioned rooms. Leaving the accumulated mail untouched, he went outside.

What he liked about Boston was that it was such a small town. That was also what he didn't like about it. He walked to the Public Garden, passing rows of townhouses more or less identical to his own, and took a seat on a bench by the lake. It was so placid he could see in it an upside-down double of every swan and paddle boat plying the water. He put a cigarette in his mouth but discovered he had no matches. The fact that he was in Boston with no employment irritated him.

After his divorce, Younger had thrown himself into his scientific work, spending days and nights in a laboratory underneath the Harvard medical school. His field in those days was microscopic infectious agents. He made his scientific name in 1913 by isolating syphilitic spirochetes in the brains of individuals who had died of general paresis, a condition previously believed to be psychiatric in origin. He saw no one. He socialized not at all.

Then something unexpected took place. He had assumed he would be a pariah because of his divorce, which was not proscribed in Boston society, but was not regarded favorably. Instead, his social reputation soared. Whether due to his respectable position at Harvard, or the notoriety attaching to his supposed affair in New York, or, most likely, the inheritance that fell into his lap from his mother's Schermerhorn relatives, Younger became a prize commodity in both Boston and New York. At first he refused all invitations. But after two years playing the reclusive scientist, he began to go out. To his surprise, he enjoyed it.

He lent his arm to coveted young women at society events. He kissed their fingers and danced with them as if he were courting. But he never was; the society girls bored him. He preferred actresses, and in New York he was infamously seen with them. Over these years, there were only three women he slept with – and even those he could stand only for short stretches of time. A moment arrived when he was simultaneously the most eligible and most hated man in two cities. Even the actresses generally ended up enraged. Every year, he expected society to revolt against him and put him under a ban. But somehow the number of mothers believing that their daughter might be the one to land him only increased. In 1917, at a party in the Waldorf celebrating the coming out of the pretty Miss Denby, the debutante's charming mother pressed him so assiduously to dance with her daughter that he made a conscious show of part-nering with every girl other than Miss Denby. He drank to such excess that he didn't remember leaving the ball and woke the next morning in a hotel room with an unknown female beside him. It turned out to be Mrs Denby.

A few weeks later, the United States declared war. He enlisted at once.

When Younger got back to his townhouse, the afternoon mail had come, and with it a letter from Colette. He opened it still standing in his hallway:

25-9-1920

Dearest Stratham,

I can't do what you ask. I realize now that everything that's happened in America has been a sign telling me to go back to Europe. God must want me to. Vows are sacred. I have to honour mine, no matter how rash or wrong I was to make it. Maybe I will see when I'm there that he is not the one. But God puts these feelings in our hearts: of that I'm sure. I beg you to understand – and to come with me. I need you.

Yours,
Colette

He didn't understand. Why say she 'needed' him when she so obviously didn't? If it was money she needed, he wished she would simply ask him for it outright.

Rummaging through his mail, Younger found a statement from his bank. With a cold eye, he observed that his balance, once a thing of six figures – that was before he'd bought his house – had shrunk to four, and the first of those four was a one. Ever since Younger had come into his inheritance, he had turned over his professor's salary and, later, his soldier's wages to one or another insufferable Bostonian charity. He had lived without thought of money. The bequest having fallen into his lap, he had determined never to let it become an anchor.

He knew he would give it to Colette – the money for her passage – fool though that would make him. All she had to do was ask. He threw on some evening clothes, and went out. At the Post Office, he dropped off the following scribbled reply:

September 25, 1920

Since it's God's will, go with Him.

– Stratham

Littlemore, arriving home late and frustrated Saturday night, found his wife in a state of distress. Her mother, a robust little woman who spoke only Italian, was next to her. 'They came for Joey,' Betty exclaimed, referring to her younger brother.

'Who did?' asked Littlemore.

'You – the police,' answered Betty.

It turned out that policemen had paid a visit to Betty's mother's apartment on the Lower East Side looking for Joey, a dockworker who still lived with his mother. Mrs Longobardi told the police he was out, which was true. They entered and ransacked the apartment, seizing newspapers, magazines, and letters from relatives in Italy.

'They say they're going to arrest him,' Betty concluded. 'Arrest him and deport him.'

'What kind of policemen?' asked Littlemore. 'What were they wearing?'

Betty translated this question. The policemen, Mrs Longobardi answered, were wearing dark jackets and ties.

'Flynn,' said Littlemore.

On Sunday morning, Younger didn't wake rested. In fact he didn't wake at all, because he had never gone to sleep. When he got back to his house, unshaven, tie askew, it was well after dawn. Making himself coffee, he decided it was high time he got back to work.

He hadn't written a scientific paper since 1917. He hadn't even contacted Harvard about resuming his professorship. But he did have notes from the experiments he had conducted during the war; there was a paper on the medical use of maggots he wanted to write; and he did have an old set of patients who would probably be delighted to make him their doctor once again. It was time to return to his senses.

He went to his study and began organizing his papers and his finances.

At dusk he jerked awake – having fallen asleep at his desk – heart pounding with a dream whose final image he could still see. Colette had come straight back to America after her Austrian voyage. She had cabled him: she didn't care for Hans Gruber after all; it was he, Younger, whom she loved. He waited for her in Boston Harbor. She came running down from the ship, but when she reached him she froze, her green eyes shrinking from him in horror. He limped to a mirror. In it he saw what she had seen. During her five weeks' absence, he had aged fifty years.

Skipping church and canceling his usual weekly visit to his father in Staten Island, Littlemore returned on Sunday to the police garage. He climbed inside the kidnappers' car and went through it minutely again, even though the vehicle had already been fully searched and inventoried by other policemen. He was rewarded with exactly one discovery. Wedged deep in a crevice between seat back and seat cushion, Littlemore found a scrap of Western Union paper. It was not a telegram, but a receipt, showing only that some message had been sent somewhere by some customer.

With a few weeks at his disposal, and a dozen men pounding the pavement, such a receipt might conceivably have been tracked to its originating office. But Littlemore didn't have the men, he didn't have the time, and sending a telegram obviously didn't count as evidence of a crime.

The telephone rang in Younger's house on Sunday evening. He answered it, cursing himself for hoping it was Colette. It wasn't.

'What are you doing in Boston?' asked Littlemore's voice.

'I live here,' answered Younger.

'I left you messages all weekend at the Commodore. You didn't tell me you were going to Boston.'

'You told me not to tell you if I left town.'

'Oh yeah – good point,' said Littlemore. The detective described the unfortunate turn of events. 'Drobac gets out of prison tomorrow afternoon. I'm sorry, Doc. And I'm worried. Seems like Drobac's lawyer knew all kinds of things about Colette, including that she was up in New Haven. How would he know that? I think they've got somebody tailing the Miss. Or maybe somebody she knows in New Haven reports to these guys, whoever they are. I'll tell you what: after Drobac gets out, I don't know where is safe for her. I think the Miss and her brother should go into hiding.'

Younger rang off, grabbed his coat and hat, and left to make arrangements. When he'd finished, he sent a wire for immediate delivery to Colette:

YOU AND LUC MUST LEAVE AT ONCE STOP DROBAC BEING
RELEASED FROM JAIL TOMORROW STOP GENUINE DANGER
STOP HE KNOWS WHERE YOU ARE STOP I HAVE BOOKED
YOU A CABIN ON THESS WELSHMAN LEAVING NEW YORK
HARBOR FIVE-THIRTY PM MONDAY FOR HAMBURG STOP
LITTLEMORE WILL BE THERE WITH TICKETS STOP TELL NO
ONE REPEAT NO ONE

Because it was a Sunday night, Younger was obliged to pay a king's ransom to get this telegram sent and to have it hand-delivered upon transmission. Unfortunately, Western Union's hastily hired delivery boy in New Haven couldn't distinguish among Yale University's dormitories, and the telegram was slipped under the door of the wrong residence.

Colette, returning to her room Sunday night after working late at the laboratory, found the door unlocked. This dismayed her. She had told Luc over and over to keep the door locked; he didn't listen to anything she said anymore. Colette stepped into the silent darkness of her dormitory room. It shouldn't have been so dark – or silent. Could Luc already be asleep? He never went to bed until she made him.

The air felt damp, heavy, pregnant. She fumbled to turn on a lamp, but couldn't find the switch. Then she heard dripping – as if it were raining, but inside. The sound came from her bedroom.

'Luc?' she called out. No answer came. She felt her way to the bedroom, found a light, switched it on.

The room was empty. The boy's narrow bed was undisturbed. On the ceiling, drops of water were forming and falling into a puddle on the floor.

One flight above lived a graduate student in divinity and his kind wife, who had often taken Luc and watched him when Colette was at work. In fact Luc had a standing invitation from these neighbors to come up to their kitchen for milk and cookies any time he wanted – an invitation he'd taken advantage of more than once. The leak was surely coming from their apartment. Luc must be up there as well, Colette thought.

She went out into the unlit common stairwell of the dormitory building and, groping in the darkness, found the handrail and climbed the steps. A light showed beneath her friends' door. She knocked; the door swung open. The small apartment was bright, silent, and still. The living-room window was open, its curtain fluttering. Colette called out the names of her friends; there was no answer.

Colette's heart began to beat faster. The divinity student and his wife shouldn't have been out; they were always home at night. Colette went to the kitchen, which was empty, but the icebox door was open, which was wrong; one always shut one's icebox door. Then she heard the sound of water running. A door from the kitchen led to the bathroom. Colette looked down: from the bottom of that door, water was seeping out onto the kitchen floor. Colette opened the bathroom door.

No one was there. The bath was running, unattended. The tub was full; water overflowed onto the tile floor. Colette didn't shut off the tap. Instead, for no reason she could have explained, she ran back to the living room, pulled open the window curtain, and looked down into the courtyard outside. Luc was there.

He was standing under a tree near a lamppost, a glass of milk in one hand, a cookie in the other, staring at a female figure who was on her knees, looking into his eyes, her wispy hair tinged red in the lamplight. The girl's lined face was strained and taut. She could almost have been pretty, if the eyes hadn't been so frightful – eyes that had seen something unspeakable or were contemplating something unspeakable. She unbuttoned her dress and pulled it open, showing the boy her throat and her naked chest. Though her face was as taut as a madwoman's, her throat and chest were unmarred, white, soft – almost radiant. The glass slipped from Luc's hands. It fell to the grass, and so didn't break, but for a moment a circle of white milk glistened in the darkness at his feet. The figure stretched out her arms as if beckoning him to her.

Colette cried out from the upstairs window. She ran into the hallway and down the stairs. When she heaved open the heavy front door, other voices in the courtyard were crying an alarm too – but they were calling out to her, not to Luc. The girl under the tree had disappeared.

The other voices belonged to Colette's upstairs neighbors – the divinity student and his wife – who breathlessly declared that they had in their possession a telegram that Colette must read at once. They had been home when an undergraduate came knocking with a message from Western Union erroneously delivered to him. The moment the couple read the urgent wire, they ran off to Colette's laboratory, telling Luc to stay behind and wait; they had rushed so precipitously that the divinity student had left his bathtub running. But when they reached the laboratory, Colette had already left.

After Colette had taken Luc back to their room, after she had read the message, after the neighbors had retired upstairs, she looked at her brother. 'Did she touch you?' asked Colette.

The boy shook his head. He pointed to his neck and made signs with his hands, which Colette understood.

'Yes, I saw it too,' she answered. 'The aura.'

Detective Littlemore returned to the law library early Monday morning. It took him several hours, but he finally found what he was looking for. Armed with this knowledge, he set off for the Astor Hotel, where

217

Chief Flynn had set up his command post. Littlemore picked up a couple of hot dogs on the way.

Inside the Astor, ignoring the protests of a secretary, Littlemore ambled directly up to Flynn's closed door, outside which his two familiar deputies were standing guard. One of them rubbed his jaw on seeing the detective.

'Big Bill around?' Littlemore asked them. Receiving no answer, Littlemore said, 'I'll just knock, if you don't mind.'

Both deputies placed their hands on Littlemore's chest. 'We mind,' said the one who had been to the detective's house.

'No problem,' said Littlemore, taking a bite of his hot dog. 'I'll come back in a few hours. Got to go to court anyway. Make out an arrest warrant. Say, you know those soldiers Big Bill stationed outside the Treasury Building? Reason I ask is the Posse Comitatus Act. You don't want a dog, do you? I got two.'

The deputies stared at Littlemore.

'See, the Posse Comitatus Act,' continued the detective, 'that's a federal law, and it says that anyone who orders any part of the United States army to deploy on US soil for law enforcement purposes – well, he's breaking the law. Anyone except the President, that is. So do me a favor. Tell Big Bill that Captain Littlemore of the New York Police Department's coming back at five o'clock with a gang of reporters and a warrant for his arrest. And tell him that the reporters are going to want to know what he's hiding inside the Treasury.'

On the fifth floor of the massive, gray, château-inspired jail known as the Tombs, the order was given at two-thirty Monday afternoon to unlock a temporary detention cell. The flesh around Drobac's eyes remained swollen and bruised. His mouth was wired shut, and a circular metal apparatus was clamped around his jaw and cheeks.

A well-dressed lawyer, highly satisfied with the proceedings, entered the cell the moment it was unlocked, accompanied by the murderer's surgeon. They each reached for one of the prisoner's arms to assist him from his cot. Drobac shrugged off their hands and rose on his own.

Littlemore stood a long way off, at the other end of a long corridor, chewing his toothpick, a barred door separating him from the cells. Several guards and officers milled about near him, including Roederheusen and Stankiewicz. Younger, having come down from Boston that morning, was there as well.

'You sure you want to see this?' Littlemore asked him.

Younger nodded.

At the end of the corridor, Drobac emerged from his cell, walking slowly, unaided, his wired chin held ostentatiously high. Lawyer and surgeon followed behind, chatting with each other.

'In that case I'll need your gun, Doc,' said Littlemore in a low voice.

'What gun?' answered Younger just as quietly.

'Right now,' said Littlemore.

Younger didn't move. Slanted light fell on Drobac and his coterie as they approached.

'Boys,' said Littlemore, raising his voice very slightly, 'restrain Dr Younger.'

Roederheusen and Stankiewicz stepped up behind Younger and seized his arms.

Littlemore reached into Younger's jacket, drew out a revolver, and handed it to a prison guard for safekeeping. 'Sorry, Doc. Cuff him.'

Arriving at the barred door, Drobac saw Younger being handcuffed. Their eyes met. If a man can smile with his jaw wired shut, Drobac smiled.

'Open the gate,' ordered Littlemore.

'Don't let him go,' said Younger, hands locked behind his back and arms still in the grasp of Stankiewicz and Roederheusen.

'Open it,' Littlemore repeated.

A guard opened the barred gate. Drobac's lawyer spoke: 'Thank you, Captain. I'm glad my little conversation with the Mayor was so effective, but I shudder to think of all the other impoverished men in here unconstitutionally. Do you enjoy breaking the law, Captain? Sign the release, please.'

A clerk handed Littlemore a clipboard. 'If your client's so poor,' asked the detective, 'who's footing your bill, Mr—?'

'Gleason,' replied the lawyer. 'I charge nothing for a case like this, Captain. It's *pro bono publico.*'

'Sure it is,' said Littlemore.

'Don't let him out,' said Younger.

'No choice,' said Littlemore, signing the release. 'The law.'

Mr Gleason accepted his copy of the release with relish. He addressed Younger: 'So you're the one who beat my client within an inch of his life. We're pressing charges, you know.'

Younger didn't reply.

'How agonizing it must be,' Gleason continued, 'to stand there believing the fantastic delusions you do. That my client is a highly trained killer. That he's going to pursue the pretty French girl no matter where she runs, from New Haven to Hamburg to the farthest ends of the earth. That one night he'll find her, slip into her bedroom, and cut her throat.'

Younger's straining at his handcuffs only caused Roederheusen and Stankiewicz to hold him more firmly. 'Not if I find him first,' he said.

'You heard that, Captain!' crowed Gleason. 'He threatened my client. I demand that you revoke his bail. He belongs behind bars. I'll have your badge, Captain, if you don't.'

'Get out,' said Littlemore.

'Very well – if you insist,' replied the lawyer. He turned to Younger again: 'My client was in jail ten days. You'll be there twenty years.'

Younger was silenced by these words. Not, however, by the threat; it was the phrase *ten days* that caught his attention. 'Littlemore,' he said as Gleason guided Drobac toward the stairwell that led to freedom. 'Have him take off his shirt.'

'His shirt?' replied the detective.

'The kidnapper has a mark on the front of his torso,' said Younger. 'A red mark, in the shape of a test tube.'

The guard posted at the stairwell door looked uncertainly at Littlemore, waiting to be told whether to let Drobac pass.

'This is absurd,' said Gleason.

The surgeon spoke up: 'Is the mark visible to the naked eye?'

'Yes,' said Younger.

'I operated on Mr Smith,' the surgeon continued, referring to Drobac, 'and I assure you he has no such mark on his torso.'

'Then he has nothing to fear from taking off his shirt,' said Younger.

'Don't be ridiculous,' said Gleason, pushing past the guard and opening the stairwell door himself. 'You heard the surgeon. My client has been released. Now, if you'll excuse us—'

'Littlemore,' said Younger.

Drobac started to pass through the door held open by his attorney.

'Hold it,' the detective called out. 'Take his shirt off.'

A half-dozen guards pulled Drobac back into the hallway and formed a circle around him.

'You have no authority,' said Gleason.

For the first time, Drobac spoke. 'Is all right,' he said in his Eastern European accent, the wires around his jaw glinting silver. 'I do it. Why not? I hide nothing.'

Littlemore looked at Younger, who raised an eyebrow.

Drobac calmly removed his jacket, slipped off his suspenders, and began unbuttoning his white shirt, never taking his eyes from Younger. When his chest was bare, everyone could see it: under his left ribs, below the thick hair of his chest, slightly angled from the vertical, was the perfect likeness of a test tube, inscribed in a deep red rash.

'How do you like that?' said Littlemore.

Drobac looked down, uncomprehending. 'What – what is?'

'A radium burn,' said Younger. 'They take ten days to emerge. Yours comes from a test tube you stole from the Commodore Hotel and put in your jacket pocket.'

'This is an outrage,' declared Gleason. 'The Mayor will hear of this.'

'Put "Mr Smith" back in his cage,' said Littlemore to the guards.

Drobac, still looking at the red mark on his torso, made a snort that managed to convey both grudging acknowledgment and condescension. 'Is all right,' he said, buttoning his shirt. 'Your prison? Is more like hotel.'

'Glad you like it,' replied Littlemore. 'You're going to be here a long time.'

Drobac only smiled through his glinting steel wires.

Outside the Tombs, Littlemore returned Younger's gun and invited him to the Astor Hotel, where he was going to meet with reporters and Chief Flynn. 'Should be some fun,' said the detective. 'Until I get myself fired.'

Younger declined, saying he had a rendezvous he couldn't miss.

'Say, Doc, do you believe in premonitions?' asked Littlemore.

'No.'

'I'm just thinking about this guy Eddie Fischer. Everybody treats him like he's crazy, but what if he's really psycho?'

'Psychic.'

'Some people believe in premonitions, don't they? Some scientists? How about when you knew the bomb was about to go off on Wall Street before anybody else did? How do you explain that?'

'Something in the air,' replied Younger.

'That's just what Fischer says. He got it "out of the air."'

'If you want to talk to a believer,' said Younger, 'go to the American Society for Psychical Research. Their office is here in New York somewhere. They're as good as it gets. Ask for Dr Walter Prince.'

'Thanks. I'll do that.'

They stood for a time without speaking.

'Sorry about the cuffs up there,' said Littlemore. 'Just protocol. I know you weren't actually going to shoot the guy.'

'I would have killed him,' said Younger.

'Christ – you can't do that, Doc. War's over.'

Younger nodded. 'Maybe there's always war. Maybe some of us just aren't fighting.'

'Uh-huh,' said Littlemore. 'Or maybe you just wanted to kill somebody.'

'Maybe.'

They shook hands and parted. After Younger's taxi had driven off, another vehicle pulled up beside Littlemore – a black-and-gold Packard. At the same time, two large men in suits converged on the detective from the steps of the Tombs. The rear passenger window of the Packard rolled down. 'Would you mind getting in, Captain?' said a voice from within.

'Depends who's asking,' said Littlemore.

The man nearest the detective put his hand between Littlemore's shoulder blades to guide him into the car. He opened his jacket just enough to let Littlemore see the butt of a gun holstered within.

'That supposed to scare me?' asked Littlemore, reaching with astonishing quickness into the man's jacket, pulling the gun out of his holster, and pointing it at his chin – while at the same time, with his other hand, drawing his own gun from his belt and aiming it at the other man. 'Where do they train you Bureau guys anyway?'

'Please, please, put your weapons away,' said the voice within the car. 'I assure you there's no need. These men are not from the Bureau of Investigation. They work for me.'

'And who would you be?' asked Littlemore.

'I'm the secretary.'

'Whose secretary?' asked Littlemore.

'President Wilson's, I suppose. My name is David Houston. I'm Secretary of the Treasury. Please come in, Captain. There's something we need to discuss.'

Littlemore got in the car.

At the harbor, Younger found Colette and Luc waiting on a pier, near the berth of the steamship *Welshman*. Beside them were three forlorn, ragged-edged pieces of brown leather luggage. The air had already begun to cool; it would be a brisk autumn evening. The ship was boarding.

After they'd greeted one another, Colette described the events of the previous night. 'It's strange,' she said. 'When I first saw her, I was frightened, but later I felt there was nothing to be afraid of.'

Silence hung in the air.

'I didn't expect you,' said Colette, brushing a lock of hair from her face. 'Your telegram said Jimmy.'

Younger nodded. He handed her the tickets.

'They let him out of jail?' she asked. 'The killer?'

'No, he's back in,' said Younger. 'And he won't be coming out for a long time. It doesn't matter. You want to take this ship.'

She looked down at her hands. 'You—' she said.

'We took a wrong turn a long time ago, you and I,' answered Younger. 'All my fault. Better this way. I doubt your soldier deserves you, but you deserve to find out.'

Her gaze fell on the tickets. 'These are for Bremen, not Hamburg.'

Younger had bought a second set of tickets, on a different ship, the *George Washington*, when he arrived at the port an hour earlier. Drobac's attorney, Gleason, seemed to know that Colette was bound for Hamburg. If so, that meant Colette's pursuers would be expecting her to board the *Welshman*.

'A first-class cabin,' added Colette, still looking at the tickets. 'We don't need that.'

Younger handed her two more white envelopes. 'This one,' he said, 'has ready money for the trip. The other contains a draft on my accounts in England that you can negotiate at any serious bank in Vienna. No, take it. You can't live on nothing.'

She shook her head and tried to return the envelopes, but Younger wouldn't take them back. He crouched and extended his hand to Luc. The boy hesitated a moment, then held out his own.

'He did it,' said Younger. 'Ruth hit his fiftieth. And fifty-first.'

Luc nodded: he knew it already.

'Take care of your sister,' said Younger. He winked: 'Every girl needs a man taking care of her.'

Secretary Houston led Littlemore up the marble steps, past the soldiers standing at attention, into the Treasury Building. Houston was a gracious and handsome man in his early fifties, his genially crinkled eyes suggesting a friendliness contradicted by everything else about him, particularly the cold soft intelligence of his Southern voice. The detective followed the top-hatted Houston through the rotunda, then down several narrow stairwells. Soldiers lined every flight, every doorway.

They entered a sub-basement and came eventually to a narrow arched stone door, so low they had to stoop passing through it. On the other side, Houston threw a switch; dim electric lights flickered on. They were in a large chamber with a low vaulted ceiling, filled with endless stacks of neatly arranged, crisscrossing bricks, glinting darkly yellow.

Houston led Littlemore on a tour through these stacks of bricks, which, like the shelves in an overfull library, left just enough space for persons to pass between them in single file. There seemed to be miles of them.

It was gold, all gold, as far as the eye could see.

'Pick one up, Captain,' said Houston.

Littlemore removed a bar from the top of the nearest pile. It was inordinately heavy for its size.

'Twenty pounds,' said Houston. 'There is no larger store of gold anywhere on earth. There never has been. Not in the Bank of England, not in the palaces of the Turk, not in the tomb of the Inca. You are looking at the metal reserves of the United States of America, on which the credit of your government, the value of the dollars in your pocket, and ultimately the liquidity of every bank in this country depend. Have you any idea how much gold is here, Captain?'

'Less than there was on the morning of September sixteenth.'

'Most astute. How long have you known?'

'I saw one of your guards lying dead outside the Treasury with a piece of gold in his hands,' said Littlemore. 'I knew you'd been robbed when I found out you tried to erase his name from the casualty list.'

'Yes, a bit heavy-handed, that,' said Houston. He took a deep breath. 'The gold in these vaults is worth approximately nine hundred million dollars. Just think. The bomb, the deaths, the incalculable misery – all that for a bank robbery.'

'That's why Flynn called in the army.'

'It wasn't Flynn,' said Houston dismissively. 'The man is a blowhard. I ordered the soldiers here, and I'm well aware it was against the law to do so. But it would have been criminal not to. I tried to get Wilson's authorization. The President, however, is not – fully active, you know.'

'Why am I here, Mr Houston?' asked the detective.

'We couldn't have you telling the press the Treasury's been robbed, could we?'

'How much did they get?'

'Oh, it's not the dollar value of the loss that counts. Gold doesn't have value because someone will give you dollars for it, Captain. Dollars have value because the United States will give you gold for them. The real value of gold is psychical. It is valuable because men believe it to be valuable. And because they do, gold gives men faith in the government that possesses it – or is believed to possess it. We could lose every ounce of gold in these vaults, and so long as people didn't know of the loss, they would continue to invest in our bonds, trade in our dollars, leave their money in our banks, and so forth. Conversely, we could hold on to every brick, but if people believed the gold reserves of this country were insecure, we could have a panic making 1907 look like a baby's fretting.'

'How'd they do it?'

'You've seen the new building adjacent to this one, Captain – the Assay Office? Deep within it we've built new secure treasure vaults, much more suitable than this musty old basement. The gold is being transferred to the new vaults. We had devised a way to make that transfer without ever having an ounce of gold leave our property.'

'A tunnel?' asked Littlemore.

'No – a bridge. An overhead bridge.'

Littlemore nodded: 'In the alley between the buildings. I saw the doors.'

'Exactly. The bridge connected their second floors. It was built specially to move this gold. Triply reinforced to carry the weight. A moving automatic belt to make the conveyance of so much metal feasible. All without ever exposing a single brick to the outside world. Or so we thought.'

'You were moving the gold on the sixteenth?' asked Littlemore.

'Yes, we were. It was a carefully guarded secret. Or supposed to be. Evidently someone knew. The workmen inside reacted quite well, by the way. When they heard the explosion, they shut the doors on either side of the bridge, as they were trained to do. The only loss was the gold that happened to be on the bridge, which burned and collapsed. The robbers must have had a truck waiting in the alley.'

'How much did you lose?'

'We still don't know exactly,' Houston answered. 'It takes time to recount 138,000 bars. In addition to the gold on the bridge, I lost a man too – the man whose name we want off your lists. He may have gone onto the bridge to try to save the gold.'

'Riggs,' said Littlemore. 'So if the bombing was a robbery, why is Big Bill Flynn chasing anarchists?'

'Nearly no one knows about this robbery, Captain,' said Houston. 'Senator Fall, for example, does not know of it. Neither does Chief Flynn.'

Littlemore thought about that: 'You're afraid the Bureau has a leak.'

'Only a handful of people knew the date on which we were transferring the gold. There are men in the Bureau who knew. Someone betrayed us.'

'Could have been someone inside Treasury,' said Littlemore. 'Could have been Riggs.'

'I can't rule that out,' replied Houston.

'You must know more or less how much they got away with.'

'Oh, more or less, certainly,' replied Houston. 'A paltry amount. We will hardly notice it, even if we never get it back. Five or six hundred bricks, give or take.'

'Which comes to?' asked the detective.

'In dollars? Perhaps four.'

'Four thousand?'

'Four millions,' said Houston.

The number hung in the air for a moment, echoing. 'What is it you want from me, Mr Secretary?' asked Littlemore.

'Why, just to refrain from telling the press about the robbery. It wouldn't do for the public to learn the United States Treasury has been breached – and certainly not that there are people inside the government with the will and wherewithal to steal the nation's gold. Wouldn't do at all.'

'Too late,' said Littlemore. 'I already told a couple of reporters there was something they might find interesting at the Treasury. Something to do with gold.'

'I know,' said Houston. 'We've received inquiries. That much is all right. I don't mind telling them the gold is here. The financial world is already aware of it. I don't even mind telling the press we've been moving the gold to the Assay vaults. I intend simply to let it out that my men happened to take their lunch break just before the explosion. A simple story. It was noon; the men had shut the doors for lunch; they heard the bomb go off; that was all. A coincidence. The great point is that there was no robbery, no breach in security, no loss of gold. Lunchtime.'

'Think anyone will buy that?' asked Littlemore.

'The gullibility of the common man constantly surprises, Captain. If everyone tells the reporters the same thing, I think we'll be all right. Especially if you tell them. You'll be doing your country a service.'

Littlemore weighed the Secretary's request. 'I want in on your investigation – who knew the gold was being moved, everything you've got on Riggs, who's selling bullion on the black market.'

'Why not?' said Houston. 'You might help. Unlike my other officers, you at least are not a suspect.'

'And one more thing. Get Flynn off my back. Any of Flynn's men come within spitting distance of my wife's family, I tell the press everything I know.'

'That will be more difficult. The Bureau is not under my control.'

'No deal then.' Littlemore put his hat back on and snapped its brim.

It was Houston's turn to weigh his options. 'Consider it done,' he said. 'I'm speaking with General Palmer tonight.'

Colette uttered not a word. She turned away and waved for a porter, who quickly loaded the three tattered suitcases onto his hand truck. The porter set off. Colette, followed by Luc, walked slowly into the crowd.

Younger, lighting a cigarette, gazed past the *Welshman* to the vast black *George Washington*, memories boiling up. It had been a great ship once. It had brought Freud to America. It had taken Woodrow Wilson to Europe. It had carried kings and queens and heads of state. Now it was relegated to commercial passenger duty once again. All greatness fades.

Colette stopped. She turned, burst out of the crowd, and ran back to him. 'I'm such a fool,' she said. 'I'm not going.'

'Get on board,' said Younger. 'You'll regret it – you'll resent it – the rest of your life if you don't.'

The ship spoke in an earsplitting blast. Seagulls took flight. The call for all passengers went out.

Colette buried her cheek on his chest.

'Go on,' said Younger. 'It won't be so hard. You can cry on my shoulder in Vienna when we get there.'

She looked at him; he looked back. 'You don't mean it,' she said.

'Why shouldn't I come?' he asked. 'You're in love with me, not Heinrich.'

She didn't deny it.

Younger went on: 'If I let you go by yourself, you might actually marry this convict. Don't think I'm coming for your sake, though. It's Heinrich I'm worried about. You don't do a man any favors by marrying him when you're in love with someone else. You'd be killing him, slowly but surely. Besides –' he removed from his jacket another ticket for passage on the *George Washington* – 'my bags are already on board.'

Colette's whole body seemed to exhale with relief, and she smiled her most irresistible smile. As the ship steamed out to open sea, the three uncorked a bottle of champagne. Even Luc was allowed to try a little.

PART 3

CHAPTER TWELVE

THE UNITED STATES should have been all fanfare and barnstorm in the autumn of 1920, all marching bands and whistle-stop. Americans were electing a new president, and the excitement always appurtenant to that event should have been redoubled in 1920 because women for the first time had the right to vote. One of the major candidates – the Republican, Senator Warren G. Harding – might even have been nominated with the fairer sex in mind.

Harding's appeal to women was not a matter of speculation. It was established fact. He had a loyal wife of sixty-one, a longtime mistress of forty-seven, another mistress of thirty, and a flame of twenty-four still head over heels in love. 'It's a good thing I'm not a woman,' Harding liked to quip. 'I can never say no.' Harding's record of political accomplishment may have been thin, but with silver hair and dashing smile, with dark eyebrows, commanding eyes, and a strong chin, he was undoubtedly a presidential-looking man.

Yet the steam had gone out of the campaign locomotive. Unease hung too palpably wherever crowds gathered. Arrests and deportations went on, yet the terrorist attack remained unsolved. Men in power – rich men, governors, and senators – demanded remobilization. Newspapers demanded war. The cloud of smoke and flaming dust that blotted the sun from Wall Street on September sixteenth had not dissipated. Its pall had spread over the entire nation.

On September 27, the day Younger and Colette left for Europe, papers around the country reported that the Soviet dictator, V. I. Lenin, had infiltrated the United States with clandestine agents to foment labor unrest, terror, and revolution. In Boston the cab drivers struck, and there was a run on the banks. In Alabama, soldiers with machine guns prevented a miners' strike. The third most popular presidential candidate, Eugene Debs, was an unabashed socialist, but at least he was in prison, having dared in 1918 to question the necessity of the war. Through it all, Prohibition parched the workingman's throat, and the still-resounding echoes of September sixteenth made people hurry as they walked out of doors in the great cities. The country was holding its breath — and didn't even know what for.

On Fourteenth Street in Manhattan, between Fifth and Sixth avenues, the Littlemores were enjoying a late-evening quarrel. It had begun in their kitchen and ended up in the street. The outdoor venue was more favorable to Mr Littlemore; inside, it had become increasingly difficult for him to duck the objects thrown in his direction — not very heavy ones, mostly, and not very accurately — by Mrs Littlemore.

Betty had not shared her husband's excitement at the prospect of moving to Washington, DC, where Littlemore had agreed to take a job with the Treasury Department. They had children in school, she pointed out. They had family in New York. Her mother and brother lived in New York. All their friends lived in New York. How could they just pick up and leave?

Littlemore did not try, after a time, to answer these questions. He just scraped the toe of his shoe against the sidewalk until his wife fell silent. 'I'm sorry, Betty,' he said at last. 'I should have talked to you first.'

'You really want it, don't you?' she asked.

'Been hoping for this kind of break my whole life,' he said.

She handed him a folded piece of paper from her pocket. 'It came today,' she said. 'It says how much we'd have to pay for Lily's operation.'

Lily, the Littlemores' one-and-a-half-year-old, had been born with a slight but complete atresia of her external auditory canals. In other words, at the center of her tiny, pretty, and seemingly healthy ears, where the aperture ought to have been, there was instead a membrane and probably, below it, a bone. The toddler responded well to sound, but if she was ever to hear and speak properly, she would have to have surgery – and soon. The surgery in turn required a specialist. The specialist required money.

'Two thousand dollars?' said Littlemore. 'To make a little opening?'

'Two thousand for each ear,' answered Betty.

Littlemore reread the letter: his wife was right, as usual. 'That settles it,' he said. 'I've got to take the Treasury job. It pays almost double what I'm making now.'

'Jimmy,' said Betty. 'It's just the opposite. We'll never have four thousand dollars, wherever you work. We're going to have to put her in a special school. They say we have to start using sign language with her right now. They got a school for that on Tenth Street. Free. It's the only one in the country.'

Littlemore frowned. He looked up and down Fourteenth Street – at the fine large buildings on the corners of the avenues, and at the plainer, smaller, walk-ups between them, in one of which was his own apartment. 'Okay,' he said. 'I'll turn the job down.'

Winning an argument invariably had a palliative effect on Betty Littlemore, who at once took her husband's side. 'Maybe we wouldn't have to move,' she said.

'That's right,' replied Littlemore hopefully. 'A lot of the investigating is going to be up here in New York anyway.'

In the end, it was decided that Littlemore would put it to Secretary Houston that he would need to split his time between New York and Washington. Houston turned out to be extremely accommodating. In Washington, Littlemore would have an office in the Treasury Department. In Manhattan, he would work out of the Sub-Treasury on Wall Street. The federal government would even pay for his train travel.

★   ★   ★

A man exiting Union Station in the District of Columbia – the largest railway station in the world when it opened, with marble floors and gold leaf dripping from its barrel-vaulted ceiling a hundred feet high – found himself, on a Sunday evening in October 1920, in a raw, vast, undeveloped plaza, with a fountain plunked down in the center and a few cars meandering dustily around it, unhindered by lanes or any law-like regularities of direction. Men were playing baseball on an adjacent weedy field. Across the plaza squatted a few dozen temporary dormitories, thrown up hastily during the war.

The effect was of leaving civilization for a wilderness outpost. Three blocks away stood the nation's Capitol, its dome tinted crimson in the failing sun – another monumental structure surrounded by an expanse of unbuilt land.

Jimmy Littlemore looked at the Capitol with a sense of awe, a suitcase in one hand and a briefcase in the other. It was his first time in Washington. He had a New Yorker's expectation that a throng of taxicabs would be jostling outside the station's doors, vying for passengers. There wasn't a single one.

As Littlemore was wondering how he would get to his hotel, he noticed a black car parked a short distance away, with a tall blonde woman leaning against one of its doors, smoking through a long cigarette holder. She was about thirty, dressed in business attire including a tightly fitted skirt, and exceptionally good-looking. When she saw the detective, she began walking his way, her gait attracting the attention of every man she passed.

'James Littlemore, I presume?' she said. 'From New York?'

'That's me,' said Littlemore.

'You look just the way they described you,' replied the blonde woman.

'How did they describe me?'

'Wet behind the ears. You're late. You kept me waiting almost an hour.'

'And you would be?'

'I work for Senator Fall. The Senator would like to see you tomorrow in his office. At four o'clock sharp.'

'Is that right?'

'That's right. Good luck, New York.' While they were speaking, her car had rolled up next to them. The chauffeur scurried out and opened a door for her. She climbed in, her long legs showing for a moment before they swung inside the car.

'Say, ma'am,' said Littlemore through the open window. 'Think you might give me a lift to my hotel?'

'Where are you staying?' she asked.

'The Willard?'

'Very nice.'

'Secretary Houston's picking up the tab.'

'*Very* nice.' She signaled the driver, who started the engine.

'What about that ride, ma'am?' asked Littlemore.

'Sorry – not in my job description.'

The car drove off, sending up a swirl of burnt orange dust that settled on Littlemore's suit. He shook his head and inquired of a couple of gentlemen nearby if they knew the Willard Hotel. One of them pointed in a westerly direction. Littlemore set off toward the setting sun, which cast a long shadow behind him.

The next morning, Secretary Houston personally pinned the badge and administered the oath that made Littlemore a Special Agent of the United States Treasury. They were in the most luxurious office that Littlemore had ever seen – Houston's own office in the Treasury Building. Gilt-framed mirrors surmounted burnished marble fireplaces. Velvet-roped draperies hung at the windows. The ceiling was painted in a celestial theme.

'Where we stand, Lincoln stood,' said Houston, 'consulting *his* Secretary of the Treasury, Salmon P. Chase.'

When instructed to swear to uphold the laws of the United States, Littlemore asked if he could make an exception in the case of the Volstead Act – the law mandating Prohibition – which Secretary

Houston did not find amusing. When taking the oath to support and defend the Constitution of the United States, Littlemore's voice caught. He wished his father could have been there.

'Let me show you around, Special Agent Littlemore,' said Houston.

The divisions of the United States Treasury were surprisingly extensive. Houston pointed out with pride his gigantic bureau of internal revenue, his anti-counterfeiting unit, his bureau of engraving and printing, his bureau of alcohol enforcement, and, finally, an elegant spacious marble hall with a row of tellers along one wall, each behind an iron-grilled window. 'This is where the Treasury pays money on demand to anyone presenting a valid note. We call it the Cash Room. Show me all the money you have in your pockets, Littlemore.'

'Let's see. I got a three-cent nickel, a couple of dimes, and a fin.'

'Only the coins are money. Your five-dollar bill is not.'

'It's a fake?' asked Littlemore.

'Not fake, but not money. It's merely a note. A promise. You'll find the promise in the small print on the reverse, between Columbus and the Pilgrims. Read it – where it says "redeemable."'

'"This note,"' Littlemore read the inscription, '"is redeemable in gold on demand at the Treasury Department of the United States in the City of Washington, District of Columbia, or in gold or lawful money at any Federal Reserve Bank."'

'Without those words,' said Houston, 'that note would be worthless paper. No shop owner would accept it. No bank would credit it. A five-dollar bill is a promise made by the United States to pay five dollars in gold to anyone presenting that note here in the United States Treasury in Washington, DC. Hence the Cash Room.'

'Not too many people cashing in,' said Littlemore. Only two customers were transacting business with the tellers.

'Which is as it should be.' Houston began walking again, leading Littlemore into a long corridor. 'No one has any reason to cash in – so long as everyone believes he can. But imagine if people began to fear we didn't have enough gold to pay off our notes. *Do* we have enough, do you suppose?'

'Don't we?'

'If all United States monetary obligations were called at once, the government would be as helpless and ruined as any bank in the middle of a panic. The system works on confidence. Picture a trickle of worried people coming here to cash in their notes. Picture the trickle turning into a crowd. Picture the crowd turning into a nation, stampeding to get their money before the nation's metal was exhausted. The government would have to declare bankruptcy. Lending would freeze. Factories would shut down. The entire economy would stop. What would happen next is anyone's guess. Possibly the states would revert to their former condition of autonomy.'

'I see why you want to keep a lid on the robbery, Mr Houston.'

'My point exactly. Here we are – this will be your office, Littlemore. Small, but you have your own telephone and access to all files of course. Here's the key to your desk. In it you'll find documents concerning the transfer of the gold from the Sub-Treasury in Manhattan to the Assay Office next door – how the bridge was built, who was involved, how it was planned, and so on. It's for you alone. Understood?'

'Yes, sir,' said Littlemore.

Houston lowered his voice: 'And I want a complete report on your meeting this afternoon with Senator Fall. Remember, Littlemore, you're my man in Washington, not his.'

On his way to the Senate Office Building that afternoon, Littlemore treated himself to a look at the Washington Monument. Adjacent to that great and solemn obelisk, he found to his surprise that the city had installed its Public Baths. From there Littlemore continued on the Mall – a straight, grassy, wide-open promenade dotted with important, majestic structures – toward the Capitol. He imagined lords and ladies strolling at a leisurely pace, with small dogs on leashes trotting behind them; in fact the Mall was empty.

At the corner of First and B Street – the address of the Senate Office Building – Littlemore saw only a small nondescript hotel at the weedy edges of the Capitol grounds. The detective was untroubled. He knew that in Washington's paradoxical cartography, there would be four different intersections where First Street meets B Street – each on a different side of the Capitol. Littlemore turned south and presently came to another corner of First and B. Here he found only a row of tumbledown wooden-frame houses, one attached to the next, with a dirt road in front of them. Garbage filled the road; flies attacked the garbage, and a whiff of unprocessed sewage sang in the nostrils. Negroes sat on the house porches. Not one white man, other than Littlemore, was to be seen. Mosquitoes abounded. Littlemore clapped one of the pests dead, near his face. When he separated his palms, he had framed between his hands the grand dome of the United States Capitol.

It was a good thing Littlemore had left the Treasury at three o'clock. He finally entered the rotunda of the Senate Office Building – which was three stories high, ringed by Corinthian columns, every wall gleaming with white marble and limestone, suffused with natural light from the glazed oculus at the apex of the richly coffered dome – at two minutes to four, just on time.

Albert B. Fall, United States Senator from New Mexico, was a hale man of sixty, tall and hard-drinking, with a drooping Western mustache white with age. Outdoors, he liked to sport a big-rimmed Western hat, mismatching his three-piece Eastern bow-tied suit. His chambers were lavish. When Littlemore was shown in, the Senator was working on his putting stroke, aiming golf balls at an empty milk bottle at least thirty feet away. The Senator's shots were missing badly.

'Special Agent James Littlemore,' declared Senator Fall without interrupting his practice. He had a large voice – the kind that could carry from an open-air rostrum or fill a legislative chamber. 'Glad to meet you, son. Heard a lot about you. What do you make of Washington?'

'Big offices, sir.'

'Big men get big offices. That's how it works. What's on your mind, boy?'

Littlemore was about to mention that the Senator had asked to see him, not the reverse, but the question turned out to be rhetorical.

'I'll tell you what's on your mind,' said Senator Fall. 'You're thinking why does this senator in this big office want to see me.'

'That's about right.'

'I'll tell you why. I want you to keep me posted on your investigation.'

Littlemore opened his mouth to answer.

'Don't you say anything, son,' interrupted Fall. 'I ain't put a question yet. I know what you'd say anyway. You'd say, "I'm sorry, Mr Senator, but the investigation is confidential. You'll have to take that up with Secretary Milksop – I mean Houston."'

There was silence in the room as Senator Fall lined up another putting stroke.

'Ain't I right?' said Fall.

'Am I supposed to answer now?' asked Littlemore.

'I'm right,' said Fall, slapping his golf ball a foot past the milk bottle into a bookcase. 'Damnation. That's it. I've had enough of this fool game. I don't play golf. Harding plays golf, so I figured I ought to give it a go. Well, he'll just have to play by himself. Mrs Cross? Get your pretty self in here.'

A door at the far end of the room opened. A tall blonde woman entered – the same attractive woman who had met Littlemore at Union Station the day before.

'Take this damn thing,' said the Senator, handing the woman his putter. 'And fix us a couple of drinks.'

'Yes, Mr Senator,' said Mrs Cross without a glance at Littlemore.

'So how's it feel to be a special agent, Special Agent Littlemore?' asked Fall, taking a seat behind his desk. 'Must feel pretty special.'

Littlemore wasn't sure how ironical this remark was intended to be. 'It's all right,' he said.

'Shouldn't be all right.' Fall leaned back in his reclining leather chair. 'Man of your age and your abilities shouldn't be content to be an agent. Got to think big. Look at that jackass Flynn. You're just as good as he is. Why shouldn't you be the director of the Bureau?'

'Whiskey, Mr Littlemore?' asked Mrs Cross.

'No, thank you, ma'am.'

Fall raised his eyebrows: 'You ain't dry?'

'No, sir.'

'Glad to hear it. Mrs Cross, give the man some whiskey. I got to tell you, Littlemore, becoming a Treasury Agent ain't the way to investigate an act of war.'

'I don't believe the bombing was an act of war, Mr Senator.'

Fall shook his head. 'Maybe it's because you back down, Littlemore. Maybe that's why you haven't made more of yourself. Men who back down don't rise up. Simple rule. Never fails. You were the only one to tell the truth about this bombing. You told Tom Lamont that the Morgan Bank was the terrorists' target. He didn't want to hear it, but you told him. Lamont was impressed; told me all about it. And Lamont ain't impressed by most. But all of a sudden you got religion. You dropped Lamont and hitched yourself up to Secretary Milksop instead. I wonder what made you change your tune.'

Mrs Cross handed a tumbler of whiskey to Senator Fall and offered another to Littlemore on a silver tray. He didn't take it. Into the Senator's glass of whiskey she poured a dollop of milk straight from a bottle.

'For the stomach,' explained Senator Fall. 'One thing I hate to see is a good man back down. Knuckle under to the people at the top. Been fighting it my whole life. Take a seat, for Christ's sake.'

Littlemore remained standing. 'Does every senator keep a firearm in his office, Mr Fall?'

'What's that?'

'You've got a pistol in your second drawer.'

Fall crossed his arms, then smiled broadly. 'Now how'd you know that? Mrs Cross, did you tell Agent Littlemore about my gun?'

'Would I do something like that, Mr Senator?' asked Mrs Cross.

'You surely would.'

'Well, I didn't.'

'How'd you know that, son?'

'You got shell packing paper next to your wastebasket, Senator Fall, which tells me you were recently loading a weapon. On your right thumb is an oil stain, from cleaning it. You're not carrying, so it's somewhere in your office. Desk's the most likely place. Second drawer's slightly open.'

'If I'm not Sam Hill's mother,' said Senator Fall. 'That's damn good, Littlemore. What else do you know?'

'I know I'm not crazy about politicians telling the rest of the country we can't drink while they got brand-new bottles of the stuff on their shelves. And I know I don't back down. I'll take that whiskey, ma'am, thank you.'

Littlemore drained the tumbler and returned it to her.

'Well, well, well,' said Fall. 'Looks like we got a man here after all, Mrs Cross. All right, Agent Littlemore, let me put my cards on the table. Houston's got you convinced you're dealing with a robbery. Ain't I right?'

Littlemore said nothing.

'Oh, I know all about the gold,' Fall went on. 'General Palmer told me about it. So let me see if I have this straight. The bombing was a robbery, so the nation's not at war. That it? I'll tell you what – we Western folks must be too plain, because I don't follow that Washington logic. There was a raid on the nation's treasure, on top of an attack on our biggest bank, on top of a massacre of the American people – and that means we're *not* at war?'

'The robbery looks like an inside job, Mr Senator,' said Littlemore. 'So no, it doesn't look like we're at war.'

'Let me tell you something, Agent Littlemore,' said Fall. 'The one thing, the one good thing, that Washington does for a man – other than setting him temporarily free from the Missus – is that it makes him an American. I ain't a New Mexican here, and you ain't a New Yorker. We're Americans. You can open your eyes now, see the big picture, do something for your country.'

'I don't follow you, Mr Senator.'

'Look around the world today. It's Bolshevik terrorists everywhere. They took down the Tsar. They took over Germany. Hungary, Austria. They're crawling all over France and Spain and Italy. Lenin says he's coming for us. Nobody listens. They already got Mexico, right next door. Now how do the bolshies work? Stand up and fight against you? No. Reason with you? No. They infiltrate. They bomb – and they *bribe*. That's their means. That's what they did in Russia, and it sure worked there. That's what they're doing here.'

'You're saying the bombers were foreign, but they paid off someone in our government to help them?'

'You don't think the Feds can be bribed?'

'To help foreigners bomb us? That would be treason, Mr Fall.'

'You got no idea what this town is like, Agent Littlemore. Gaudy and statesmanlike on the outside, rotten to the core on the inside. Ten grand will buy you a US congressman. We senators are a little pricier. Everybody in this town's got an angle. Everybody's looking to make out. Even Mrs Cross here is looking to make out, aren't you, honey?'

Fall extended his empty shot glass in Mrs Cross's direction. She refilled it – and topped it off with milk. He drank it, grimacing.

'This is war, Littlemore. We're under attack. They blew us to hell on September sixteenth. *They blew us to hell!*' Fall slammed his fist on his desk; the sound echoed between the bookcases. He lowered his voice: 'And they'll do it again. Why wouldn't they?'

'You think Russia is behind the bombing, Senator?' asked Littlemore.

'You bet I do. Who else would dare to make war against the United

States of America? They know we sent our army into Siberia last year. Why, they practically got the right to attack us back. What other country has a motive? What other country would want to bring us down?'

'I don't know, Mr Fall.'

'Well, I do,' said Fall. 'Listen to me. I'm going to tell you how history should go, son – how the history of the rest of this century should go. We got a million-plus army of soldiers, trained, ready to be mobilized right now. We could take down this Soviet dictatorship. This is the time. This is the *only* time. They just got whipped in Poland. They got a civil war on their hands. The Russian people don't want a dictatorship. Why, Lenin's got fifty, sixty thousand people in jail already just for speaking up against Bolshevism. The Russian people want freedom. We can help them. And if we don't, son, nobody will be able to stop this red juggernaut. We got a little window here, and it's closing fast. These communists don't just want Russia. They're mean, nasty sons of bitches – you mark my words – and they want to rule the world. That's right: they want to rule the world. They hate freedom. They hate Christ. They will fill the world with darkness for a hundred years. And there ain't no one in this government doing a damn thing about it. Wilson's a cripple. Only thing he cared about was his League of Nations. Palmer's on his way out. Bill Flynn's an idiot. Houston's a moneychanger. Who's protecting the country, goddamn it? Who's protecting the world?'

The Senator was roused again. His fist shook in the air. The sound of applause – a single pairs of hands, slowly clapping – surprised Littlemore. It was Mrs Cross.

'You cut that out,' Fall said to her, calming down. 'She thinks I take myself too seriously. Maybe I do. Here's the point. You want to get somewhere in this town? You got to hitch yourself to the right horse. Warren Harding's going to be elected president in three weeks. Houston's not going to be secretary of shee-it after that. I am. You want to do something for your country? Houston only cares about the gold. I care about freedom. I care about whether our citizens are going to be able to walk their streets in peace or get blown up by our enemies. That jackass Flynn with his Italian anarchists! It was the Russians, damn them, and if we can prove it, the country will go to war. That's why I need you, Littlemore. If you show Houston evidence – hard evidence – proving the Russians did it, know what he'll do? Nothing. He'll bury it. Just let me in on at that evidence if you find it. That's all I ask. Will you do that?'

Littlemore had not answered when they heard a knock at the main door to the Senator's chamber. The door opened, revealing a harried secretary and a well-dressed man behind her, straining to get past her. The woman had managed only to say, 'I'm sorry, Mr Senator, I told him you were busy,' when the man, completely bald except for a tuft of hair behind each of his ears, pushed brazenly and clumsily past her.

It was Mr Arnold Brighton, owner of factories, oil wells, and mines, who had contributed twenty-five thousand dollars to the Marie Curie Radium Fund.

'My people are being run out of Mexico,' declared Brighton without introduction. 'They're Americans, Fall. They're in danger.'

'Day late, nickel short, Brighton,' said Fall. 'Make an appointment. Get in line.'

'I tried to make an appointment,' complained Brighton, sounding genuinely aggrieved. 'They said you were busy.'

'I *am* busy,' shouted Fall. 'We're electing a president here, in case you haven't noticed.'

'I guess I'll be leaving,' said Littlemore.

'Wait just a minute, Littlemore,' said Fall. 'We didn't finish.'

'Is that Detective Littlemore?' asked Brighton. 'I've been meaning to thank you, Detective. Without your help, I – I – what was it again? Oh, my. I've forgotten. What was it I wanted to thank Detective Littlemore for?'

'How the hell would we know what you were going to thank him for?' roared Fall.

'Where's Samuels?' asked Mr Brighton plaintively. 'Samuels is my assistant. He would remember. Does anyone know where Samuels is?'

Fall seemed to exercise a great power of self-restraint in order to lower his voice: 'I'm in the middle of an important conversation, Brighton. Step outside and talk to my secretary.'

'But this Obregón fellow is taking over my mines in Mexico,' said Brighton. 'The oil wells will be next. Everything. He's sending in soldiers – with guns, for heaven's sakes! These are American work-ingmen. There have been beatings and death threats. You've got to do something. I know I didn't give money to Harding. It's not my fault. Everyone told me the other man, Cox, was going to win. I'll give now. Whatever amount you ask. Tell me where to send it. Just drop a few bombs on Mexico City – perhaps on their capitol and in the nicer parts of town – I'm sure they'll see the light.'

Fall took a long time before answering: 'You turn my stomach, Brighton. Know that? I ain't for sale. The Republican Party ain't for sale. The US army ain't for sale. I'm not going to let Harding get bogged down in Mexico, and I'm not going to use the army to take care of your business.'

'You won't help Americans in Mexico?' asked Brighton.

'They're your employees,' replied Fall. 'You help them.'

Brighton looked confused, at a loss. 'Is that all?'

'You bet that's all. Now git.' Fall took Brighton by the arm and ushered him into the other room, from which Littlemore heard Brighton asking if anyone knew where Samuels was.

'I'll be going too, Mr Fall,' said Littlemore when the Senator returned.

'I asked you a question, Littlemore,' replied Fall. 'Will you show me your evidence if you tie the bombing to the Russians?'

'I can't promise that, Mr Senator. But I'll think about what you said.'

On the steps of the Senate Office Building, Mrs Cross – seeing Little-more out – said, 'Well, didn't you charm the Senator?'

'Is that right?' asked Littlemore.

'That's right. You stood up to him. He likes that. You could go far in this town. If you learned how to dress.'

'Something wrong with how I'm dressed?'

She reached out and fixed his jacket collar, one wing of which was saluting rather than lying down flat. 'What party are you, Agent Littlemore?' she asked. 'Are you a Democrat, like Secretary Houston? Or a Republican, like Senator Fall?'

'I don't belong to any party, ma'am.'

'No? Well, who do you like, Cox or Harding?'

'Haven't decided. My wife likes Debs.'

'How interesting,' said Mrs Cross. 'I wouldn't mention that again, if I were you.'

'Which – that I have a wife, or that she's for Debs?'

'That depends on whether you're talking to a woman or a man. Goodbye, New York.' The well-heeled Mrs Cross walked in what might have been described as a businesslike sashay, the graceful motions of which, when viewed from behind, defied any man, even a married man, to turn away. Littlemore watched her disappear liltingly into the Senate Office Building.

No sooner had Mrs Cross sashayed out of sight than a man's voice called out, 'Detective Littlemore, is that you? Samuels was out here all along, waiting for me.' It was Brighton, standing next to a luxurious car with a closed passenger compartment and a roof that stuck out over the driver. Brighton seemed to consider his private secretary's whereabouts a cause of public concern. 'Why would he a do a thing like that?'

'I'm guessing it's because you told him to, Mr Brighton,' said Littlemore, descending the steps.

'Really?' Brighton stuck his head below the protruding roof. When he reemerged, he said, 'By Jove, you're right. I did ask him to. How did you know?'

'Wild guess.'

'It's so fortunate I ran into you. Samuels reminded me what I wanted to thank you for. It was for Samuels himself. Your report cleared him of wrongdoing after that unfortunate shooting of the mad girl. You saved me no end of trouble. I couldn't manage without Samuels, you know – not for a day.'

'Just doing my job, Mr Brighton,' said Littlemore. 'The girl had a knife. The witnesses said she attacked first. Your man acted lawfully.'

'How is she?'

'Still in the hospital. Been there ever since she was shot.'

'Not her,' said Brighton. 'I meant Miss Rousseau. Such a lovely girl. I nearly fainted when that madwoman assaulted her.'

'Miss Colette's fine, so far as I know.'

'Is she poor?'

'Poor?' asked Littlemore.

'I'm not like you, Detective. No woman will ever fall in love with me for my personal qualities. My father told me so many years ago, after I took over the business. I'm looking for a girl who will marry me for my money.'

'I know a couple hundred girls like that.'

'Really?' Brighton blinked as if he couldn't believe the detective's good luck. 'You couldn't introduce me to them, could you?'

'Sure. My wife loves to match-make.'

'How strange,' Brighton reflected. 'The only girl I can think of at present is Miss Rousseau. So comely. Do you know where she went? She promised to come to Washington with me, but Mrs Meloney says she simply vanished.'

'Couldn't tell you.' This was doubly true. Littlemore neither knew where Colette was, nor would he have told Brighton if he did.

'That other creature – the madwoman.' Brighton shuddered. 'I've never seen anything so hideous. Did she tell anyone what's wrong with her?'

'No. She's been unconscious since the shooting.'

'How can I thank you for Samuels? What about five thousand dollars?'

'I'm sorry?'

'His freedom is worth much more than that to me, I promise you.'

'You can't give me money in exchange for police work,' said Littlemore.

'I don't see the logic in that,' replied Brighton, removing a thick wallet from his breast pocket and withdrawing a single large-sized Federal Reserve note with a blue seal and a picture of James Madison on it. 'Where's the incentive to do good work if a man can't be rewarded for it? Surely you could use five thousand dollars.'

Littlemore took a deep breath through his nostrils, thinking of his daughter Lily. 'I can't take it, Mr Brighton. I can't take a dime.'

'How absurd. Well, what about a ride? At least I can offer you a ride. I'm on my way to the train station. Can I take you somewhere?'

Littlemore, who was going to the station himself, accepted. When Brighton discovered that Littlemore too was destined for New York that evening, he beamed and insisted they travel together.

Samuels pulled the limousine up at a loading dock in the rear of Union Station. Brighton explained that this was the only way to get the automobile onto the train.

'They let you bring your car onto the train?' asked Littlemore as they stepped out of the vehicle.

'I can bring anything I like,' answered Brighton. 'It's my train. I have a parlor car, a bedroom car, a billiards car, a kitchen car, and a car car – hah, hah – a car car, isn't that good? We'll have great fun, Detective. No one ever rides with me.'

'Afraid I can't, Mr Brighton.'

'What? Why not?'

'If I ride your private train,' said Littlemore, 'I'm accepting a pretty fancy service from you. It's like you're buying something for me.'

'But what good is my money if I'm not allowed to buy things with it?'

'Some things you can't.'

'That's ludicrous,' said Brighton. 'The Commissioner of Police, Mr Enright, has taken my train. The Attorney General has taken it. Senator Harding rode it three weeks ago.'

'That's different.'

'Why?'

'Because –' Littlemore began before interrupting himself. 'I don't know why, to tell you the truth. But that's the way it is.'

'I have an idea. You could you do extra work for me – you know, when you're off-duty. That can't possibly be against the law, can it?'

'No,' Littlemore acknowledged reluctantly. 'A lot of the men moonlight.'

'There we are then! You'll do something useful for me, and I'll pay you five thousand dollars for it. What do you say? The ride to New York will be your interview. We'll figure out what service you can render me. I'm not sure what; Samuels is so good at everything. He used to be a Pinkerton man, you know. But there must be some valuable service you can perform.'

Littlemore watched Samuels steer the limousine up a wide ramp. 'I guess I might be able to do something,' said the detective.

'What about my people in Mexico?' asked Brighton. 'You know it was quite true what I told Senator Fall. I own hundreds of thousands of very productive acres in Mexico, and their government is trying to take it all away from me.'

'I don't doubt it, Mr Brighton.'

'Didn't I hear Senator Fall say you work for the federal government now? Perhaps you can help me with Mexico. Confiscation is theft, you know – outright theft. Could you send some federal policemen in?'

'Listen, Mr Brighton. First of all, I got no jurisdiction over Mexico. Second, whatever I do for you, it can't have anything to do with my government work. Third, I'm not taking any money today. I'll just ride up to New York with you, and we'll see if we can figure out something you need that I could do for you. Okay?'

'I know: Let's play billiards,' declared Brighton. 'Come on – it's only good when the train's at rest. Samuels is bunk at billiards. I could pay you for being my billiards partner!'

The Sixth Avenue Elevated rattled by a half block away, shaking the floors and the bed in which Littlemore and his wife were lying.

'What's the matter?' asked Betty, seeing her husband's open eyes.

'Nothing.'

'It's after two, Jimmy.'

'I feel like I took my first bribe.'

'You mean because you rode in Mr Brighton's train? You're the only policeman in New York who would think there was anything wrong with that.'

'He offered me five thousand dollars. Enough for Lily. He put it in my hand.'

'Did you take it?'

'No.'

The noise of the train receded into the distance. The bedroom was completely silent.

'What did he want you to do?' asked Betty at last.

'Nothing. He wanted to pay me for something I already did.'

'He offered you five thousand dollars for nothing?'

'It was for police work,' said Littlemore. 'I'm sorry, Betty. I couldn't take it.'

'You listen to me, James Littlemore,' said Betty, sitting up. 'Don't you take any dirty money. Not for me, not for Lily, not for anything.'

Littlemore shut his eyes. 'Thanks,' he said.

Betty lay down again. A long while passed.

'Did I make enough of myself, Betty?' asked Littlemore.

'Enough? Nobody works harder than you. You put food on our table every day. You got us an apartment on Fourteenth Street.'

'Mayor Mitchel was mayor of New York City at thirty-four,' said Littlemore. 'Teddy Roosevelt was Police Commissioner at thirty-eight. I can't even afford to fix my own daughter's hearing.'

'They had famous fathers, Jimmy. Your father –' Betty hesitated – 'well, you did everything on your own.'

Littlemore didn't speak.

'And you're still going places,' said Betty. 'Look at this new job of yours. None of the girls have a husband like mine. You should see the looks in their eyes. You're like a god. Captain Littlemore of the New York Police Department. Special Agent Littlemore of the United States Treasury.'

'Like a god,' said Littlemore, smiling, wiping his eyes in the darkness. 'That's me all right.'

The morning papers confirmed Brighton's complaints. The President-elect of Mexico, General Álvaro Obregón, had ordered troops into American-owned silver mines. He was threatening to do the same with the much more lucrative oil wells, claiming that Americans had bought their subsoil rights through illegal, corrupt transactions with the pre-revolutionary regime.

The American Society for Psychical Research had a perfectly unspir-itual office on East Twenty-third Street in Manhattan, lined with scientific publications, most prominently its own. No signs of the occult were anywhere in evidence. Dr Walter Franklin Prince, the acting director, was equally mundane in appearance. He was a large-faced, affable man of about sixty with a receding hairline, and he smoked a pipe with an unusually large bowl.

'Thanks for making time, Dr Prince,' said Littlemore the next morning, shaking Prince's hand. 'Friend of mine told me you were the outfit to talk to about supernatural stuff.'

'Delighted to assist,' replied Prince. 'My secretary, Miss Tubby, tells me you doubt whether Mr Edwin Fischer really could have seen into the future.'

'That's right, but I'm listening.'

'Certainly he could have. Premonitions of disaster are commonplace.

In 1902, I myself dreamed in precise detail of a train wreck four hours before it occurred. In 1912, Mr J. C. Middleton, having purchased tickets for the maiden voyage of the *Titanic*, dreamed two nights in a row of the ship's foundering and of its passengers drowning in the cold sea. He refused to travel and lived.'

'Didn't happen to tell anybody about his dreams before the ship went down, did he?'

'I wouldn't mention it otherwise. I have no truck with after-the-fact clairvoyants. Mr Middleton was so alarmed that he immediately told his wife and several friends. Their affidavits are in my drawer. I've been looking into the Fischer case myself, and based on the evidence, I'm convinced his premonition was authentic.'

'Fischer says it came to him "out of the air,"' said Littlemore. 'That make any sense to you?'

'He could not have expressed it more felicitously. When we see a twinkling in the night sky, Captain, what are we seeing?'

'Um – I'm going to say a star.'

'We're seeing the past. The universe as it existed centuries ago. The past surrounds us at every moment, although we can rarely see it. So too with the future. It's all around us, in the form of waves or perturbations quite invisible to the naked eye – like radio waves, actually. Many of us fleetingly detect these currents, for example in the hair on the back of our necks. In time, science will discover their molecular structure. But there can be little doubt about their source.'

'Their source?'

'Death, Captain,' said Dr Prince. 'Death releases this energy into the air. If a true catastrophe is looming, the disturbance becomes such that a sensitive individual may become highly troubled by it. He may be aware of exactly when and where it will occur. He may see an aura around people who are soon to die. Or he may see images of the disaster beforehand, as I did, and as Mr Middleton did. That is what happened to Edwin Fischer.'

Littlemore nodded. He didn't accept, but he didn't judge. 'Can they ever know more?' he asked. 'Like who's behind it?'

'I've never heard of that. There is evidence that the souls of the murdered, reached in the spirit world, can tell you who killed them, but I know of no cases documenting such foreknowledge in the living. Are you interested in contacting a medium? I have a very gifted one.'

'I'll take a rain check on that, Dr Prince.'

'Would it be helpful to know when the attack was conceived?'

'Could be very helpful,' said Littlemore. 'You think Fischer might know?'

'In cases of deliberate slaying, premonitions almost never come before the murderer has formed the intention to kill. Often the initial premonition will come at that very moment. Ask Mr Fischer when he first had his precognition.'

'Thanks, Dr Prince – I may do that.'

In the Astor Hotel, in mid-October 1920, an increasingly belligerent Director Flynn of the Federal Bureau of Investigation held yet another press conference. Flynn's repeated claims of imminent prosecution had not worked to his advantage. The case had not cracked. No one had been charged. An air of skepticism and defeated expectations had begun to infect several gentlemen of the press.

As Flynn saw it, the fault was not his. It lay rather with the news-papers, for reporting his setbacks. Every time one of his leads came to nothing, the newspapers made a story of it, which wasn't the kind of behavior Flynn expected from loyal Americans. Embarrassing the federal government's efforts to defeat its enemies was a criminal offense. That's why Eugene Debs was in jail. Flynn could have hauled any one of these reporters into custody. He knew what they were saying to each other on the telephone – because his agents were listening in. He felt they owed their continuing and undeserved liberty entirely to his largesse.

'Each and every one of you boys,' said Flynn, 'ought to be on your knees in thanks to me. But I ain't going into that today. Instead I'm going to sell more newspapers for you. We got it all sewed up now. Here's your story: yesterday afternoon, my office received information establishing the identity and whereabouts of the political prisoners, which you goons were too busy writing about mental cases to even realize you didn't know who they were.'

Pencils hung frozen in midair as comprehension sought in vain to work its way through this declaration.

'Don't you remember nothing, you saps?' asked Flynn helpfully. '"*Free the political prisoners*" – that's what the anarchist circulars said. Well now, just who exactly are these political prisoners? Figure that out, and you bust the whole case wide open.'

'But last time you said Tresca did it, Chief,' said a reporter. 'Then Tresca gives a public speech in Brooklyn, and you don't even bring him in. What gives?'

'Why, I ought to show you what gives,' rejoined Flynn, neck straining at the buttoned collar of his white shirt. 'I never said Tresca did it. All's I said was he was a suspect. Got that?'

'Director Flynn,' said another man, less disheveled than the others, 'my readers want me to tell you that you're a fine American.'

'Thank you, Tommy. I appreciate that. You're a fine American.'

'My readers,' continued Tommy, 'feel a lot safer since you began rounding up the foreigners who are trying to take over this city.'

'Now that's how to be a newspaperman,' said Flynn. 'Listen good, the rest of you. Once we get our hands on the political prisoners, which we already got our hands on, we'll have this whole bombing wrapped up like a Christmas present. That's your story. Signed, sealed, and delivered. You print that.'

On Friday, October 15, Littlemore returned to Police Headquarters on Centre Street to pack up a few things. His men Roederheusen and Stankiewicz stopped in. They carried their hats as if attending a funeral.

'Spanky,' said Littlemore, shaking each by the hand. 'Stanky.'

'We're going to miss you, Cap.'

'Knock it off,' said Littlemore. 'Now don't forget. The alley is the key – the alley between the Treasury and Assay Office. Look for people who ran into the street on September sixteenth, or went to their window, and saw a big truck carrying a massive load out of that alleyway onto Pine Street. That's how the bombers made their getaway.'

'Why would the bombers be in a truck?' asked Stankiewicz.

'Carrying a load of what?' asked Roederheusen.

'Can't tell you yet, boys,' said Littlemore. 'But find out what that truck looked like and where it went, and you can break this case. You know where to reach me.'

The officers put on their hats unenthusiastically. 'Say, Cap,' said Roederheusen on his way out, 'you asked me to locate that Mexican guy – Pesqueira? The consulate says he's gone. Left for Washington last week.'

'Not interested anymore, but thanks.' Littlemore strode down the corridor to Commissioner Enright's office, knowing it was likely to be the last time. He rapped at Enright's door and, when a voice from inside gave him permission, entered.

'Captain Littlemore,' said Enright from his desk. 'Not captain much longer, eh?'

'Already got sworn in down in Washington, Mr Enright. Just packing my things.'

The Commissioner nodded. 'I knew your father, Littlemore.'

'Yes, sir.'

'A good man. Imperfect, as we are all are. But a good man.'

'Thank you, sir.'

'Your badge, Captain. And your weapon.'

Littlemore placed his badge on Enright's desk. It hurt so much he almost couldn't let it go. 'The gun's mine,' he said.

'Well, I'm not happy to do the formalities,' said Enright, 'but by the power vested in me as chief of the New York Police Department, I hereby revoke your commission. Mr Littlemore, you're no longer a member of the Force.'

Littlemore said nothing.

'Do us proud, my boy,' said Enright.

CHAPTER THIRTEEN

A FTER A DAY at sea, an ocean liner steaming out of New York becomes its own and only point of human reference. No other vessels interrupt the vast waters. Under a cloudless morning sky, Colette and Younger strolled the upper deck, the swell unsteady enough to make her accept his arm. The ship's engines set up a dull, churning roar behind them.

'What did they want with me?' she asked.

'The redheads or the kidnappers?'

'All of them.'

'The more I think about it,' said Younger, 'the more I think the note we got at the hotel – the note from Amelia – was a trap. Bait. We thought Amelia never came back to the hotel the next morning. But perhaps she did, with the kidnappers.'

'Why?'

'Maybe it's their business – kidnapping girls, selling them.'

'Selling them?'

'We have a term for it: white slavery. Perhaps they were going to lure you somewhere; Amelia would prey on your compassion, telling you she needed your help. They expected you to be alone. Instead I was with you. So they changed plans. They followed us to Wall Street. Amelia was caught in the bombing. But her friends kept watch, and when you went back to the hotel, they took you.'

'Why me?'

'Because you're a foreigner. No family in America, no connections. Young and beautiful would be further qualifications.'

'I am not beautiful. How would they know I was a foreigner with no family?'

'How did they know you lived in New Haven? Or that you were going to Hamburg? One thing is certain: they have money. Enough to investigate people.'

Unexpectedly, she rested her head on his shoulder. 'At least we're safe on this ship. I can feel it. I wish we never had to reach Europe.'

Younger had made inquiries with the ship's bursar, from whom he learned that he'd been the last one to buy tickets. Colette, it seemed, was right. The ship was safe; no one had followed them aboard. 'We don't have to get off when the ship gets to Bremen,' he suggested. 'We could stay on for the return voyage. At New York, we could stay on again. Go back and forth forever.'

'Don't say anything else,' she answered, closing her eyes. 'I'm going to dream about that.'

He looked at her lovely face: 'Yes, if I were running a white slavery ring, you'd be at the top of my list.'

Later that morning, Younger emptied onto the deck the contents of a large sack he'd brought along with his luggage. There was a baseball, a bat, a jumble of wooden pegs and metal plates, and assembly instructions. A half-hour later, he had constructed a batting tee – a freestanding pedestal for holding a baseball in place, about waist high, so that a batter can practice his swings at it. Younger then fashioned a bag of netting around the baseball, tying off this bag with a long cord of rope borrowed from a seaman. The other end of the rope Younger secured to a winch. He then set the bagged ball atop the tee and gave Luc a lesson in hitting. After each swing, they retrieved the baseball, soaking, by reeling in the rope.

Soon a good number of male passengers wanted a go, doffing their hats and undressing to their shirtsleeves to take their cracks. Naturally, the handful of other boys on the voyage were eager to try as well. Younger made them ask permission first from Luc, who solemnly granted it, and who for the rest of the journey thereby became an indispensable member of the little gang of boys, despite his muteness.

Of all the men and boys who had a go at the batter's tee that day, Younger hit the most towering drives. But the next morning several of the ship's seamen joined in. One of these was a muscular swab who had played for the Brooklyn Robins during the war and who, taking his shirt off altogether, packed so Ruthian a wallop into his first swing that the rope was not long enough. The netting broke; the ball was lost. Younger tried several substitutes – an orange, a globe of wood cut by the ship's carpenter, a golf ball lent to them by another passenger – but there's nothing quite like a baseball, and that was the end of that.

As the days of oceangoing passed one to the next, Younger found he couldn't make any further headway with Colette. His relations with her were intimate enough, but only in a friendly way. She was affectionate, but distant. And she became more so as they drew nearer to Europe.

Sometimes he would catch her staring out to sea into a future he couldn't penetrate. Or was it a past – a memory of falling in love with a devout, ailing soldier in Paris, to whom she had given her heart, and whom she hadn't seen for more than two years?

'You're his hero, you know,' she said to him one day, coming out of such a reverie.

'Whose?'

'Luc's.'

'Am I?' said Younger. 'Who's yours?'

'I have two: Madame Curie and my father. I'm lucky that way. The Germans killed my father when he was still a hero to me – fearless, strong, noble in every way. Even the Germans couldn't take that from me. But Luc barely remembers him. I used to try to remind him about Mother and Father – tell him stories of Father's strength and bravery.

But he wouldn't listen. He isn't even curious. That's what he really needs – a father.'

'And you're doing your best to find him one?'

She didn't answer.

'Do you really think he loves you?' Younger went on. 'Heinrich, I mean.'

'Hans.'

'Heinrich hasn't written you a single letter in two years. That doesn't sound like love to me.'

'It doesn't matter whether he's written me.'

'You mean you love him regardless? You don't. I'm sorry, but you don't. If you loved him, you'd be thinking of one thing only: how he'll react when he sees you. You'd be in a panic to know whether he still cares for you. You'd be looking in mirrors. You also wouldn't concede that he hasn't written you. You'd tell yourself that he wrote to the hospital in Paris, but that you never received the letters. Instead you say it doesn't matter.'

She didn't answer.

'Is he that handsome?' asked Younger. 'Or did you give yourself to him, and now you think you have to marry him on that account?'

Colette looked away: 'Don't talk about him anymore. Please.'

'What do you owe him? You nursed the man when he was sick, but you act like he was the one who saved *you*. As if you owed him your life.'

'You can't understand what I owe him,' she said. She looked at him: 'Do you want me to say I love you more than him? That I'll give him up for you? I won't. I'm sorry. You shouldn't love me. You should just – leave me alone.' She got up and went to her cabin and didn't return.

On the last night of their voyage, as he contemplated the unfathomable force drawing Colette to her soldier from thousands of miles away, Younger tried to decide which was the greater illusion – the false motion of the stars, which seemed over the course of a night slowly to cross the sky, or the false motionlessness of the earth, which was in reality soaring around the sun at unthinkable speed.

How could it be that a young man whom Colette had known for only a few months exerted such power over her, or that this French girl exerted such power over him – Younger – against his will, against his reason, against his judgment? He seemed to be in orbit around her, circling her, closing on her, then falling away, always with some final, unbridgeable distance between them. Does the earth find its orbit a cause of unending torment?

The Amityville Sanitarium on Long Island was spotless and white and healthful, but Edwin Fischer, its newest resident, did not seem content. Gone was the gregarious good cheer so conspicuous when he was taken into custody in New York City a month earlier.

'How are they treating you, Fischer?' asked Littlemore, taking a seat in the visiting room.

'The Popes have always been against me,' replied Fischer. 'Are you Roman Catholic, Officer?'

'Catholic? My wife is.'

'None of the Popes has ever been a true Catholic. They pretend, of course, but it's always been a lie. They are using their powers against me. Why did you come here?'

'Funny – I'm asking myself that same question right now.'

'Shall I tell you the reason the Popes wish to keep me confined?'

'Because you're crazy?'

'They don't believe I'm an agent of the United States Secret Service.'

'You're not.'

'Why do you say that?' Fischer looked genuinely hurt. 'I resent that very much. Are you a Secret Serviceman?'

'No.'

'Are you the Secretary of the Treasury?'

'Why?' asked Littlemore.

'If you were, you'd be in charge of the Secret Service.'

'I don't think so.'

'You don't think you're the Secretary of the Treasury?' replied Fischer. 'Most people are sure, one way or the other.'

'I happen to work for the Secretary of the Treasury, and I don't think he's in charge of the Secret Service.'

'Then he's an impostor. I know why you're here.'

'Is that right?'

'You're here to get me out of this place.'

'No, I'm not.'

'Yes, you are. And to ask me when I first received my premonition of the Wall Street bombing.'

Littlemore sat up.

'I'm correct?' asked Fischer.

'Son of a gun. How'd you know that?'

'Were you at the train station when the police brought me from Canada, Captain?'

'No. So when was it – your first premonition?'

'I love train stations. Whenever I go to a new city, I wander around the station for hours. It makes me feel at home. Grand Central Terminal is like a second home to me.'

'Great. When was your first premonition?'

'You'll do something about the Popes?'

'I'll do what I can.'

'The end of July, I think. I know it was before the East–West matches. It was right after I decided not to go to Washington. You must know I'm an adviser to Mr Wilson?'

'That would be President Wilson, I'm guessing.'

'In 1916, I advised Mr Wilson that if he didn't stop the war, many would die. That's how I got to be a Secret Service agent. He wished to meet with me, but his aides wouldn't permit it. Doubtless he regrets that decision profoundly today.'

'Sure he does. So who do you think was behind the bombing, Fischer? Who did it?'

'Anarchists, of course. Bolsheviks.'

'Are you positive?'

'Absolutely.'

'How do you know?'

'I read it in the papers.'

A nurse interrupted them, to take Mr Fischer back to his room.

Their train slipped with a satisfied shriek into Vienna's Westbahnhof on a mid-October evening. The Austrian trains, once the pride of an empire, were shells of their former selves. They ran on half rations of coal – the other half having been sold off by corrupt officials and needy conductors. Chandeliers and decorated paneling had been ripped away, evidently by thieves.

A single cab was waiting outside the station under a bright half-moon – an elegant two-horse carriage. Although Younger sat next to Colette, she kept her distance, facing away from him and looking out at Vienna. Luc sat across from them, one suitcase under his legs and another beside him. It was a lovely, old-world night. In the distance, over the roofs of handsome buildings, the electric lights of the Riesenrad – the giant Ferris wheel of the Prater, Vienna's famous amusement park – described a high slow arc in the air. The wind carried strains of a faraway waltz and merry laughter.

'Vienna is gay,' said Colette – wistfully, Younger thought.

Colette had spoken in French. The coachman answered in the same language: 'Yes, we are gay, Mademoiselle. It is our nature. Even during the war we were gay. And unlike the last time you were here, we are no longer eating our dogs.'

The driver presented his card to them. He was the very same nobleman – Oktavian Ferdinand Graf Kinsky von Wchinitz und Tettau – who had taken them to their hotel on their first stay in Vienna. But on his card, the words *Graf* and *von*, indications of his illustrious birth, had been crossed out.

'Titles of nobility have been abolished,' he explained. 'We're not allowed them even on our cards. Yes, things are improving. Things are certainly improving.'

They heard a far-off keening behind them, followed by a thunderous crash.

'What was that?' asked Colette, starting almost out of her seat.

'It's nothing, Mademoiselle,' replied the coachman. 'It comes from the Wienerwald, the Vienna woods, the loveliest woods in the world. They are chopping down its trees.'

'At this hour?' said Younger. 'Who?'

'Everyone, Monsieur. It's illegal, but people have no choice. There is no more coal to burn. Only wood. They go at night to avoid arrest. When winter comes, many will have no heat at all. You've come from Paris?'

'New York,' said Younger.

'Is Monsieur American?'

Younger allowed that he was.

'I beg your pardon; I thought you were French. Then you must accept this ride with my compliments. Austria owes you its deepest thanks.'

Younger was surprised at this offer and said so.

'A defeated country does not ordinarily express gratitude toward its foe?' asked the coachman. 'It's our children I'm thanking you for. Your relief packages are still their chief source of food. Do you know Mr Stockton – your chargé d'affaires? I drove him to the station last month. He had just received a letter from the Chief Justice of our Supreme Court, asking if the judges could have a relief package too.'

'What will happen,' asked Colette, 'to the children if they have no heat this winter?'

'They'll die, I imagine, many of them. Here we are – 19 Berggasse. I hope Dr Freud is well.'

Younger, letting himself out and extending his hand to Colette, raised an eyebrow at their exceedingly knowledgeable coachman.

'When foreigners visit the Berggasse,' explained the driver, 'there can be only one reason.'

Younger asked if he would be so kind as to wait for them while they called on the Freuds. Oktavian said he would be most willing.

It was Freud's wife's sister, Minna Bernays, who answered the door to the second-floor apartment. Although they were expected, Miss Bernays wouldn't let them in, explaining that Dr Freud and his wife, Martha, had retired early. She was asking if they could come back tomorrow when a deep male voice intervened, declaring his retirement to be much exaggerated.

Their greetings were cordial. Much was made of Luc being a full head taller. 'Well, Minna,' observed Freud, 'Martha was mistaken, as I predicted she would be.' To Younger and Colette, he explained: 'My wife was certain the two of you would be married before the year was out.'

'The year's not over yet,' said Younger.

'She meant 1919,' Freud replied drily.

'Then tell her there is still hope for 1920,' said Younger.

'I've given you no reason to hope, Stratham,' Colette rebuked him. 'Not for any year.'

Younger, stung, resolved to make light of it: 'In that case I'll schedule the wedding for midnight December thirty-first,' he said, 'which doesn't belong to any year.'

Colette turned to Minna Bernays and said, 'He's hopeless.'

'First she chides you for hoping,' Freud replied to Younger, 'then for being hopeless. Women – what do they want?'

Sigmund Freud looked his age, sunk deep in an armchair in his study. A furrow knit his white brows into a scowl. His usually frenetic chow, Jofi, curled sympathetically at the master's feet. They had talked of the Wall Street bombing, the kidnapping, and the collapse of the finances of the psychoanalytic association. Freud's son Martin had finally been released from prison. 'His first act of freedom,' Freud said, 'was to relinquish it. He got married.'

Colette thanked Freud for agreeing to treat her brother.

'I haven't agreed to treat him,' answered Freud. 'I wrote you, Fräulein, stipulating my one condition. You didn't answer.'

Colette made no reply.

'I'm too old and too busy for half measures,' said Freud. 'I take very few new patients now; I only have time to train others to do so. Every new hour I take on is an hour lost for my own work. Psychoanalysis, Miss Rousseau, is not accomplished in a few days. You must be prepared to stay in Vienna for a very substantial period.'

'But I – have no means, no work,' said Colette.

'That's your concern,' answered Freud, his sharpness surprising Younger. 'If I'm to treat your brother, I must have your word that you will remain in Vienna this time as long as it takes.'

'I'm sorry,' said Colette. 'I don't know.'

Freud rose slowly, went to the window, opened it. A fresh night breeze tousled his white hair. From the little courtyard below, where Count Oktavian's carriage waited, came the stamping and neighing of horses. Freud took a deep breath. 'So,' he said, his back to Younger and Colette. 'Have you ever dreamt, Fräulein, of a child being beaten?'

'I beg your pardon?' said Colette.

'Have you?'

Colette hesitated. 'How did you know that?'

'Sometimes without knowing who is doing the beating?'

'Yes,' said Colette.

'It is a surprisingly common dream in women who feel they should be punished for something,' said Freud. 'Well, it's clear you didn't come to Vienna specifically to have your brother see me. It follows you have some other business. Based on your remark to Younger in the foyer, I can only conclude that you are here to find and marry your fiancé, the one who was in jail the last time you were here. That would explain your uncertainty about whether or how long you will be in Vienna. You don't know where he lives now – perhaps not in Austria at all – is that it?'

Colette was astonished.

'It's all right,' Younger said to her. 'He does this sort of thing all the time.'

'The real mystery,' said Freud, 'is how you managed to persuade Younger, your fiancé's rival, to join you on such a journey. I must say I find that impressive – and puzzling.'

'You're not the only one,' said Younger.

'Well, none of this affects my position,' said Freud. 'In case, Fräulein, you decide you are serious about finding employment here, I'll give you the address of Vienna's Radium Institute. I'm told it is excellent, and they hire women without compunction. I'm also going to give you the name and address of an old friend, a neurologist.' A smile, brief and not cheerful, passed over Freud's face as he wrote them a note. 'He has a treatment for war neuroses far more expeditious than mine. I can't vouch for what he does, but many believe in it, and since you seem interested in attempting a quick cure for your brother, Miss Rousseau, it would be remiss on my part not to mention him. As for you, Younger, it's high time we settled our unfinished business. I have an hour free at eleven tomorrow morning. I'll see you then.'

'I told you he could be brusque,' said Younger as their carriage clopped down the cobblestoned Berggasse toward the Danube canal.

'He's so very sad,' answered Colette.

'Freud? Tired, I think,' replied Younger. 'And angry – I'm not sure why.'

'Pragmatic, I would have said,' reflected Oktavian, their coachman. 'Professional.'

'I've never seen such sad eyes,' said Colette.

'I didn't find them sad at all,' replied Younger.

'Ah, there, you must take me out of it,' declared Oktavian. 'I could hear him from the window, but I couldn't see his eyes.'

'That's because you never know what other people are feeling,' Colette said to Younger. 'It's a good thing you gave up psychology. You're like a blind man.'

CHAPTER FOURTEEN

AMONG THE GRANDER edifices on Vienna's Ringstrasse was a five-story, pink-and-white confection of an apartment building, the first floor of which housed the elegant Café Landtmann. In the main salon of that coffeehouse, below a receding boulevard of crystal chandeliers, Younger met Freud at eleven the next morning. The head waiter had greeted Freud as if he knew him personally and guided them to a table at a window with elaborate drapery, through which they could see the magnificent state theater across the street.

'So,' said Freud, taking a seat, 'do you know what I want to discuss with you?'

'The Oedipus complex?' asked Younger.

'Miss Rousseau.'

'Why?'

'Tell me first,' said Freud, 'what you thought of my old friend Jauregg, the neurologist.'

Younger, Colette, and Luc had visited Dr Julius Wagner-Jauregg in his university office earlier that morning. 'His treatment for war neurosis is electrocution,' said Younger.

'Yes. His team reports considerable success. Was he surprised I had sent you?'

'Very. He said you testified against him at a trial of some kind last week.'

'On the contrary, I testified *for* him. There was an allegation that he had essentially tortured our soldiers into returning to the front. The

270

government commissioned me to investigate. I reported that his use of electrotherapy had been perfectly ethical. I explained, of course, that only psychoanalysis could uncover the roots of shell shock and cure it, but that this was not yet known in 1914. My friend – and his many supporters – spent the rest of the hearing attempting to destroy the reputation of every psychoanalyst in Vienna.' A waiter brought them two small gold-rimmed demitasses of coffee and a basket of pastries. 'Foolish of me. I'd somehow forgotten how intense a hostility we still provoke. But never mind. Did he persuade you to attempt electrocution on the boy?'

'He made a case for a single treatment at low voltage. He believes shell shock is a kind of short circuit inside the brain – and that a brief convulsive charge can clear the circuitry.'

'I know. And since you disbelieve in psychology, you should be favorably inclined.'

Younger pictured the confused and harrowed expressions he had seen in the faces of shell-shocked soldiers. The scientist in him knew that the cause of their suffering could indeed have been a cross-firing in their neural circuitry. But something in him rebelled at this diagnosis – or at least at the treatment. At last he said, 'I don't believe there's anything wrong with the boy's brain.'

'Ah – you think the problem is in his larynx?'

'I doubt it,' said Younger.

'Well, at least you have one thing right. What was Miss Rousseau's opinion? No, let me guess. She was distracted and had no firm opinion. She wanted you to decide.'

'How did you know that?'

'Would you say she is self-destructive?' asked Freud.

'Not at all.'

'Really? My impression was that you had a taste for such women.'

'I make exceptions,' said Younger.

'She's not attracted to abusive men?'

'If you mean me, her attraction to abusive men is regrettably weak.'

'I don't mean you,' said Freud.

'Her fiancé – Gruber?'

'The man is a convicted criminal.'

Younger looked out the window. 'She only remembers a sweet, injured, devout soldier she knew in a hospital.'

'A maternal affection? Not likely.' Freud stirred his coffee. A scowl came to his already deeply furrowed brow. 'Was I too severe with her last night?'

'She can take it. Why were you severe?'

Freud removed his glasses and wiped them clean with a handkerchief, lingering on each lens. 'She reminds me of my Sophie, my second-to-youngest,' he said. 'Beautiful, headstrong. Sophie became engaged at the age of nineteen. To a thirty-year-old photographer. It was as if she couldn't get out of the house fast enough. I believe I was taking out on Miss Rousseau an anger I harbor against Sophie for leaving us so soon.'

'Sophie – she's the one who lives in Germany?'

'She's the one who is dead.'

Freud's spoon tapped the rim of his glass, repeatedly, unevenly.

'I didn't know,' said Younger.

'It happened last January. The flu. She was living in Berlin, she and her two little boys and her husband, whom I never treated as well as I should have. When we received word she was ill, there were no trains running – not even for an emergency. The next we heard, she was gone.' He took a deep breath. 'After that, fundamentally everything lost its meaning for me. To an unbeliever like myself, there can be no rationalizations in such circumstances. No justifications. Only mute submission. Blunt necessity. For several months, my own children – my other children – and their children –' Freud stopped, gathering himself – 'I could no longer bear the sight of them.'

Outside, the Ring was in its full daytime bloom. Cars and streetcars rolled by. A charming carriage trotted past. A governess strolled with a perambulator.

'Well, the intention that man be happy was never part of his creation,' said Freud. 'You will say it's superstition, but I have a foreboding about Miss Rousseau. What is her goal in coming to Vienna?'

'You guessed it last night. This Gruber fellow was just released from prison.'

'Come – you can't have forgotten all your psychology. What is her object?'

'To see if he still loves her, I suppose. Or perhaps if she still loves him. She made a promise. She feels she has to keep it.'

'Nonsense. I don't trust her motivation. Neither should you. Do you know what specifically her soldier was imprisoned for?'

'No.'

'I do. She told me herself – in tears, the day after you left Vienna last year. He beat up an old man. So at least the police say. I advised her that a ruffian who marches with the Anti-Semitic League was not a fit husband for her. I counseled her not to see him again. I thought she took my advice.'

'Evidently she reconsidered,' said Younger.

'There is a condition into which many young women fall. They attach themselves to violent men. They forgive any mistreatment. They think it love; it isn't. What they really want is to be punished for their sins, real and imagined – or for someone else's. There's something wrong with Miss Rousseau's attachment to this Gruber. I sense it. My advice to you is not to let her out of your sight. She's throwing herself into the arms of a criminal.'

'Maybe he'll beat her, and she'll come to her senses.'

Freud raised an eyebrow. Younger wondered if his own habit of doing so – raising a single brow – was copied from Freud. 'You feel,' said Freud, 'she's made her bed with this man, and you're inclined to let her sleep in it?'

'I don't control where Miss Rousseau sleeps.'

'You wish to see her punished – for choosing another man. You retaliate by letting her go.'

'Letting her go? I crossed an ocean trying to change her mind.'

'You can't change her mind. But you might be able to protect her.'

'From what?' asked Younger.

'From this Gruber. From a decision she'll regret the rest of her life.'

Younger, back at the Hotel Bristol, found a note waiting for him:

> *Dear Stratham:*
>
> *I'm running to catch a train. I didn't go to the Radium Institute. I went to the prison, and they told me that Hans had left Vienna and gone to Braunau am Inn. I think it's his hometown. There's only one train a day for Braunau, and it leaves in half an hour. I expect to be back tomorrow. Luc is upstairs in my room. Please look after him. Some day I hope you'll understand.*
>
> *Yours,*
>
> *Colette*

Younger stared at the note a long time. He ran his hands through his hair. Then he had a messenger sent for Oktavian Kinsky, the aristocratic carriage driver.

An hour later, Younger and Luc were waiting in the hotel lobby when Oktavian appeared, nattily dressed in the leather jacket and crisp cap customarily worn by chauffeurs of open-air automobiles. 'I know you wanted a motorcar, Monsieur,' said Oktavian, 'but this was the best I could do on short notice. Quite sufficient, however. I'll have you in Braunau in six hours.'

He pointed outside, where, in front of the hotel, stood a gleaming motorcycle with polished chrome trim and an attached wood-paneled sidecar.

'No good,' said Younger.

Oktavian saw the problem: Luc was dressed for travel as well, and the sidecar would hold only one passenger. 'Is the young fellow coming? I didn't realize.'

Younger walked outside. Oktavian and Luc followed him. 'The boy and I will go ourselves,' said Younger.

'But the vehicle isn't mine,' Oktavian replied. 'I don't think—'

'You'll have it back tomorrow. I guarantee it. I'll take this too, if you don't mind.' Younger relieved Oktavian of his leather jacket. 'And the cap.'

'Oh, dear,' said Oktavian.

The top of the sidecar had a hole in it for the passenger's torso. It opened into two leaves, revealing a cushioned seat and a small storage compartment. Younger fitted the leather jacket onto Luc, pulled the cap down over his ears, deposited him onto the seat, and closed the two leaves, locking them into place. Not long after, they were on the open road.

As he drove, Younger taught Luc how to lean into the curves to increase their speed. The jacket and cap were comically oversized on the boy, but they kept him warm. Younger said nothing about the purpose behind their mission, and Luc didn't ask. All in all, it wasn't bad riding – until the rains came.

The first crack of lightning split the sky in front of them without warning. A thunderclap rent the air immediately afterward, like a howitzer exploding directly over their heads. Luc seized Younger's arm in alarm. Younger momentarily lost control of the handlebar, the motorcycle swerving and nearly spinning out beneath him. When he'd straightened them out, Younger barked at the boy roughly. 'When you're scared,' he added, 'move slower, not faster.'

The walled village of Braunau, on the river Inn, was quaint and utterly German in character, a mere stone's throw from Bavaria. Colorful pointed-roof houses adjoined one another in picturesque little town squares, all presided over by a high-steepled church. There was no railway station – just a platform and ticket booth.

Younger pulled his motorcycle up to that platform in the gathering darkness. He wiped the grit from his eyes and the water from his forehead, wishing he'd had goggles. The trip hadn't taken six hours. It had taken ten – a combination of the rain slowing them down, the necessity of feeding Luc, and their getting lost on three different occasions. Younger opened the top of the sidecar and pulled Luc out; the interior was drenched, as was the boy.

Younger asked the ticket agent if there were any blankets on hand. There were. Younger threw them to Luc, ordering him to take off his wet clothes and dry himself. 'The train from Vienna,' Younger said to the man. 'Has it come?'

'Yes – two hours ago,' answered the agent.

'Did you happen to see a girl, dark hair, traveling by herself, get off that train?'

'French?' asked the agent.

'Yes.'

'Very beautiful?'

'That's her.'

'*Nein.*'

Younger waited; no further information came. 'What do you mean, *nein*?' he asked.

'I wasn't here when the Vienna train arrived, Mein Herr,' said the man. 'But your fräulein must have been on it. I sold her a ticket.'

'A ticket where?'

'She bought a one-way on the night train to Prague. No baggage. You only just missed her; the train left less than an hour ago. Most unusual. Imagine, a girl like that traveling at night by herself.'

Younger ran his hands through his hair. 'I'm looking for a Hans Gruber. Do you know where he lives? Or his family?'

Younger found the house the ticket agent had described to him – a small, fenced, rustic affair, clean but dilapidated. The roof looked like it might collapse at any moment. A thick-set, hard-eyed old woman answered the door.

'Frau Gruber?' asked Younger.

'Yes,' she said. 'What do you want?'

'I'm a friend of Hans's.'

'Liar.' The old woman's voice was both shrewish and shrewd. The sight of the blanket-wrapped boy at Younger's side did nothing to soften her. 'Go away. He's not here. He's in Vienna.'

She tried to shut the door, but Younger stopped her. 'That's not what you told the girl,' he said. 'You told her Prague.'

She narrowed her eyes suspiciously. The old yellow teeth broke into a nasty laugh. 'You think I don't know what he'll do with her? I know his tricks. He'll take the shirt from her back. He'll make her whore for him and throw her in the rubbish bin when she's used up. Just like all the others.'

Younger's reaction to these predictions was surprisingly ambivalent. On the one hand, he felt Colette might actually be in danger if she married Gruber. On the other, he felt the odds of her marrying Gruber had distinctly decreased. 'Tell me where in Prague I can find him.'

'I know why you're here,' said the old woman. 'He owes you money. I see it in your eyes. Well, he owes me first.' She shook her head bitterly. 'Taking the family stipend all these years, just because the government addresses the envelopes to him. Then he dares come back here and sleep under my roof. Get out of my doorway or I'll call the police. You expect me to help you get money from Hans? Anything he has belongs to me.'

'How much?' asked Younger.

'What's that?'

'How much does he owe you?'

The old woman was only too happy to work out the sum; it was a large one. Younger took from his wallet, in crowns, a significantly larger amount. Her eyes twinkled.

Younger left the woman's house with an address in Prague and with Luc clad in a dry and clean, if ancient, brown wool suit of boy's clothing. From the ticket agent, he had a good idea how to get to

Prague. 'You get some sleep in there,' he said to Luc as the latter climbed into the sidecar. 'We have a long road ahead.'

Luc fastened his eyes searchingly on Younger.

'All right, there's no mystery to it,' said Younger. 'Your sister is looking for a man she met during the war. They were supposed to be married. We're following her.'

Luc still looked at Younger.

'No, I don't know what I'm going to do if we find her,' said Younger. 'It's probably pointless anyway. By the time we get to Prague, they're likely to be in a church with the wedding bells already pealing. At which point I'll look pretty foolish.'

The boy tapped Younger's arm. He fished around inside the compartment for something to write on and found some of Oktavian's engraved cards. On the back of one, he wrote a message and handed it to Younger. The card said, 'My sister wants to marry you.'

'That is demonstrably false,' answered Younger, mounting the motor-cycle and kick-starting it.

Luc tapped at his sleeve and handed him another card. This one said, 'I don't like my sister.'

'Yes, you do,' said Younger.

It was nine in the morning when, in a light rain, they rattled over the cobblestone streets of Prague's Nové Město, or New Town, where 'new' refers to the green days of the mid-fourteenth century. The jumbling of epochs throughout the great city was incongruous. Gothic churches jostled with ornate neoclassical domes; baroque palaces sported box-like towers from the Middle Ages; and the streets were studded with nineteenth-century statues of eighteenth-century generals rearing back on their steeds, swords in hand. In the drizzling rain, all was gray; even the gold spires on the churches and the salmon-pink houses seemed gray.

Younger's eyes were bloodshot. He had driven through the night. Next to him, slumped over in the sidecar, Luc lay sleeping.

On a wide avenue bordering the slow and turbid river Vltava, Younger pulled up outside a café showing signs of life. He got out, lit a cigarette, and crossed the avenue to a parapet where he could look out at the water. Downriver, boats passed into tunnel-like vaults below a medieval stone bridge. Yawning, Luc – awakened by the vehicle's halt – joined him. Across the river, the land sloped up to a considerable height, at the summit of which, reflecting the glinting rays of a morning sun, stood the sprawling Pražský hrad, the castle of Prague.

'It's the largest castle in the world,' Younger said to Luc. 'Before the war, it was home to emperors and kings. It's empty now – being rebuilt, they say. Renovated for government use. Smell that? Something's baking in that café. Let's go have a look.'

It took them another hour to find the street that old Frau Gruber in Braunau had written down for Younger. The Czech language was incomprehensible to him; even when he found someone with whom he could get by in German, no one recognized the street name. This may have been because the street was located in the oldest quarter, which was a maze of labyrinthine alleys, or because Younger couldn't make its pronunciation intelligible.

At last they found the little street, near an ancient stone gunpowder tower. From surrounding rooftops, a tribunal of life-size saints, carved from centuries-darkened marble, gazed down on them in postures twisted in either bliss or agony. Two- and three-story houses, hundreds of years old, lined the narrow street, their opposing balconies so close that the occupants might almost have been able to shake hands across them.

Younger knocked at the house posted with the number he was looking for. He wasn't sure what he would do if someone answered, but no one did. He tried the door; it was locked. He also tried questioning passersby, asking for Hans Gruber. They had no idea what he was saying – or if they did, the name meant nothing to them.

'We'll just have to wait,' he said to Luc. A short way down the street, he parked the motorcycle in a space between two old buildings and lit a cigarette.

By early afternoon, Colette still had not appeared. Nor had anyone fitting the description of Hans Gruber. It occurred to Younger that old Frau Gruber might have lied to him about the address. He didn't think so. Another possibility was that she had made a mistake about the address, but if that were true, then Colette would make the same mistake and eventually turn up – assuming she hadn't beaten them there, which Younger considered very unlikely, given the propensity of the Austrian trains to break down and arrive at their destinations up to twenty-four hours late.

At a nearby store, Younger bought a loaf of bread and some thick slices of ham. When he returned with these goods, the boy handed him another message: 'Am I a coward?'

Younger fixed a sandwich for the boy and another for himself. 'I'm going to answer you with a bromide,' said Younger. 'In English, a bromide is a platitude, a commonplace – something everybody knows. Actually, it's also a bromine salt, but never mind that. Being afraid doesn't make you a coward. That's the bromide – but it happens to be true.'

Luc wrote on a new card: 'You're never afraid.'

'Oh, yes I am,' said Younger. 'I'll tell you a secret. Bravery consists of not letting anyone else know how scared you are. Sorry to have to tell you, but by the time they're your age, some boys have already proven they're heroes. You might as well know the truth. I knew a boy once – no older than you – who did about the bravest thing I've ever seen. This boy had been kidnapped. He was tied up. And he still had the presence of mind to point my attention to a test tube of uranium dioxide that happened to be rolling off a table at just that moment. Saved us from being killed by a rather ugly fellow. Actually a very ugly fellow. So ugly he looked better with his hair on fire.'

★   ★   ★

Night had fallen when Luc woke him up. The street was now full of light and noise from several boisterous taverns. The air was cold. Younger's mouth tasted stale; his whole body was stiff. Luc pointed eagerly: a slim female silhouette in a lightweight coat was approaching the house with determined steps. It was Colette. She knocked on the door. This time someone answered, and she disappeared up a flight of stairs. Younger waited, scanning the windows overhead for signs of life.

He was considering what to do next when Colette reappeared in the doorway and proceeded down the street, passing directly opposite Younger and Luc. A few steps on, she turned and vanished into a stone archway.

They followed, cautiously. The archway led to a surprisingly large, crowded, open-air beer hall in the courtyard of what might have been an abbey centuries before. A small orchestra played merrily. Lanterns hung from branches. Men sang, unpleasantly loud and off-key. Women were plentiful, but none was unaccompanied except Colette. There was dancing on a flagstone dance floor. Colette, it seemed, was looking for Gruber.

Younger was sorely tempted to show himself. But he suspected that if he presented himself straightaway, before she had even met her Heinrich, Colette would be furious and indisposed to listen to him. His interference might even, Younger reflected, make her more stubborn. It seemed better to let Gruber sink his own ship. If Frau Gruber was right, Heinrich would be a cad and a ladies' man – a type that might possibly have fooled Colette when he was sick and wounded, but that would surely repulse her now. And if Colette wasn't repulsed, there would be time for Younger to confront her later and to make a last appeal. In addition to which, Younger had to admit to a certain curiosity; he wanted to see how Colette and Gruber would behave when they saw each other.

So Younger installed himself with Luc in a dark corner of the crowded garden as far as possible from Colette. He pulled the oversized driver's cap low over the boy's head, although in the darkness and crush of bodies, there was little chance of Colette spying them. She seemed preoccupied, in any event, with her own business. Under one of the hanging lamps, conspicuous in her solitude, Colette took a seat on a bench at one end of a long wooden table. Almost ostentatiously, it seemed to Younger, she removed her coat and revealed a dress like none in which he had ever seen her before.

Her arms were bare, her back exposed. Her hemline, which almost revealed her knees – no, which *did* reveal her knees when, seated, she crossed one leg over the other – conspired with her high-heeled shoes to attract virtually every male eye in the beer garden. Never did a back express so clearly that it was made to be looked at. The men at the table behind her manifestly thought so. They pounded each other on the shoulders, pointing to the newcomer, and made the predictable male noises and gestures.

Among those men, despite never having laid eyes on him before, Younger instantly recognized Hans Gruber. He was unmistakable: the only tall, blond, strapping, blue-eyed man in the garden. He was an exceedingly well-looking man – in his late twenties, rakish in clothing, confident in demeanor, generously ordering drinks not only for himself but for a coterie of friends as well.

From another direction, a stranger with a greasy mustache stumbled up to Colette's table, apparently meaning to engage her in repartee, but tripping over her bench in his haste. Colette swiveled deftly, so that the man fell not into her lap but onto the table instead, howling at the blow to his shin and knocking over a collection of glasses and bottles. In the ensuing quarrel, Colette showed not the slightest interest, removing a cigarette holder from her purse. Younger had never seen her smoke.

A cupped pair of male hands appeared with a lit match. The hands belonged, of course, to Hans Gruber. Colette accepted the light. She looked up at him and spoke, but the noise of the place was such that Younger could only see the moving lips. It was not obvious to Younger that Gruber recognized her. Or perhaps, as his hands lingered near her lips and they spoke together, their faces not far apart, he was recognizing her just now.

They continued conversing for a while – she smoking, he occasionally thrusting off other men who sought an audience with her. Gruber ordered a drink for her; it was delivered; Gruber paid for it; she drank it. Presently he led her to the dance floor. And dance they did, with Hans's right hand caressing Colette's waist.

Younger grimaced, inwardly.

Their dancing lasted an hour or more, punctuated by rambunctious consumption of alcohol in abundant quantity, not only by Gruber, but by Colette and two short, stocky friends of his, who lacked female companionship of their own but seemed to take as their goal the furtherance of Gruber's conquest. At one point Gruber downed a triple stein of sudsing beer in one go, cheered on by chants of his name. During a lull in the music, Gruber helped Colette into her coat and led her merrily out of the beer garden, his two friends trailing behind them, laughing uproariously.

Younger let them pass out of the garden before setting off after them. He and Luc got to the street just in time to see Colette entering the back of an open-roofed four-seater. Gruber got in next to her, and the car drove off. Gruber sang loudly – and not badly, Younger had to admit – his arm draped over Colette's shoulder. Younger hurried to the motorcycle.

Six-pointed stars and Hebrew letters on storefronts indicated that they had entered a Jewish quarter. Younger could not have said exactly what he was doing – surreptitiously trailing Colette and her beau as they drove through Prague – but he kept at it. Younger had followed Gruber's car on a meandering, inebriated path. More than once, the car rolled up onto the sidewalk before rediscovering the street.

They were now on a boulevard called Mikulasska Street, lined with trees and art nouveau facades lit capriciously by gas lamps. An old woman scurried across the street, carrying something heavy in her arms, as if running for cover.

'What's she doing out at this hour?' asked Younger, speaking his thoughts aloud.

Shouts came from unseen precincts. Packs of boys could be seen running down side streets. Up ahead was a commotion. Gruber's car stopped just past the disturbance. Younger came to a halt as well, next to a ring of more than a dozen young men on the large sidewalk. At the center of their circle, a gentleman in evening clothes – a slight man with glasses and a walking stick – was being pushed and taunted. Someone yanked away his cane and threw it at a shop window, breaking the glass.

'Festive,' said Younger.

Gruber hopped out of his car and ran toward the crowd. He pulled aside one gawker after another to reach the center of the circle, where the taunted gentleman in evening clothes stood. '*Jüdisch*?' asked Gruber.

The frightened man didn't reply. The onlookers seemed as suspicious of Gruber as they were hostile to the gentleman.

'*Jüdisch*?' Gruber repeated, not malignly, but as if it were an important point of information.

Luc looked at Younger, who explained quietly, 'He asking if the man's Jewish.'

The bespectacled gentleman in evening clothes evidently understood the German word. He nodded just perceptibly: perhaps he nursed a hope of rescue from the foreigner. The admission was costly. Gruber removed the man's glasses, let them fall to the ground, and crushed them under his shoe. The crowd erupted with approving shouts. The gentleman tried to back away, but Gruber caught him by a lapel and punched him in the face, causing him to fall backward through the broken windowpane. The crowd cheered still louder. Hans, wiping his hands, pushed through the circle of onlookers and returned to his car.

Younger considered going to the aid of the assaulted man, but Gruber was even then climbing back into his car. Probably Colette had no knowledge of what he had just done. Younger could see her in the backseat, letting Gruber throw his arm around her again. The car restarted and drove away. Younger left the fallen man to his fate.

Gruber's car rolled slowly up the boulevard. Younger followed, keeping his distance. After several blocks, they entered an old square in the center of which a bonfire burned. People clapped their hands and sang around it. Others, loaded with piles of heavy tomes, emerged from an old and considerable building on the opposite side of the square. When these people reached the bonfire, they fed it with the books.

'It's a good old-fashioned pogrom,' said Younger.

Gruber's car crossed the square, circumventing the revelers, and about a half mile farther on, pulled up at the gate of a small, grassy park. Younger stopped a block or so behind him. The interior of the park was dotted with wrought-iron lampposts and scattered trees, whose russet leaves shimmered silver in the moonlight. Gruber and Colette got out. His friends remained within, drinking and carousing.

'Wait here,' said Younger to Luc.

Younger dismounted and slipped through the darkness to the perimeter of the park, where he encountered a high, barred, iron fence. Through the bars, he could make out Colette and Gruber strolling arm in arm. Younger moved along the fence, watching them penetrate farther into the center of the park. Gruber was carrying on in rapid German; Colette laughed flirtatiously, although Younger had trouble believing she could understand what he was saying. To Younger's disgust, Gruber twirled Colette every now and then as if they were still dancing in the beer garden.

They stopped under the soft light of a gas lamp. Gruber slipped her coat off and let it fall to the ground. He turned Colette around so that he faced her back. His put his hands on her stomach and seemed to be nibbling at her ear. Younger recalled an evening when he himself had done something similar: Colette had been rather less acquiescent. Roughly, Gruber turned her round again. They were face-to-face. He

285

stroked her mouth with his thumb. Colette's purse fell to the grass. Gruber drew her in, bent to kiss her – then abruptly staggered back, palms raised in the air.

Colette was holding a small pistol. There had been no report; she hadn't shot him. But she pointed it straight at his heart with two hands. She was saying something to him in German. From her cadence Younger had the impression she was reciting memorized words, but she spoke too quietly for Younger to understand. Gruber dropped to his knees, pleading, begging. Colette was breathing hard; her shoulders heaved up and down. Then she grew still, her pistol aimed at Gruber's eyes, the range point-blank.

But she hesitated. A full thirty seconds she hesitated, Gruber supplicating all the while. At last she took a backward step, then another and another, until she turned and fled into the darkness.

Younger heard a collision and a muffled cry. A moment later, Hans's stocky friends appeared in the cone of light falling from the lamppost. Between them, they held a struggling Colette, her feet not quite touching the ground. She must have run right into them. One of the men had a fat hand covering her mouth; the other pressed Colette's own gun into her ribs.

Gruber got up. He spat, wiped his nose on his sleeve, and took the pistol from his friend. He slapped Colette across the face, called her a foul name in German, and inserted the gun into her mouth.

'You there, Gruber!' bellowed Younger, straining at the bars of the fence. 'Let her go!'

His voice took the men by surprise. They heard Younger, but couldn't see him. Gruber spun around, waving the pistol blindly in Younger's direction.

'We're coming for you, Gruber,' shouted Younger. 'We're going to rip your heart out of your chest and stuff it in your mouth and make you eat it.'

Younger was of course lying: there was no 'we.' Or so Younger thought until a little figure dashed up next to him and fought its way through the bars of the fence, which were too tightly spaced for a man, but not for a boy. Younger grabbed Luc by his leather jacket just as he squeezed through. His feet spun like a flywheel, slapping at the ground, but he went nowhere.

The sound of these footsteps had an immediate effect. Evidently believing that he was being chased, Gruber broke for the park gate, ordering his friends to bring the girl. The two men obeyed at once, dragging Colette between them. Younger, yanking Luc back through the fence, sprinted away as well, carrying the boy over his shoulder. He had farther to go, but he reached the motorcycle almost as quickly as Gruber and his friends reached their car.

'Stay when I tell you to, damn it,' ordered Younger, jamming Luc back into the sidecar and this time pinning the boy's arms and shoulders into the closed interior, so that he couldn't squirm out. 'Brave lad.'

Younger fired up the motorcycle's engine and pulled out in chase.

Gruber had taken the wheel of his car. He drove savagely through the narrow streets. He didn't slow when he sideswiped a parked car or even when he sent pedestrians diving out of his way. In fact he sped up once when a man in the middle of the street had nowhere to go; on impact, the man was sent sprawling. In the backseat, Colette was sandwiched between Gruber's two friends, who held her fast.

Younger pursued, but could not close the distance between them. Suddenly they emerged onto an avenue bordering the river, where Younger, opening the throttle, was able to make up ground. Gruber turned under a Gothic pointed arch onto a medieval bridge, hurtling past twisted baroque statues on either side, again sending pedestrians scurrying away. As they reached the far side of the river, Younger was right behind him.

But Gruber made a sharp turn off the bridge, and though Younger tried to follow, the motorcycle skidded out beneath him, spinning a hundred and eighty degrees and slamming into a shuttered wooden stall. Younger had the bike going again in a moment, but he had lost ground. Down the street, Gruber turned hard again, tires screeching, heading uphill. Following, Younger entered a neighborhood with zigzagging streets that grew increasingly steep. For a moment Younger lost Gruber's car completely. Then, in the distance, he saw it take a hairpin turn and disappear up a steep alley.

Younger raced to follow. The street underneath turned into a cobblestone ramp lined by houses on one side and a stone wall on the other. They were ascending to a great height. Low steps intervened every fifty feet or so; Younger bounced in the air every time they climbed over one of them, with Luc in the sidecar airborne next to him. They flew by a roadblock, which was broken and swinging: Gruber's car had obviously smashed through only moments before.

At the summit, Younger entered a huge dark plaza. He stopped the bike. The massive Gothic cathedral of St. Vitus loomed up one side, and the enormous Prague castle on the other, engulfed in shadows.

The plaza was empty, littered with rocky debris and construction equipment. In some places the ground had been dug out in vast holes. In other places mounds of earth were piled twelve feet high. All was silent. Strange oblong shapes broke up the moonlight. There was no sign of Gruber.

Younger didn't like it. Gruber's car could be hiding anywhere, while if Younger drove into the open plaza, he and Luc would be exposed – wide-open targets. A flock of birds screamed from a distant corner of the square, rising and peeling away, but Younger heard no motor, nor saw any vehicle lights. 'Maybe they aren't here,' said Younger quietly, not believing his own words.

He killed his headlight. With a light hand on the throttle, he guided the motorcycle around the dug-up terrain, skirting the large equipment and the dangerous pits. Still there was no sign of Gruber. They came to two great conical mounds of earth, close together. Younger rolled the motorcycle between them.

Just ahead was a vast and panoramic vista overlooking all Prague

– its river, its bridges, its many districts sparkling with lights. At the edge of the precipice, there had been a retaining wall, but it was demolished. Younger began to fear that he really might have lost his prey.

The response to this inward conjecture was the roar of an engine behind them and a crash. Gruber's car had rammed them from the rear, forcing them several feet closer to the cliff. Gruber backed up and rammed them again. Younger had no escape route, caught between the two hillocks on either side of them and the precipice ahead. Gruber's car now locked against the rear of the motorcycle and sidecar; its engine screamed, pushing them forward. Younger's brakes had no effect. He put the bike in reverse and gunned the motor. This slowed their forward motion, but didn't halt it. They came to the very edge of the precipice – and lurched to a stop. The remains of the demolished retaining wall, maybe five or six inches in height, had saved them.

Gruber backed up one last time. Younger tried to yank Luc out of the sidecar by the collar of his leather jacket, but the boy was crammed into it too well. Younger couldn't get him out. He heard the roar of Gruber's car; he heard its gears engage. Younger jumped onto the top of the sidecar. He seized the boy by the armpits, pulling and twisting at him just as the final impact came, which punched the motorcycle over the curb. Younger was thrown into the air, with the boy in his arms, as the motorcycle plunged over the cliffside and banged down the mountainous slope, flipping over, hitting ground and flipping again, finally crashing into a stone wall at the bottom of the hill, where it exploded into flame.

Younger looked down at the explosion from a spot a few yards down from the top of the cliff. He and Luc had rolled down the treacherous slope together until Younger arrested their descent by the clever stratagem of slamming into a tree trunk. The explosion sent pieces of the motorcycle high in the air, several of which rained down on either side of Younger and Luc. The boy wasn't breathing properly:

his eyes were wide, but he wasn't taking in breath at all. Younger had a heart-stopping instant. Then Luc began to gasp brokenly.

'You're all right,' said Younger. 'Just the wind knocked out of you. Stay here.'

Younger ran up the slope. When he climbed back into the plaza, he saw Gruber's car at the other end – about to leave the square by the same cobbled lane they had come up. Younger put fingers to mouth and whistled piercingly in the night.

Gruber's car stopped. Younger whistled again. The car backed up and wheeled around, its headlamps illuminating Younger, perhaps a hundred feet separating them. For an instant there was no movement except the wind ruffling the tails of Younger's long overcoat. The great towers of the castle were shrouded in darkness; moonlight cast a faint glow on the flagstones. Younger opened his arms wide, beckoning Gruber to come at him.

The car's engine clamored. Younger began walking forward. The car jerked into motion; Younger broke into a trot. Gruber accelerated; Younger ran. In the center of the plaza, when the collision was imminent, Younger leapt high in the air. The car's hood passed under him. He hit the windshield with his shoulder, shielding his face behind an arm.

The glass gave way, knife-like shards flying into Gruber's face, and the car spun out of control. The front passenger seat broke from its anchorage when Younger smashed into it, plowing into one of the men in the backseat, who cried out in pain, his legs pinned or perhaps broken.

Next to that pinned and unarmed man, in the middle of the back-seat, was Colette. 'Stratham?' she said.

'Don't move,' he replied.

Gruber's second stocky friend, on the other side of Colette, had her pistol in his hand and tried to point it at Younger as the car skidded to a halt. Younger seized that hand, placed his own thumb over the gunman's trigger finger, and forced the man's first two shots to fire harmlessly into the air. Then he thrust the man's arm across Colette's chest, so that the gun pressed directly into the ribs of the other man – the pinned man. Younger squeezed off three shots, after which he jackknifed the gunman's arm so that the pistol pointed at the gunman's own temple. The last look on the fellow's face was incomprehension; he didn't seem to understand how a weapon he himself was holding could be aimed at his head. Younger caused the pistol to fire.

Gruber, in the front seat, had been desperately scraping glass from his bloody face and eyes. At the sound of the gunshots, he thrashed wildly at his door, unable to find the latch. At last he began climbing over the door instead.

Younger got hold of Gruber's ankles and stood up on the front seat of the car, holding Gruber upside down. Gruber's hands scraped at the flagstone like the paws of a rodent trying to burrow into the earth. Younger lifted him several feet off the ground and dropped him, face-first, onto the stone.

The blow stunned Gruber, but didn't knock him out. Younger saw on the dashboard the steel shaft that had separated the two panes of the windshield. He grabbed it, jumped over the door, and hoisted Gruber off the ground, holding him up against the car. Gruber's face was bloody, his eyes frightened. Colette, prying herself loose from between the two dead men, climbed out of the car as well.

'I guess the engagement's off,' Younger said to Colette, without looking at her.

'He wasn't my fiancé,' she answered. 'He—'

'I know what he is,' said Younger.

'No,' said Colette, 'he—'

'I know,' repeated Younger.

'Luc,' cried Colette. The boy was standing only a few feet away, lit up by the car's headlamps.

Younger looked at the cowering Hans Gruber. 'I'm trying to think,' Younger said to him in a low voice consisting mostly of breath, 'of a reason to let you live.'

'It wasn't me,' said Gruber. 'It was all of us. Everyone did it.'

'That's not a reason,' said Younger in the same unvoiced voice.

'They ordered us to do it,' said Gruber imploringly.

'I don't believe you,' said Younger.

'Stratham—' said Colette.

'The only thing I can think of is your cravenness,' Younger observed, studying Gruber's pleading face. Younger thought it over. Then he said, 'But that's not a reason either.'

Younger ran the steel windshield shaft through the underside of Hans Gruber's chin straight up into his skull. The blue eyes froze. Younger looked at those eyes for a long moment – then let the corpse slump to the ground.

'We'll take his car,' said Younger.

Dragging the other two bodies out of the backseat, Younger left all three corpses in a heap. Luc gazed down at the dead men. Then he took his sister's hand, and the two of them got into the vehicle. As they crossed a bridge over the Vltava in their windshield-less vehicle, sirens and alarms began to wail.

Several hours later, Younger opened a sleeping compartment aboard a rumbling train. A single candle cast an unsteady light. On the lower bunk, both Luc and Colette were stretched out. The boy was sleeping.

'Is that you?' Colette whispered in the darkness.

'Yes.' Younger loosened his tie, went to the washbasin, rinsed his face. They had just crossed into Austria. He had waited in the corridor to see if any police boarded. None had.

'You're a good killer,' she said unexpectedly.

He picked up Luc and laid him in the upper bunk. The boy stirred but didn't open his eyes. Colette, startled, sat up, and pulled the sheet protectively up to her neck. She was afraid, evidently, that he was going to lie down next to her.

He was about to reassure her that he had moved the boy only because he had found another compartment for himself, so that she and Luc didn't have to share a bunk. But the words didn't come out. Instead he was seized with fury. He tore the sheet from her. Dressed only in a slip, she drew her knees close to her and encircled them with both arms, green eyes sparkling faint and anxious in the candlelight.

He shook his head. 'What does a man have to do before you trust him?' he asked. 'Die?'

'I trust you.'

'That's why you're acting like I'm about to rape you.'

She drew farther back into the shadowy corner of the bunk, clutching the silver chain she always wore around her neck.

He could not have explained his own violence. If it was rage, he had felt its kind only a few times, during the war. He reached down, took her by the wrists, pulled her up standing before him, and yanked the chain from her neck. She said nothing. He spoke quietly, his words just audible over the noise of the locomotive: 'I admire it – I do. You lied to me for years. You did it so well, pretending to be aggrieved at how much I kept from you. And now you play the little God-fearing virgin again, with your cross in your hands and your faith that He'll protect you. Didn't anyone tell you that good Christian girls don't hunt a man down for six years to kill him?'

'It's not a cross,' she said.

He opened his palm: at the end of the silver chain was a locket.

'It's how I knew his name,' said Colette. She took the locket from him, prized its two halves apart along a tiny hinge, and removed from within a small thin metal oval. 'When we found Mother, her fist was clenched. I opened it, one finger at a time. This was inside. She had torn it off the man who – who killed her.'

Younger held the little oval: it was a soldier's dog tag. Angling it, he made out the etched letters spelling *Hans Gruber*.

'I wore it every day,' she said, 'since 1914. If I had told you the truth, would you have let me come to Vienna to find him?'

He didn't answer.

'Wouldn't you have tried to stop me?' she asked.

'Yes.'

She turned to the compartment's window and twisted at its catch. It wouldn't turn. She pulled at it with both hands. Finally the upper pane dropped open, and a ferocious wind blew in with the roar of the rushing night. She fell back into his arms, her long black hair blowing about, getting in her eyes and his. He saw the delicate line of her cheek and the anxious radiance of her eyes looking up at him, flickering in the candlelight. He held her close, so close her chest was pressing against his, and put his lips to hers. For a moment her whole body surrendered to him; then she pushed herself away, took the dog tag from him, and flung it out the open window. It disappeared into the night without a trace, without a sound.

She turned to face him, shivering in the cold air that swirled through the compartment, hair billowing, bare shoulders catching the light of the candle. He could see that she wouldn't resist him. If he put his hands on her, she would let him: Was it a debt she felt she owed him? He glanced at the slumbering form of the boy and shut the window.

For his part, Luc – not asleep – waited for the unpleasant sound of kissing or other things that grown-ups do. It never came. Instead he heard the door open and close as Younger left the compartment.

CHAPTER FIFTEEN

IT IS OFTEN wondered by Americans, not to mention residents of the nation's capital, whether the city of Washington is *in* the District of Columbia or *is* the District of Columbia. The answer in 1920 was neither. There was no city of Washington.

When the United States first placed its capital on the banks of the Potomac River between Maryland and Virginia at the end of the eighteenth century, the land devoted to the enterprise was a perfectly shaped square, or diamond, each side of which was exactly ten miles in length. The whole of this diamond was called the territory of Columbia. In that territory were three municipalities: the early settlement of Georgetown, the formerly Virginian city of Alexandria, and the new capital city of Washington.

More than a half century later, as the United States struck numerous futile compromises between North and South, one such bargain was negotiated in the territory of Columbia. Alexandria, poor and intensely pro-slavery, was retroceded back to the slave state of Virginia, while the trade in human property was abolished everywhere else in the territory. As a result, the capital lost its geometric perfection as well as about a third of its hundred square miles. Meanwhile, the cities of Georgetown and Washington grew to a point where they began to encroach. Accordingly, in the 1870s, Congress repealed the charters of those two municipalities, combining them instead, together with the rest of the territory, into a single District of Columbia.

From that point on, there was, formally speaking, no city of

Washington at all. But no one has ever scrupled over that nicety, and Washington continues to be spoken of and believed in by all, just as if it were a real city.

'Progress report, Littlemore,' said Treasury Secretary Houston in his mild Carolinian voice on a late October morning, having summoned the detective to his sumptuous office, which was larger than many New York apartments Littlemore knew. 'I should very much like to claim some progress just now.'

'In time for the election?' asked Littlemore.

'Correct.'

'I wish I had more for you, Mr Houston.' Littlemore was frustrated; none of his leads was panning out. 'My boys still haven't found anybody who saw the getaway truck leaving the alley after the bombing. But they will. Somebody had to have seen it. Meantime, I've been investigating everybody who had anything to do with the gold transfer. The only one that sticks out is Riggs, and he's gone.'

'Riggs?' asked Houston. 'Who's that?'

'Your officer who died on September sixteenth.'

'Oh, yes. What about him?'

'Riggs applied for a passport last July,' said Littlemore. 'Planning a little foreign travel.'

'So he was one of the criminals!' declared Houston.

'Looks like it,' said Littlemore. 'Unfortunately I can't find anybody who knew him. No wife. No family. He was hired by Treasury here in Washington in 1917. Transferred to New York last year. Who would have transferred him, sir?'

'I have no idea. I became Secretary only this year.'

'Could you find out?'

'I don't see why not.'

Littlemore rubbed his chin. 'I wonder if they could have taken the gold out by sea. The harbor's right near Wall Street. Have we been checking the ships sailing out of New York?'

'*Have* we?' said Houston. 'Customs inspects every single container of cargo loaded onto outgoing ships. Gold is very heavy, Littlemore. It would be impossible to get twelve thousand pounds of gold onto a vessel without our knowledge.'

'Okay, let's say they didn't sail it out. They took it away in their truck. What then? You're the expert, Mr Houston. If you're sitting on all that metal, what do you do with it?'

'Melt it down. Re-bar it.'

'Why?'

'Every Treasury bar is engraved with our marks. To sell that gold, the thieves need to erase those marks, and the only way to do that is to melt it down. Once melted and re-barred, gold is untraceable. That's what they do with Soviet metal.'

'The Russians have gold?'

'Vast amounts – from the Tsars' treasure houses. It's contraband. Can't be sold anywhere in the civilized world. Even I'm not allowed to buy it. What the Russians do is smuggle it here by ship, melt it, bar it, and then sell it to us.'

'Us? You mean the Treasury?'

'Certainly. The United States Treasury will buy any and all gold presented to it, no matter in what quantity, and we pay the best price of any country in the world. Except for Russian gold, which we won't touch – provided we can identify it as Russian. We just intercepted a shipment the other day. Didn't you read about it? Over two million dollars in Russian metal hidden on a Swedish ocean liner. Customs found it. I sent the Swedes packing. The ship's back at sea now, taking the Russian gold home with it.'

'Mr Houston, you better bring that ship back in.'

'What for?'

'Classic bait and switch,' said Littlemore. 'That Swedish ship sailed out of New York carrying a cargo of gold with your authorization. But maybe beneath a few bars of Russian metal, the rest of it wasn't Russian. Maybe it was your gold – the stolen gold.'

'I don't believe it.'

'Bring that ship back in, Mr Houston. Then we'll know for sure.'

'I can't intercept a ship on the high seas and haul it back to New York.'

'Why not? Send out a few cruisers. We used to do it all the time during the war.'

'We're not at war now, Littlemore. It's very delicate these days. Tensions are high. We don't want an international incident, for heaven's sake.'

'Then just board her, Mr Houston. Open the crates of gold. Check the bars and make sure they're Russian. That's all.'

'Don't tell me how to do my job,' said Houston. 'We're talking about a passenger ship. A thousand people aboard. It would be in every newspaper all over world if I were wrong. And what would I say I was looking for? Stolen Treasury gold – and let everyone know about the theft?'

'You don't have to say. People will think you're looking for arms or something.'

'It's pure speculation. I'm not going to send the United States Navy on a wild-goose chase.' He drummed his fingers on his desk. 'What did Fall want from you?'

'To let him know if I found evidence linking the robbery to Russia.'

'He'd like that, wouldn't he?' Houston grunted contemptuously. 'Warmonger.'

It was a privilege of federal officials that they received priority over civilians when placing long-distance telephone calls. For example, an agent making a call to New York from the Treasury in Washington could usually reach his party in less than a quarter-hour. More important, ever since the federal government seized control of the nation's telephone companies in 1918 and began dictating rates, such calls were essentially free of charge.

Littlemore took advantage of these perquisites to call the American

Society for Psychical Research. A short time later, an operator rang him back with Dr Walter Prince on the line.

'Question for you, Doctor,' said Littlemore. 'Did you by any chance talk to Ed Fischer after I met you in your office?'

'Certainly,' said Dr Prince, his voice distant and broken up by the accumulated static of two hundred miles of telephone wire. 'I visited him at the sanitarium later that very day.'

'Did you tip him off that I was going to ask him when he first got wind of the bombing?'

'I mentioned there was a policeman interested in that information, yes.'

'I should have known,' declared Littlemore. 'He had me thinking he pulled off one of his magic tricks. Thanks, Dr Prince. That's all I needed.'

'I feel you are expressing skepticism about Mr Fischer's gifts, Captain.'

'Why would I be skeptical about a guy who thinks he's a Secret Service agent and the Popes are out to get him?'

'The gifted often feel persecuted, Captain. They are often unstable. It doesn't make their premonitions less valid.'

'Sorry, Dr Prince, I'm not buying.'

'Then how do you explain his foreknowledge of the bombing?'

Littlemore answered with a vituperation that surprised himself: 'I can't explain it,' he barked. 'But you know what? I don't care if he's the ghost of Christmas future. He's no use to me.'

The Willard Hotel, on Pennsylvania Avenue just down the street from the White House, used to be President Ulysses S. Grant's favorite watering hole when he needed a brandy after a long day at the office. Businessmen or their hirelings would lie in wait for the President in the flush hotel lobby, pouncing on Grant to make their case, ply him with liquor, and in general explain how much they could do for his Administration if only some vital permit were issued or lucrative contract signed. Grant called them 'lobbyists.'

Littlemore was making his way across this high-ceilinged lobby when a familiar, tall female figure approached him, clad in a well-fitted feminine version of a man's suit.

'Enjoying Washington, Agent Littlemore?' she asked below a sparkling chandelier.

'Evening, Mrs Cross,' said Littlemore.

'New necktie?'

Littlemore looked down. He was ordinarily a bow tie man, but in his first weeks on the job, Littlemore hadn't seen a single other Treasury agent who wore one. He'd mentioned this to Betty, who gave him a full-length tie as a present. 'You're going to tell me it's not tied right?' he asked.

'It's tied just fine. A little too tight.' She loosened it; he was able to breathe easier. 'That's better. Senator Fall wants to see you. I'm here to take you to him.'

Without waiting for an answer, Mrs Cross turned and walked toward the hotel's front door. Littlemore followed her sashaying form, first with his eyes, then with his legs. Outside, she climbed behind the wheel of a waiting car.

'You're the driver?' asked Littlemore, seating himself beside her.

'I'm the driver.' She started the car. 'Does that make you nervous?'

'I'm not nervous.'

Mrs Cross drove Littlemore along the Mall. Just before the Capitol, she turned and entered a poor neighborhood similar to the one into which he had mistakenly wandered his first day in Washington. She came to a halt behind another car in a small, unlit street sandwiched claustrophobically between opposing walls of brick row houses. Lights were on in several windows, but curtains made it impossible to see within. 'Maine Avenue,' said Mrs Cross. 'Used to be called Armory Place. Also known as Louse Alley. Good luck.'

From the car in front of them, the driver emerged and opened a passenger door, allowing Senator Fall to stretch himself out onto the street, a white ten-gallon hat over his drooping white mustache.

Littlemore stepped into the alley and joined him. Mrs Cross remained in her car, engine humming softly.

'Like 'em colored, Littlemore?' asked Fall. 'Best colored girls in the city are in this street. That's how come I love this town. Just three blocks from the Capitol.'

'Why are we meeting here, Mr Senator?'

'Seems your boss, Secretary Milksop, complained to President Wilson today that I was interfering with his investigation. I figured we should find a more out-of-the-way place to powwow.' Fall began walking up the street, with Littlemore at his side and the Senator's car following slowly behind them. 'What do you know about these two boys that Flynn's after?'

'What two boys?' asked Littlemore.

'Couple of Italians up in Boston. What the hell are their names? All I can think of is a sack of spaghetti.'

'Sacco and Vanzetti?'

'That's it,' said Fall.

'They were arrested for murdering a payroll clerk,' said Littlemore. 'What's Flynn got to do with them?'

'He thinks they're the political prisoners from the anarchist circulars.'

'That's crazy,' said Littlemore. 'When Reds say political prisoners, they mean Debs and the other anti-war guys Palmer and Big Bill put behind bars. Everybody knows that. You'd have to be some kind of boneheaded anarchist to say "Free the political prisoners" if you wanted to free two guys arrested for killing a payroll clerk in Boston. Nobody would know what you meant.'

'Well, Flynn's got something on them,' said Fall. 'He's planted an informant in their cell.'

'Where's he getting these ideas? He's not smart enough to be that stupid all by himself.'

'I was hoping you'd know. Now this house here —' Fall pointed to a large but run-down corner house — 'this one used to belong to a gal named Hall. Served Piper champagne in crystal glasses. Rich as us senators. They still tell stories about her girls. Well, it all played out like I said, didn't it? You found out the Russians were involved in the bombing, and Secretary Milksop buried it.'

'I didn't find Russian involvement, Mr Senator.'

'If the bombers used even a few bars of Russian metal to trick Customs, that's Russian involvement. How do you think the bombers got their hands on Soviet gold? I'll bet the whole crew of that Swedish ship turns out to be Russian.'

'Do you know everything I say to Mr Houston?' asked Littlemore.

'Pretty much. Walls have ears in this town, Littlemore. Got to know what the other guy knows if you want to stay ahead of him.'

'We're not sure the Swedish ship has the stolen gold,' said Littlemore.

'And Houston ain't going to lift a finger to find out, is he? Well, I am. I already talked to Baker, the Secretary of War. He'll speak with his old friend Daniels, the Navy Secretary. I'll have a couple of warships on that Swedish ocean liner within forty-eight hours. We'll know soon enough what she's carrying.'

Littlemore chewed his toothpick. 'That's impressive, Mr Senator.'

'We're the United goddamn States of America. What are we supposed to do after they bomb the crap out of us? Wring our hands? Turn the other cheek? Hope they just go away?' Fall signaled his driver and spat on the pavement, wiping his mouth with a handkerchief. 'This damn Mexican situation's heating up. They're too greedy, these Mexicans. What do they want to take all our oil for? It's going to take some serious ambassadoring to keep Harding out of trouble.'

'What will Harding want to do, sir?'

'Whatever I tell him.' The Senator stepped into his car. 'I'll let you know what we find on the Swede. Mrs Cross will give you a lift back. You should get to know her. Not as tough as she pretends.'

'How long you been working for Senator Fall?' Littlemore asked Mrs Cross as she drove past row after row of the bunker-like, concrete, 'temporary' War and Navy buildings squatting on the Mall – temporary by official description, permanent by appearance.

'A few years. I work for several of the senators. Mr Harding, for example.'

'For Harding? Wow.'

'I do quite a lot for Mr Harding. On loan from Senator Fall, of course.'

'You could end up in the White House.'

'I've ended up in the White House many times.'

Littlemore thought that over. 'You got a first name, Mrs Cross?'

'Grace.'

'Nice name.'

'It's a state I left long ago. Everyone leaves their home state when they come to Washington. Here we are. The Willard Hotel. Good night, New York.'

The next morning, Littlemore received a telephone call in his closet-sized office at the United States Treasury. The operator informed him that New York City was calling. It turned out to be Officer Stankiewicz from police headquarters.

'What is it, Stanky?' said Littlemore.

'It's Fischer, Cap,' said Stankiewicz. 'He keeps calling and calling and sending wires for you. Says you're supposed to be getting him out of the sanitarium.'

'Oh, for the love of Pete,' replied Littlemore.

'He says you were going to talk with his brother-in-law – a guy named, what was it, Bishop or something? Anything you want me to do?'

'Just ignore him. He'll stop.'

'Okay. How's Washington?'

'Wait a second,' said Littlemore. '"Bishop or something"? Did the name sound like Bishop, or did it remind you of Bishop?'

'Yeah, Bishop or something.'

'No, I'm asking you if – do me a favor. Go get Fischer's file. I'll hold.'

A few minutes later, Stankiewicz was back on the line: 'Got it.'

'Okay, find me the name of Fischer's brother-in-law,' said Littlemore. 'He's the guy who went to Canada and had Fischer locked up as a lunatic. His name should be on the Canadian papers.'

'Okay, here it is: Pope. Robert Pope. That's why I thought Bishop.'

'How do you like that?' said Littlemore. 'The Popes.'

The Treasury's personnel department was located on the second floor. Littlemore was already familiar with it; he had been poring over personnel files for three weeks. 'Say, Molly,' he asked one of the girls in that office, 'is Treasury in charge of the Secret Service?'

'Sure is,' said Molly. 'Why?'

'A guy said that to me a couple of weeks ago, and I didn't believe him,' replied Littlemore. 'Seems he was right about a lot of things.'

A few minutes later, Littlemore was upstairs in a filing room flipping through decades of United States Secret Service employment records. He knew in advance he would eventually find the name he was looking for, improbable though it was. And he did.

The folder was virtually empty, containing only a bare indication of the year of hiring and the location of service. The year was 1916, the place New York City. After that, a few more dates were penciled in, terminating in late 1917.

Littlemore dropped the manila folder on Secretary Houston's desk. 'It might have helped, sir,' said Littlemore, 'if you'd mentioned to me that the one man trying to warn people about the bombing was an employee of ours.'

Houston reacted with astonishment.

'You didn't know Ed Fischer was an agent?' asked Littlemore.

'I had no idea. I told you – I only became Secretary in February of this year.'

'How does somebody get to be an agent?'

'The Director of the Secret Service makes those hires.'

'Who's the director?'

'Bill Moran.'

'Can I talk to him?'

Houston called for his secretary and ordered him to find Mr Moran. In the ensuing silence, Houston stood at a window, hands crossed behind his back, surveying the White House grounds. 'I won't miss this job, Littlemore. How am I supposed to balance an eight-billion-dollar budget with revenues of four billion? We live beyond our means. Neither a borrower nor a lender be – that's what my father told me. Now that's all I do – borrow and lend.'

'You're not going to miss being a Cabinet member? You're on top of the world, Mr Houston.'

'What, because I hosted a dinner for the British Ambassador last night? My wife likes that sort of thing. I can't stand it. Every word out of one's mouth a lie. Well, it will all be over in five months, when Harding takes office. I may resign sooner. Go abroad. Yes, I think I might.'

Houston's secretary came back in with William Moran, head of the United States Secret Service. Mr Moran positively denied having hired Edwin Fischer. 'There – you see,' said Moran, looking at the file. 'Fischer was hired in 1916. I didn't take over until the next year.'

'Who was the director before you?' asked Houston.

'Flynn was.'

'Flynn?' repeated Littlemore. 'Not Big Bill Flynn?'

'Sure,' said Moran. 'Before he became Chief of the Bureau, Bill Flynn was head of the Secret Service.'

On November 2, 1920, having run full tilt through the vast, echoing Union Station to make his train, Littlemore settled into his seat, breathing hard, and realized that it was Election Day. He further realized that he wouldn't be voting. His train would arrive in Manhattan well after the polls had closed. The thought caused him a surprisingly sharp pang of disappointment.

As the train passed one small town after another, Littlemore felt an inexplicable sympathy: with the small frame houses, with the smoke rising from their chimneys, with the little piles of firewood stacked outside, residue of a man's labor – sympathy with all the quiet, hard, uncounted lives of which no stories would ever be written. Then Littlemore imagined the citizenry in each of these towns lining up to vote for their country's leaders. It filled him with pride – and with a sense of estrangement at missing it for the first time. But then Littlemore was not even certain he was entitled to vote. Technically he might now be a resident of the District of Columbia, and Washingtonians did not vote for the nation's president.

Not that his vote mattered. That was the oddity of democracy: nothing mattered more than voting, and voting didn't matter. In any event, Warren Harding, the Republican, was certain to win; the Democratic candidate, James Cox, had about as much chance as Eugene Debs, the Socialist candidate, who was still in prison. Which meant that Secretary Houston, a Democrat, would not be a secretary much longer, while the Republican Senator Fall would soon be Secretary of State.

Women all across America celebrated on that November Tuesday, when for the first time they exercised the national suffrage. At many polling booths, men stepped aside to make way for the womenfolk as an act of courtesy, but the women wouldn't have it, insisting on taking their place in line and waiting as long as the men had to. Back home in their kitchens and parlors, they gathered in little groups, treating themselves to sparkling cider, a lawful substitute for prohibited champagne.

Blacks were not received quite so chivalrously at the polls; nor did the revelry subsequent to their voting have the same genteel character. When, for example, two black men had the temerity to exercise their suffrage in Ocoee, Florida, the Ku Klux Klan decided to set an example. Two black churches were sacked, a black neighborhood was burned to the ground, and some thirty or sixty black people were killed, one of them strung up a telephone pole and hanged by the neck.

But the country elected itself a new president, and there was great festivity and a galvanization of energies throughout the land.

Back in New York, the next day, Littlemore paid another visit to the Federal Bureau of Investigation's temporary field offices at the Astor Hotel.

'Look what the cat drug in,' said Bill Flynn, Chief of the Bureau. 'It's Littleboy.'

'I need to ask you some questions, Flynn. About Ed Fischer.'

Flynn addressed the two large, dark-suited men who, as always, stood on either side of his desk. 'A New York cop wants to ask *me* questions? Is this jerk-off looking to get his head busted in?'

'Hey jerk-off,' inquired one of Flynn's deputies, 'are you looking to get your head busted in?'

Littlemore displayed his United States Treasury badge.

'Let me see that,' said Flynn. He inspected the badge. 'World's going down the toilet, that's all I got to say.' He threw the badge onto the floor at Littlemore's feet. 'Too bad I don't answer to T-men.'

'You'll answer to me, Flynn.' Littlemore handed him a letter, signed by Secretary David Houston of the United States Treasury, instructing Flynn to respond fully to any questions Special Agent Littlemore might ask concerning Flynn's tenure as Director of the Secret Service. Flynn read the letter, then let it too fall to the floor.

'I got news for you, hotshot,' he said. 'I don't take orders from Secretary Houston either. I take my orders from General Palmer. Get out of here.'

Littlemore took another letter from his pocket. This one was signed by Attorney General A. Mitchell Palmer.

'Son of a bitch,' said Flynn. He spoke to his deputies again: 'Okay, you boys clear out.'

'Have one of them pick up my badge first,' replied Littlemore.

'What are you goons standing around for?' Flynn said to his deputies. 'Pick up the man's badge.'

'Okay, so I hired him,' Flynn acknowledged several minutes later. 'So what? The guy was a nut-ball.'

'How'd you meet him?'

Big Bill Flynn, whose barrel chest and gut didn't need any additional fortification, unwrapped a red-and-white-striped candy from the bowl of treats that sat on his desk. 'Fischer starts sending letters to Wilson in 1916, okay? Your usual anti-war garbage. But there's something funny about them, like he knew the President personally. So I send a couple of my boys to check him out and tell him to knock it off if he doesn't want to end up in jail. You know.'

'Sure.'

'So my boys tell me the guy is soft in the head, but he works for the French in one of their outfits.'

'The French High Mission.'

'That's it — leave it to the Frogs to hire a nut-ball, huh?' Flynn's torso heaved with mirth at his riposte.

'Only a moron would hire a nut-ball,' agreed Littlemore.

'Yeah, that's a good one, only a moron would—' Flynn interrupted himself, comprehension dawning. 'Why, I ought to—'

'How'd you get involved?'

Flynn grumbled, but continued: 'When I heard where Fischer worked, I figured it couldn't hurt to have somebody planted in French governmentary circles. So I played the guy, buttered him up, told him he could be an agent for the Secret Service. Told him he was a spy. You know, the whole drill. When I took over the Bureau, I kept him on the string. But the guy was cracked. I never got anything from him. Saw him no more than half a dozen times. Total waste.'

'Where would you meet him?' asked Littlemore.

'Why?'

'Just answer the question, Flynn.'

'Here in New York. Train station.'

'When was the last time?'

'This summer. June or July. After the Convention. General Palmer sent McAdoo to meet with some Republicans at Grand Central to see if they could work something out. Fischer was totally off the deep end. Never saw him again.'

'Did Fischer say anything to you about Wall Street?' asked Littlemore.

'Are you kidding?'

'I'm not kidding.'

'No, he didn't say nothing about Wall Street. You think I would have let the NYPD have him if he knew anything? I'll tell you the funniest thing. After the bombing, Fischer's brother-in-law, a guy named Pope, he calls the Bureau. Says that Fischer is claiming to be an under-cover federal agent. Wants to know if there's any truth to it. I get on the phone and say it's a crock. Pope thanks me, says he just wanted to be sure, and has Fischer locked up the next day. He's been in the loony bin ever since. Ain't that a laugher?'

A message was waiting for Littlemore when he returned to his office in the Sub-Treasury on Wall Street, informing him that Senator Fall had called for him from Washington. Littlemore rang the operator.

'That you, Littlemore?' asked Fall some minutes later over the static.

'Yes, sir, Mr Senator.'

'We intercepted the Swedish ship. No gold.'

'You mean no Treasury gold?' asked Littlemore.

'No Treasury gold, no Russian gold, no fool's gold,' answered Fall. 'No gold at all. The Captain said the harbor authorities in New York told him to leave it on the dock.'

'He's lying. Secretary Houston made them take it back. Did the navy guys search the ship?' asked Littlemore.

'Of course they searched the ship. High and low.'

'But—'

'I'm too busy, Littlemore,' said Fall. 'You figure it out. Get back to me when you do.'

Fall rang off. It made no sense, Littlemore thought. Why would they leave the gold on the dock – wherever the gold came from? Could someone in Customs be working with the thieves? Littlemore put his coat on. He'd have to go down to the harbor himself. As he was leaving, his telephone rang again. A Mr James Speyer was asking for him downstairs.

'What can I do for you, Mr Speyer?' asked Littlemore in the rotunda of the Sub-Treasury.

'You can give me my painting back,' answered Speyer in his German accent. 'At the police station they didn't know what I was talking about. They told me you worked at the Treasury now.'

Littlemore apologized, explaining that he had put the Rembrandt in a special lockup to ensure its safety. 'We could go over and get it now, if you want,' he said.

'Excellent. My driver can take us.'

Inside Speyer's car, Littlemore asked, 'How's the wife?'

'Better, thank you.'

'Business in Hamburg work out okay?'

'Capitally,' said Speyer. 'The funds are all in Mexico now – despite the Morgan people's best efforts.'

'I hear things in Mexico are getting pretty hot.'

'They certainly are,' agreed Speyer. 'Bad for Arnold Brighton; good for me.'

'You know Brighton?'

'I know his oil fields in Mexico are worth hundreds of millions. I just returned from Mexico City, as a matter of fact. Peculiar to be somewhere where America is so hated. More than even in Germany. I suppose we might feel the same way about them if they'd occupied our capital and taken half our country.'

'We did that to Mexico?' asked Littlemore.

'The Mexican-American War, Detective. Or the American Invasion, as they call it south of the border. My Rembrandt had better not be damaged.'

At police headquarters on Centre Street, Littlemore led Speyer to a special safe room in the evidence storage locker. Once the layers of protective wrapping were peeled away, the painting itself looked small and fragile. 'Undamaged, Mr Speyer?'

'Undamaged,' Speyer agreed.

The men stared at the self-portrait. It was from the artist's older age, showing him wrinkled and red-cheeked, with pouches under wise, misty eyes.

'How'd he do that?' asked Littlemore.

'Do what?'

'He looks like he knows he's going to die,' said Littlemore. 'Like he – like he –'

'Accepts it?'

'Yeah, but at the same time like he isn't ready to go yet. If they hate Americans so much, why don't they hate you down in Mexico, Speyer?'

'Because they think I'm German,' replied Speyer with a smile, pronouncing the last word *Cherman*.

At the harbor, Littlemore spoke with a Customs agent, who denied that the Swedish ship had left its contraband gold on the dock. 'You're sure?' asked Littlemore. 'The Swede sailed out of the harbor with all the gold on board?'

'Wouldn't know about that,' said the agent. 'When we find dirty goods, we alert the departments. Maybe the goods get impounded, maybe they get destroyed, maybe they go back on board. That's up to the department.'

'What department?'

'If it's guns, the War Department. Liquor, the Revenuers. This was gold, so Treasury.'

'Who do you notify at Treasury?'

'All's I do, Mister, I send in the piece of paper. You want more, talk to Treasury.'

On Wall Street late that afternoon, as Littlemore mounted the steps to the Greek facade of the Treasury Building, a messenger boy from the Morgan Bank tapped him on the shoulder.

'Detective Littlemore?' said the boy.

'Yeah?' said Littlemore.

'Mr Lamont wants to see you right away. In his office.'

'Good for him,' said Littlemore, continuing up the steps.

'But he wants you now, sir,' said the boy. 'You're supposed to follow me.'

'Tell Lamont he can come to my office,' answered Littlemore.

The phone was already ringing when he got upstairs.

'Let me guess, Lamont,' said Littlemore into the mouthpiece. 'Your man tailing Speyer told you I met with him today.'

'Are you aware,' asked Lamont, 'that James Speyer is profiting from the Mexican confiscation of American property in Mexico?'

'Not my problem,' said Littlemore.

'But the man's anti-American. Surely you see it now. Why haven't you arrested him in connection with the bombing?'

'Come off it. I'm not arresting somebody just because he's your competition in Mexico.'

'We've been over and over this, Littlemore,' said Lamont. 'Speyer threatened me. He threatened to retaliate against the Morgan Bank. Two weeks before the bombing.'

'It wasn't Speyer,' said Littlemore. 'I told you: it was a man named Pesqueira, and it didn't have anything to do with the bombing.'

'It *was* Speyer. Did you ever talk to Pesqueira? Talk to him. You'll see that Speyer's lying. James Speyer's a traitor. He wouldn't care how many American lives were lost. A year ago I got a cable from Mexico. It was the middle of September 1919. Speyer was in Mexico City celebrating their Independence Day. He was urging the Mexican government to seize American mines and oil wells, telling them that he would provide the funds to keep them in operation.'

'Mr Lamont,' said Littlemore. 'This is the last time I'm going to say it: not my problem. So long.'

Chapter Sixteen

Their train broke down north of Vienna, coming to a halt in the woods. Hours and hours went by. Finally another train – every seat of which was already occupied – pulled up next to them; they rode the rest of the way to Vienna upright and jam-packed. When they finally arrived, it was evening. In the motorized taxi they took from the station, Younger ordered the driver to stop in front of the opera house, about a block short of the Hotel Bristol.

'What is it?' asked Colette. Then she saw: a knot of policemen was gathered in front of the hotel, eyeing everyone who entered or exited. Younger instructed the driver to make inquiries, explaining, truthfully, that he didn't want to check into a hotel where they might be in danger.

From across the avenue, still in the taxi, they watched their driver consult with an officer and nod in comprehension as he received an account of what the police were doing there.

'They can't be looking for us,' said Colette.

'No?' said Younger.

Their taxi driver was now pointing an accusatory finger at his own automobile. The officer peered in their direction through the darkness. Then he and a colleague began walking slowly toward them.

'Well – shall we give ourselves up?' asked Younger.

'But we've done nothing wrong,' said Colette.

'Nothing at all,' said Younger. 'Leaving a pile of dead bodies next to Prague castle, fleeing the country – we can explain everything. If they don't believe us, we can show them Hans Gruber's dog tag as proof.'

Colette's hand went to her throat, where Hans Gruber's military tag had been clasped for six years. The police officers were getting close. 'The engine's still running,' she said.

Younger jumped into the front seat, put the car in reverse, and floored the gas pedal. The policemen broke into a run, chasing them.

'Where will we go?' Colette asked, holding on to Luc in the back-seat.

'One catastrophe at a time,' answered Younger, turning the car around. Tires screaming, they roared off down the Ringstrasse. The policemen, panting, abandoned the chase.

Sigmund Freud, opening his door at 19 Berggasse, took a long puff at his cigar before speaking. Younger's face bore several cuts, and his overcoat looked as if he had rolled down a mountainside in it and then smashed through a car's windshield for good measure. Colette's cheek was bruised. Only Luc, scrupulously washed and brushed by his sister on board the train, was no worse for wear, although his knees were skinned and his brown wool suit, with short trousers, gave him a strangely provincial look.

Freud addressed Younger: 'I assume you and Miss Rousseau didn't give each other your injuries?'

'The police—' Younger began.

'Are looking for you – I know,' said Freud. 'Your friend Count Kinsky came by to warn you. He says the police believe you may have killed a man in Prague.'

'Three,' said Younger.

'I beg your pardon?' asked Freud.

'I killed three men.'

'I see,' said Freud. 'Miss Rousseau, tell me Younger didn't kill your fiancé in a fit of jealous rage.'

'He wasn't my fiancé,' said Colette.

Freud raised both eyebrows: 'Younger killed the wrong men?'

'No,' she answered. 'He killed the right men.'

'I see,' said Freud again.

'Dr Freud,' said Younger, 'I should warn you it may not be wise to let us in. I don't know how things are here, but in America it's a crime to take a murderer into your house.'

'Did you commit murder?' asked Freud.

'I may have,' said Younger. 'I believe I did.'

'It wasn't murder,' Colette replied sharply. 'And if it was, I only wish you could have murdered him a thousand more times.'

'Ah,' said Freud. 'Well, don't just stand there. Come in.'

A fire crackled in an old-fashioned porcelain stove in the Freuds' sitting room. Younger and Freud were drinking brandy. Tea had been served to Colette, but she ended up taking brandy as well, out of Younger's snifter. They had told Freud the entire story, and silence had fallen.

'What a lovely tablecloth,' said Colette.

'Is it?' asked Freud.

'The lace,' she answered. 'It's lovely.'

'I'll tell Minna you said so; she sewed it,' replied Freud. 'Would you like a blanket, my dear?'

Colette was holding herself as if outside on a chill night. 'Why didn't I kill him?' she asked with sudden animation. 'Why was I such a weakling?'

'You don't know?' said Freud.

'No.'

Freud began trimming a cigar, watching Colette out of the corner of his eye. He offered one to Younger, who declined. 'The conventional answer,' said Freud, 'would be that your conscience rebelled at the last moment, convincing you that revenge is a sin.'

'Revenge *is* a sin,' she said.

'Everyone wants revenge,' answered Freud. 'The problem is that we usually seek it against the wrong person. At least you sought it against the right one. But your religious compunctions – they're not the reason you didn't kill him.'

'I know,' she agreed. 'I believed it was the right thing to do – with all my heart. I still do. I shouldn't, but I do. But then why couldn't I pull the trigger?'

'For the same reason, I suspect, your brother doesn't talk.'

Colette looked at Freud, perplexed.

'Do you have something else to tell us, my dear?' asked Freud.

'What do you mean?'

'Your brother has something to say,' said Freud. 'As a result of which he says nothing.'

'I – you know what's wrong with my brother?' asked Colette.

'I know exactly what's wrong with him,' said Freud, drawing on his cigar. 'But first things first. You have only two options, as I see it. Turn yourselves in or leave the country.'

'We can't turn ourselves in,' said Younger. 'We'd be handed over to the police in Prague and jailed for who knows how long. Eventually they'll find Gruber's mother, so they'll learn we were looking for him. They'd ask us why. If we told them the truth, they'd conclude that Colette was bent on a revenge killing, which would be true – and which would be murder, even if we could prove what Gruber did in the war, which we can't. If we refused to tell them why we were looking for him, they'd know we were hiding something, and then they probably wouldn't believe anything else we said. Either way, we might end up convicted.'

'Then you have to get out,' said Freud. At that moment, the lamps in the room flickered. 'Blast it – we're going to lose power again. It happens at least once a week.'

Freud waited, cigar poised in the air. The flickering abated; the lights stayed on.

'Perhaps we'll be all right,' he resumed.

'Please, Dr Freud,' said Colette. 'Can you explain what's the matter with my brother?'

'I'll tell you what I know, Fräulein, but the concepts will be new to you and strange. Brandy?' Taking his time, Freud refilled his own and Younger's glasses.

'Well, where to begin?' said Freud. He was seated again, his legs crossed, in one hand a cigar, in the other his brandy. 'Twenty-five years ago, I discovered a path to unseen provinces of our mental life, which I may have been the first mortal ever to enter. There I found a hell of inexpressible fears and longings, for which men and women might have burned in earlier eras. A man cannot expect such insight more than once in a lifetime. But last year, I made a new discovery that, in my more vainglorious moments, I think might even surpass the first. No one will believe it, but that will be nothing new. It came to me from studying the war neuroses – indeed in part from studying your brother, Miss Rousseau. Not that your brother has a neurosis, strictly speaking, but his condition is similar. I want to be clear about one thing: he requires treatment. Wherever you go next, you should not simply leave him as he is. His case is straightforward enough. I could cure him myself, I expect, in – I don't know – eight weeks.'

'Cure him?' repeated Colette. 'Completely?'

'I should think so.'

Colette didn't know how to respond.

'You sent us to Jauregg,' said Younger. 'Why?'

'Many choose to treat their psychological disorders mechanistically. Miss Rousseau has to decide if she really wants her brother analyzed. I'm not sure she does. Twice now, she has brought her brother to Vienna but refused to commit herself to the time an analysis would require. And perhaps she's right: after all, it may not be pleasant for her.'

'For me?' asked Colette. 'Why?'

'I told you last year,' said Freud. 'The truths that psychoanalysis unearths are never irrelevant to other family members. Fräulein, you know what it is to yearn for revenge. Your brother is taking revenge too – by not speaking.'

'On whom?' asked Colette.

'Perhaps on you.'

'Whatever for?'

'You can't tell us?' asked Freud.

'I can't imagine what you're talking about,' answered Colette.

'It's just speculation, my dear. I don't know the answer.'

'But you said you knew what was wrong with him,' said Colette.

'I do. I understood it last summer, two months after you left. It was child's play, as a matter of fact. Younger, what is the boy's most revealing symptom?'

'I have no idea,' said Younger.

'Come – I just gave it away.'

Younger chafed at Freud's habit of luring him with analytic conundrums, particularly under the present circumstances, but all the same, the lure took. Child's play? 'His game,' said Younger. 'Something to do with his fishing reel game.'

'Exactly,' said Freud. 'Miss Rousseau told me that her grandmother played a German hide-and-seek game with her brother when he was little. He is saying *fort* and *da* when he unspools and rewinds his reel – *gone* and *there*. What does it mean?'

Younger thought about it: 'When did he start?'

'In 1914,' said Freud.

'He's reliving the death of his parents,' said Younger.

'Obviously. Over and over. But why?'

'To undo the feeling of loss?'

'No. He isn't undoing anything. He's making himself experience the single worst moment of his life again and again.'

Cigar smoke had filled the candlelit room with its heavy, heady odor.

'It's the key to the riddle,' said Freud. 'All the war neurotics repeat. They have a kind of compulsion – a repetition compulsion – a need to reenact or reexperience the trauma that has given rise to their condition. And they're all repeating the same thing: death, or the moment when they came closest to it. Normally, we have defenses – fortifications, physiological and psychological – that keep our mortality away from us, out of our consciousness. If these fortifications are breached, if in a moment of unexpected trauma, mortality punctures these defenses, its terror rushes in and starts a kind of mental conflagration – a fire very difficult to extinguish – but a fire to which a man wants to return again and again. The shell-shocked man will relive his trauma when asleep; or in broad daylight, he will conjure a bomb going off in the noise of a door slamming; he may even reenact the episode through bodily symptoms.'

'Why?' asked Younger. 'To discharge the fear?'

'For a long time I tried to understand it that way,' replied Freud. 'Discharging fear would be pleasurable. At least it would lessen displeasure. Every psychological phenomenon, I thought, was motivated at bottom by the drive to increase pleasure or lessen displeasure. But I was trying to fit facts to theory, when I should have been fitting theory to facts. I had just begun to understand it when you were last here. The war taught me something I should have seen ages ago: we have a drive beyond the pleasure principle. Another instinct, as fundamental as hunger, as irresistible as love.'

'What instinct?' asked Colette.

'A death instinct. More tea, Miss Rousseau?'

'No, thank you.'

'You mean a desire to kill?' asked Younger.

'That's one side of it,' said Freud. 'But fundamentally it's a longing for death. For destruction. Not only someone else's; also our own.'

'You think people want to die?' asked Colette.

'I do,' said Freud. 'It's built into our cells, our very atoms. There are two elemental forces in the universe. One draws matter toward matter. That is how life comes into being and how it propagates. In physics, this force is called gravity; in psychology, love. The other force tears matter apart. It is the force of disunification, disintegration, destruction. If I'm correct, every planet, every star in the universe is not only drawn toward the others by gravity, but also pushed away from them by a force of repulsion we can't see. Within an organism, this force is what drives the animal to seek death, as moths seek a flame.'

'But you can cure it – this death instinct?' asked Colette.

'One cannot cure an instinct, Miss Rousseau,' said Freud. 'One cannot eliminate it. One can, however, make it more conscious and in this way relieve its pathological effects. When an instinct creates in us an impulse that we don't act on, the impulse does not go away. It may subsist unaffected. It may intensify. It may be turned to other objects, for better or worse. Or it may produce pathological symptoms. Such symptoms can be cured.'

'I wouldn't have thought,' said Younger, 'that Luc's muteness aimed at death.'

'No, his muteness has another function. That would be the point of analyzing him – to uncover that function. It's undoubtedly connected to his parents' death, but there's something more too. Possibly their death reminded him of a scene he had witnessed even earlier. Did your father mistreat you, Miss Rousseau?'

'Mistreat me? In what way?'

'In any way.'

'Not at all,' said Colette.

'No? Did he favor you?'

'Luc was his favorite,' said Colette. 'I was a girl.'

Freud nodded. 'Well, it's a pity you can't remain in Vienna, but I don't see how it's possible. Vienna is a much smaller city than New York. You'll be noticed here. The police will have everyone watching; someone will report you.'

'May I ask you a question, Dr Freud?' asked Colette.

'Of course.'

'These two forces you describe,' she said. 'They're good and evil, aren't they? The instinct for love is good, and the instinct for death is evil.'

Freud smiled: 'In science, my dear, there is no such thing as good or evil. The death instinct is part of our biology. You're familiar with chromatolysis – the natural process by which cells die? Every one of our cells brings about its own destruction at its allotted time. That's the death instinct in operation. Now if a cell fails to die, what happens? It keeps dividing, reproducing, endlessly, unnaturally. It becomes a cancer. That's what cancer is, after all – cells afflicted with the loss of their will to die. The death instinct is not evil, Miss Rousseau. In its proper place it's every bit as essential to our well-being as its opposite.'

That night, after Freud had retired and Colette and Luc were installed in one of the children's old bedrooms and the apartment fell silent, Younger smoked a cigarette on the veranda. He had felt claustrophobic inside; on the little balcony overlooking the courtyard, he felt claustrophobic outside as well. A door opened within; Younger imagined it might be Colette, coming to join him.

'No – it's only me,' said Freud's voice behind him. The older man stepped out onto the veranda. 'So what do you think of my death instinct?'

'I'm for it,' said Younger.

Freud smiled. 'You're still at war, my boy. You never demobilized. Ten years ago, I wouldn't have foreseen you as the instinctual kind. You were more – repressed.'

'I read somewhere that repression is unhealthy. A world-famous psychologist has proven it.'

'Whose ideas you don't accept.'

'Ten years ago,' said Younger, reflecting, 'I saw your ideas as moral anarchy. Exploding all propriety. But you were right. I guess I don't believe in morality anymore.'

'Ah yes, that's what my critics say: Freud the libertine, Freud the amoral.' He inhaled the night air – a deep breath of age and judgment. 'It's true, I'm no believer in Sunday school morality. Love thy neighbor as thyself is an absurd principle: quite impossible, unless one has a very unusual neighbor. But when it comes to a sense of justice, I believe I can measure myself with the best men I've known. All my life I've tried to be honorable – not to harm, not to take advantage – even though I know perfectly well that by doing so I've made myself an anvil for others' brutality, their disloyalty, their ambition.'

'Why then?' asked Younger. 'Why do you do it?'

'I could give you a plausible psychological explanation,' said Freud. 'But the truth is I have no idea. Why I – and for that matter my children – have to be thoroughly decent human beings is beyond my comprehension. It is merely a fact. An anchor.'

There was a slight pause before Younger said: 'You think I need an anchor?'

'No. You have one already.'

'You mean a sense of justice?'

'I meant love,' said Freud. 'Which is why this bombing of yours worries me.'

'The Wall Street bombing?'

'Yes. It may be a harbinger of something new. Not its violence – that's to be expected. I was reading the other day a description of one of those happy quarters of the earth where primitive societies flourish in peace and contentment, knowing no aggression. I didn't believe a word of it. Where there are men, there will be violence. Fortunately, the death instinct almost never operates alone. Our two instincts are nearly always obliged to work together – which gives sexuality its violent character, but also tempers the death drive. That's what makes your bombing so troubling.'

'Because it was unalloyed?'

'Exactly,' said Freud. 'The death instinct unbound. Freed from the life instincts, freed from the ideals by which the ego assesses its actions – conscience. Perhaps the war has unleashed it, or perhaps an ideology. Men have always worshipped death. There are death gods in every ancient religion. Goddesses as well, some of them quite beautiful, like Atropos with her shears, cutting life's threads – which is further evidence, by the way, of man's attraction to death. They haven't caught the perpetrators, have they?'

'Of the bombing?' asked Younger. 'Not yet.'

'Perhaps because they're dead.'

It took Younger a moment before he understood: 'You think they killed themselves in the blast – deliberately.'

'Maybe they did, maybe they didn't,' said Freud. 'Maybe they'll give others the idea. But yes, that's what worries me.'

Early the next morning, while Freud was out for his daily constitutional, Oktavian Kinsky called. 'I've come to offer you my services, Mademoiselle,' he said to Colette in the Freuds' sitting room. 'I heard what happened outside the Hotel Bristol last night. I thought I might find you here, and I also thought you might want discreet transportation to the railway station.'

'You're very kind, Count Oktavian,' said Colette. 'I don't know how to thank you.'

'Not at all, Mademoiselle,' he replied. 'A nobleman's first duty is not to the police, but to the beautiful woman the police are pursuing.'

'Especially the nobleman who reported the woman to the police in the first place,' said Younger.

'Stratham,' Colette rebuked Younger. 'Why would you say that?'

Oktavian was abashed. 'I'm afraid he's right.'

'They found your business cards,' said Younger.

'That's just it,' replied Oktavian abjectly. 'Several of my cards were discovered near the scene of your – your misadventure. The Czech authorities wired the Vienna police, who put me in a cell as if I'd committed a crime. They said a man named Hans Gruber had been killed in Prague. They asked me if I knew him. What was I to do? Naturally I explained that you, Miss Rousseau, had journeyed to Braunau in romantic pursuit of Herr Gruber, and that Dr Younger had driven to Braunau in romantic pursuit of you, together with your brother, in a motorcycle I'd rented for him. I'm sure the police have everything wrong, as they always do. I told them that neither of you could possibly have been involved in a killing. I'm so sorry; it's all my fault.'

'No,' said Colette, 'it's our fault the police came for you.'

'Did you tell them,' asked Younger, 'that we were acquainted with the Freuds?'

'Certainly not,' said Oktavian. 'One doesn't reveal confidences to the police. By the way, where is my motorcycle, if you don't mind? I understand you arrived at the hotel last night by taxi. Did you leave the motorcycle at the station?'

'The police didn't tell you?' asked Younger.

'Tell me what?'

Younger beckoned to Luc. 'Count Kinsky wants to know where his motorcycle is,' Younger said to the boy.

Luc pulled from a pocket a small round mirror with a piece of snapped metal at one end. Oktavian took the offering with blinking eyes. From his other pocket, Luc produced a bent wheel spoke.

'Oh, dear,' said Oktavian.

'Enjoyed it immensely,' said Younger. 'Agile little vehicle.'

'Oh, dear,' Oktavian repeated, swallowing drily. 'Well, they say debtor's prison is not nearly so unpleasant as it used to be.'

'Wait – there's one more item,' said Younger, withdrawing from his jacket a bank draft, which he made out to Oktavian Kinsky.

Oktavian stared at the draft. 'This isn't enough for a motorcycle, Doctor,' he said. 'It's enough for a motorcycle and three new automobiles.'

'I know,' said Younger. 'And still not enough to repay you.'

There was nothing to pack. Their belongings were all at the hotel and therefore irretrievable. In the courtyard, they were saying goodbye to Minna when Freud returned from his morning walk, accompanied by his wife, Martha.

'You're going already?' Freud asked Younger and Colette.

'Yes,' replied Younger. 'Oktavian is taking us to the station. Every moment we stay, we put you in danger.'

'Mrs Freud and I have been discussing it, Miss Rousseau,' said Freud. 'Let the boy remain behind. With us.'

'I couldn't,' said Colette.

'Why not? It would be a boon to Martha. We haven't had a child in the house for a long time.'

'But I couldn't,' repeated Colette.

'It might make your escape easier,' interjected Oktavian. 'The police are looking for a couple with a little boy. They're sure to be keeping watch at the railway stations.'

'I've never been away from Luc,' said Colette.

'Never?' repeated Freud. 'You left him to go to Braunau just the other day. With no assurance you would ever return.'

Colette frowned. 'There was only one thing in the world I would have done that for. And now I—'

'Fräulein,' said Freud gently but pointedly, 'you have had your brother in your care for six years and never obtained treatment for him. This was probably wise on your part, wise beyond your years, because the care he would have received almost anywhere in the world would have been useless or even detrimental. But you will be doing him a great disservice now if you deny him the treatment he needs. He is at a precarious age. If he remains as he is for much longer, it will likely have permanent effects on his adulthood.' Freud paused. 'I have an additional, medical reason for my proposal. Your brother will have a better chance at a cure if he is treated in your absence.'

'In my absence?' repeated Colette. 'Why?'

'He improves when away from you,' answered Freud. 'Younger, did the boy communicate with you when you were traveling with him?'

'Yes – he wrote me notes.'

'You didn't tell me,' Colette said to Younger.

'It's natural, Miss Rousseau, for the boy to do better outside his immediate family – and natural on your part to resent it.'

'I don't resent it.'

'No? Well, I can tell you nothing else right now, but you are almost certainly involved in his symptoms. Your behavior for the last six years and his are intertwined in some fashion. You may even be the cause of his condition.'

Younger could see that Colette was distraught. 'Can I speak with Stratham for a moment?' she asked.

'Of course,' said Freud.

They withdrew to the stairwell. 'Tell me I'm not the cause,' she whispered, desperately. 'Am I the cause?'

'I don't know.'

'What should I do?'

'Leave him here, without question,' said Younger. 'We may not make it out of Austria. If we're caught and he's with us, they'll put him in some kind of Czech institution – an orphanage or worse. He could be there for years.'

'But how will we get him back?'

'If we get out?' said Younger. 'Easily. We'll send someone for him.'

Colette steeled herself, and they returned to the courtyard. She hesitated – then put the question to her brother, asking what he wanted to do. The boy looked at Younger.

'You want my opinion?' asked Younger.

The boy nodded.

'Stay behind.' Younger decided to put it in terms of the courage Luc would need: 'It will be hard on you, but you'll be helping your sister and me. After we reach safety, you'll follow.'

Luc thought about it. His eyes were deep – deep enough, Younger suspected, to have seen through his tactic. Then the boy took a few steps until he was standing between Freud and his wife. He looked up at Colette, his expressionless face indicating that he had made his decision.

'Wire us the moment you can,' said Freud.

★   ★   ★

Outside the Westbahnhof railway station, policemen stood guard, demanding papers from everyone who went in.

'It's worse than I thought,' said Oktavian. 'I don't see how you'll get through.'

'The Czechs hold an anti-Semitic riot, and it's we whom they want to arrest,' said Younger disgustedly. They were still inside Oktavian's carriage. 'Is there another train station?'

'Several,' replied Oktavian, 'but the police are sure to be there too. There is another way, Doctor, if you're willing. Aeroplane. A French company began service just last month. The airstrip is small and nearly always deserted. The police may not think of it. The aeroplanes are quite safe, they say, but very dear.'

'What would you think of flying?' Younger asked Colette.

'Luc looked happy to be left behind, didn't he?' she answered. 'Almost as if he were glad to be away from me.'

Vienna's airport – the only one in Austria – consisted of a dirt landing strip with a single craft on it: a double-winged monoplane with the largest propeller on its nose Younger had ever seen. Oktavian was right: there were no policemen. Neither, however, was there anyone else, so far as they could see. No passengers, no ticket agents, no crew. The only building was locked.

Venturing around the back, they found two men drinking coffee and schnapps. One turned out to be the pilot, a Frenchman, who jumped eagerly from his chair when Oktavian inquired about the possibility of two passengers flying immediately to the nearest port.

'We're supposed to fly to Paris,' said the pilot with a Gallic shrug, 'but we're not particular. I could take you to Bremen.'

'Bremen would be fine,' replied Younger.

They agreed to a price. The pilot downed his schnapps and clapped his hands. 'Off we go then,' he said.

The aircraft boasted eight passenger seats. When the pilot had settled into the cockpit, he took an additional swallow from a hip flask and signaled a thumbs-up to his partner, who gave the propeller a strong tug. The engine churned into life. Oktavian, looking less enthusiastic about the plan he had originated, said goodbye to Younger and Colette at the foot of a small ladder leading into the passenger compartment.

'It's strange, Mademoiselle,' said Oktavian. 'All this time I've felt I knew you from somewhere else. A long time ago. You have no relatives in Austria?'

'Perhaps you knew my grandmother,' said Colette. 'She was Viennese.'

'That's it,' cried Oktavian. 'I must have met her. Yes, I can almost remember the event. I knew I had seen your face before. She was of noble birth, your grandmother?'

'Oh, no, she was very poor.'

'I would have sworn it was at some fine ball, and with some fine gentleman.'

'That can't have been my grandmother, Count Oktavian.'

'Well, it will come to me. But you mustn't call me Count. I don't count for anything.'

Taking off, the aircraft rolled alarmingly, but it achieved a semblance of stability on reaching altitude. They peered down at the blanket of snow beneath them – which was not snow, but clouds.

'I've never seen the top of a cloud before,' said Colette. 'Do you think God minds?'

'I doubt He'd begrudge us a view of His handiwork,' answered Younger. 'I'd be more worried about your toying with His atoms.'

'Why do you so mistrust radium?' she asked. 'You made me wear that absurd suit in Professor Boltwood's laboratory. Everyone else thought I looked like a sea diver.'

'Everyone else should have been wearing one too.'

'I wonder if it could explain radioactivity,' mused Colette. 'Dr Freud's death instinct. We don't have any idea why radium atoms split apart – but then we don't know why other atoms don't. Perhaps there is one force holding the particles together, and another one driving them apart. It would be just what Dr Freud described: two fundamental forces, one of attraction and one of repulsion.'

'Which is stronger?' asked Younger.

'I would say the force holding them together,' said Colette. 'That would explain why radioactivity releases so much energy.' A thought came to her: 'But that energy, when it's released – that could *be* the death force. Perhaps the splitting of the atom is death itself, in pure form. It could communicate the death force to other atoms, causing them to split apart.'

'And you wonder why I don't trust it,' said Younger.

'That could also explain radium's effect on cancer,' replied Colette with growing excitement. 'No one has ever explained how radium cures cancer. Even Madame doesn't know. But Dr Freud was right: cancer cells are cells that have stopped dying. When radium is placed inside a tumor, perhaps it releases the death force, spreading it out over the whole tumor, transmitting it to the cancer cells, which makes them begin dying again. What are you doing?'

As Colette spoke, Younger had become distracted by a separate train of thought until finally he had risen from his seat. 'Pilot,' he called out. 'You said this plane was supposed to fly to Paris?'

'*Oui*, Monsieur,' said the pilot.

'Take us there.'

'Paris?' asked Colette. 'Why?'

'To see one of your heroes.'

Chapter Seventeen

U NDER THE HEADLINE 'Invited to Mexico,' Littlemore read the
following front-page story:

*An invitation to President-elect Harding to visit Mexico was
extended at a conference last night between Senator A. B. Fall of
New Mexico, and Elias L. Torres, envoy from President-elect
Obregon of Mexico. The invitation contemplated Senator Harding's
attendance at the inauguration of President-elect Obregon in Mexico
City on the twenty-fifth of this month. Whether the invitation
will be accepted seems very uncertain and tonight there was no
official statement from the President-elect. Senator Harding is
exceedingly anxious to restore amity between Mexico and the
United States, but his close advisers doubt the propriety at this
time of the President-elect going to foreign soil.*

Littlemore was riding a train back down to Washington. He stared out
the window for a long time.

On arriving in Washington, Littlemore took a taxi directly to the
Library of Congress, just down the street from the United States
Capitol. There he asked for some basic facts and history concerning
the country of Mexico; the librarian directed him to the *World Book
of Organized Knowledge*. A half-hour later, his pace quickening,
Littlemore went to the Senate Office Building.

'What's the matter?' asked Fall when Littlemore was let in to see him.

'I read the Mexico story in the paper, Mr Senator.'

'Now that's something I'm proud of,' said the Senator, stretching his arms and leaning back in his chair. 'The two presidents-elect of the two largest democracies in the world. It'll be a first. Harding doesn't want to go, but I'll persuade him. Obregón will pull his troops out of the mines and let us keep our oil wells, and all will be right with the world.'

'I don't think Mr Harding should go, sir.'

'You're giving *me* advice on foreign policy?'

'What if it was Mexico, Mr Fall?'

'What if what was Mexico?'

'What if it was Mexico, not Russia?'

There was a long pause. 'You ain't talking about the bombing, are you, son?' asked Fall.

'Remember what you asked me the first time I met you? What country stood to gain from the bombing, what country had the motive, what country would have felt it had the right to attack us?'

'Sure I remember.'

'Nobody had a bigger motive to bomb J. P. Morgan than the Mexicans,' said Littlemore. 'Morgan's been bleeding them dry – keeping every banker in the world from lending to Mexico for six years. That's not the only motive either. From what I hear, they hate us pretty good down there, sir. Been looking to pay us back for a long time.'

'What for?'

'The Mexican-American War.'

'What kind of—? That's ancient history, boy. Nobody even remembers that war.'

'They remember it, sir. We took almost half their land. Invaded them. Occupied Mexico City. Killed a lot of people. There were some atrocities. I think they think we look down on them, Senator Fall. On top of which they think we're taking all their silver and oil, getting rich while they're dirt poor.'

Fall considered. 'I was going to say that's the most ridiculous thing I ever heard, but maybe it ain't. This new envoy Torres – I'll tell you the truth, he didn't rub me the right way. Like he was hiding something.'

'Let's say they were getting ready to nationalize our oil wells,' Littlemore went on. 'They'd have to show us that even though our army can lick theirs, they can hurt us in a different way – a new way – that an army can't stop. Hurt us badly enough so it wouldn't be worthwhile to invade.'

'You're saying the bombing was supposed to show us how they'd fight if we invaded?'

'I'm saying that if you look at it from Mexico's point of view, it starts to make sense. An attack on Morgan. Revenge for our invasion. And a warning of what kind of damage they can inflict on us if we move in with our army after they take back the oil. All three at once.'

'In that case they'd have to be first-class idiots,' said Fall, 'because they forgot to tell us they were the ones who did it.'

'They wouldn't want to say it right out,' answered Littlemore. 'Then we'd *have* to send the army in, which is what they don't want. So they'd leave us a sign showing they did it, without giving us any proof.'

'But they didn't leave a sign.'

'They did,' said Littlemore. 'Do you know when Mexican Independence Day is?'

'No.'

'September sixteenth.'

Fall was silent for several seconds. 'You sure about that? Not the fifteenth, not the seventeenth?'

'September sixteenth, Mr Senator. And it's a big day for them, just like it is for us.'

'Well, I don't use the word *irony* much, but ain't that an irony? They were trying to show us they ain't so puny, but they're so puny we didn't even get the message.'

'Something else, Mr Fall. Two weeks before the bombing, Mr Lamont of the Morgan Bank was threatened. Lamont got it mixed up though. He thought a banker named Speyer was the one making the threat, but it wasn't Speyer. It was a Mexican consul – a guy named Pesqueira – who said that if Morgan didn't start letting money back into Mexico, there would be hell to pay.'

A thought came to Fall's eyes: 'Why, this envoy Torres, he may have been playing me for a fool. I believe I *was* a fool. They blow us to pieces, and I get the President of the United States to make peace with them – after they've seized our mines. Maybe they *are* planning to go for the oil next. Damn my eyes for a blind man.'

'We don't have any proof, Mr Fall. Not yet. And the missing link is still the gold.'

'That's right – what about the gold?' Fall's eyes moved back and forth. 'It can't be, Littlemore. You're telling me that by coincidence our gold was being moved on Mexican Independence Day?'

'I don't think it was coincidence, Senator. Like you said, maybe the Mexicans paid off somebody in our government – somebody in a position to arrange when the gold would be moved. I'm going to the Mexican Embassy, Mr Fall. I'm going to talk to this Torres. And Pesqueira.'

'By God, son, if you get to the bottom of this, I'll get you an embassy of your own. Where'd you like to be ambassador?'

'Not my line, Mr Fall.'

'Then how does Chief of the Federal Bureau of Investigation sound?'

The Mexican Embassy, a substantial four-story house on I Street, had a damp and insalubrious odor in its foyer. Discoloration streaked its walls.

'You got mold in here, ma'am,' said Littlemore to the receptionist.

'I know,' she replied. 'Everyone says. Can I help you?'

The detective learned that Elias Torres, the new envoy, had not yet presented his credentials at the embassy, but was expected tomorrow. Señor Pesqueira, however, was upstairs.

★   ★   ★

Roberto Pesqueira was a small man with well-oiled black hair, fair skin, an ink-thin mustache and small but perfectly white teeth. He showed no signs of unease when Littlemore introduced himself as an agent of the United States Treasury. If anything, he looked as if he might have been expecting the visit.

'I have reason to think you threatened a man in New York City two months ago, Mr Pesqueira,' said Littlemore.

'What man?'

'Thomas Lamont. Two weeks before the Wall Street bombing.'

Neatly folded white handkerchiefs were piled on one corner of Pesqueira's desk. He removed one of these and applied it to his teeth. 'Your emperor,' said Pesqueira.

'I beg your pardon?'

'Señor Lamont is the king on your throne. Everyone else is his lackey. Wilson, your so-called President, is his lackey.'

'You don't deny the threat?'

'The Morgan Bank strangled my people for six years,' said Pesqueira. 'Your government propped up a corrupt dictator in my country for twenty years. You occupy my country. You steal California from us. You warn us you will make another war if we do not change our constitutional laws. And you accuse me of threatening?'

'I'm just doing my job, Mr Pesqueira.'

'Really? You must have forgotten the first two words of the law of nations.'

'What would those be?'

'Diplomatic immunity. Your law doesn't apply to me. You cannot arrest me. You cannot search my home. You cannot even question me.'

'Nope. You're a *consular* agent, just like Juan Burns was,' said Littlemore, referring to a Mexican consul jailed in New York City for illegal weapons purchases in 1917. 'You don't have diplomatic immunity.'

'Forgive me, you are not as ignorant as I assumed; one gets so used to it with Americans. But I am not a consular agent anymore. My office is here now, as you can see, in the embassy – and all embassy officials, I'm sure you know, enjoy the immunity of the diplomat. Technically, you are on Mexican soil right now. You cannot even be here without my consent. Shall I call the police, Agent Littlemore?'

Littlemore hurried back to Senator Fall's chambers and, notwithstanding the protest of one of the Senator's assistants, knocked on Fall's door and strode through.

'Don't you come busting in here, boy,' said Fall, seated at his desk, white handlebar mustache contrasting sharply with a florid countenance.

'Sorry, Mr Senator,' said Littlemore. 'I need to know where I can find the Mexican envoy you were telling me about – Torres. Right away.'

'Why?'

'He's not on staff at the embassy yet. Can't claim diplomatic immunity. Can we find out where he's staying?'

'That's the sort of thing I'm good at,' said Fall. 'Go sit yourself down in my waiting room. Could take a little while.'

Littlemore went to the Senator's waiting room, but he didn't sit. He paced. He looked at his watch. He got a cup of coffee. Finally, over two hours later, the businesslike but exceedingly good-looking Mrs Cross emerged with an address and a car key. 'Mr Torres has taken an apartment on Crescent Place,' she said. 'Senator Fall says you can use one of his motorcars, if you like. I'll show you where it is.'

In the basement of the Senate Office Building, an electric monorail shuttled people through an underground passage to and from the Capitol. Mrs Cross led Littlemore to a parking garage, where she climbed into the driver's seat of an open-roofed sedan.

'Excuse me, ma'am,' said Littlemore. 'I think I better do this on my own.'

'Because it might be dangerous?'

'That's right.'

'I like dangerous,' she answered. 'Besides, you're in a hurry; do you have any idea where Crescent Place is?'

'No.'

'Then you're wasting time. Get in.'

Mrs Cross slowed as they approached a narrow lane in a fashionable neighborhood. They were on Sixteenth Street. In their rearview mirror, the gates of the White House were visible in the distance far behind them. Mrs Cross turned into the curving lane and parked in front of a small apartment house. Dusk had begun to fall.

Littlemore found the name, 'Elias Torres,' handwritten in relatively fresh ink next to the mail slot for apartment 3B. Climbing to the third floor, Littlemore rang the bell. Mrs Cross stood behind him.

'Who it is?' called a Spanish-accented voice from within.

'Federal agent James Littlemore,' said Littlemore. 'Is that Elias Torres?'

'Jace.'

'What did you say?'

'I am Elias Torres.'

'I want to ask you a few questions, Mr Torres.'

'What about?'

'About the bombing of Wall Street,' answered Littlemore.

There was a pause. 'All right. A minute. I am putting on the shirt.'

'I'll give you thirty seconds,' said the detective. Littlemore put his ear to the door. He heard rushed footsteps and a window being thrown open.

'He's running,' said Mrs Cross.

'I know,' replied Littlemore.

'Aren't you going to do anything?' she asked.

'Yup – wait to make sure he's on his way.' Littlemore banged on the door. When no response was forthcoming, the detective took out a pick and metal file and went to work on the lock. 'We don't want Torres, Mrs Cross.'

'Why not?'

'He just arrived from Mexico,' said Littlemore, working his file between doorjamb and bolt. 'Hasn't moved into his embassy office yet. No diplomatic immunity. We can search whatever boxes and government papers the guy brought with him: that's what we want. But without a warrant, you can't just break into somebody's place and search his stuff – unless of course your suspect is attempting to flee.'

Littlemore popped the bolt.

'You play by the rules, New York,' said Mrs Cross.

'Somebody has to.' A breeze was blowing the curtains of the living-room window. Littlemore looked out: the window opened onto a fire escape. 'That's where he went.'

The apartment was newly and cheaply furnished. The only decorations were a few wall-hung watercolors of clowns and bulls, along with a vase of flowers sitting on an inexpensive table. Littlemore went through the rooms, the closets, the drawers. He found nothing – only a smattering of clothes and personal effects. Mrs Cross stood in the living room, smoking a cigarette. 'Sharp move,' she said, 'letting him run.'

'Not looking too smart, am I?' asked Littlemore.

'Tidy Mexican gentleman,' said Mrs Cross, making use of a clean ashtray on the dining table. 'He might have swept his floor a little better.'

Littlemore followed her line of sight. At the base of the wall, a small mound of sawdust was visible. Five feet above this sawdust, hanging on the wall, was a watercolor of a bullfight.

'Got him,' said Littlemore.

He lifted the picture off its hanger. A hole had been drilled behind it – a hole large enough for a man to stick his hand into. Which is what Littlemore did, drawing out therefrom a cardboard cylinder. The corners of rolled-up documents poked out from either end of the tube. Littlemore pulled the sheets free and flattened them out on the table, holding them down so they didn't curl.

Some of the documents were photographs. Another was a letter, in

Spanish, bearing the stamp and letterhead of a Mexican governmental department. One was a diagram.

'Holy cow,' said Littlemore. 'Holy mother of cow.'

'Why are we going down the fire escape?' asked Mrs Cross, descending the metal stairs a few treads behind Littlemore.

'Because if anybody's waiting for us, they'll be out front.'

'Who would be waiting for us?'

'If I'm Elias Torres and I left these documents behind, I'm coming back for them. With some friends. And some guns. Hold this.'

Handing Mrs Cross the cardboard cylinder with the documents inside it, Littlemore let himself down a short metal ladder, at the end of which he had to jump the last several feet to the ground. He was in the building's rear lot, which appeared to be empty.

'Throw me the tube,' he said quietly, 'and come down.'

She complied, but when she reached the last rung of the ladder, still some six feet off the ground, she looked at him and said, 'Now what?'

'Let go,' he answered. 'I'll catch you.'

She hesitated.

'Jump, for Christ's sake,' he whispered.

She did; he caught her. She had one hand on his chest: 'You're stronger than you look.'

'Is that a compliment?' he asked. 'Don't answer. Just keep quiet.'

He led Mrs Cross around the apartment house, keeping her behind him, pressing himself against the wall when they came to the street. Peering around the corner, Littlemore saw four men, hats pulled low over their heads, outside the front door of the building. One sat on the hood of the sedan in which Mrs Cross and he had arrived; the man seemed to be carelessly polishing his shoe. Littlemore drew his gun.

'Wait,' whispered Mrs Cross. 'I'll go. They don't know you're with a woman. I'll pick you up on Avenue of the President.'

'Where's that?'

'It's Sixteenth Street.' She pointed the way. Then she walked boldly out into the street, displaying not a hint of anxiety. As she sauntered near the car, the men elbowed each other. One whistled; another asked her questions of a personal nature, which Mrs Cross did not answer. When she let herself into the car and started the engine, the man sitting on the hood leaned over the windshield.

'Where do you think you're going, honey?' he said. Perhaps he thought she couldn't pull out with a man on her hood. If so, he was mistaken.

'If you can hang on, you'll find out,' answered Mrs Cross. She put the car into drive and shot from the curb, dumping the man onto the pavement behind her. Without turning to look, she gave the four men a wave of her hand and turned at the first corner. Littlemore, in the meantime, had taken advantage of the distraction to walk off, unnoticed, in the other direction.

Mrs Cross and Littlemore, coming from opposite directions, met on Sixteenth Street, renamed Avenue of the President by its socially ambitious residents. Littlemore glanced over his shoulder before climbing in the car: no one was following them.

'Where to?' she asked.

'Your senator – where would he be right now?'

'Mr Fall? Home – at the Wardman Park Hotel. It's not far from here.'

'Go,' said Littlemore. He checked behind them again. 'Not bad, Mrs Cross.'

'Why did you ask my first name if you aren't going to use it?' she replied.

The central lobby of the thousand-room Wardman Park on Connecticut Avenue, which sprawled out in several wings on a bucolic sixteen-acre hill, was bright and crowded with brand-new automobiles as well as a throng of onlookers ogling them despite the lateness of the hour.

340

'An auto show,' said Littlemore disparagingly. 'The whole world's foul, and all these people can think about is a new car.'

'Why Agent Littlemore,' said Mrs Cross, 'this is a new and darker tone for you. I thought you looked at things on the bright side.'

'They got a hundred elevators in this place. Which way?'

'Follow me.'

On the eighth floor, Senator Fall himself opened the door to his rooms, dressed in a dark red smoking jacket. Mrs Cross walked right in, making herself at home. Littlemore stood in the doorway. 'You found something?' asked Fall.

Littlemore nodded.

'Have you shown it to Houston?'

'I can't,' said Littlemore.

As Littlemore spread out the documents on Senator Fall's dining table, Mrs Cross placed two tumblers of whiskey over ice in front of the men. She poured another for herself. 'What are the photographs of?' she asked.

'Looks like a military training camp somewhere in Mexico,' said Littlemore. 'That's a shooting range there. These are machine rifles. This one shows people working with fuses and detonators.'

'What's this list of names?' asked Fall.

'I'd say those are people who spent time at the camp. See, it shows how long they spent, what dates, and what weapons training they got. They're from all over the world. They got Italians, Russians – you name it.'

'It's a goddamn terrorist boot camp,' said Fall, 'right under our noses.'

'Do you see these two names, sir?' asked Littlemore.

'Sacco and Vanzetti,' said Fall.

'Looks like Flynn was onto something after all,' said Littlemore. Then he placed a different, thicker sheet of paper on top of the others. This one had a pen-and-ink sketch on it, carefully drawn, with arrows and labels in Spanish.

'My God,' said Fall.

'What is it?' asked Mrs Cross, sipping her whiskey.

'A diagram for arranging shrapnel around a bomb loaded in a wagon – a horse-drawn wagon.'

No one spoke.

'And that's not even the kicker, Senator Fall. Look at this one.'

Littlemore pointed to a document bearing the letterhead of the Controller-General of Mexico and, at the bottom, that gentleman's signature. Between these two formalities were several paragraphs of flowery Spanish. Senator Fall read them.

'You understand what this letter says, son?'

'Yes, sir. It's an authorization to transfer $1,115,000 to the accounts of three United States senators and one United States Cabinet member.'

'Are you one of the three, Senator dear?' Mrs Cross asked innocently.

Fall swatted Mrs Cross on her flank. 'No, I ain't. It's Borah, Cotton Tom Heflin, and Norris – the three biggest friends in Congress of those bandits running Mexico.'

'Senator Borah – the one having an affair with Alice Roosevelt?'

'Is that the only thing you women think about?' asked Fall.

'It might explain why Mr Borah needed extra money,' replied Mrs Cross. 'Which Cabinet member was getting rich?'

'Mr Houston, of the Treasury,' answered Littlemore.

Toward midnight, important men began arriving at Senator Fall's apartment at the Wardman Park Hotel. Retiring to a private study, they engaged in discussions from which Littlemore was excluded, although the detective was asked in several times to repeat the circumstances in which he'd found the documents. The meeting went on for hours. To judge from the sharp and raised voices, the discussion was contentious – occasionally acrimonious. At one point, Littlemore heard Senator Fall arguing that President Taft had 'done no less' for Wilson in 1912.

Mrs Cross identified some of the men to Littlemore: Mr Colby, the Secretary of State; Mr Baker, Secretary of War; Mr Daniels, Secretary of the Navy; Mr McAdoo, whom Littlemore had met with Commissioner Enright and the Mayor; and Mr Daugherty, the man expected to be Harding's Attorney General. 'Senator Harding himself would be here,' she said, 'but he's vacationing, lucky man. Not that he would have made any decisions anyway. These are the men who make the decisions.'

'So this McAdoo – he's the President's son-in-law? He must be as old as Wilson himself.'

'Girls like older men in this town,' replied Mrs Cross. 'Eleanor must have been about twenty when she became engaged to him. He was over fifty. But a very handsome over-fifty. You don't approve of a girl taking an interest in older men?'

'Wonder how the President felt about it,' said Littlemore, thinking of his own daughters.

'They say it broke his heart. Mr McAdoo was a member of Mr Wilson's Cabinet at the time. But Mr Wilson let him go and then, last June, took the Democratic nomination away from him. I believe Mr McAdoo might have been our next president otherwise. Poor Eleanor. I wonder how she feels now.'

'Wilson fired his own daughter's husband from the Cabinet?'

'Oh, Mr McAdoo came out all right. He's a very prominent lawyer. He's here because he knows the location of the biggest oil wells in Mexico, which belong to one of his clients. I believe Mr Brighton is an acquaintance of yours? You rode his train to New York. It's quite nice, isn't it?'

'How does everybody know what I'm doing?' asked Littlemore.

'Were there any girls on Mr Brighton's train?'

'No, there weren't.'

'Too bad. There were the one time I was invited. Well, I'm taking a rest.' It was past two in the morning. At the foot of the stairs, she turned: 'Would you mind coming upstairs, Agent Littlemore? I need to ask you something.'

Senator Fall's apartment had two floors. Evidently the bedrooms were upstairs. Littlemore went to the stairwell. The motion of Mrs Cross's figure ascending a flight of steps was even harder to turn away from than it was on flat ground. He followed her and found her in a guest bedroom, unfastening her earrings. 'Close the door,' she said.

'Why?' asked Littlemore.

'I told you – I need to ask you something.'

He closed the door. She undid her blond hair and shook it out. 'What's your question, Mrs Cross?' he asked.

She approached very near him. With her heels, she was almost exactly his height. 'Does Mrs Littlemore know how important her husband's going to be?'

'Does Mr Cross know how his wife spends her nights?'

'There is no Mr Cross anymore. He died in the war.'

'I'm sorry about that, Grace, and I'm flattered, I really am, but I can't. There are rules about this kind of thing.'

'Rules?' She slipped off her shoes, one at a time, and looked up at him, putting her hands on his chest. 'This is Washington, Agent Littlemore. The rules don't apply here.'

'Maybe not,' he said, removing her hands. 'But I still play by them.'

At five-thirty in the morning, the meeting broke up, and the well-dressed gentlemen took their leave. There was little talk, and much seriousness of expression, as the long dark overcoats made their way out of Senator Fall's apartment.

'I'm too old for this,' said Fall to Littlemore after all had departed, pouring himself another drink and easing himself into a chair. 'The war order will go out tomorrow. It'll take a while to get the troops to the border. I told them we'll need half a million soldiers.'

'A half million?' repeated Littlemore.

'Baker thinks we can do it with a fifth as many, because he's not thinking about what we're going to be doing after we win. We're going to have a country to run, for Christ's sake.' Fall took a drink, grimaced. 'Where's Grace? I need milk. Wilson's people don't want to make it public yet that Mexico bombed Wall Street. That's what I was fighting with them about. They're afraid the people will panic if they realize that the enemy can blow the hell out of our cities. I told them the American people aren't a bunch of sissies. They'll demand war when they find out. Anyway, for now Baker's not going to say anything about the bombing. They're going to play it in the papers as a response to Obregón grabbing our mines.'

'What are they going to do about Mr Houston and the three senators?'

'Nothing yet.'

'I thought they wouldn't. All we've got is an authorization from the Mexicans to transfer funds. It's not proof any money ever changed hands. It's not proof of any crime at all. We need more.'

'You've done your country a great service, son.'

'Thank you, Mr Senator,' said Littlemore.

The sun was rising when Littlemore left. The November air was sharp and clean; the smell of burning leaves was everywhere. Littlemore walked the two miles back to his hotel. When he got there, he showered, trying to figure out how he would behave around Secretary Houston and what he'd need to do at the Treasury. He stayed under the steaming water a long time.

CHAPTER EIGHTEEN

'I THINK YOU must like keeping me in the dark,' Colette said to Younger in their lurching airplane, shouting to make herself heard over the propeller's roar.

Younger had refused to give Colette any explanation of his changing their destination from Bremen to Paris except to say that he had questions only Marie Curie might be able to answer. Far below he could see the twisting Danube, whose course the pilot was evidently following. 'Yes, it must be frustrating,' he replied to Colette, 'when you've been such a model of transparency yourself.'

When they finally reached Paris, they passed so close to Mr Eiffel's tower they seemed almost about to graze it. At the airstrip a few other planes warmed themselves in the afternoon sun, haphazardly arranged, and there was even a ticket office, but the entire place was deserted. The pilot, himself a Parisian, eventually gave them a lift to the city center in a ramshackle car.

Colette pointed out favorite sights as they crossed the bridge to the Trocadéro and its spectacular crab-shaped Oriental palace, where, around calm reflecting pools, top-hatted men and parasol-carrying women promenaded. She gave the pilot directions to the Radium Institute. 'You must remember,' she said to Younger, 'that Madame is not in the best health anymore, and her sight is failing.' Colette shook her head. 'They almost rumored her to death a few years ago. Now she is the toast of Paris, and they all try to pretend it never happened.'

★   ★   ★

Viewed from the Rue Pierre Curie, the Radium Institute looked more like a comfortable bourgeois house than a scientific laboratory. 'When I first went through these doors and saw Madame's equipment inside,' said Colette, 'I thought it must be the grandest, finest laboratory in the world. Then I saw your marble halls of science in America. It must seem like nothing to you.'

Inside the equipment was indeed of very high quality: banks of electrometers, gas burners, twisted-necked glass beakers, all sparkling with scrupulously maintained sterility. Colette, after greeting old friends, eventually led Younger to the doorway of a room with a high ceiling, a large window, and a desk rather than a laboratory table. A gray-haired woman stood inside this room, instructing an assistant who was carefully packing equipment into a box.

Colette knocked on the open door and said, 'Madame?'

Marie Curie turned and stared: 'Who is it?'

'It's Colette, Madame,' said Colette.

'My child,' cried Madame Curie, beaming with delight. 'Come here. Come here at once.'

Marie Curie, fifty-two, looked older. Her upper lip was pinched with little vertical lines, her hands were spotted, her fingertips red. She wore her gray hair in a tight bun. A simple black dress covered her entirely, from tight collar to long sleeves to floor-length skirt. Her posture, however, was straight and proud, and she had one of those brows so clear, so fine, that it conveys a serenity beyond the slings and arrows of human misfortune.

'These dreadful cataracts,' Madame Curie went on. 'My surgery is next month. The doctors promise me a complete recovery. Let me look at you close up – why, you're lovelier than ever.'

Colette introduced Younger and explained to Madame Curie that he wished to ask her a few questions, if she could spare the time.

'Dr Stratham Younger,' said Madame Curie, shaking his hand. 'I know that name. Were you one of the soldiers who took training with us last year?'

'No, Madame, but I treated many with your X-ray units in France. America owes you an unrepayable debt.'

'I remember now,' she said. 'You were the one who initiated the entire program. I saw your name in the correspondence. I can't thank you enough. Your army kept us afloat last year when we had no other funding.'

Colette looked at Younger in surprise.

'The benefit was ours,' replied Younger. 'Your mobile radiological apparatus is far superior to anything we have. Which I only knew because Miss Rousseau was kind enough to volunteer her services to our men.'

'You never told me you worked with Americans,' Madame Curie said to Colette. 'We all have our secrets, don't we? Let me make some tea. How do you find America, my child?'

'Anything is possible there,' answered Colette. 'For good or bad – that's how one feels. You should see their radium refinery. Black smoke pours from the chimneys. Trucks roll up one after the other, depositing ore brought by train from mines in Colorado, two thousand miles away. The factory runs day and night – using your isolation process, Madame. They work with an ore called carnotite, not pitchblende. They say there is enough carnotite in America to make nine hundred grams of radium.'

Madame Curie went still for a long moment. 'Nine hundred grams,' she said at last. 'What I might do with ten. Forgive me. I'm not bitter. But you know that Pierre and I could have patented our discoveries long ago, when no one on earth had ever heard of radium or dreamt of radioactivity. Everyone told us to take out patents on our isolation processes, but we refused. That's not what science is for. Radium belongs to all mankind. Still, had we behaved a little more selfishly, I would not be without radium today, and with just a little radium we could do such things – cure so many – save the infant who might have grown up to be the next Newton. I have none left at all now. Only radon vapor. We have so many experiments waiting to be performed. Patients by the dozen whom we turn away.'

No one spoke.

'And how is the irrepressible Mrs Meloney?' Madame Curie asked Colette, resuming her energetic and cheerful tone. 'She is certainly one of your anything-is-possible Americans. Is there any chance she'll raise enough money to buy a gram of radium for us?'

'I'm afraid the fund is still short, Madame,' said Colette sadly. 'Very short.'

'Well, I never believed it would happen,' replied Madame Curie. 'She has a good heart, Mrs Meloney, but she is not very scientific in her thinking. Don't worry. If there is no American gram of radium for us, I won't be unhappy. I won't have to travel across the ocean and make a lot of speeches. You know how I hate that sort of thing. I'm much too tired for it. But what can I do for you, Dr Younger?'

'I had hoped,' said Younger, 'with your permission, Madame, that I might make a drawing for you. I took some radiographs of a young woman's neck not long ago. The X-rays made a pattern I had never seen before. I can draw it, though, and I was hoping you might be able to tell me if it means anything to you.'

'Madame is not a roentgenologist, Stratham,' Colette chided him. 'She works with radium, not X-rays.'

'It's quite all right,' replied Madame Curie. 'Let him make us his drawing. I'm curious.'

Younger was given pen and paper; he proceeded to draw. He filled a page with the strange, undulating, cross-hatched shadow pattern that he had seen after X-raying the McDonald girl. When he had finished, Madame Curie held the sheet of paper close to her eyes, then far away, then close again. 'The X-rays,' she said, 'didn't pass through the woman's neck.'

'Exactly,' replied Younger. 'Something blocked them.'

'Or rather interfered with them,' replied Madame Curie. 'You're sure what you saw were X-rays of a person – not an object of some kind?'

'I took them myself. The young woman had a growth on her neck and jaw. Granular. Larger than any such growth I'd ever seen.'

'I know this pattern. Quite well.'

'It's radium, isn't it?' asked Younger.

'Radium?' repeated Colette.

'Without question,' said Madame Curie.

'But how—?' asked Colette.

'Radium is roentgenopaque – impervious to X-rays,' explained Madame Curie. 'What's more, the gamma rays emitted by radium atoms have physical properties virtually identical to X-rays. As a result, the two sets of waves interfere with one another. When an object containing radium is X-rayed, what we see is an interference pattern – this pattern.'

'What would happen,' asked Younger, 'to a person who had radium inside her body for an extended period of time?'

Madame Curie set the drawing down. 'You must understand one thing about radium,' she said, 'how little we comprehend it. Nature kept it hidden for so very long. Within the atoms of radium, there is a cauldron of forces we can't see, a source of almost immeasurable power. Somehow the release of these atomic forces has profound effects on living things. On inanimate lead, radioactivity has hardly any impact at all. On a piece of lifeless paper, the same. But on the living, the effect is profound, unpredictable. Administered properly, it holds un-precedented medical potential. I myself discovered the radium treatment for cancer; in France, when we insert a needle of radium into a cancerous tumor, it is referred to as Curietherapy.'

'In America too, Madame,' said Colette.

'Some think that radioactivity may be the long-sought fountain of youth,' Madame Curie went on. 'Unquestionably it has curative power. But radium is also one of the most dangerous elements on earth. Its radiation seems to interact in some unknown fashion with the molec-ular structure of life itself. It is a fearsome poison. If a person were to ingest it in any quantity, the case would be hopeless. There is absolutely no means of destroying the substance once it enters the human body.'

★　　★　　★

Outside the Radium Institute, Colette said, 'But how could Miss McDonald have radium inside her?'

'On September sixteenth,' answered Younger, 'where were you before you met Littlemore and me – before we all went down to Wall Street?'

'I had just visited the radium clinic,' said Colette, 'at the Post-Graduate Hospital.'

'Where they use Curietherapy,' he said. 'You were telling Littlemore and me about it that morning. I knew the McDonald girl didn't have syphilis.'

'What are you saying?'

'She has cancer. A cancer of the neck or jaw.'

'Wait – you think she was a patient at the radium clinic?'

'Let's say Miss McDonald had cancer. If her doctors knew what they were doing, they would have sent her to the Post-Graduate Hospital for treatment; it's the best radium clinic in the city. But something might have gone wrong there. Maybe they botched the treatment and couldn't find the needle of radium they put inside her. Didn't I read about the Post-Graduate Hospital losing ten thousand dollars' worth of radium not long ago? Maybe they lost it inside that girl's neck. After a few weeks, she'd be in agony. She goes back to the clinic and begs them for help. They deny any wrongdoing; they refuse to admit their mistake. Suddenly she sees you. Somehow she gets it into her head that you can help her. She decides to follow you.'

'How could I help her?'

'I don't know, but what other explanation is there?'

A thought occurred to Colette: 'But Amelia left us the note at our hotel the night before – for the kidnapping ring, according to you. You're saying Miss McDonald had no connection to Amelia?'

'I don't know. But someone has to remove the radium from Miss McDonald's neck. God knows what it will do to her. I'll wire Littlemore.'

★   ★   ★

They found an international cable office in the Place de la Concorde. Younger dashed off a telegram to Littlemore:

MCDONALD GIRL HAS NEEDLE OF RADIUM IN NECK STOP CHECK WITH POST-GRADUATE HOSPITAL ON TWENTIETH STREET TO SEE IF SHE WAS PATIENT THERE STOP THEY MAY KNOW WHERE IN NECK RADIUM IS STOP RADIUM MUST BE REMOVED AT ONCE REPEAT AT ONCE

'The radiation will burn her throat away,' said Younger as they waited on line for the telegraph operator. 'It could have reached her brain by now. That's probably why she can't regain consciousness.'

'There's no evidence that radium has any effect on the brain,' objected Colette. 'You always overstate radium's danger. Madame is exposed to more radiation than anyone, and she doesn't wear one of your diver's suits.'

'Madame Curie didn't seem particularly healthy to me. She's pale as a lamb. Fatigued. You told me her blood pressure is low.'

'She's a scientist. She stays inside all day.'

'Or else she's anemic,' said Younger. 'She probably has radiation in her bloodstream after all these years.'

'Next you'll say radium caused her cataracts.'

'How do you know it didn't?'

Younger sent the cable. Outside the office, Colette saw a hotel on the other side of the Place de la Concorde. 'Can we get rooms there?' she asked.

'The Crillon?' said Younger, flinching inwardly. 'Why not?'

At Marie Curie's invitation, they attended a crowded dinner party that evening: a celebration of Poland's newfound independence and miraculous victory against the Bolsheviks. The celebration was held in a small apartment – Younger never found out whom it belonged to – where the guests ate standing up. Toasts were raised, a great deal of

Polish was spoken, and an even greater quantity of flavored vodka was drunk.

Madame Curie took Colette under her wing the entire evening as if the girl were her daughter. Colette was still wearing the stylish dress, with its low-cut back, that she'd worn in Prague. It was true that she had nothing else to wear, but Younger nevertheless considered the dress too revealing. Plumed and pomaded Polish men flocked continuously around Madame Curie, doubtless moved by the opportunity to converse with one of the world's greatest scientists. The men bowed deeply when introduced to Colette; they twisted the ends of their moustaches; they kissed her hand. Invariably Colette averted her eyes, flashing a glance at Younger as if she knew he would be watching, which he was.

After midnight, Younger lay on his four-poster bed in the Hôtel de Crillon, smoking. His jacket he had flung to the floor, but otherwise he was fully clothed. Even his shoes were on.

He had shown Colette to her room. She was skittish in the hallway, nervous, unable to work the key. He thought the strong drink might have gone to her head, except that he was pretty sure she had only sipped at it. When at last he had taken the key from her and opened the door, she practically fled into the room, leaving Younger in the corridor, with the door ajar. He closed it for her and went to his own room.

Younger stared at the gilt ceiling and at the dancing particles of smoke illuminated by the lamplight. Then he got up, extinguished his cigarette, and returned to the hallway.

He unlocked Colette's door. Her sitting room was empty. He walked past the stiff and formal Empire furniture. At the threshold of the bedroom, he saw the door to her bath cracked open. Through it, he caught glimpses of her moving back and forth, wrapped in two white towels — one for her hair, one for her torso. Apparently she hadn't heard him; she had been in the bath.

She opened the bathroom door, saw him, and froze. Her long neck was bare, her shoulders bare, her slender arms and legs bare, her skin wet.

He walked toward her. She backed away, into the bathroom, against a wall, shoulders lifted in apprehension. There was nowhere to go. The air was thick with moisture from the hot water, the mirror blurred by condensation. He took her by the arms. She struggled; he had to use more force than he expected, but he was prepared to, and he did. Their kiss went on a long time. When it was done, her body had softened, her eyes had closed, and the towel about her hair had fallen to the floor. He picked her up, carried her to the bed, and laid her down on the crisp sheets.

Colette's hair spread out darkly over the pillows. Moonlight from the window silvered her limbs, still gleaming with moisture. One of her hands lay on her chest, the other over her waist, holding the white bath towel in place. He kissed her neck. He heard her murmur, 'Please.' He heard, 'No.'

Younger said, 'Do you want me to stop?'

She answered in a whisper: 'I don't want you to ask.'

He ran his hand through her long hair. He tilted her chin and kissed her mouth. Later she called out to God, biting her lip to keep her voice down, so many times he lost count.

Still later, as they lay next to one another in the moonlight, her cheek resting on his chest, she said, 'Do you forget?'

'Forget what?'

'This. Does it fade away?'

Her head rose and fell with his breath.

'I remembered this before it happened,' he said. 'I saw it before.'

'Me too,' said Colette, smiling. 'Many times.'

She found Younger downstairs the next morning, eating breakfast at a white-linen table in a grand salon with rococo columns and a floor of checkerboard black and white marble. Daintily robed cherubs cavorted on the ceiling. Colette looked simultaneously happy and alarmed.

'Have you seen the policemen?' she asked quietly. 'They're everywhere.'

'Nothing to worry about,' replied Younger. 'Just another American male wanted for murder. Movie star, I'm told. His wife, also a movie star, was found dead on their bed on top of a hundred fur stoles, naked. It was their honeymoon. Something to eat?'

'Madame took me aside last night before we left,' said Colette, troubled, as she sat down across from him. 'I've never seen her that way. She never shows anyone her feelings.'

'What happened?'

'She burst into tears. She said that Monsieur Langevin doesn't love her anymore because she's old. That she gave up her name for him. That she let the whole world condemn her. All she wants now is her science, her experiments. But without radium, she says, she's nothing. She told me she's ready to die.'

A waiter whisked into view, set a place for Colette, and with a flourish unfolded a linen napkin for her. She barely noticed. Then she saw the piece of paper next to Younger's plate.

'You received a wire?' she asked. 'Is it from Dr Freud?'

'No. Littlemore. I went back to the cable office this morning to see if he'd replied.' Younger showed her the cable:

WHERE HECK HAVE YOU BEEN STOP YOU HAVE COURT DATE
NOVEMBER TWENTY SECOND STOP TWO PM STOP YOU
BETTER BE HERE

'Court date?' asked Colette. 'What for?'

'For assaulting Drobac.'

'Assaulting *him*?' she protested. 'He kidnapped me. He killed that woman on top of the building.'

'Yes, but he hasn't been convicted yet. In the eyes of the law, he's an innocent man.'

'You mean you could go to jail?'

'Littlemore says it's very unlikely,' he answered.

'What are you going to do?'

'Go back. I have to.'

'Why?' she asked. 'Just stay away until they convict him.'

'Littlemore got me out of prison after they arrested me. If I don't appear in court, it will be bad for him. Very bad. I have to go.'

'I'm coming with you.'

'No,' he said. 'It could still be dangerous for you.'

'How? Even if anyone were looking for me, they couldn't possibly know I came back into the country.'

'Someone was watching you in New Haven. Whoever it was may still be there.'

'I won't go to New Haven.' Colette sat quietly for a long time. At last she said, 'I have to come with you; I'm going to raise the money for Madame's radium. Mrs Meloney told me I could do it. She said I just had to be nicer to one rich man, and we could make up the whole shortfall. Besides, Luc will be with Dr Freud for at least two months. I can't stay here by myself and worry about him.'

That afternoon, they caught a train to Rouen from the Saint-Lazare station. The next day, they went on to Le Havre, where they boarded a ship for New York.

With her hand at his elbow, Colette allowed Younger to lead her on an exploratory tour of their ocean liner. They wandered through a glass-domed rotunda, observed ladies and gentlemen playing *belote* in the hall of Louis XIV, and took tea in a blue-tiled Moorish saloon. In an empty smoking room, they kissed beneath a gently swaying crystal chandelier. And many levels down, as a hard rain began to fall, causing passengers to scurry indoors, they saw a thousand human beings confined to less opulent and more redolent quarters.

'You're corrupting me,' said Colette as they climbed the stairs back to the upper deck – the first-class deck. A steward readmitted them into the Louis XIV hall.

'You like it.'

'I feel like Dante,' she said, 'emerging from the inferno, with you as my Virgil.'

'No, you're Beatrice, and you'll rise to heaven while I end up below. But,' he considered, 'I'd pay the price again. I'd pay it every time.'

'What price?'

'Eternal damnation,' he answered, 'for a night in your arms.'

'Only one night?'

That evening, despite a fierce storm outside, the ocean liner erupted with merrymaking, toasts, and the blowing of party whistles. In all the dining rooms and lounges of every class, bands and orchestras played American music while the rain beat on the portholes.

'What's happening?' asked Colette. They were descending the grand red-carpeted stairwell into an Edwardian ballroom. Dancers whirled around the floor.

'The United States has elected a new president,' said Younger.

'Who won?'

'A man named Harding.'

They took a seat at a table in silence.

'What's the matter?' she asked him.

'Nothing.'

'All right,' she said. 'Then ask me to dance.'

He did.

Well after midnight, they returned to their luxurious stateroom. 'Only one room for both of us?' she asked him, cheeks flushed. 'Monsieur is very presumptuous. Is my corruption never to end?'

The next morning, in their cabin bed, she was happier than he had ever seen her. Lying on their backs, she made him extend a leg in the air and put hers alongside it. She tried to persuade him that despite the difference in their overall height, her leg was almost as long as his. Certainly it was smoother and more appealing in shape.

In the afternoon, however, as they strolled through the ship's exotic outdoor palm court – open to first-class passengers only – she grew contemplative. 'What does Dr Freud mean,' she asked, 'when he says I may be the cause of Luc's condition?'

'I don't know,' said Younger, telling the truth.

'I always thought I could take care of him.'

'You did take care of him.'

'But what if I did the wrong thing keeping him with me all these years?' she asked. 'What if I wanted him to be different? What if I wanted him to be mute?'

'Why?'

'So that I wouldn't have to be alone.'

'Oh, stop it,' Younger replied. 'Pure self-indulgence.'

'You're the one who said I didn't love him.'

'I never said that,' replied Younger.

'You said it with your eyes,' she answered. 'Because I left Luc behind when I took the train to Braunau. You thought killing Hans Gruber was more important to me than taking care of my own brother.'

Younger didn't answer. He hadn't thought any such thing, but she must have.

'If I had died,' she said, 'you would have raised him, wouldn't you?'

'That's why you wanted me to come to Vienna.'

She tightened her grasp around his arm. 'You would have done it – raised him – wouldn't you?'

'If you had died chasing Heinrich?'

'Yes.'

'No, I would have put him in a home for deaf-mutes. Where he belongs. So that he wouldn't remind me of you. But then he couldn't have reminded me of you because I would have killed myself. Besides, you wouldn't have wanted me to raise him: I'm a pauper. Have I mentioned to you how much I have left?'

'No.'

'I don't have anything left. Our stateroom took the last of it. Fortunately, that comes with meals for two, so we won't starve until we reach America.' He stopped, disengaged himself from her arm, and put his hands in his pockets. 'I'm serious. I'm ashamed of my poverty. I should have told you about it. I'm not penniless. I still have my house in Boston, and I believe Harvard will take me back as a professor. But I seduced you under false pretenses. No, I did. The worst cad could not have behaved more basely. All this luxury – first-class cabins, grand ballrooms – you'll never see it again. You'd be perfectly justified to leave me now that you know the actual state of things.'

'What a long speech,' she said, taking his arm again. 'And so foolish. I like you much better poor.'

PART 4

CHAPTER NINETEEN

TELEGRAPHIC INSTRUCTIONS FLEW from station to station, east to west, across the United States on the morning of November 18, 1920 – the day after Littlemore found the secret cache of Mexican documents. Their point of origin was the War Department in Washington, DC. The most important of these wires was issued to Fort Houston in San Antonio, Texas. It ordered Major General James G. Harbord, commander of the Unites States Army, Second Division, to mobilize for immediate deployment to the Mexican border.

―

Colette Rousseau held Younger's hand at the ship's rail, steaming into New York Harbor that same morning. All around them, passengers crooned over the fantastical Manhattan skyline, lit by the morning sun. 'This time, even I think your skyscrapers are beautiful,' said Colette.

Over the course of the voyage, they had discovered certain intimacies about each other. She would insist, at night, on his extinguishing every light and candle before emerging from the dressing room in her slip and darting into bed, where she would pull the bedclothes up to her chin. She had an additional scruple – that he was not to be naked in her presence. She seemed to like it when he took off his shirt, but that was as undressed as she was prepared to have him.

'Strange,' said Younger. 'I was going to say that this time even I find them unsettling.'

★   ★   ★

From coast to coast, the newspapers that morning were filled with strange items concerning Mexico. There were rumors – unattributed to any official sources – of a military mobilization and of an imminent threat that American-owned oil wells were to be nationalized. From Washington, the following was reported:

> The Mexican Embassy issued a statement last night declaring that it had been authorized by General Obregon, President-elect of Mexico, to deny that Elias L. Torres, who last Tuesday extended an invitation to Senator Harding to visit Mexico, was acting on behalf of the Mexican government. 'The Mexican Embassy,' the statement said, 'is in receipt of a telegram from General Obregon, in which he categorically denies that Elias Torres is his representative.'

No further details were offered to explain this curious report.

Also that morning, in an antiseptic room in New York City, with perfectly white walls and a single hospital bed in the middle, a girl with long red hair opened her eyes. She tried to speak, but something in her mouth prevented her from doing so. She would have removed this impediment, but her wrists were tied to the bed rails with leather straps.

'Will she be clean?' asked a male voice. Whoever spoke was out of her sight. She tried to turn her head, but couldn't.

'Yes,' answered a man she could see, wearing a white medical coat.

'The last one wasn't clean.'

'It's acidic. It will clean.'

'Will it hurt?' asked the male voice, out of her sight.

'Probably,' said the man in the white jacket.

'Can you give her something?'

'For the pain – now?'

'Please.'

The white-coated man came to her bedside. She felt his hands on her arm and then the prick of a needle. Presently, her fears and wretchedness subsided. A warmth spread through her body. It felt pleasant, comforting. She wanted more.

The man she hadn't seen – and, as the room began to swim, still couldn't see clearly – now came to her bedside. He gently parted her lips. Between those lips, a gag pulled against her cheeks, tightly tied.

The man inserted something bristly into her mouth. It was a toothbrush. He was brushing her teeth, above and below the gag. He went about it methodically, thoroughly, minutely. He brushed in tiny circles, first her incisors, then her canines, then her molars, front and back, upper and lower.

The doctor had been wrong: it didn't hurt at all. It wasn't even unpleasant. At least not at first. Then she felt a burning on her tongue and in her throat. The gag caused her to choke. Tears began to run from her eyes. The man stroked the tears from her eyes, gently. He parted her hospital gown and looked at her white, soft throat and bosom.

'I like this one,' he said. 'No defects. Can't you give her more?'

'She'll be unconscious,' said the man in the white coat.

'I don't want her unconscious. Can you make her – almost unconscious?'

She felt another prick in her arm. Soon the man with the toothbrush set to work again, finding every crevice and crown of her teeth, cleaning her, cleaning. The paste burned her terribly, but she didn't mind it anymore. The pleasant, generous warmth spread deeper into her limbs and chest and elsewhere. Then everything became confused, tangled, and she couldn't understand what was happening. She was pulled, mentally as well as physically, in two different directions; someone was now scrubbing at her neck and shoulders with the same astringent paste, which hurt and which she wished would stop, but there was also more of the heavenly flooding warmth, which she wanted to last forever.

★ ★ ★

Littlemore went to Secretary Houston's office first thing that morning. Denied permission to enter, he waited in the hallway, reading the newspapers, until, an hour later, Houston appeared.

'Can't you see I'm busy, Littlemore?' asked Houston as he hurried down the corridor, the detective in his wake.

'Is it the Mexican business, sir?'

'Mexican business?' Houston stopped. 'What do you know about it?'

'Been reading the papers.'

The Secretary set off again, followed by Littlemore. 'Well, what is it?' asked Houston.

'Just wondering who chose the date for the transfer of the gold.'

'What? Why?'

'I think it may unlock the whole puzzle, sir.'

'The date? I don't see why,' said Houston. 'Everyone inside the Department knew when the gold was going to be transferred. In any event, it was before my time. The move had been planned for years. The new Assay Office was designed specifically for the purpose. Long before my time.'

'You didn't have anybody advising you on the date, Mr Houston – making suggestions, reviewing the timing?'

'Advising me on the date? I had nothing to do with it.'

On checking in, Younger immediately had the hotel operator ring police headquarters. Informed that Captain Littlemore no longer worked there, he obtained a number for the detective in Washington. Some minutes later, he reached Littlemore in his Treasury office.

'What are you doing in Washington?' Younger asked.

'Long story,' said Littlemore. 'What were you doing in France?'

'Long story. Did they get the radium out of the McDonald girl?'

'Not exactly. I told her doctor what you said; he looked at me like I was nuts. He said she has syphilis, not radium. And I checked with the Post-Graduate Hospital. They've got no record of her.'

'She doesn't have syphilis. What's the doctor's name?'

'Lyme,' said Littlemore. 'Dr Frederick Lyme at the Sloane Hospital for Women. Listen, Doc – Drobac's out of prison.'

The line crackled; Younger said nothing.

'You still there?' asked Littlemore.

'I'm here,' said Younger. 'What is this, the Perils of Pauline? How can he be out of prison?'

'Because you jumped bail, for Pete's sake,' said Littlemore, 'and took the Miss and the boy with you. His lawyer told the court you fled the country. Whereabouts unknown. The Miss was the complainant. How are we supposed to prosecute a kidnapping when the victims have left the jurisdiction? I told them you'd be back, but the judge ruled we had to let him go.'

'So the murderer's on the street while I'm to stand trial?'

'It's not a trial. It's a bail revocation hearing. The judge ordered it after he heard you were out of the country. If you don't show, your bail gets revoked, a warrant issues for your arrest, and I have to pay up on your bail bond. You got to be there, Doc.'

'I'll be there.'

'Say – I'm catching the afternoon train back to town. Why don't you and the Miss come over for dinner?'

A bellboy rang, delivering to Younger and Colette a packet of telegrams that had arrived during the last week. 'From Freud,' said Younger. 'I let him know where we'd be staying.'

'Open them up,' said Colette eagerly.

The first of the telegrams was sent only a few days after they boarded their ship for New York:

7 NOV. 1920

BOY FINE. TWO BRITISH PUPILS HAVE TAKEN LIKING TO HIM. VISITED ZOO. STRONGLY SUSPECT INVOLVEMENT OF FATHER IN BOY'S SYMPTOMS. PLEASE CONSULT MISS ROUSSEAU AND ASK

AGAIN WHETHER SHE RECALLS ANY MISTREATMENT OF HER OR
BROTHER AT FATHER'S HANDS.

FREUD

'Mistreatment of me?' said Colette. 'That's the second time he's asked. What does he mean?'

Younger, who knew exactly what Freud meant, didn't answer that question. 'What about Luc? Did your father ever — I don't know — beat him?'

'Father doted on Luc. He was the kindest man in the world. What does the next one say?'

Younger opened the second telegram:

11 NOV. 1920

IGNORE PREVIOUS WIRE. BOY HAS BEGUN SPEAKING TO ME. FOR
NOW HE WHISPERS, BUT I EXPECT COMPLETE CURE. WEEKS NOT
MONTHS. MORE SHORTLY.

FREUD

'*Mon dieu*,' said Colette excitedly. 'Open the next one.'

Younger did so:

13 NOV. 1920

BOY HAS RECURRENT DREAM. HE IS BACK IN BEDROOM OF HOUSE
WHERE BORN. IT IS MIDDLE OF NIGHT. GOES TO A WINDOW. SEES
WOLVES LURKING IN TREE WATCHING HIM. DREAM IS REVERSAL
OF LATENT CONTENT. BOY DREAMS OF BEING LOOKED AT
BECAUSE HE SAW SOMETHING HE WAS NOT SUPPOSED TO SEE.
UNDOUBTEDLY FATHER INVOLVED, BUT ALMOST CERTAINLY ALSO
SISTER.

FREUD

Colette was perplexed. 'Why am I involved?' she asked.

'There's one more,' said Younger. He read it:

17 NOV. 1920
SETBACK. LUC HAS STOPPED SPEAKING. WILL NOT COMMUNICATE
WITH ANYONE NOT IN WHISPER NOT IN WRITING NOT EVEN BY
GESTURE. PLEASE URGE MISS ROUSSEAU NOT TO BE ALARMED.
TEMPORARY REGRESSION NOT UNCOMMON IN ANALYSIS. POSSIBLY
POSITIVE SIGN.

FREUD

'How could it be a positive sign?' asked Colette.

'If it was brought on by their getting close to the source of the problem.'

'What does that mean?'

Younger ran a hand through his hair. 'I don't believe in psycho-analysis. I told you.'

'But if you did believe, what would it mean?'

'The way Freud would see it is this,' he said. 'Luc has a memory from early childhood – from a time when he saw something forbidden or wished for something so wrong he had to suppress all conscious-ness of it. This memory doesn't like to stay hidden; it tries to escape the repression, to force its way into consciousness. That's what produces a patient's symptoms.'

'What don't you believe?' she asked.

'I don't believe in the wishes that Freud attributes to children. And I don't believe in repressed childhood memories coming to light years later. It's like a – like a too-neatly-tied-up ending in a novel.'

Colette considered for a moment – and announced that she trusted Dr Freud.

Newspapermen so crowded the office of Senator Albert Fall that Littlemore was barely able to squeeze in. The reporters' primary question was whether the Senator could confirm that United States troops were deploying to the Mexican border.

'That's right, gentlemen,' said Fall. 'The Second Division is on its way.'

'What are their orders, Mr Senator?'

'Can't say,' answered Fall. 'But let's not get all out of joint. I'm heading to Mexico myself. Going to attend Señor Obregón's inauguration. I'm sure all parties would like to see our disputes resolved peacefully.'

'What will you tell General Obregón, Mr Senator?'

'I'll tell him to keep his hands off our oil. And that having America as your friend is a whole lot smarter than having us as your enemy.'

After the conference, Littlemore voiced surprise at Senator Fall's planned visit to Mexico City. 'Don't you think it might be dangerous, Mr Fall?'

'I'd imagine so,' replied the Senator. 'For somebody.'

On the express to New York, Littlemore read a stack of afternoon newspapers, which, since he knew more than the journalists did, filled him with a sense of unreality but also of foreboding, as if he had a clairvoyant's foreknowledge of an impending catastrophe that could not be averted. In Washington, the papers reported, Roberto Pesqueira, confidential agent of the Mexican Embassy, had to be forcibly restrained at a meeting of American businessmen after insisting on his country's right to its own natural resources. In Los Angeles, Mexicans were purchasing munitions in dangerously large quantities. In Mexico itself, American citizens had begun fleeing the country.

Littlemore next removed from his briefcase the architectural plans for the Assay Office in lower Manhattan. The new vaults of the Assay Building were closer to impregnable than any bank he'd ever seen. They were eighty-five feet below ground, reinforced with three separate layers of steel and concrete, accessible only by a single door through a four-foot-wide tunnel, and surrounded by alarm systems, weapons caches, even food and water supplies in case of siege. The plans had been approved in 1917 by then-Secretary of the Treasury William G. McAdoo. A different Treasury Secretary's signature appeared at the bottom of the other document Littlemore had on his lap.

It was a work order authorizing the transfer of the nation's gold reserves from the Sub-Treasury in New York City to the adjacent Assay Office via overhead bridge commencing the night of September 15, 1920. The detective had found the order crumpled in the back of a filing drawer. It was signed, as Littlemore knew it would be, by Secretary David Houston.

Younger and Colette went to the Littlemores' that night for dinner. 'What are you doing in Washington, Jimmy?' asked Colette. 'It must be very important.'

'Not much – just starting a war,' he replied. They expected him to say more, but he didn't.

After dinner, while the women did the dishes, Younger and Littlemore sat without speaking at the table, the detective scraping his fork back and forth along his dessert plate. 'Littlemore,' said Younger.

'Huh?'

'You're out-silencing me.'

'Wars don't always go the way they're planned, do they?' asked Littlemore.

'They never go the way they're planned,' said Younger.

'Remember when you said that the Wall Street bombing was a way to assassinate the people? What do they want, the assassins? How about those Serbs who assassinated that Austrian duke guy in 1914? What did they want?'

'War.'

'They got it, didn't they?'

'Beyond their wildest dreams.'

★   ★   ★

The next morning, newspapers reported that Senator Fall, who the previous day had announced his intention to attend the inauguration of General Obregón, had been denied the visa required for entry into Mexico by confidential agent Roberto Pesqueira of the Mexican Embassy. In response to questioning, Mr Pesqueira would say only that the Senator was an enemy of the Mexican people.

Meanwhile, the United States army was massing on the Mexican border. Dispatches from Mexico City asserted that President-elect Obregón had come down with a sudden and unexplained illness, preventing him from attending his scheduled preinaugural events.

Colette had arranged a meeting that morning with Mrs William B. Meloney, chairwoman of the Marie Curie Radium Fund. Younger made her pack her things before they left.

'Why?' asked Colette.

'We're changing hotels.' In part this move was precautionary. Younger hadn't told anyone but Freud where he and Colette would be staying, but someone keeping an eye on the harbor might conceivably have spotted them. Or someone monitoring the transatlantic cables might possibly have seen Freud's wires. Younger's chief motivation, however, was pecuniary. He needed cheaper lodging.

They took the subway to Mrs Meloney's house on West Twelfth Street. Younger insisted on accompanying Colette there. Then he headed uptown, making Colette swear not to leave before he returned.

When Littlemore came down from the elevated train on his way to work that morning, he was so deep in thought that he got out at his old station, Grand Street, by mistake. He was halfway to police head-quarters before realizing his error. There was something the detective didn't like, but he didn't know what it was.

At the Sloane Hospital for Women on Fifty-ninth Street, Younger gave his name and asked for Dr Frederick Lyme. A short time later,

Younger was greeted by a man of about forty, prematurely gray, with wide-rimmed glasses, a clipboard, and a stethoscope over his white jacket.

'What can I do for you, Dr Younger?' asked Lyme, taking his glasses off and placing them in a pocket.

'I'm here about the McDonald girl. You spoke with a policeman named Littlemore; I'm the one who sent him. The girl has radium inside her neck. She needs an operation immediately.'

'Radium,' said Lyme lightly. 'How could Miss McDonald possibly have gotten radium inside her? I already told the policeman the idea was quite absurd. I have nothing further to say. Good day.'

'Cancer,' said Younger, 'is the most likely cause of the growth on her neck. If she was diagnosed with cancer, she could very well have taken a radium treatment for it. I believe the needle of radium is still in her neck.'

Lyme put his clipboard to his chest: 'Miss McDonald never took any radium treatments, and cancer did not cause her tumor. Syphilis did. Surely you're aware that third-stage syphilis produces gummas – granulomas, growths – which can appear anywhere on the body. Syphilis was also the cause of her dementia. She had already begun raving. She had delusions of persecution. Perhaps she said something?'

'No.'

'Syphilis was found in 1913 to be the cause of general paresis,' said Lyme. 'Or don't you keep up with the literature?'

'I'm familiar with the finding,' said Younger. 'Dr Lyme, I took X-rays of the girl.'

'How? When?'

'When she was at Bellevue. The X-rays clearly indicated the presence of radium.'

'Ridiculous. Your X-ray machine was obviously malfunctioning. Either that or you didn't know how to operate it.'

'I've confirmed the diagnosis with Madame Curie herself in Paris. There was no malfunction; radium produces the specific fluoroscopic pattern I found on her X-rays. At least open up the tumor and have a look. It can't hurt her.'

'It can't help her either,' said Lyme. 'She's dead. Now if you'll excuse me.'

When he finally reached his office on Wall Street, Littlemore had the operator ring Senator Fall's chambers in Washington. It took over an hour before he managed to speak with the Senator. 'What if the Mexican government didn't order the bombing, Mr Fall?' asked the detective. 'What if it was just one or two rogue Mexican officers?'

'You're not getting cold feet, are you, son? The war's going to be a cakewalk. Our boys will be home by Christmas.'

'Obregón says Torres had no connection to the Mexican government,' said Littlemore.

'What do you expect him to say after what you found in Torres's room?' the Senator replied.

'There's no proof, Mr Fall.'

'Courtroom talk. Wars aren't fought in courtrooms. You keep your eye on the ball, son. We got the signature of the Mexican financial minister on letterhead paper and a goddamn terrorist boot camp run by their military. That's more proof than we need.'

'What if it was just some bad apples, not the whole government?'

'I'll be honest with you,' said Fall. 'I don't care if the bombing was ordered by El Presidente de la Republico or El Ministerio de la Financio. What difference would it make? We still got to clean out Mexico City. Hunt down the sons of bitches who bombed us. Wipe out that boot camp. If Obregón wasn't behind it, that means he can't control his bad apples, so we got to put in somebody who can – before they spoil the whole damn barrel.'

Static filled the line.

'Tell you what, son,' said Fall. 'I'm coming up your way to meet with Bill McAdoo on Saturday. Got to figure out what we're going to do about Houston. Tricky business funding a war when your Secretary of the Treasury is being paid off by your enemy. We always have dinner at the Oyster Bar. Why don't you meet us there?'

'The Oyster Bar?' said Littlemore.

'You know the Oyster Bar – in the terminal?'

'Sure, I know it. Sounds good, Mr Fall.'

A short while later, Littlemore was still standing by the telephone.

Younger knocked at the door of Mrs William Meloney's townhouse on West Twelfth Street, which was filled with purring cats and shelves full of testimonials to Marie Curie.

'These are letters,' Mrs Meloney explained to Younger, 'from cancer patients who have been cured with radium therapy. I'm collecting them for Madame Curie when she arrives. One is from a botanist who wants to send Madame Curie an entire hothouse of flowers. We must raise the rest of the money. We simply must.'

'It's all arranged,' said Colette with excitement. 'We're going to visit Mr Brighton's luminous-paint factories tomorrow – one in New Jersey, one in Manhattan. Mrs Meloney says there's a chance at a very large donation.'

'Mr Brighton,' said the older woman knowingly, 'is very close to contributing an even larger amount than he did before. As much as seventy-five thousand dollars. He told me so himself. All it will take is a little feminine push.'

'Seventy-five thousand dollars – can you believe it, Stratham?' said Colette. 'That's more than we need. The radium will be paid for.'

On their way back uptown, Younger told Colette about his visit to Sloane Hospital. 'Lyme insists it was syphilis,' he muttered. 'I should have asked to see the Wassermann test. I've never heard of tertiary syphilis in a girl that age.'

Littlemore walked down the steps of the Sub-Treasury and into Wall Street. Next door, soldiers were still stationed in front of the Assay

Office, where deep in basement vaults the nation's gold reserves were stored. He crossed the street to the Morgan Bank.

Wall Street was crowded as always. Though in the way of the hurrying pedestrians, Littlemore walked slowly up and down the length of the sidewalk outside the bank, inspecting the places on its exterior wall where the concrete had been scored and gouged in the bombing.

Everyone had assumed this damage was caused by the bomb and the shrapnel. Littlemore examined the pockmarks more closely. It was strange that they were concentrated below and around a first-floor window. Some of the uneven gouges – particularly the larger ones – might well have been the product of shrapnel, but most of the pockmarks were small and round, as if the concrete had been repeatedly struck by bullets.

Littlemore went next to City Hall. In the basement land offices, he pored over the gas, water, sewer, and subway maps for lower Manhattan. It took him hours. He was pretty certain he wouldn't find anything, and he didn't. Ordinary plumbing, power, and gas lines ran under Wall Street. No sewer pipes crossed from Wall to Pine. A subway had been announced for Nassau Street in 1913, with a station at the corner of Broad and Wall, near where the bomb went off. But unlike the other eighty subway routes announced in 1913, the Nassau line had never been built.

The hotel into which Younger moved was the kind that provided in every room a set of old, unmatching utensils and an electric hot plate. Seeing these implements, Colette declared that she would cook. She took Younger shopping – at a greengrocer's, a butcher's, a baker's. It was, she said, like being in Paris. Or would have been, if there had only been a bottle of wine to buy.

The Littlemores had dinner in their Fourteenth Street apartment all together – parents, grandmother, and innumerable children. Littlemore's mind was not on the meal. Twice he called James Jr by the name of Samuel, which was their youngest boy, and he called Samuel Peter, even though Peter didn't look anything like Samuel, being twice his age. Betty, feeding Lily in the high chair, had never seen her husband so distracted.

'You know,' said Younger to Colette as they ate across their tiny candlelit dining table, 'there's another possibility.'

'Of what?'

'Of how radium cures cancer.' He cut into the chop she had made him. 'What if there's a kind of switch in every one of our cells that turns on or off the process of cell death – and what if radioactivity flips it? In cancer cells, the switch is off; the cells don't die; that's why they keep replicating, endlessly. When radioactivity hits those cells, it turns the switch on, so the cells start dying again. That cures the cancer.'

'But then in good cells, radioactivity would – it would—'

'Turn the switch off,' said Younger. 'Make the cells stop dying. Cause cancer.'

'Radium doesn't cause cancer.'

'How do you know?'

'One medicine can't both cure a disease and cause it. That's impossible.'

'Why?'

'Do you know why you are so suspicious of radioactivity?' asked Colette. 'I think it's because you didn't discover it. If you had been the first to think of God, you'd believe in Him, too.'

In her antiseptic room, the girl with long red hair knew what it meant when the man in the white coat came in. She strained against the leather straps; she tried to scream, but the gag muffled her mouth.

She also knew from the man's presence that she would soon feel the pinprick of a needle in her arm, and after that the gratifying warmth that would spread so comfortably up and down her limbs.

Soon the other man was brushing her teeth again, upper and lower, front and back, taking his time.

A folded note slid under Younger's hotel room door well after midnight. Younger read it, threw on some clothes, and went down to the front desk. 'You're out late,' he said.

'What's the world's strongest acid?' asked Jimmy Littlemore, chewing his toothpick.

'Strongest for what purpose?' asked Younger.

'Cutting through metal.'

'Aqua regia. It's a mixture of nitric and sulfuric acids.'

'Can you travel with it?' asked Littlemore. 'You know, bring it with you?'

'It's safe enough in glass. Why?'

'I might need some help,' said Littlemore. 'Could be a little dangerous. You around tomorrow night?'

Younger looked at him.

'It's important, Doc.'

'To whom?' asked Younger.

'To the country. To two countries.'

Younger still didn't answer.

'The war,' added Littlemore.

'The war's going to be a mismatch,' said Younger. 'A single division of ours is larger than the entire Mexican army. Our generals could go in blindfolded, and we'd still win it.'

'Not trying to win it,' said Littlemore. 'Trying to stop it.'

The front pages of the newspapers the next morning were full of the escalating crisis in Mexico. President-elect Obregón had not been seen in public for two days. On the border, the United States army, Second Division, had beaten to full war strength. American warplanes had begun crossing into Mexican airspace, patrolling south all the way to Mexico City.

The *Wall Street Journal* demanded an immediate invasion to protect American interests. So did the governor of the great state of Texas. In Washington, high-ranking gentlemen in the Wilson Administration, together with men whose offices would be correspondingly lofty under Harding, issued a joint statement addressed to General Obregón, President-elect of Mexico. The statement set forth the conditions necessary to a peaceful resolution of the crisis, including an amendment to the Mexican Constitution prohibiting confiscation of American-owned subsoil interests.

According to rumors circulating on both sides of the border, the American war was to commence the next day, with the goal of occupying Mexico City by November twenty-fifth, the day of General Obregón's inauguration. It was widely asserted that the Americans would allow the inauguration to go forward – but with an individual of their own choice taking office.

Younger accompanied Colette once again to Mrs Meloney's house on West Twelfth Street, where a car was waiting to take them to Mr Brighton's luminous-paint factory in Orange, New Jersey. The driver was the redoubtable Samuels. Younger said goodbye, waiting on the curb until he was sure no one had followed them. Then he took the subway uptown. The day was brisk and overcast.

Passing warehouses and slaughterhouses, Younger walked to Tenth Avenue, where he entered Columbia University's College of Physicians and Surgeons, the medical school attached to the Sloane Hospital for Women. Younger knew two researchers who worked there. He found one of them – his name was Joseph Johanson – in his laboratory. Younger asked him to call the hospital to see if he could pull the charts on a female patient named McDonald under the care of Dr Frederick Lyme.

'There's no Dr Lyme at Sloane,' replied Johanson.

'There was yesterday,' said Younger. 'I talked to him.'

Johanson looked dubious but made the call. Presently they learned that there was indeed a patient file for a Quinta McDonald, but that all her charts were gone, having been removed on instructions from the family. What remained was a death certificate, which indicated that the patient had died five days previously from syphilis.

'Who signed the death certificate?' asked Younger.

Johanson relayed the question to the nurse, who reported that the signature appeared to be that of an attorney by the name of Gleason. She also said that she had never heard of a Dr Lyme at the hospital.

'Wait a minute: Frederick Lyme – I know that name,' said Johanson after ringing off. He took down from a bookcase a large loose-leaf binder: a directory of the faculty of Columbia University. 'Let me just – here he is. He's not a doctor. He's in physiology. Not even a Ph.D.'

'Why would a physiologist,' asked Younger, 'be treating a patient in your hospital?'

Colette and Mrs Meloney, received like dignitaries by Mr Arnold Brighton at his luminous-paint factory in New Jersey, were each presented with a diamond stickpin – a token, Brighton said, of his appreciation. Mrs Meloney was delighted. Colette tried to look it.

The factory, Brighton proudly showed them, operated under the scrupulous supervision of laboratory scientists, who took care that precisely measured micrograms of radium were properly added to the drums of blue and yellow paint, which were then sealed and spun to ensure uniform hue and dilution. Lead screens separated the radium-infused paint from the rest of the factory floor. Radioactivity detectors were located in various spots to sound an instant alarm in case of a radiation leak.

Mrs Meloney brought up the subject of the Marie Curie Radium Fund.

'Yes, Marie Curie,' said Brighton reverently. 'You can't quantify what the world owes that woman. Even Samuels would have difficulty measuring it. He's a gifted accountant, my Samuels. You wouldn't guess it from looking at him. It just shows you can't judge a man by his cover. Isn't that right, ladies?'

Colette and Mrs Meloney agreed that you could not.

'Was I saying something?' asked Brighton.

'Our debt to Madame Curie,' prompted Mrs Meloney.

'Yes, of course. The profit from my radium mines in Colorado, the profit from my luminous-paint sales – I owe it all to Marie Curie. Of course, I do own a few other little things here and there.'

'Mr Brighton,' Mrs Meloney explained to Colette, 'is one of our nation's great oilmen.'

'That's how we discovered radium in Colorado,' said Brighton cheerfully. 'We were sinking exploratory lines for oil.'

Mrs Meloney gently reminded Brighton of the Fund.

'Fund?' he asked. 'What Fund?'

'The Radium Fund, Mr Brighton.'

'The Fund, the Fund, of course,' he said. 'Marvelous idea, yes – I can't wait to meet Madame Curie. And I can't wait for you to see my factory in Manhattan, where we put the paint on the watch dials. I am one of the largest employers of women in New York, Miss Rousseau, did you know that?'

Colette politely denied such knowledge. With a theatrical sigh, Mrs Meloney declared, 'What a pity that Madame Curie will not be coming to America after all. The Fund is still woefully short of what it needs. Sixty-five thousand dollars short, despite the magnanimous contribution with which you started us off, Mr Brighton.'

'Sixty-five thousand dollars short,' repeated Brighton, with strange good cheer. 'It would be a great relief to know whether I will be making another donation, wouldn't it?'

'We are most eager to know, Mr Brighton,' replied Mrs Meloney.

'No more so than I, Mrs Meloney,' said Brighton. 'No more so than I.'

Colette and Mrs Meloney exchanged glances at this mysterious remark.

Younger called next at Columbia University's Department of Physiology, located on the grand new campus far uptown, where one of the buildings bore his mother's maiden name. The secretary in the small physiology building confirmed that Frederick Lyme was a member of the faculty.

'What's his specialty?' asked Younger.

'Toxicology,' said the secretary. 'Industrial toxicology.'

'Is he in?'

'Mr Lyme is out all day with clients.'

'Clients?' repeated Younger.

'Yes – the people he consults for.'

'Who would they be?'

'I'm sorry,' said the secretary. 'You'll have to speak with Mr Lyme about that.'

At the Sub-Treasury on Wall Street, Littlemore welcomed into his office a lean, tall, towheaded man with an infectious smile. The fellow was, according to his own estimation, very well indeed. He thanked Littlemore for dealing with the Popes and arranging his release from the Amityville Sanitarium. 'What can I do for you in return, Detective?' asked Edwin Fischer.

'You can meet me uptown tonight,' said Littlemore.

CHAPTER TWENTY

ON LATE NOVEMBER evenings a change comes to the air of lower Manhattan. Biting currents from the Atlantic pour into the harbor at the southern tip of the island. There, the massive skyscrapers function as wind tunnels, channeling and compressing the turbulent air until its force is so great it will halt a grown man in his tracks and, if he doesn't put his shoulders to it, send him reeling.

Littlemore, passing the dark Sub-Treasury Building in the shadows of Wall Street, was used to that wind. The sign of this acquaintance was that he walked at a sixty-degree angle when facing it and never took his hand from his hat. Secretary Houston, arriving by car at the neighboring, brilliantly lit Assay Office, still guarded by a platoon of federal troops, was not used to it. The sign of this unfamiliarity was that he lost his top hat the moment he stepped out of his long black-and-gold Packard.

Another well-dressed gentleman emerged from the car as well. Although their conversation was in whispers, the wind carried snatches to Littlemore, who could hear Houston assuring the man that payment would be forthcoming. The gentleman shook Houston's hand and crossed the street to the Morgan Bank.

Secretary Houston surveyed the rank of infantrymen in the glare of military klieg lights. His top hat lay only a foot from one of the soldiers, who stood at sharp attention, making no motion to come to the Secretary's haberdashery assistance. Houston strode to the building's steps to retrieve his hat, but as if the Secretary were the straight man in a vaudeville prank, at the moment he bent to pick it up, a malicious wind plucked up the hat and spun it into the shadows of the street. It happened to come to rest near the detective, who dusted it off and, stepping into the light, offered it to the Treasury Secretary.

'Agent Littlemore,' said Houston. 'Lurking in wait is becoming habitual with you. I don't think I approve. How did you know I would be here?'

'From your calendar,' replied Littlemore.

'You went through my private calendar?'

'Your secretary left it open on the desk. Was that Mr Lamont, sir?'

'Yes. The bankers are gathering in force tonight. Never a good sign.'

'The war with Mexico?'

'Obviously.'

'Worried about it, Mr Houston?'

'Blast it – why does everyone keep asking me that? I'm worried to the extent that the nation's treasure will be called on. What do you know about this Mexican business? More than what you read in the papers, I think. Where are you getting your information, Littlemore? And what are you doing here?'

'Just wanted to have a look inside the Assay Office, Mr Houston.'

'Why?'

'Maybe the stolen gold's hidden inside there. That would explain why no one saw the getaway truck. They wouldn't have seen a getaway truck if there was no getaway truck.'

'Nonsense. I've been in the Assay Office a dozen times since September sixteenth. The gold's not here.'

The detective scratched the back of his head. 'With nearly a billion dollars of gold in this building, sir, you can tell that the four million we're looking for isn't here?'

'Yes, I can. I can also tell that the period of your usefulness to me has come to an end. But that won't disturb you, since you haven't been working for me for some time already. You're Senator Fall's man, aren't you? What did he promise you?'

'Did you happen to look for the gold in the hidden safe room on the second floor, Mr Houston? The one behind the wall of the super-intendent's office?'

A new expression flashed momentarily in Houston's eyes. Littlemore's practiced eye recognized it at once: guilt. Houston whispered angrily: 'How do you know about that room?'

'From the architectural plans, Mr Secretary. You gave them to me. I also found the work order you signed, authorizing Riggs and the rest of your boys to start moving the gold on the night of September fifteenth.'

'What is that supposed to prove?'

'Nothing. Mind if I come with you into the building, sir?'

Houston turned his back to Littlemore and, braving the wind, mounted the stairs, calling out to the two soldiers posted closest to the imposing front door, 'No one enters this building, do you under-stand me? No one.'

The Secretary's voice sounded strangely thin in the wind-rent air. The soldiers threw each other a glance. As Houston neared the front door, they stepped into his path and blocked hm.

'What is this – a joke?' asked Houston. 'I meant no one *else* enters the building. Stand aside.'

The soldiers didn't budge.

'I said stand aside,' repeated Houston.

'Sorry, sir,' said one of the infantrymen. 'Orders.'

'Whose orders?'

'Mr Baker's, sir.'

Even from behind, and notwithstanding the Secretary's overcoat, Littlemore could see Houston's entire body realign. 'Mr Baker – the Secretary of War?'

'Yes, sir.'

'You must be mistaken.'

'No, sir.'

'This is an outrage. This is my building. The Secretary of War has no authority to keep the Secretary of the Treasury out of a United States Assay Office.'

'He has authority over us, sir.'

Houston strode forward, daring the soldiers to stop him. They did. Houston attempted to push through; they thrust him bodily backward – two uniformed young men manhandling the sixty-year-old Secretary, who was clad in black tie and tails. Houston fell to the ground, top hat rolling onto the cement, then sailing away once again into the night. When he stood, his face was darkly colored. Houston descended the steps, unsteadily, and made for his car. The driver hurried out and opened the back door. Houston climbed in without a word. Littlemore put his hand on the door as the driver was about to close it.

'I know what you're guilty of, Mr Houston,' said the detective.

'You're fired,' said the Secretary. 'Give me your badge. That's an order.'

Littlemore handed over his badge. This one wasn't as hard to part with as the last.

'Now get away from my vehicle,' ordered Houston.

'And I know what you're not guilty of,' added Littlemore, pressing a large, folded piece of paper into Houston's hand. 'Be there, Mr Secretary. Bring some men.'

Once Houston's car was out of sight, Littlemore walked from the Assay Office to the corner of Broad and Wall Streets. He stopped when he reached Younger, who was leaning against a corner of the Equitable Building, hatless, cigarette smoldering in the sharp wind.

'What was that about?' asked Younger. He was holding two covered paper cups of coffee, which he handed to the detective.

'Just getting myself fired,' said Littlemore. 'I guess it's better this way. Now it won't be a disgrace to the federal government if you and I get arrested.'

'We're committing a crime?'

'Want to pull out? You can.'

'One question,' said Younger. 'Are we going down an elevator into an underwater caisson which is about to be flooded, leaving us no way out except to turn ourselves into human geysers?'

'Nope.'

'Then count me in.'

'Thanks.' The two men headed back down Wall Street toward the Sub-Treasury, leaning into the wind. 'I got to say,' said Littlemore, 'I like this city.'

'What are we doing, exactly?' asked Younger.

'See that little alleyway between the Treasury and the Assay Office? That's where we're going.'

'The soldiers are going to let us through?'

'No chance,' said Littlemore. 'They're not letting anybody in. The alley's locked off by a fifteen-foot wrought-iron gate. There's another gate just like it at the other end, on Pine Street. More soldiers on that side too.'

'So how do we get there?'

'Got to go up before you come down.' Littlemore led Younger up the Sub-Treasury steps. No soldiers stood guard there; the Treasury Building had been emptied of its gold and would soon be decommissioned. But a night watchman remained outside its doors, and Littlemore greeted the man by name, handing him a cup of coffee. Thanking Littlemore, the guard rapped on the door, which a few moments later was opened by another lonely guard, to whom Littlemore gave the second cup of coffee. Then Littlemore took Younger through the rotunda to a staircase in the rear.

'What do those men think you're doing?' asked Younger.

'I work here,' said Littlemore. 'I'm a T-man, remember? Leastways, I was until a few minutes ago.'

After climbing four and a half flights of stairs, Younger and Littlemore stepped out onto a flat rooftop. The wind was so strong it knocked them sideways. They went to a parapet facing the Assay Office, which was only about three yards from them. At their feet were several long coils of rope, attached to the stone crenellations adorning the parapet. Next to the rope was a pile of additional equipment: crowbars, pulleys, friction hitches – all deposited there by Littlemore the night before.

Below them, at street level, was the alleyway between the Treasury and Assay buildings. To the right and left, at either end of the alley, illuminated by klieg lights, infantrymen manned the wrought-iron gate. The soldiers were facing out to the street, their backs to the alley. Gesturing to the pulleys and hitches, Littlemore asked quietly, 'You know how to use this stuff, Doc?'

Younger nodded.

'All right then,' said Littlemore.

The two men knelt down and fitted rope ends through the pulleys. Rappelling is not very difficult even without special equipment; with a friction hitch, which allows the descending man to play out rope at his discretion, it's simple. Younger, who had learned the skill in the army, formed a loop with a short length of his rope and stepped into it with his heel.

Littlemore, picking up the crowbars, followed suit.

The two men rappelled down the side of the Treasury Building, kicking off the wall every ten feet or so in the darkness. The well-oiled pulleys made almost no sound as the rope played through them, but it wouldn't have mattered if they had creaked. The wind's howling would have covered the noise in any event.

'Over here,' whispered Littlemore when they reached the cobblestones. He led Younger to a large manhole cover, which he had first seen the day of the bombing. 'Let's try the crowbars.'

The manhole cover bore the familiar logo of the New York City sewer department.

'We're going into the sewers?' asked Younger.

'This is no sewer,' whispered Littlemore. 'I checked the city maps yesterday. This is how they got rid of the gold – down this hole. That's why there was no getaway truck.'

The manhole cover had two small slats into which Younger and

Littlemore each inserted the bent tip of a crowbar. They tried to pry it up, but the iron circle wouldn't budge.

'Didn't think that would work,' whispered Littlemore. 'It's locked from the inside; you can't open her up from out here.'

'Hence the acid,' replied Younger.

'Yeah – hence,' said Littlemore.

Younger withdrew three slim cases from his coat. The first contained an empty glass beaker, a pencil-thin glass tube, and a pair of laboratory gloves. Inside each of the other two cases, lined with crushed blue velour, was a well-stoppered vial of transparent liquid. Wearing the gloves, Younger opened these vials and poured a portion of each into the beaker, creating the acid he'd described to Littlemore. No chemical reaction attended this admixture – no change of color, no precipitation, no smoke. To the mouth of the beaker Younger now attached the burette – the thin tube – and began drizzling the acid along the perimeter of the manhole cover. Angry bubbling commenced at once on the iron surface, with an accompanying acrid reddish smoke.

'Don't get it in your eyes,' said Younger.

By the time he was halfway around the manhole cover, Younger had exhausted the beaker's supply. He had to mix another few ounces of the aqua regia, requiring him briefly to hand over to Littlemore the two glass vials, unstoppered, while he took apart his apparatus. At that moment, a particularly savage gust of wind blew through the alley.

'Shoot,' whispered Littlemore. Younger looked up. White bubbles were sudsing on the top of the detective's black shoe. Somehow keeping his voice to a whisper, Littlemore gasped, 'It's going through my shoe! Do something, Doc – it's on my foot. It's burning into the bone!'

'That's not my acid,' said Younger.

Littlemore's gasping came to an abrupt halt.

'What is that,' asked Younger, 'baking soda?'

'Anyone else would have fallen for that,' said Littlemore, genuinely annoyed. 'Anyone. How'd you know it was baking soda?'

Younger looked at Littlemore a long time. 'Give me those,' he said, referring to the glass vials in the detective's hands. Soon the entire perimeter of the manhole cover was seething with corrosion. 'Now we wait.'

A few minutes later, Younger rose and took up a crowbar, offering the other to Littlemore. They strained to wrench loose the manhole cover, but with no success. 'Maybe the acid's not strong enough,' said Littlemore.

The two men stood over the manhole cover. Littlemore gave it a stomp with one foot. As he was about to administer another, Younger said, too late, 'I wouldn't do—'

Littlemore's shoe punched loose the acid-cut manhole cover. They could hear it rushing away from them, as if sucked down into a vacuum. For an instant Littlemore remained poised over the now-open manhole, one foot already inside it, body twisting and wavering, struggling for balance. Then he said, 'Shoot' – and fell in.

As Littlemore disappeared down the hole, his flailing arms grabbed Younger's ankle. Younger was almost able to arrest their fall, but he couldn't hold on, and a moment later he too vanished down into the earth, leaving only a crowbar lying across the manhole.

Younger found himself sliding down a chute at an alarming speed. There was no light at all. There was, however, sound: that of his own body smashing into curved walls, and that of Littlemore yelling in front of him. They flew around hairpin bends and sailed over bumps, plummeting downward in the sightless black.

Mr Brighton kept them in suspense all day about his plans for the Radium Fund. Every time Mrs Meloney veered round to the subject, he deflected it – whether artfully or absent-mindedly, Colette couldn't tell.

They dined in the Garret Restaurant, high over the southern tip of Manhattan, overlooking a sanguine sunset on the Hudson. On their way down the elevator, Mrs Meloney declared herself a nervous wreck from eating in so lofty a perch and insisted she must go home. Colette said that she would go as well.

'Don't be silly, dear,' said Mrs Meloney. 'You must visit Mr Brighton's dial factory. He is especially proud of it – and justly so.'

'Please say you will,' said Brighton.

'Is there time?' asked Colette. 'Dr Younger will be waiting for me at Trinity Church at nine-thirty.'

'Waiting at the church?' asked Brighton. 'Why – are you – you're not getting married, are you, Miss Rousseau?'

'Getting married tonight?' laughed Mrs Meloney. 'Mr Brighton, girls do not marry at night. And if they did, they would not spend the day of their wedding visiting paint factories. Not to mention the fact that Trinity Church will be good and locked up at this hour.'

'Oh, dear,' said Brighton. 'There's so much I don't know. But I do have keys to Trinity Church. I'm on the board of directors. Would you like to see the interior, Miss Rousseau? It's very fine.'

'I've seen it, Mr Brighton,' said Colette, who had spent several hours inside the church on September sixteenth.

'Miss Rousseau doesn't want to see the church, Mr Brighton. She wants to see your factory.' Mrs Meloney turned to Colette: 'There's plenty of time, my dear. The factory is quite close by. And from the factory, the church is only round the corner. Now don't disappoint him – or me. Please.'

Mrs Meloney left in a taxi. 'Do you like to walk, Miss Rousseau?' asked Brighton.

Colette was suddenly tongue-tied. So long as Mrs Meloney had been there, Colette had not quite understood herself to be spending time with a man solely in pursuit of his money. Now she did feel that way, and it seemed to infect everything she said or didn't say with a false and hypocritical tinge. 'I like walking very much,' she replied.

Brighton offered her his arm. Colette pretended not to see it, but Brighton didn't see her not seeing it, and left his elbow suspended so long that Colette was obliged finally to take it. Brighton seemed strangely tall walking next to Colette; their gait never managed to synchronize. Samuels maintained a respectful distance behind them.

'We'll be right on time,' said Brighton cheerily. 'My second shift of girls is just finishing up. I do want you to see the factory in action. But you must be cold, Miss Rousseau.' The wind had kicked up bitterly; Colette had not dressed for it. 'Here – I brought another little present for you. They will help keep you warm.'

Brighton drew a gift box from his coat. Inside was a double-tiered diamond necklace matching the stickpin he had given her earlier.

'Oh, dear,' said Brighton, 'it's the choker. I meant to give you the gloves first. Never mind. May I?'

He clasped the necklace on Colette, who, wishing Mr Brighton had spent the money on the Radium Fund instead, stammered out a thank-you, sensing to her dismay that if she didn't accept his gifts, he would never make another contribution to the Fund. It was the first time Colette had ever worn diamonds; they felt cold against her neck. Perhaps she might sell it later and donate the money in his name?

Brighton handed her a second box. This one contained a pair of thin, long-sleeved gloves, the color of fresh cream and made of a leather suppler than any she had touched before. 'Try them on,' he said.

'I can't, Mr Brighton. They're much too—'

'Too long to put on without taking your coat off? Yes of course. Allow me.'

He removed her light overcoat. Not wanting to give offense, she pulled on the gloves, which came up past her elbows. 'My coat, Mr Brighton,' said Colette.

'Yes?'

'Would you please put it back on? I'm cold.'

'Cold – of course – how absurd,' said Brighton. 'There you are. Do you like them?'

She looked at her elegant fingers, clad in ivory leather. 'I don't know what to say.'

'The pleasure is mine, I assure you. Now if I can speak frankly, Miss Rousseau, I know what you want most in the whole world. Mrs

Meloney told me. You want me to help buy radium for Madame Curie. Don't you?'

'Yes, if you're willing, Mr Brighton.'

'I'm most willing!' he cried. 'I'll buy the entire gram myself.'

'You will?' she said excitedly.

'If you will,' he said.

'If I will what?' she asked, excitement giving way to consternation.

'Marry me,' replied Brighton.

Colette didn't know whether to burst into laughter or tears.

'I know I'm not what girls consider handsome,' said Brighton. 'But I'm very rich. I can give you everything you desire. Think about that. Everything is no little thing.'

'We don't even know each other, Mr Brighton.'

'That's not true. I know you perfectly, because you are perfection itself. I don't ask you to love me. That doesn't matter at all. Let me worship you. Say yes, and I will wire one hundred thousand dollars to Mrs Meloney's account this minute.'

The staggering sum hung momentarily in the air. 'But surely you will consider a donation even if I say no?' she asked.

'I will not,' declared Brighton forthrightly. 'I've given twenty-five thousand dollars already, and I did that only to be present at your lecture. Why would I give money to a Frenchwoman I've never met? I have no reason to. But if you marry me, my dear Miss Rousseau, your wish will be my command. Say two grams if you like. Say ten.'

'Ten grams of radium?' she repeated, unable to believe what she had heard.

'From my own mines. Why not? The market value would be a million dollars, but for me the cost would be much less.' When Colette didn't answer, Brighton added, 'Oh my, is all this considered immoral? Am I acting immorally?'

Colette shook her head, her dark brows frowning severely.

'Thank goodness. I never know what's going to be thought immoral. They say people should marry for love. I don't know what they're talking about. I want you to share my home, Miss Rousseau. To travel with me on my train. To be on my arm when I dine with the President. Is it unreasonable that I should want the most beautiful, intelligent, innocent creature on earth to be my wife – or that I should offer her whatever I can to induce her to consent? Here we are at my factory.' Samuels opened the door for them. 'Come in, please. Ah, look at all the girls leaning into their work. What a beautiful sight. But what was I saying? Oh yes. Ten grams of radium, to be used as you direct. Samuels! Prepare a money wire for the account of Mrs William Meloney. I have a telegraph machine here in my office. Say you'll marry me, and I'll wire a hundred thousand at once. Samuels has advised me against it, I want you to know. He says it's rash to pay money in return for your mere promise. In fact Samuels had a very strong misimpression of you at first, Miss Rousseau. I can't begin to tell you what he thought. But if you give me your word, I know you'll keep it. What – are you crying? May I hope with tears of joy?'

Colette begged Mr Brighton for some time by herself.

'Certainly, my dear,' said Brighton. 'Samuels will need a few minutes to prepare the wire.'

Four stories below Wall Street, in a cavernous, unlit, dirt-floored chamber, two men worked an immense blast furnace. Their faces were blackened with soot; each wore a thick, heavy full-length leather apron. One stoked the furnace with large, heavy bars of gold. The other handled a set of iron molds into which flowed a stream of molten yellow metal coursing down a half-pipe from an aperture high up on the furnace. When a newly molded bar of gold was formed and ready, this man would throw it, using tongs, onto a mountain of such bars that filled the subterranean chamber in front of the furnace. Both men wore goggles; in the sparks and unnatural light thrown off by the furnace, their arms and foreheads shone with sweat.

About fifteen feet behind these workmen was a wall, and in this wall was a perfectly round hole, and from this hole came a sound that drew the workmen's puzzled attention. It was a metallic sound, echoing and distant – a faraway clanging. The noise grew louder and louder and still louder until it reached a horrendous pitch and out from the hole shot a large iron disk. It was a manhole cover with jagged edges, and it hit the dirt floor of the chamber at a dangerous speed, rolling past the legs of the astonished smelters, disappearing under their work-table, and climbing the gold bar mountain almost to its pinnacle, at which point it turned round and rolled back down, rattling to rest at the workmen's feet.

The two smelters removed their goggles. They stared down dumb-founded at the intrusive object, then looked at each other: a new sound was coming from the hole in the wall. This sound was not metallic. It was more like a tumbling, with the interspersed shouting of a human voice, and it too began quietly, distantly, only to grow nearer and louder and nearer still until Jimmy Littlemore shot feetfirst through the hole, followed immediately by Stratham Younger, the two men skidding and rolling in a jumble of arms and legs until they too lay at the smelters' feet.

Littlemore looked up at the two workmen, spat the remains of a toothpick as well as some dirt from his lips, and said, 'You're under arrest.'

Younger, lying on his stomach, did not know to whom the detective had addressed his remark, but he added, 'In the name of the law.'

Littlemore drew his gun from his shoulder holster and said, 'Drop that thing –' this was a reference to the red-hot tongs – 'and put your hands in the air.'

The speechless smelters complied at once.

Littlemore stood, pulled a set of handcuffs from his back pocket, and tossed them to Younger while keeping his gun trained on the two workmen. 'Cuff one of these guys.'

'Which one?' asked Younger.

'I don't care. The bigger one.'

The workman who had been feeding the furnace was the larger of the two. Younger handcuffed his wrists behind his back. Littlemore turned the other smelter around and pushed him forward a step.

'March, fellas,' said Littlemore, directing them around the furnace and toward the mountain of gold bricks. 'Let's see if this place leads where I think it—' he stopped, interrupting himself. 'Did you hear that, Doc?'

'Hear what?'

Littlemore was looking at the mound of gold, which was about fifteen feet high. Suddenly, at the top of that little mountain, the heads of three men appeared, and next to each one a pistol. The one in the middle had scars running from the corners of his mouth to the corners of his eyes – as if he had recently undergone facial surgery. 'Shoot!' he shouted in a strong Eastern European accent. 'Shoot all!'

'Get down!' cried Littlemore.

The gunmen didn't have a clear shot at either Younger or Littlemore – who each had one of the smelters in front of him – but they evidently didn't care. All three fired, ripping bullets into the bodies of the two workmen as Younger and Littlemore dove for cover. Younger overturned the heavy wood worktable and sat with his back to it. Littlemore crouched behind the furnace.

'A shoot-out,' said Younger as bullets slammed into his table and ricocheted off the blast furnace. 'I'm at a shoot-out without a gun.'

Littlemore craned around the furnace and fired two shots, which kept the gunmen at bay but did nothing else. 'That guy,' he said. 'Was that who I thought it was?'

'Yes,' said Younger. 'Tell me you have another gun.'

'Nope,' said Littlemore. Incoming bullets tore pieces from the bottom of the furnace, causing it to list slightly and to emit a dreadful steam shriek. 'Any ideas, Doc? Any play we can make with Drobac?'

The massive blast furnace was held up by a three-legged base. One of these legs now gave way with a loud crack; the furnace clunked down at a crazy angle.

'Offer him reduced bail?' suggested Younger.

'Good thinking,' replied Littlemore, firing another shot at the mountain of gold.

'I don't think it's very safe,' Younger called out, 'their shooting a lot of bullets into a blast furnace.'

'That's helpful,' said Littlemore, reaching around the crooked furnace and firing his last two shots.

The detective now had to reload. Drobac knew it or guessed it. 'Charge furnace,' he yelled.

All three gunmen came scrambling over the hillock of gold. At the same time a second leg at the base of the huge furnace collapsed, and the entire iron behemoth began to topple away from Littlemore – straight at Younger – with a fantastic screech of bending and breaking metal.

Littlemore and Younger were about to die. Younger was lying exactly where the red-hot furnace, spewing molten gold, would fall to the ground. Littlemore was reloading his revolver as three gunmen rushed at him down a mountain of gold and the furnace that had provided him with cover was toppling over.

Younger saw the manhole cover at his feet. 'Shield,' he shouted, hoisting up the manhole cover and heaving it through the air before diving away as several tons of iron crashed to the dirt floor and a deadly shower of gold barely missed his legs and feet.

In a single motion, Littlemore slapped the new cartridge into his gun, caught the manhole cover, and turned to face the three gunmen just as the furnace fell completely away from him. All three gunmen fired repeatedly at Littlemore, but the manhole cover stopped their bullets, and Littlemore returned fire, killing one, then another, but not the third – Drobac – who slammed into the detective shoulder-first. Littlemore fell hard on his back with the heavy manhole cover on top of his chest, and Drobac on top of the manhole cover.

Littlemore's arms were pinned. Drobac had a knee on the manhole cover, pressing it down on the detective while he brought his gun to Littlemore's temple. Drobac smiled and squeezed the trigger. His gun, however, didn't fire; he too was now out of bullets. Cursing, he threw his gun to the side. 'Is all right,' he said. 'I have other.'

Drobac drew a second gun from his jacket.

'Goodbye, policeman,' he said.

'Hey, Drobac,' said Younger, standing next to the collapsed furnace and kicking at the iron half-pipe sticking out from it.

Drobac turned at the sound of Younger's voice. It's unlikely he understood what he saw: a cast-iron half-pipe, dripping with molten gold, one end attached to the furnace, the other end swinging toward him. The pipe struck him square in the forehead. The blow would have been no more than an annoyance if liquid gold, at a temperature of two thousand degrees, had not coursed down his forehead, his nose, his cheeks, his neck. Drobac tried to scream, but what came out was nothing like a human scream: the yellow metal stream had already burned through the flesh of his cheeks and entered his mouth. He raised his hands to his bubbling face, tried to scream again, fell backward, and, with black smoke rising from his head, lay twitching, smoldering, on the dirt floor.

Littlemore squirmed out from under the manhole cover and scrambled to his feet, staring at the convulsing Drobac. 'Think I should arrest him?' asked Littlemore.

'I think we should get out of here,' said Younger, gesturing toward the fallen iron beast of a furnace. It was glowing red and seemed to be getting redder by the instant. The heat in the room was appalling.

'Jesus – she's going to blow,' said Littlemore. 'There's got to be a door somewhere on the other side of that gold.'

They ran around the mountain of gold bars, passed a table covered with playing cards and whiskey glasses and, at the other end of the subterranean chamber, came to a steel door. There was no knob or handle or latch. They pushed at the door – threw their shoulders into it – but it wouldn't open.

From the furnace, a low sound began to issue, so deep it was like the note of a cathedral organ. Then the note grew deeper still. Out of the two men's sight, a smoldering body, cheekless, lipless, stretched out a hand and grasped a gun lying on the floor nearby.

'That's not good,' said Younger, referring to the organ sound filling the air. 'I don't think that's good.'

'Wait a second,' replied Littlemore. He ran back to the card table, grabbed one of the chairs, and returned just as quickly. 'We're going to be all right. I told Houston to listen for us.'

He smashed the chair against the door and did it again and again. The chair broke into pieces, but the door didn't budge.

Next to the furnace, the faceless creature rose slowly to its feet in the pulsing crimson light of the overheated furnace. Several of Drobac's teeth, along with a fragment of his jawbone, were visible.

The low note pulsing from the furnace grew so deep that no man-made musical instrument could have made it. It also began to swell in volume. Littlemore smashed the remains of the broken chair against the door.

Drobac staggered to the side of the mountain of gold. The bellow from the furnace had become so loud that it vibrated the floor and shook Littlemore up and down. Leaning against the gold bricks, Drobac caught sight of Younger at the far door. He raised his pistol with two hands, arms wavering, unsteady.

Littlemore, unable to bear the noise, covered his ears with hands. The steel door remained shut. He and Younger looked at each other.

The gun in Drobac's trembling hands grew still. He squeezed the trigger.

All at the same moment, the furnace exploded, the gun fired, and the door swung open. Younger and Littlemore were blown through the doorway into a corridor crowded with men, as a bullet flew somewhere above their heads. In the furnace room, Drobac's body slammed into the gold bricks and burst into flame, while the wood beams supporting the walls and ceiling were engulfed in fire as well. The beams collapsed; the ceiling caved in. The room was an inferno.

'Shut that damned door,' ordered Secretary Houston at the top of his voice as tongues of fire lashed into the corridor.

The steel door was slammed and bolted, suddenly muffling the deafening rage of fire. The corridor was silent. Younger and Littlemore, rising, found themselves stared at by a half-dozen Secret Servicemen and an equal number of well-dressed bankers, including Thomas Lamont.

'What's in there, Littlemore?' asked Houston.

Lamont, not Littlemore, answered: 'It's nothing but an old abandoned foundation. We closed it up long ago. No one's been in there for decades. I don't know how you even knew where to find it, Houston.'

'I didn't; my man Littlemore told me where to go,' said Houston. 'And he told me to bring Secret Servicemen in case you tried to stop me, Lamont. What did you find, Littlemore?'

'Just some gold,' said Littlemore. 'I'd say about four million dollars' worth.'

There was a buzzing among the well-heeled bankers.

'It's not Morgan gold, I promise you that,' declared Lamont. 'The J. P. Morgan Company has nothing to do with this.'

'Four millions in gold are lying in a room adjoining a sub-basement of the Morgan Bank,' Houston said to Lamont, 'and you say your company doesn't know about it?'

'It was an old foundation under Wall Street,' replied Lamont. 'We don't own the lot. We have nothing to do with it. Any number of people could have tunneled into it.'

One of the other bankers spoke up: 'Maybe it's *your* gold, Houston. There have been rumors about a theft from the Treasury on September sixteenth.'

'Treasury gold?' said Houston, affecting incredulity. 'Don't be ridiculous. Every ounce of my gold is accounted for and has been since the day I took office. Every bar and every coin. The Treasury has never been breached. Two of you men –' Houston addressed his Secret Service agents – 'stay here and guard this door. No one goes in under any circumstances. Tomorrow when the fire has burnt itself out, we'll see.

My suspicion, Lamont, is that it's another shipment of your contraband Russian gold.'

'I tell you Morgan has nothing to do with it,' said Lamont.

As soon as they were back out on Wall Street, leaving the palatial Morgan Bank, Houston asked Littlemore in a hushed and anxious tone, 'Does the gold have our insignia on it – or did they melt it?'

'Melted almost all of it,' answered Littlemore.

'Thank heavens,' replied Houston.

'If you don't want people to know it's Treasury gold down there, Mr Houston, you'd better plug up the hole in your alley.'

'What hole?' asked Houston.

Littlemore pointed across the street to the alleyway between the Sub-Treasury and the Assay Office, where the wrought-iron gate had been thrown open, and a troop of soldiers were inspecting the open manhole – from which smoke now poured out. Houston was about to hurry there with his remaining Secret Servicemen when he stopped and pulled a badge out of his pocket. 'I'm sorry I doubted you, Littlemore. Take your badge back. I'm reinstating you.'

'No thanks, Mr Houston,' said Littlemore. 'I'm done with the Treasury for a while. Got a little police work I need to do anyway.'

Houston rushed off, leaving Younger and Littlemore by themselves. Younger lit a cigarette. The two men sported filthy faces, dirty hair, and torn, blackened clothing.

'At least it would be police work,' Littlemore muttered, 'if I were a policeman.'

CHAPTER TWENTY-ONE

COLETTE WANDERED, lost in thought, onto the factory floor, a large high-ceilinged open room, where rows and rows of young women, hunched over long tables, used fine-pointed brushes to dab luminescent paint onto the razor-thin hands of fashionable watches. Between every two girls, an electric lamp hung suspended by a long wire from the ceiling, throwing harsh light onto their close and arduous work. But the girls' studious hush was probably due less to concentration than to the entrance of Mr Brighton, their employer, a few minutes before.

Colette herself contributed to their silence as well. A young lady in a diamond choker and elbow-length white gloves – who came in with the owner – was not a typical sight for the working girls. They eyed her warily as she passed among them.

Colette didn't notice. She had only one thought in her head: ten grams of radium. It would change Madame Curie's life. It would save countless people from death. Devoted to science, rather than watch dials or cosmetics, it could yield discoveries about the nature of atoms and energy heretofore undreamed of.

To be sure, it was absurd that Mr Brighton should propose to marry her, having met her only three times in his life. Or was it? She had known she wanted to marry Younger the first day she met him, when he brought the old French corporal out of the battlefield.

Of course she could never marry Mr Brighton. She wasn't obliged to do that, not even for Madame Curie – was she? She owed Madame everything: Madame Curie had taken her in, given her a chance at the Sorbonne, saved her when she was starving. But that didn't mean Colette had to sacrifice her life and happiness for her – did it?

True, she didn't hate Mr Brighton. He might even be a little endearing in his forgetfulness, his childlike enthusiasms. And he was obviously generous. But she would be dreadfully unhappy if she married him. She would die from such unhappiness. No, she wouldn't die. And what did her happiness count against the lives that would be saved, the scientific progress that could be achieved, if she said yes? What right did she have to say no, to live for herself, when millions of young men had given more than their happiness – had given their lives – in the war?

'Don't, Miss,' said one of the girls close by her.

'I'm sorry?' said Colette.

'Don't lean on that,' said the girl. 'It's the lights for the whole factory. Some of us got work to finish. You want us all to be in the dark?'

Colette looked behind her. In the middle of the wall was a metal bar with a red wooden handle – a master light switch, apparently, which she had been on the verge of accidentally shutting off. When she turned round again, Colette became conscious that all the girls were staring at her, and not welcomingly. Several were chewing gum. One or two wiped hair from their eyes with smudged wrists, the better to see Colette's slender arms and her pretty neck effulgent with diamonds. The girl who had spoken seemed the least interested in her. She returned to her work, snipping a stray hair from her paintbrush with the curving blades of a pair of scissors. Then the girl dabbed the brush into a dish of green paint, placed its tip between her lips, and drew it out again, nicely pointed.

'Stop!' cried Colette.

'Who – me?' answered the girl.

'Don't put that in your mouth,' said Colette.

'That's how they teach us, honey,' said the girl. 'You point the brush with your mouth. Sorry if it ain't refined.'

The girls, Colette now saw, were all pointing their brushes the same way – with their lips. 'Where are your gloves?' she asked. 'Don't they give you protective gloves?'

'Only one of us in this room got gloves,' said the girl.

A loud bell rang. The girls jumped from their chairs. Amid an eruption of female talk and laughter, they cleared their desks, putting away paints and brushes and unfinished watch dials. As the girls hurried to the coat rack and made for the door, one of them stopped next to Colette. She glanced furtively about and said, 'Some of us are afraid, ma'am. A couple of girls took ill. The company doctors say it's because they got the big pox, but they weren't the types. They weren't the types at all.'

'What?' said Colette, not understanding the girl's idiomatic English. But the girl hurried away. Colette tried to pull off her leather gloves; they fit her too tightly. She tried to undo the diamond choker, but couldn't find its clasp. She gave up in frustration, and as the working girls emptied out of the factory she ran to Brighton's office, calling out his name.

'Yes, Miss Rousseau?' replied Brighton eagerly as she neared him. 'Are you going to make me the happiest man on earth?'

'The girls are putting the brushes in their mouths,' said Colette.

'Of course they are. That's the secret to our technique.'

'They're swallowing the paint.'

'How wasteful,' replied Brighton. 'Do you remember which ones? Samuels will make a note of it.'

'No – it will poison them,' said Colette.

'You mean the paint?' cried Brighton. 'Not at all. Don't be silly. How could I sell a product to the public if it were too dangerous for my girls to work with?'

'Do you monitor the radiation levels here – as you do at your paint factory?'

'There's no need, my dear.'

'But you can't let them put it in their mouths. It will get into their jaws. It will get into their teeth. It could –' She broke off in mid-sentence, her breath stopping cold as a series of images cascaded through her mind: a tooth wrapped in cotton, eaten away from within; a girl with a tumor on her jaw; another girl in New Haven, with a greenish aura emanating from her neck. A darkness crossed over Colette's eyes, which she tried to keep out of her voice: 'Oh, I suppose it doesn't matter. When the quantities of radium are so minute, I'm sure it does more harm than good. I mean more good than harm. It's so late, isn't it? My friends will be wondering where I am. Mrs Meloney must be very jealous.'

'Jealous?' said Brighton.

'Of all the radium your girls get on their skin.'

'Oh, yes,' he answered, laughing aloud. 'She would be green with—'

'She knows, sir,' said Samuels, drawing a gun.

No one spoke.

'Oh, my,' said Brighton. 'What does she know, Samuels?'

'Everything.'

'Are you quite sure?' asked Brighton. 'She said Mrs Meloney would be jealous of our girls.'

'She was lying,' said Samuels, gun pointed at Colette.

Brighton shook his head in disappointment. 'It's useless to lie, Miss Rousseau. Samuels can always tell. How he knows is a mystery to me. I never have any idea myself. Samuels, would you please put your gun very close to Miss Rousseau?'

Samuels approached Colette from behind and pressed his gun against the small of her back. Brighton came to her, his body strangely large and poorly knit together. He touched the shiny nail of his little finger to her chin and gently angled her face to one side, so that he could better see her diamond-studded neck. Colette tried not to react.

'Look,' said Brighton appreciatively. 'So clean.'

He stroked the underside of Colette's jaw; he ran his fingernail down her breastbone; he cupped his palms and shaped them around the outside of her chest. Colette, horrified, remained immobile.

'Does she like it, Samuels?' asked Brighton. 'I think she may be nervous. I wish I were better with facial expressions, Miss Rousseau. I have a great deal of trouble understanding them. If only Lyme were here. He has a relaxant that makes girls much more receptive to me. Have you ever been kissed, Miss Rousseau? On the mouth?'

Colette made no response.

'Can you make her answer?' Brighton asked Samuels.

Samuels thrust the gun harder into her spine.

'Yes, I've been kissed,' said Colette.

'But you've never – you've never – ?'

Colette didn't reply.

'No, don't answer,' said Brighton. 'You're right not to. The words would dirty your lips. I'm sure you never have. You're purity itself. Now, Miss Rousseau, I'm going to get started. I want to so very badly, and I no longer think we're going to be married. I hope you don't mind that Samuels sees us; just put him right out of your head. Please don't make any violent movements. Samuels might shoot.'

Brighton leaned down, evidently to kiss her. Colette waited as long as she could bear it, even until Brighton's mouth was actually upon her, before she thrust an elbow into Samuels's stomach, pushed Brighton with all her strength – causing the ungainly man to fall to the floor – and bolted from the office. The factory floor was empty now; she rushed through it to the main door. But the doorknob wouldn't turn; it was locked. Desperately, Colette looked around, and she saw something that gave her an idea. If she'd been able to run, she could have reached it in a moment. But a voice froze her.

'Stop where you are, Miss Rousseau,' ordered Brighton. 'Please don't make Samuels shoot you.'

Colette turned. 'Miss McDonald worked here,' she said, 'didn't she?'

'You mean the one with that – thing on her neck?' said Brighton. 'Yes, she did. A lovely girl. I thought for a time she might be my wife, before that hideousness grew on her.'

As Brighton and Samuels came nearer, Colette took a step back from them, along the wall, as if out of fear. 'Radium got into her jaw,' said Colette. 'You knew. You kept it a secret to sell your watches.'

'No, my dear,' replied Brighton earnestly. 'I don't care about the watches. It's the radium itself. If the public were to learn that radium causes that sort of thing to grow on a girl's neck, no one would want any radium products anymore. The price of radium would fall ninety percent – back to what it used to cost. For a mine-owning man like me, that would be a substantial loss. Very substantial.'

'Amelia worked here too,' said Colette, taking another step backward. 'She was losing her teeth.'

'Yes. Most unattractive. I was very angry at her. She was almost your undoing, you know. Samuels was certain Amelia had told you all our secrets. That's why we had to – to take action against you.'

'You had me kidnapped,' she said, still backing away.

'It was the most efficient thing in the world. We had some foreigners in town for another task – Serbs, weren't they, Samuels? – very well suited for the job.'

'You tried to kill me – and then proposed to me?'

'That is one of my great strengths, Miss Rousseau. I admit my mistakes. I learn from them. It was all a misunderstanding. Do you know why Amelia tried to see you at your hotel? It's because some of the girls overheard you at our factory in Connecticut saying that my company was killing people. But you didn't mean my paint was doing any harm. You meant that luminous watches divert radium from medical uses. How preposterous – that misunderstanding nearly killed you! It was I who came to your rescue. You owe your life to me, Miss Rousseau. I saw Samuels's mistake immediately after I heard you at the church. That's why I ordered the attacks against you to stop.' Brighton shook his head ruefully. 'But now look how things have turned out. What a pity. Samuels, can we keep her in the infirmary? If I can't marry her, that would be my second choice.'

'They'll come for her,' said Samuels.

Brighton sighed: 'You're right, as always.' While Samuels kept his gun trained on Colette, Brighton went to a metal barrel positioned on top of a worktable. Opening a tap at its base, he filled a glass measuring cup with greenish paint. 'Since you aren't receptive to me, Miss Rousseau, would you mind at least opening your mouth and holding quite still? Please say you'll cooperate. It will make things so much easier.'

Colette didn't answer. She was touching the wall with her hands behind her back, feeling for something. Where was it?

'Does your silence mean yes?' asked Brighton. 'I would be very impressed with you. Girls are usually so unreasonable. Most people are. I remember as a boy I would propose something perfectly sensible, and my parents would say it was "wrong." They would get that look on their faces. What does it mean – wrong? It's as if they were suddenly speaking in tongues. I don't believe the word has any meaning. I've asked people many times to explain it to me; no one can. They just give examples. It's gibberish. I look at people sometimes, Miss Rousseau, and honestly I think they're all cattle. I may be the only one with a mind of his own. Samuels, open Miss Rousseau's mouth.'

'You're going to make me drink your paint?' asked Colette, aghast, taking another step back

'Please don't be concerned,' said Brighton. 'We've done it before; it works splendidly. The paint will make you sick, and we'll rush you to the Sloane Hospital for Women, where a specialist named Lyme will treat you. He'll give you something that will keep you from speaking. You'll get weaker, and your hair may fall out. That will make you very unattractive, but it's all right – I won't come to visit. You'll be diag-nosed with syphilis, I imagine. Then you'll die. It all goes very smoothly, I promise you. Won't you please open your mouth? You'll be doing me a great favor.'

'Mr Brighton, I beg you,' she said, turning her back to him. 'Shoot me now. Get it over with.'

'But I can't,' answered Brighton. 'If we shot you, Miss Rousseau, either your body would have to disappear, which would raise all sorts of questions, or else we'd have to turn you over to the police with bullets in you, which would raise even more. I assure you, the paint is much –'

Brighton never finished this sentence. Colette, her back to the two men, had taken hold of the red wooden handle of the light switch – the master switch, which the working girl had warned her of earlier – and she plunged the factory into darkness. Immediately she dropped to all fours as shots rang out and bullets ricocheted off the metal plate above her.

'Stop shooting!' ordered Brighton. 'There's nowhere she can go. Get the lights back on.'

Colette could see nothing except the glass measuring cup of radio-luminescent paint in Brighton's hands, glowing greenish yellow, casting an eerie light on his nose and chin. She darted to him, seized the cup with both hands, and threw the paint in his face.

'Get it off me!' yelled Brighton. 'Get it off!'

Colette rushed to the far wall, which had four great windows in it. The dimmest hint of light was coming back to the factory floor. Samuels had thrown the master switch, but the overhead lamps, with their thick filaments, only gradually came to life. Samuels stood next to Brighton with a handkerchief, trying vainly to rub the glowing paint off his employer's face.

'Never mind!' said Brighton. 'Where is she?'

Colette picked up one of the girls' stools and smashed it into the windowpanes, opening a gaping hole. Samuels fired in her direction, but the darkness saved her. She scrambled out of the window, the leather gloves preventing the glass shards from cutting her too deeply, and let herself drop to the street below. Heedless of direction, heart pounding, Colette ran from the factory. She didn't hear anyone pursuing her; still she ran on.

Turning a corner, she found herself on a short, narrow, empty street without a single streetlight. She came to a small park. She ran across it, under several trees, until she reached an old, high, massive stone building with wooden doors. It was Trinity Church. She was at a side entrance: the doors were locked. Breathing hard from running, she beat on the doors with all her might, but no one answered. Again she ran off into the night.

'Got to go to Grand Central,' said Littlemore to Younger as they walked down Wall Street toward the subway station at the corner of Broadway, where, directly facing them at the end of Wall Street, the dim Gothic spires of Trinity Church loomed up in the night sky. 'Want to come?'

'I'm meeting Colette,' said Younger. 'Here at the church.'

'Hope you aren't planning to take her some place fancy,' said Littlemore, looking at Younger's scarred clothing.

'Strange – where is she? She should have been here by now.' They were still a half block from the church, but there was a streetlamp outside its entrance, where Younger had expected Colette to be waiting.

'Say, how's the Miss doing?' asked Littlemore. 'Wasn't she meeting some bigwig tonight?'

'Arnold Brighton.'

'No kidding. You know, I wonder if—'

Littlemore had not finished this sentence when Colette came running frantically around the side of the church. She stopped at the iron lamppost, body heaving for lack of breath. Younger called out her name.

'Stratham?' she answered, full of alarm. Although Colette was visible to the two men, they were in darkness, invisible to her. She set off toward the sound of Younger's voice. 'Thank God.'

The twin doors of Trinity Church burst open, revealing an arched portal flooded with light from within the church. Beneath that arch stood Arnold Brighton, his face a glowing chartreuse orb, his eyes starkly white by contrast. Next to him was Samuels.

'There she is!' cried Brighton, pointing to the figure running down Wall Street. 'Shoot her!'

Samuels fired. Colette disappeared from below one streetlight and reappeared below the next. She hadn't been hit. Younger stepped forward to gather her in, trying to put his back between her and the gunfire even as Samuels fired twice more. Colette fell hard into Younger's arms. He whirled her off her feet and carried her into the darkness of a storefront alcove.

Littlemore had taken cover behind a mailbox, checking all his pockets for a gun, but he had none, having lost his firearm underground. Now he scrambled on all fours to Younger as Samuels's bullets flew over his head. 'Is she all right?' he asked.

'I'm fine,' answered Colette, still in Younger's arms. Samuels held his fire, evidently unable to see his targets.

'You with the girl,' said a different voice directly behind them, boyish but trying to sound commanding. 'Let her go.'

Younger turned. The speaker was a fresh-faced soldier who had come running to investigate the gunshots. He pointed a rifle nervously at Younger, its bayonet much closer to his chest than Younger liked.

'Are you there, Miss Rousseau?' Brighton called out from the glaringly illuminated arch. 'Samuels, do you see her?'

'Oh, give me that,' muttered Younger to the soldier. In one motion, he set Colette on her feet, seized the boy's rifle, kneeled, took aim at the doorway of Trinity Church, and fired. His shot hit Samuels in the joint of his shoulder, nearly amputating his arm.

'You got him, Doc,' said Littlemore.

'Did I?' Younger shifted his aim just slightly.

Samuels fell to his knees, blood flowing prodigiously from his subclavian artery.

'What's the matter with you?' asked Brighton, looking down at his secretary with a mixture of perplexity and indignation. 'It's only one arm. Shoot with the other.'

Younger fired again.

Brighton's eyes opened wide. A dark red circle appeared in the middle of his green forehead. 'Oh, my,' said Brighton, before collapsing.

Younger threw the rifle to the soldier's feet. 'How quickly can you get us an ambulance?' he asked Littlemore. 'Colette's hurt.'

She was in fact badly cut on her legs, and her long-sleeved gloves were ripped in several places, revealing lacerations to her palms and forearms.

'I'll find a car,' said Littlemore, sprinting away. Within a minute, a dozen soldiers were running down Wall Street toward Trinity Church, where the bodies of Brighton and Samuels lay bleeding, and Littlemore had returned in Secretary Houston's Packard. Younger made Colette get inside.

'But they're only scratches,' she protested.

'We're going to a hospital,' said Younger, lowering himself next to her in the backseat.

She looked at him and smiled. 'All right. If you think we should.'

'Which hospital, Doc?' asked Littlemore, behind the wheel.

'Washington Square,' said Younger. 'Wait – I thought you were going to stop a war tonight. Did you?'

'Not yet,' answered Littlemore.

'Well, go stop it.' The two men looked at each other. 'Someone else can drive. She'll be all right. Go.'

'Thanks,' said Littlemore, who persuaded Houston's chauffeur to drive the car.

As they set off, Colette rested her head on Younger's shoulder. She didn't see him wince. 'It's finally over, isn't it?' she asked.

'Yes,' he answered. 'I think it is.'

It wasn't until Younger had failed to respond to the next several things she said that she noticed his closed eyes and touched the back of his shirt and felt it dampening with blood. Colette screamed at the driver to hurry.

At Grand Central Terminal, under the celestial ceiling of the main concourse, Littlemore found Officer Stankiewicz in plain clothes, together with Edwin Fischer, waiting for him at the round central information booth, which was capped by a gold sphere with clocks on all four sides. Littlemore shook hands with Stankiewicz, thanking him for doing unofficial duty. 'Everything okay?' asked Littlemore.

'So far, so good,' said Stankiewicz.

'Anybody make you?' asked Littlemore.

'Hard to tell up here, Cap. Too many people.'

Littlemore nodded. The station was bustling with the comers and goers of a Saturday night in New York City. A constant din of loud-speaker crackle filled the concourse with announcements of train numbers, destinations, and tracks.

'Okay, Stanky,' said Littlemore, 'you're going to Commissioner Enright's place. He's expecting you. Here's the address. And bust it; there's no time to lose. When you get back, meet me downstairs exactly where I showed you. Fischer, you're coming with me.'

Littlemore glanced around the concourse, then tapped his knuckles on the information counter. The attendant, whom the detective greeted by name, shuffled to a gate and let Littlemore and Fischer in.

'Why are we going in the information booth?' asked Fischer. 'Are we looking for information?'

'We're going down to the lower level. If they've got people watching the stairs and ramps, they won't see us.'

In the center of the round booth was a gold pillar with a sliding door, which Littlemore opened. The detective cleared away boxes of old schedules, revealing a narrow spiral staircase.

'A hidden stairwell,' said Fischer. 'I didn't know this was here.'

'You're in for a lot of surprises tonight,' replied Littlemore.

The spiral stairs led past a landing littered with empty liquor bottles. When they arrived at the bottom, they were behind another, smaller information window. Littlemore opened it and joined the throng of passengers in Grand Central's lower level. He led Fischer to an intersec-tion of two broad and crowded corridors, where Officer Roederheusen, also in plain clothes, was waiting in an inconspicuous corner under a tiled, vaulted ceiling. Across the gallery was the Oyster Bar.

'They still in there?' Littlemore asked.

'Yes, sir,' said Roederheusen. 'Still eating.'

'Anybody see you?'

'No, sir.'

'Good job,' said Littlemore. 'Fischer, you and I are going to wait here until the Commissioner comes. Spanky, you go down to Washington Square Hospital on Ninth and see how Miss Rousseau's doing. Just stay put there unless Doc Younger needs anything, in which case you get it for him.'

Twenty minutes later, Stankiewicz returned with Commissioner Enright.

'This had better be good, Littlemore,' said Enright.

'It will be, Commissioner,' replied Littlemore. 'Stand right here, sir. Keep an ear to the wall. You too, Fischer, just like we talked about. Don't move.'

'An ear to the wall?' repeated Enright indignantly.

'Yes, sir. Keep your ear right here.'

The detective crossed the lower-level concourse, wending through the crush of bustling passengers, many of them carrying on in extraordinarily loud voices, as New Yorkers like to do. When he got to the Oyster Bar's entrance, he turned around, confirming that he could no longer see Enright, Roederheusen, or Fischer, who, on the other side of the wide and busy gallery, must have been almost a hundred feet away. Littlemore ducked into the restaurant.

He found them at a table covered with nacreous and crustacean remains: Senator Fall, Mrs Cross, and William McAdoo, the former Treasury Secretary who was now a lawyer. No bottles were visible, but it was clear from the Senator's exuberance that considerable drink had been consumed with the repast.

'Agent Littlemore!' cried Fall. 'Savior of his country. Exposer of corruption. You've missed dinner. You've missed great tidings. You've

– you look ridiculous, son. What have you been doing, spelunking?'

'I need to talk to you, Mr Fall,' said Littlemore.

'Talk away. I think you're getting cold feet, boy, I really do.'

'Can we speak alone, Mr Senator?' replied Littlemore, still standing.

'Anything you want to say to me, Littlemore, you can say in front of my friends.'

'Not this.'

Fall was irritated, but he stood up. 'All right. I'm coming. But first give me one more dose of that dark medicine, woman.'

Mrs Cross inconspicuously removed a flask from her purse and put a splash into Senator Fall's glass. She topped off Mr McAdoo's as well. 'Whiskey, Agent Littlemore?' she asked.

The detective shook his head and, after Fall had downed his drink, led the Senator out of the crowded restaurant. He stopped at a discreet spot against the wall in the terminal concourse, a few feet from the doors of the Oyster Bar. 'I know who stole the gold, Mr Fall,' said Littlemore.

'The Mexicans,' replied Fall. 'You already figured that out.'

'Not the Mexicans, sir.'

'Houston?'

'It was Lamont,' said Littlemore.

'Impossible.'

'I saw the gold tonight. In the basement of the Morgan Bank.'

'Keep your voice down,' whispered Fall. 'You tell anybody yet?'

'Yes, sir,' said Littlemore quietly.

'Who?'

'You.'

'Apart from me, goddamn it,' said Fall.

'You mean Mr Houston?'

'Yes – did you tell Houston?'

'I came straight here, Mr Fall.'

'Good. Let's keep a lid on this, Littlemore. Don't want to cause a panic. Tell you what: Just leave it to me. I'll make sure the right people find out.'

'Got you, Mr Fall. Keep a lid on it. But somebody better talk to Mr Lamont right away.'

'Don't you worry, son – I'll talk to him.'

'What'll you say?' asked Littlemore.

'I'll tell him – why, I'll tell him—' Fall had difficulty finishing the sentence. 'Damn it, you're the one who said I should talk to him.'

'I figured you'd want to tip him off,' said Littlemore.

Fall didn't flinch. 'What did you say?'

'You know when I knew, Senator Fall? It was when you told me that you and Mr McAdoo always have dinner at the Oyster Bar. I realized that Ed Fischer was in Grand Central when you two met here a few months ago, after the Democratic Convention. A lot of people think Fischer's crazy, but everything I heard him say turned out to be true.'

'Are you drunk, Littlemore?'

'Then I saw the whole thing. Finding those Mexican documents was way too easy. Torres's apartment – it was a fake, wasn't it? A setup. That's why you had Mrs Cross come with me – to make sure I'd find the hole in the wall where the documents were hidden. What a sucker I was. Sure, a Mexican envoy is going to bring incriminating documents with him from Mexico in a cardboard tube – nothing else, no files, no suitcases, barely any clothes, just those documents – and then leave them for me in an open wall safe after I knock on his apartment door. Torres wasn't really a Mexican envoy at all, was he? You invented him. That's why Obregón denied the guy's existence.'

Fall took out a cigar. 'You're all twisted up, son. Not thinking straight.'

'From the very start,' said Littlemore, 'Lamont tried to put me onto Mexico. Every time I talked to him, something having to do with Mexico would come up. I just didn't see it. Same with you, Mr Fall. You pretended you thought the Russians were behind it, but you were steering me to Mexico the whole time. Brighton was in on it too, wasn't he? You and he staged that scene in your office for my benefit, when he was complaining about the Mexicans seizing his oil wells. Then Lamont calls me again and conveniently mentions that Mexican

Independence Day is in the middle of September. You were doing the same thing with Flynn, sending him hints about Sacco and Vanzetti, hoping he'd put together their Mexico connection, but he never did. So you had to make me think I'd found proof – the documents in Torres's wall. But they're all fakes. Forgeries.'

Fall lit his cigar, taking his time. He glanced left and right and spoke almost inaudibly: 'The Mexicans bombed us, Littlemore. Massacred us. You're the one who figured it out. Let's say those documents are fake. Let's just say. If that's what Wilson and his Secretary of War needed to see the light and send in the troops, that's the way it had to be.'

'Except the Mexicans weren't behind the bombing,' said Littlemore.

'What are you talking about?'

'You were behind it.'

Fall blew a cloud of smoke over Littlemore's head. 'You think I bombed Wall Street – killed all those people – to steal a little gold from the Treasury? You're out of your mind, boy. No one will believe you.'

'The gold was icing,' said Littlemore. 'The cake was war. Invading Mexico, getting rid of Obregón, installing your own man as president, taking the oil fields. That would have been worth maybe half a billion dollars to your pal Brighton. And a few hundred million more to Lamont. And who knows how much to you.'

'That's big crazy talk, boy. You could get in trouble talking big and crazy like that.'

'You're making a war for their oil.'

'*Their* oil?' Fall hissed. 'That's *our* oil you're talking about. We bought it, we paid for it, and now a bunch of Reds are trying to steal it. You think the Mexican people like being ordered around by a gang of God-hating, gun-toting bandits? The Mexicans'll thank us. They'll cheer our boys when we march into Mexico City.'

'Sure they will,' said Littlemore. 'They love the US of A., just like you do.'

At that moment Mr McAdoo came out of the restaurant, along with Mrs Cross, who was carrying Senator Fall's overcoat.

'What's going on, Fall?' asked McAdoo. 'Is there a problem, Mr Littlemore?'

'No problem. Senator Fall and I were just talking about how you and he planned the Wall Street bombing.'

'I beg your pardon?' said McAdoo.

'You were the one who knew about the gold,' Littlemore said to McAdoo. 'You were Secretary of the Treasury in 1917 – before you started working for Brighton. You knew exactly how and when the gold would be moved. You knew Riggs. You probably had him transferred from Washington to New York.'

'Don't answer him, Mac,' said Fall. 'Ignorant talk – that's all it is.'

'Answer him?' said McAdoo. 'I would sue him for slander if it weren't so palpably risible.'

'How much did they promise you?' Littlemore asked McAdoo. 'Or were you just getting back at Wilson?'

McAdoo bristled. 'Why would I want to "get back" at my own father-in-law?'

'Maybe because he took the nomination from you?' answered Little-more. 'You were going to be the next president of the United States. Must have been so close you could taste it. But Wilson took it away. All because you married his little girl, thinking it was your ticket to the White House. Kind of backfired, that move. Wilson stayed a step ahead of you all the way, didn't he?'

'Let it go,' Fall said to McAdoo. 'He's just baiting you.'

'Woodrow Wilson,' replied McAdoo, 'will go down in history as a president so bedazzled with his role as Europe's peacemaker that he didn't see the war being made against us by our neighbor to the south – the first president since 1812 to permit an attack on American soil.'

'Sure, if only there had been an attack,' said Littlemore. 'But there wasn't. You just made it look that way. You figured you'd hire some men to bomb Wall Street, make it look like the Mexicans did it, rustle up a little war – and come out a billion dollars richer. Lamont owns the land across from the Treasury Building. He digs a tunnel to the one spot where the gold is vulnerable while it's being moved – the overhead bridge between the two buildings. Then on September sixteenth, Mexican Independence Day, you pulled the trigger. You covered your tracks too. Nobody knew. But you made one mistake. You were overheard by Ed Fischer.'

Fall laughed out loud. Then the Senator spoke more quietly: 'That's your evidence? We were overheard by a certified lunatic? I hate to break it to you, son, but I never talk anywhere I can be overheard.'

'You've talked here before. In this corner. Outside the Oyster Bar.'

'How would you know?' replied the Senator. 'And what if I have? Nobody can hear us.'

'Ed Fischer can,' said Littlemore. Lowering his voice to the quietest whisper, the detective added: 'Come on out, Fischer. Tell Mr Fall whether you can hear him.'

'Indeed I can!' cried Edwin Fischer's voice from across the crowded gallery. Soon they could see him practically bounding through the crowd. 'It's just like before,' he said jauntily when he reached them. 'The same voices – out of the air!'

'What on earth?' said McAdoo. 'What is this?'

Fall looked at Fischer as if he were a species of exotic bird that ought to be exterminated. 'Is this your idea of a joke, Littlemore?'

'I don't think Commissioner Enright finds it funny, Mr Senator,' said Littlemore as Fischer was followed by Enright and Stankiewicz. 'Commissioner Enright, could you hear the Senator and Mr McAdoo talking just now?'

'Every word,' said Enright.

'Stanky – did you hear them?'

'Sure did, Cap.'

'Eddie?'

'"I hate to break it to you, son,"' quoted Fischer, imitating Fall's Western twang, '"but I never talk anywhere I can be overheard."'

'Good gracious,' said Mrs Cross. 'They really could hear you.'

'It's a trick,' said Fall, looking up at the ceiling and down to the floor. 'You got a wire here somewhere. It's a policeman's trick.'

'No wire, Mr Senator,' said Littlemore. 'It is a neat trick though. We detectives discovered it a couple of years ago, after the Terminal opened. If you stand right where we're standing now, just outside the Oyster Bar, folks on the exact opposite side of the hall can hear everything you say, loud and clear, even if you whisper and even if there's a crowd in between. I asked Fischer earlier today if that's where voices came to him.'

'It was my favorite place,' declared Fischer. 'I used to hear so much out of the air.'

'You and Mr McAdoo,' said Littlemore, 'had dinner here in July. Big Bill Flynn was with you. Flynn met Fischer that night – here in Grand Central. Afterward, Fischer came down to his spot over there and listened. The two of you must have been on your way out of the restaurant. You stopped. You whispered, positive that nobody could hear you. But you were wrong.'

'The Treasury owed me millions,' McAdoo protested. 'That's all I ever said. It was a purely hypothetical—'

'Shut up, Mac,' interrupted Fall sharply. His countenance softened into a broad smile: 'Mr Fischer, I don't believe I've had the pleasure. You're the tennis champion, am I right? Heard a lot of fine things about you. Albert Fall's the name. You ever been introduced to me, son? Or to Mr McAdoo here?'

'Never,' replied Fischer, sticking out his hand, 'but I'm delighted to make your acquaintance.'

The Senator didn't shake Fischer's hand: 'Then you can't be sure it was us you heard back in July – especially if the voices you heard were whispering.'

'I didn't say I was sure,' replied Fischer candidly. 'But your voices certainly sound similar.'

Fall laughed again. 'Congratulations,' he said to Littlemore. 'Your evidence is a lunatic who never saw us before but thinks maybe possibly he heard voices similar to ours whispering something last summer. You couldn't indict a flea with that evidence. Mac, Mrs Cross – time to go.'

'If I'd been trying to indict you, Fall,' replied Littlemore. 'I would have waited and brought you down when I had more. Instead I just blew my whole case against you.'

As Mrs Cross draped his overcoat on him, Fall asked, 'And why would you do that?'

'Because I need something from you.'

The Senator chuckled: 'Boy, are you ever mixed up. In future, when you want something from me, I'd recommend you try a different tactic.'

'Really?' said Littlemore. 'I got two witnesses here, one of whom is the Commissioner of the New York Police Department, who will confirm that Fischer could hear you and Mr McAdoo from all the way across the hall and that Fischer recognized your voices as the ones he heard talking about the Wall Street bombing three months before it happened. Not enough to convict, but plenty enough for a newspaper. Especially when people start looking into your Mexican documents. It'll take a while to prove the forgery, but we will. You'll deny you knew they were forged, but my witnesses will tell the papers they heard you say you didn't care if the documents were forged or not. How do you figure the headlines will read? Senator Fall Takes Country to War on Tissue of Lies?'

Fall didn't reply.

'That kind of story could put a serious crimp in a man's legal career, Mr McAdoo,' Littlemore continued. 'Not to mention his getting back into politics.'

'Let's hear what the detective wants,' said McAdoo.

'Meantime,' continued Littlemore, 'those three senators and Mr Houston – the ones who, according to your forged documents, were taking bribes from the Mexican government – I'm guessing they won't let you off the hook so easy, Mr Senator. When they find out what you did, they'll want to hold hearings or something, won't they? With all that going on, I can't see President Harding naming you to his Cabinet. Can you, Mrs Cross?'

'No, I can't,' she agreed.

Fall took a long draw at his cigar. 'What is it you want me to do?'

'Call off the war.'

'I don't make that kind of decision,' said Fall gruffly. 'Harding isn't even president yet.'

'You better find a way, Mr Senator,' said Littlemore. 'Otherwise, you can kiss your Cabinet position goodbye.'

A piece of tobacco leaf was caught between Fall's front teeth. He sucked it in and spat it out to the floor of Grand Central Terminal. He looked at McAdoo, who nodded. 'There will be no war,' said Fall. 'Hope you're proud of yourself, boy.'

The Senator buttoned his overcoat. He turned to go.

'The one thing I'll never understand,' said Littlemore, 'is how you could kill so many of your own countrymen. You didn't need to pick noon. You could've done the bombing anytime – at night. You're not just a traitor, Fall. You're some kind of monster.'

The Senator faced the detective. 'How do you know the bomb was supposed to go off at noon?' he asked. 'Mistakes happen in war. Don't they, McAdoo?'

'Don't ask me,' replied McAdoo. 'I wasn't responsible.'

'Maybe the bombers were told to do their work at a minute after midnight on the sixteenth,' said Fall, 'when the Mexicans would be celebrating their puny independence. Maybe nobody was supposed to die. But maybe the bombers were told twelve-oh-one, and maybe where they came from, twelve-oh-one doesn't mean a minute after midnight.'

Littlemore whistled. 'Your boys blew the bomb twelve hours late. That's why Fischer was off on the date. He heard you say the bomb would go off the night of the fifteenth.'

'*Our* boys?' asked Fall. 'Don't know what you're talking about, Littlemore. I was just speculating. But let me tell you what ain't speculation: you're handing the Reds the biggest victory they ever had. Oil is mother's milk, son. The countries that have it are going to be big and strong. The ones that don't are going to wither and die. Know how much oil we Americans produced yesterday? One million two hundred thousand barrels. Know how much we consumed? One million six hundred thousand barrels. That's right – every day, we're short four hundred thousand barrels of oil. Where's that extra oil coming from? Mexico. We'll get our oil; trust me on that. One way or the other, we'll get it. This country has enemies, Littlemore. I ain't one of them. Evening, Commissioner.'

Enright said goodbye to the Senator.

Unseen by anyone else, Mrs Cross winked at Littlemore. 'Good night, New York,' she said. 'You do play by the rules, don't you?'

'You really can't connect them?' Commissioner Enright asked Littlemore a few minutes later. 'To the bombing?'

'We've got nothing on them,' said Littlemore. 'The only witness who can tie Fall to the bombing is Fischer here, and no judge will let him testify.'

'How about the gold?' asked Enright. 'Can't we prosecute them for theft?'

'There's no theft if the owner won't admit his property was taken,' said Littlemore. 'Secretary Houston's going to deny that the Treasury got robbed. I saw him do it tonight.'

'I know what to do!' interjected Fischer. 'I'll tell Wilson. He'll be very unhappy with Senator Fall. I'm one of the President's advisers, you know.'

'You did good tonight, Eddie,' replied Littlemore. 'Thanks.'

'You're most welcome. By the way, the Popes are trying to condemn me again.'

'The Popes?' asked Enright.

'I know what he means, Commissioner,' said Littlemore. 'It's okay, Eddie. I'll help you out.'

'Well, perhaps all this will make good crime fiction someday,' observed Enright. 'I might do something with it myself. Mr Flynn is publishing my work, you know.'

'I'm sorry?' said Littlemore. 'Big Bill Flynn?'

'His days as Chief are numbered now that the Republicans are in,' said Enright. 'He's starting a literary magazine. Intends to call it *Flynn's*. I'm to be his first writer. I'll have several detective stories for him. Set in New York.'

Littlemore had no reply for a moment. Then he said, 'Don't put that in one of your stories, sir.'

'Don't put what?' said Enright.

'That the Police Commissioner of New York City is going to write detective stories for the fat-headed Chief of the Federal Bureau of Investigation, who's starting a literary magazine and naming it after himself after botching the biggest investigation the country's ever seen. Nobody would believe it.'

The Washington Square Hospital was a small, comfortable private facility with only two floors, connected by a wide central marble staircase. Littlemore was taking those stairs two at a time when he came upon Colette on the landing, looking out a large window. She saw him in the reflection and turned to him; the diamond choker, still on her neck, sparkled brilliantly.

'Glad to see you're okay, Miss,' said Littlemore before taking in her expression. 'What's wrong?'

'Nothing,' she answered. 'Everything's fine. He's going to be fine.'

'Who?'

At that moment a surgeon came slowly down the steps, cleaning his hands with a long wet cloth. His sleeves were bloodied. 'Miss Rousseau?' he asked. 'I'm very sorry, but—'

'I don't want to hear it,' Colette shouted, running upstairs. 'He's going to be fine.'

The surgeon shook his head and continued down the stairwell, leaving Littlemore by himself on the landing, trying not to believe the inferences he'd already drawn. Colette's footsteps trailed off down the corridor upstairs.

'Wait a second,' Littlemore called out half a minute later, unsure whether he was addressing Colette or the surgeon, then broke into a run downstairs. 'Wait just a darn second.'

The surgeon stopped midway down the hall: 'Are you a friend of Dr Younger's?' he asked.

'Sure, I'm a friend,' said Littlemore. 'What's wrong with him?'

'He was shot.'

Littlemore saw in his mind's eye Younger stepping between Colette and Samuels's gunfire. 'In the back,' he said.

'Twice,' agreed the surgeon. 'There's nothing I can do for him. I'm sorry. Does he have family?'

'What do you mean, nothing you can do? Operate on him.'

'I have,' said the surgeon, wiping his forehead. 'The bullets struck his ribs and lodged in the thoracic cavity. I don't dare try to extract them, because I don't know where they are. I'll tear his heart and lungs to pieces before I find them.'

'Can't you X-ray him or something?'

'X-rays are useless,' said the surgeon. 'The bullets haven't come to rest. Every breath he takes moves them. By the time we have images, the bullets will be somewhere else. They won't stabilize for at least seventy-two hours.'

'That doesn't sound so bad,' Littlemore said, refusing to accept the grim fatality with which the surgeon spoke. 'Roosevelt kept a bullet in his chest for almost ten years.'

'The situation *is* like Roosevelt's,' the surgeon reflected, 'except for the infection. Dr Younger's neutrophils are at about eighty percent. He has fever. Roosevelt's wound healed with no infection at all. That was the remarkable thing about it.'

'What are you saying, Doc? Help me out here.'

'I'm saying your friend must recover from his infection,' replied the surgeon. 'We are powerless against this sort of thing. All our instruments, all our science, all our medicines – powerless. He should live through the night. We'll test his blood again tomorrow morning. If the neutrophils decrease, all may yet be well.'

Littlemore tapped at the door and entered a silent hospital room. Colette was standing by the bedside, dousing Younger's forehead with a cold compress. Younger was lying on his stomach, eyes closed, cheek lying directly on the bed, with no pillow. His breathing was shallow, his face unnaturally livid, his entire body shivering.

'How's he doing?' asked Littlemore.

'Well,' said Colette. 'Very well. He's sleeping.'

Neither spoke for a while.

'What are neutrophils, Miss? The doctor was telling me—'

'Doctors are fools,' declared Colette.

Silence again.

'Neutrophils,' said Colette, 'are white blood cells, the most common kind. When there is an infection in the body, the neutrophils increase in number to fight it. Normally, they make up about sixty-five percent of the white cells.'

'How bad is eighty percent?'

'It's not bad; it's good,' said Colette. 'It means he's fighting his infection. His neutrophils will be in the seventies tomorrow, the high seventies. You'll see. Then they will come down more and more each day until they're normal. Did Mr Brighton live?'

'No. Neither did Samuels.' Littlemore looked at Younger's shivering body. 'Did they say anything about the kind of bullets, Miss?'

'Why?'

'It can make a big difference. The worst thing is if the bullets were hollow-points. Those mushroom on contact. They're real bad. Can't even use them in warfare. It's illegal. The bullet that hit Teddy Roosevelt wasn't a hollow-point, so it didn't mushroom when it him. When we policemen heard that, we knew he'd be okay.'

Colette remained quiet a long time. 'That's the word the doctors used,' she said at last. 'They said the bullets mushroomed.'

Before dawn, string-tied stacks of newspapers hit the streets, announcing in bold headlines a reconciliation between the United States and Mexico.

The American army at the border was standing down. Confidential Mexican agent Roberto Pesqueira declared in Washington unequivocally that American investments in his country would not be nationalized. United States law enforcement officers were said to have discovered and foiled a nefarious but unspecified plot to unseat General Obregón.

Younger's blood was drawn first thing that morning. He was still unconscious, but his fever had stabilized, although his body seemed wracked, weakened. Colette was there; Littlemore had gone home to his family.

A half-hour later, the surgeon from the night before came in. 'Eighty-six percent,' he said.

'It's a mistake,' answered Colette.

'No mistake. I'm sorry.'

'It doesn't matter,' said Colette. 'The count will improve by this evening. He's doing better. Much better. I can tell.'

Littlemore and Betty came back to the hospital at sunset. They had been there, one or the other, on and off, throughout the day. Littlemore's face was deeply drawn. They ran into Colette at the front door.

'I'm buying cigarettes,' explained Colette, smiling. 'He asked for them.'

'He's awake?' said Betty.

'Wide-awake,' said Colette. 'He's so much better.'

'I'll get him the smokes, Miss,' replied Littlemore, a tremendous weight lifting from him. 'You go back upstairs.'

'No, it's fine. He said he was hoping to talk to you.'

'To me?' asked Littlemore.

'Yes.'

'Doc doesn't talk to me. He doesn't talk to anybody. His neutrophils went down?'

'They're very strong,' said Colette. 'Ninety-five percent.'

'Ninety-five?' repeated Littlemore dumbly. 'But I thought—'

'It shows how hard he's fighting the infection. It's a good sign. But I think – I think – I think maybe you should hurry, Jimmy.' Colette turned and hid her face from them, but she didn't cry. 'Is there a tobacco nearby?'

'I know a place,' said Betty, understanding the French girl's meaning. 'I'll show you.'

A nurse was preparing a syringe when Littlemore entered the room. 'This will make you much more comfortable,' she said to Younger.

Younger was still lying on his stomach. His face, resting on one cheek, was turned toward the door; he saw Littlemore. His back, exposed from the waist up, had thick plasters in two places. His shining forehead was as pale as his white sheets, and he shook badly. 'No,' he said. His voice was strong, but he made no movement. 'No shot.'

'Afraid of a little shot, a big man like you?' said the nurse. 'Don't worry. You'll feel much better soon.'

Younger tried to lift himself; his arms looked powerful, but evidently it was too painful. He closed his eyes. 'No shot,' he repeated to Littlemore.

'Ma'am,' said Littlemore, 'he doesn't want the shot.'

'It's for his pain,' answered the nurse, paying no attention.

Younger shook his head.

'Sorry, ma'am, can't let you do that,' said Littlemore.

'Doctor's orders,' she replied as if those magic words preempted all further discussion. She tapped the syringe, forced a drop of clear liquid from the needle, and was just about to inject Younger when Littlemore seized her wrist and led her, protesting, out the door.

'Thanks,' said Younger.

Littlemore noticed matches and a packet of cigarettes on a table. 'I thought you were out of smokes.'

'One left,' said Younger.

'Want it?'

'Sure, let's do all the clichés. I reject the morphine. You put a cigarette in my mouth.'

'Is that a yes or a no?'

'No,' said Younger.

'You're not going to die on us, Doc, are you?'

'Thinking about it.'

A silence followed. Younger's teeth began to chatter. With an effort, he brought the noise to a halt.

'How's the job?' asked Younger.

'Job's good,' said Littlemore. 'Don't have one, but it's good.'

'Family?'

'Family's good.'

A steady dripping came from the intravenous tubes on the other side of the bed. They could hear traffic outside the closed window.

'That's good,' said Younger.

'You wanted to talk to me?' asked Littlemore.

'Who told you that?'

'The Miss.'

'Ridiculous,' said Younger. His teeth began to rattle again.

'I'm lighting you that cigarette,' said Littlemore. He did so, fingers not as steady as they usually were. 'There you go.'

'Thanks.' Younger smoked; it settled his clattering teeth. 'You realize there's a silver lining.'

'Oh, yeah — what?'

'If I die fast enough, you'll be in the clear at my hearing tomorrow. They can't make you pay a man's bail bond posthumously.'

'I already talked to the DA,' said Littlemore. 'He dropped the charges against you.'

'Ah. Excellent. Then my death will be completely pointless.'

There was a long pause.

'Good thing I'm not a believer,' said Younger, smoke curling into his eyes.

Another silence.

'Not even to my own family,' said Younger.

'What's that?' asked Littlemore.

'Nothing,' said Younger. 'Ash?'

Littlemore took the cigarette, tamped it into an ashtray, and returned it to Younger's mouth.

'I wasn't kind, Jim,' said Younger quietly.

'What are you talking about?'

'I was never kind. Not to one person. Not even to my family.'

'Sure you were,' said Littlemore. 'You took care of your mom when she got sick. I remember.'

'No, I didn't,' said Younger. 'And my father. All he ever wanted from me was a show of respect. That's all. Never gave it to him.' He laughed through the smoke. 'Funny thing was I did respect him. I wasn't like you. You visit your father every weekend. You make him part of your life. You talk about Washington.'

'My dad?' said Littlemore.

'Yes.'

'My dad?'

Younger looked at him.

'My dad's a drunk,' said Littlemore. 'He's been a drunk his whole life. He cheated. And he was crooked. Got kicked off the force for taking bribes. They took his badge, took his gun. Everything I ever said about him was a lie.'

'I know.'

'I know you know,' said Littlemore. 'But you let me tell my lies.'

Neither spoke.

'That was kind,' added Littlemore.

Younger grimaced. His head jerked back; his teeth clenched. The cigarette broke off, and the lit end flew in a little arc like a miniature rocket, bouncing off the sheet near his chin, then falling to the floor. At the same time, the door to the room opened.

'I'll get that,' said Colette, hurrying in, brushing a hot red ember off the sheet and cleaning up the floor. She placed her palm wordlessly below Younger's lips. From his mouth, he let slip the unsmoked butt end of the cigarette, which fell into her hand. He began to shake again and sweat.

No one said anything.

At last Littlemore asked, 'You in a lot of pain, Doc?'

'I never understood it,' said Younger.

'What?' asked Littlemore.

'Why I was alive. Why any of us were.'

'You understand now?' asked Colette.

Younger nodded. 'Not happiness. Not meaning. It's just—'

He stopped.

'What?' asked Colette.

'War.'

'Only some people aren't fighting,' said Littlemore, remembering something Younger had once said to him.

'No. Everyone's fighting. And I know what it's between, this war.' He looked at Colette.

'What?' asked Littlemore.

'Too late,' said Younger. He lost control of his torso, which began to convulse. Fresh blood appeared on his bandages. Whether the expression on his face was another grimace or a smile, Littlemore couldn't tell.

Colette stared. Betty called for the nurse.

In the middle of the night, Colette knelt alone at Younger's bed. A candle burned on the table. 'Can you hear me?' she whispered.

His eyes were closed. He was still prone, his back rising and falling so shallowly there was hardly any respiration at all. His forehead was drenched. A hollow light glowed in his cheeks.

'If you die,' she said quietly, 'I'll never forgive you.'

He lay there.

Abruptly she stood, letting go his hand. 'Go ahead and die then if you're so weak,' she cried. 'I thought you were strong. You're a weakling. Nothing but a weakling.'

'Not very sympathetic,' he said softly, without opening his eyes.

She gasped and covered her mouth. She took his hand again and whispered in his ear. 'If you live,' she said, 'I'll do anything you want. I'll be your slave.'

'Promise?'

'I promise,' she whispered.

His eyes blinked open – and shut again. 'Incentive. That's good. Nevertheless, I'm dying. You have to go.'

'I'm not going anywhere.'

'Yes, you are,' he said, making a great effort to speak. 'I need to tell you what to do. I won't be awake long enough. Get Littlemore. Tell him to take you to a fishing tackle store.'

'What?'

'Break in if you need to. They'll have maggots – for bait. I should have thought of it before. Make sure they're from blowflies. Anything else will eat me alive. Tell the surgeon to open me up where the bullets entered. Cut as far down as he can. Drop the maggots in. Keep the incision open – use clamps. There's got to be plenty of air. Drain the wounds every couple of hours. After three days, clean them out.'

Dr Salvini, chief surgeon of the Washington Square Hospital, initially objected vigorously to the idea of embedding fly larvae to feast next to his patient's heart. But he knew Younger was dying, and in any event Colette gave him no choice.

'Um, what if they lay eggs in there?' Littlemore asked Colette early the next morning, peering at the seething stew in the troughs of Younger's back.

'First we have to hope they clean out the infection,' she answered quietly.

'I know,' said Littlemore, 'but what if the eggs hatch after he's sewed up?'

'They're larvae,' said Colette. 'They can't lay eggs. They only eat.'

'Oh – sounds good,' said Littlemore, swallowing.

How Younger held on over the next forty-eight hours, no one knew. His fever reached a hundred and five. He had no food, nearly no drink. They had to tie him to the bed rails because his convulsions were so violent.

On the third day, his fever broke. When the engorged maggots were flushed out of the wounds, Salvini was astonished to find clean, pink, healthy tissue, with all the necrotic detritus and seepage gone.

They took another set of X-rays. This time, Colette herself computed the depth and location of the bullet fragments – correctly to within a tenth of a centimeter. The bullets had indeed mushroomed, but they were stable and largely intact. Salvini didn't even have to break any more of Younger's ribs to extract them.

The following morning, fresh air and dappled sunlight poured in through the window of Younger's hospital room, the curtains of which were now thrown open, affording a pleasant view of Washington Square Park and its autumnal trees. Younger was awake, propped up by pillows. He had lost weight, but his skin had regained its color, and he could move again.

Colette came in, radiant, carrying a baguette and a paper bag filled with other groceries. 'I found a French bakery,' she said. 'I brought you croissants. Can we live here?'

'Where did you get those diamonds?' he asked, looking at her choker.

Colette shook her head, breaking the baguette. 'These hideous diamonds. I can't get them off. I've even taken my baths with them.'

'I like you in them,' replied Younger. 'I command you to keep them on. Day and night.'

'But I don't want to,' she said.

'Some slave,' he answered. 'Come here.'

She bent to him. Younger reached behind her and – with infuriating male handiness – unclasped the necklace. She kissed his lips. He handed her a telegram brought by Officer Roederheusen from the Commodore Hotel. Colette read it:

26 NOV. 1920

BOY CURED. HAVE BOOKED CABIN FOR HIM S.S.
SUSQUEHANNA ARRIVING NEW YORK 23 DECEMBER IN
COMPANY OF YOUR FRIEND OKTAVIAN KINSKY. PLEASE
ADVISE IF THIS PLAN SUITABLE.

FREUD

Chapter Twenty-two

O N December twenty-third, in the icy early morning harbor air, below an overcast sky, they stamped their feet – Younger and Colette; Jimmy and Betty Littlemore – and waited for the steamship *Susquehanna*. Winter had come. A dusting of overnight snow had given New York City a fairy-tale veneer, belied by the heavy, forbidding waters of the port, dotted with skins of fruit and other refuse.

The men stood on the dock. Colette and Betty conversed near the harbor buildings, which sheltered them from the sharp winds. Younger, whose rib cage was trussed in bandages below his suit, asked the detective for the time.

'Quarter of eight,' said Littlemore, rubbing his hands for warmth. 'Where's your watch?'

'Sold it.'

'Why?'

'To pay the hospital,' said Younger. 'And to pay Freud for Luc's ticket.'

'Does Colette know?'

'She knows I'm cleaned out,' said Younger.

'I can top that. Betty and I are packing up the apartment. Had to choose between paying the rent and feeding the kids. I was for paying the rent, but you know women. At least you can make some dough as a doctor.'

Younger smoked. 'You'll go back to the Police Department. You're a captain in Homicide.'

Littlemore shook his head. 'Department's on a payroll freeze. Maybe next spring.'

'Maybe we could rob a bank,' said Younger. 'How's that girl – the one Brighton was keeping prisoner?'

'Albina? Better. Colette visiting with her helped a lot. Want to know how it all started?'

'Sure.'

'There were three sisters – Amelia, Albina, and Quinta. They all went to work for Brighton in 1917. Within a couple years, girls at his factories started taking sick – their teeth are falling out, they're having trouble walking, there's something wrong with their blood.'

'Anemia,' said Younger.

'Brighton knows it's radium, so he builds a kind of hospital room upstairs in his factory where his own doctor would examine them – except it wasn't a doctor; it was Lyme. When that growth first showed up on Quinta's neck, Lyme told her she had syphilis. Brighton magnanimously offered to treat her for free in the infirmary, but Lyme was just doping her up. Amelia was next. Her teeth were coming loose. But she was tough. When Lyme told her she had syphilis too, she knew it was a lie. She went to Albina and told her something terrible was happening. They snuck Quinta out of the infirmary and got the heck out of the factory. Brighton had men all over looking for them. The girls knew it and were scared. So they went into hiding. Amelia took a bunch of scissors from the factory, which they carried around just in case. Then they heard about Colette. They heard she'd been telling people that the radium paint factories were killing people, and they thought maybe she could help them. You know the rest.'

'Why did Albina take her shirt off in front of Luc?'

'After she followed the Miss to Connecticut? It was her skin: her skin was glowing in the dark. She wanted Colette to see it, but the Miss wasn't there, so she showed Luc instead. She was afraid Brighton had men watching for her in New Haven; that's why she ran. She was right too. They caught her and brought her back to New York. Darn it – I should have known Amelia's tooth had radium in it.'

'Why?' asked Younger.

'Remember how your radiation detector gizmo lit up when you pointed it at me – right at my chest – in front of the hotel?'

Younger saw it: 'I gave you the tooth.'

'It was in my vest pocket,' said Littlemore.

The two men stood silently for some time. 'What about your senator?' asked Younger.

'Fall? *He's* doing fine. Going to be in Harding's Cabinet. Not Secretary of State – they're going to give him some less high-profile position, but still in the Cabinet.'

'Who says crime doesn't pay?' said Younger.

'He'll pay. I had a look through Samuels's books. I found a hundred-thousand-dollar cash payment from Brighton to Fall; I'll nail him with it sooner or later. But for now nobody can touch him. He's got something on Harding.'

'What?'

Littlemore looked around to be sure they were out of anyone's earshot. 'Harding's got a woman problem. The Republican Party just paid twenty-five thousand dollars to keep one gal quiet. Now there's another girl in bed with him, and only Fall knows about her.'

'How?'

'Because she works for him. Good-looking girl. Ever since I quit as a T-man, she's been feeding me all kinds of Washington secrets. She says Houston's got something to tell us.'

'Us?'

'Yeah – you and me.'

The men were quiet again for a while.

'You were right about the machine gun,' said Littlemore.

'How's that?'

'Turns out the bombers blew up Wall Street twelve hours after they were supposed to. So they had a little problem: the manhole was locked.

There they were in the alley, with all that gold and no place for it to go. One of them runs across the street and fires his machine gun into a wall of the Morgan Bank, trying to get somebody to open up the manhole. Apparently it worked. I told Commissioner Enright about it, and he sent Lamont a letter telling him to keep those bullet holes unrepaired. He says Morgan can tell everybody it's a memento, but if they repair the holes, he'll arrest them for destroying evidence.' Littlemore looked out to sea. 'Where's that ship?'

'Late.'

'It's funny,' said Littlemore. 'People are already forgetting September sixteenth. When it happened, it was like nothing would ever be the same. The country was frozen. Life was going to be different forever.'

'At least we didn't go to war. A manufactured war on a country that had nothing to do with the bombing – God knows the price we would have paid for that, if you hadn't stopped it.'

'Yeah – I should be famous,' said Littlemore. 'Instead I'm broke.'

'We could go to India.'

'Why India?'

'Poverty is holy in India.' Younger ground out his cigarette under a heel. 'So no one gets punished for it. The bombing.'

'I don't know about that. Where did you and I first see Drobac?'

'At the Commodore Hotel – after they kidnapped Colette,' answered Younger.

'Nope.'

Younger shook his head: 'Where then?'

'A horse-drawn wagon passed you and the Miss and me when we were walking down Nassau Street the morning of September sixteenth. Remember – about three minutes before the bomb went off? With a load so heavy the mare could barely drag it behind her? Drobac was the guy driving that wagon.'

'*Bonjour*,' said Luc, looking up at his sister that night.

The *Susquehanna* had arrived twelve hours late. The boy, sprucer and cleaner than Younger had ever seen him, had just come down the gangway, hand in hand with Oktavian Kinsky, into the bright electric lights of the dock. There were no stars in the sky, nor any moon. The cloud cover was too thick.

For an instant Colette was paralyzed. It was the first time she'd heard her brother speak in six years. She could not fit the voice to Luc; it was too mature, too self-possessed, as if a stranger had taken over her brother's body and were speaking through his mouth. Then somehow the voice and the steady eyes and the serious face came together all at once: it was he. She opened her arms and gathered him in.

'*Bonjour?*' she repeated, hugging him. 'How can it be *bonjour* in the middle of the night, you goose? And your hair – you let them cut it?'

Luc nodded gravely.

Oktavian greeted Younger and Colette – the Littlemores having departed hours before – like long-lost friends. 'I'm here to start a fleet of hired cars,' Oktavian declared. 'That sort of thing is not frowned on in America, I'm told.'

'On the contrary,' agreed Younger. 'And you'll have to fight off the American ladies, Count, at least the ones I'm going to introduce you to. They worship aristocracy.'

'But you abolished your titles of nobility over a hundred years ago,' said Oktavian.

'People always want what they can't have,' said Younger.

'Not me,' said Colette.

That night, they stayed with Mrs Meloney, who generously opened her home to them. Colette had persuaded Mrs Meloney to help the dial workers at the luminous-paint factories – and the good woman had taken to the business with all her usual industry and alacrity.

At Brighton's Manhattan plant, the dial painters were being tested for radiation exposure. Over half the girls were radioactive, especially in their teeth and jaws; several of them glowed in the dark. Pointing of brushes with the mouth had been forbidden. Protective gloves were made mandatory. Radiation detectors were being installed. Brighton's bank accounts had been seized, and his assets were being held for the benefit of girls who developed illnesses as a result of their work in his factories.

Younger and Colette put Luc to bed. 'I have something to tell you,' the boy said to his sister.

'I know,' answered Colette. 'Dr Freud told us.'

'He told you?'

'Only that you had something to say. He wouldn't tell us what.'

'But now that I'm here,' said Luc, 'I don't want to say it anymore.'

'Sleep for now,' replied Colette. 'Tomorrow you can tell us.'

Tomorrow, however, the boy was still less talkative. Oktavian took rooms at a modest but decent hotel in Manhattan and began looking into the letting and buying of livery vehicles. They said goodbye to him and that evening boarded a train for Boston.

As the train rumbled quietly north, a light snow fell outside their window. 'Luc,' said Colette, 'now is a good time.'

The boy shook his head.

'You can whisper it in my ear, if you want,' said Colette.

'Rubbish,' declared Younger. 'He can't whisper it. He's not a child. He's lived through a war. He saved our lives. You're a man, Luc, not a little girl. Stop this nonsense and speak up.'

Luc frowned. He looked taken aback – and undecided.

Younger pulled out a letter from his jacket. 'This is from Dr Freud,' said Younger. 'You trust Dr Freud, don't you?'

Luc nodded.

'He warns us that you might go quiet in America,' Younger went on. 'He says you'll be worried that your sister doesn't want to hear what you have to say.'

Luc stared steadily at Younger.

'He says we should remind you that he's spent thirty years of his life telling people what they didn't want to hear. He says that the fact that someone doesn't want to hear the truth is very rarely a good reason for silence. He also says that your sister does want to hear what you have to say.'

Luc turned his gaze on Colette. 'You do?' he asked quietly.

'Very much,' said Colette.

'You don't know what it is,' said Luc.

'Whatever it is, I want to hear it.'

'No, you don't.'

'I do,' said Colette.

'No, you don't.'

'Yes, I do.'

'Wonderful,' said Younger. 'The boy speaks for the first time in his life, and the two of you quarrel like schoolchildren.'

'Father was a coward.' Luc had spoken simply but definitively.

Colette started. Her fingers clenched. 'Father? A coward?'

The boy looked at the snowflakes melting on the train's window. 'I was at the house when the Germans came,' he said.

A shadow fell across his sister's face, and she began a question: 'You mean—?'

'Yes,' Luc interrupted her.

'But we—'

'Were in the carpenter's basement,' he completed her sentence. 'I left in the middle of the night. You didn't hear me. I went back to the house. I looked in through the window next to the shed.'

Colette stopped moving altogether. She may even have stopped breathing.

'German soldiers were inside with Father. Three of them. One was tall with blond hair. Do you remember where Mother and Grandmother were hiding?'

'Yes.'

'Father was saying to them, "Please don't kill me. Please don't kill me." He started to cry.'

'That doesn't make him a coward,' she answered.

441

'Father pointed to the cabinet. I think he was trying to show the Germans where the silver was. They opened the cabinet, but I guess they didn't care about the silver. They turned around and yelled at Father again. The tall one aimed his rifle at him. Father pleaded with them not to shoot.' The train rattled around a curve. 'Then Father pointed to the rug.'

'You saw him point to it?'

'He pointed to it and then he got up and he pulled it away so the German soldiers could see the trapdoor.'

Colette said nothing.

'They opened it. They found Mama. And Nana. They hit Mama on the face. Then the tall one shot Father. Another one shot Nana.'

'What did you do?' she asked quietly.

'I ran into the house. Mama was screaming. They were holding her down on the floor, pulling at her dress. One of the Germans hit me, I think. I don't remember anything else. The next morning—'

'Don't,' said Colette, putting her arms around her brother and closing her eyes. 'I know.'

'I didn't want to say anything,' said Luc.

They spoke little for the remainder of the ride. Colette said almost nothing at all. In Younger's coat pocket was the letter from Freud, which he hadn't shown her. Colette therefore hadn't seen the little folded note that Freud had included along with it; nor had she read the letter's last paragraph, which said:

Miss Rousseau is keeping something from her brother as well. I believe I know what it is, but it's not for me to say. She'll tell you in her own time. When she does, give her the enclosed note.

As ever,
Freud

After they had arrived at Younger's house in Boston and shown Luc his new bedroom and tucked him in, Younger and Colette went to their own bedroom. She let him undress her, which he liked to do. Then he took off his shirt, revealing the thick white bandaging wrapped round and round his chest.

'Is it painful?' she asked.

'Only if I breathe,' he said. 'I'm joking. I don't feel it at all.'

'Can you?' she whispered.

He could. She had to cover her mouth with his hand to keep from waking Luc. She dug her fingernails into his arms. He thought he might be hurting her, but she begged him not to stop.

A long while later, she spoke quietly in the dark: 'I didn't want to say anything either.'

'You knew?' said Younger. 'What your father had done?'

She nodded.

'You saw it too?' he asked.

'No,' she said. 'Father told me himself. The next morning. He was still alive when we found them. He confessed to me. He pleaded with me to forgive him.'

A clock ticked.

'I didn't,' she said. 'I couldn't. Then he was gone.'

Tears ran down her cheeks in silence; Younger could feel them on his chest.

'God help me,' she whispered. 'I didn't forgive my own father.'

'The oldest bear the most,' said Younger.

'Now you know,' she said to him, wiping her eyes. 'Now you know my very last secret.'

Hours later, at daybreak, he was buttoning a shirt when Colette, still lying in bed, asked him a question: 'Did I do everything wrong?'

'I have something for you,' he answered. 'From Freud.'

He gave her the note. She sat up and read it, holding the bed sheet over her chest. She stared at the note a long time before handing it back to him:

My dear Miss Rousseau,

If you are reading this, it means, assuming I'm right, you have revealed to Younger that you knew of your father's unfortunate conduct before your brother told you of it. Do not condemn your father too harshly. A man is not to be judged by his actions at gunpoint.

Neither should you judge yourself. True, if you had told your brother what you knew, his condition might possibly have abated sooner. But it might also, perversely, have become more entrenched. The fact is you each tried to protect the other from a truth the other already knew. This was irony, not tragedy.

You may have perceived that your brother has harbored a resentment against you. That is natural. He may have disliked you, or thought he did, for not knowing what he knew (as he believed) and thereby making him keep it a secret. Children expect adults to know what they know; when we disappoint them, they think the worse of us. But then even as adults we eventually come to scorn those from whom we have kept the truth, and we resent those for whom we have made the largest sacrifices. For these reasons, if you are even now undecided about whether to tell your brother that you knew his secret all along, you know what my advice to you would be.

There is one more thing I want to say. You wondered in my presence why you didn't kill the man who murdered your parents. It was from just this fact that I deduced what you were hiding. The reason is simple. You felt, even if you didn't know it, that you would be insulting your father if you did what he lacked the courage to do. It was kindness toward your father that motivated you, not kindness to the murderer. (This also leads me to believe that you feel you wronged your father some time in the past, although the nature of this wrong I'm unable to decipher.) Fortunately, at that moment you were with a man who didn't labor under your compunctions. If you are half as wise as I believe you to be, you won't refuse that man's affections a second time.

Freud

★   ★   ★

On December 25, 1920, a long-distance telephone connection was established between a private home in Washington, DC, and another in Boston, Massachusetts. It was almost midnight.

'Is that you, Jimmy?' asked Colette. She and Younger both had their ears to the receiver. A Christmas tree stood in front of them, decorated with toy soldiers and glittering hand-painted paper globes.

'It sure is, Miss,' answered Littlemore, voice crackling, 'and Betty too. Is Doc there?'

'I'm here,' said Younger. 'What is it?'

'You wouldn't believe this house we're in. Guy who owns it owns the *Washington Post*. Wife owns the Hope Diamond. It's a big Christmas party. Secretary Houston invited us down. Harding's here. There's so many senators you'd think it was the Capitol. Lamont's here too. Looking pretty blue – like a guy who lost millions at the track. But you know what? Things are picking up. In the country, I mean. They got dancing girls here from New York. They're playing a new kind of music. Something in the air. The twenties may not be as bad as I thought.'

'You took the Treasury job again?' asked Younger.

'Nope. We're just guests. Betty's the one who likes Washington now. Probably because Harding's been all over her the whole night.'

'What about you and that Mrs Cross?' replied Betty.

'Not interested,' said Jimmy.

'*She* is,' replied his wife. 'The harlot.'

'Did you call for any particular reason?' asked Younger.

'It's Christmas, Doc.'

'Merry Christmas.'

'Everybody's giving out presents here,' said Littlemore.

'You're not the only ones,' replied Younger, looking at the diamond on Colette's finger, which had once belonged to his mother.

'Guess what?' said Littlemore. 'You got a present too.'

'I did?' asked Younger. 'From whom?'

'Houston. He asked me if you found the gold with me. I said yes. Then he asked me if you were a law officer.'

'Why?'

'Well, they finally dug it all up, and Lamont swears the gold doesn't belong to Morgan, and Houston swears it doesn't belong to the Treasury, so officially it doesn't belong to anybody. It's unclaimed. They got laws for that. They call it treasure law. The law is that unclaimed gold goes to the finder – unless he's a law officer. I told him you definitely weren't a law officer. Told him you were more a law breaker.'

There was silence on the line.

'Did you hear me, Doc?'

'*All* the gold goes to the finder?'

'Unless he's a law officer,' said Littlemore.

'How much was there?'

'A little over four million.'

'I can't accept it,' said Younger. 'It belongs to the United States. Tell him I give it back to the Treasury.'

'I already did.'

'You did?' asked Younger.

'I knew you wouldn't accept it.'

'Yes, but you might have let me exercise my own generosity.'

'There's something you don't know,' said Littlemore. 'Back in October, Lamont over at Morgan tried to sneak into the country two million dollars of Russian contraband gold. Customs caught him, but Houston secretly had the Treasury take delivery of it. That was illegal, but Houston didn't want Morgan to take a two-million-dollar loss; he thought it would be bad for the country. Houston was going to have the Treasury pay Morgan for that gold until he found out Lamont was behind the September sixteenth robbery.'

'What are you talking about, Littlemore?' asked Younger.

'Bear with me here. Houston's not going to pay Lamont a dime for the Russian gold now. The Treasury's just going to keep it. Lamont can't object, because the Russian gold was contraband in the first place. So Houston only needs two million more for the Treasury to be made whole.'

'I think I'm following you,' said Younger. 'The Treasury is short two million dollars in gold. What's the point?'

'Point is, when I told Houston you wouldn't accept all that gold we found, he says, well, the Treasury's only short two million, so why don't we use the European rule?'

'Which is?'

'Finder gets half. Government gets half.'

Again there was silence.

'I'm not taking anything you don't get,' said Younger. 'As a matter of fact, you weren't a law enforcement officer when we found it. Houston had just fired you.'

'I mentioned that to him.'

'What did he say?' asked Younger.

'You and I are splitting two million dollars of gold. Merry Christmas.'

AUTHOR'S NOTE

THE WALL STREET bombing of September 16, 1920, would remain the most destructive act of terrorism in the United States until the Oklahoma bombing of 1995. Unlike the latter, however, and unlike the attacks of September 11, 2001, the Wall Street bombing was never solved. Its perpetrators were never caught. No one was ever prosecuted. In 1944 the Federal Bureau of Investigation concluded that the explosion 'would appear' to have been 'the work of Italian anarchists or Italian terrorists,' but this was conjecture, and the identity of those responsible remains unknown to this day.

Let me emphasize that my 'solution' to this mystery is imaginary. There is absolutely no historical evidence for the notion that the true masterminds behind the bombing were Senator Albert Bacon Fall, Thomas W. Lamont of the J. P. Morgan Co., or former Treasury Secretary William G. McAdoo. These men are real historical figures; the latter two are properly credited with significant public service and important accomplishments. The background facts that I recount about them are true. My story, however, about their responsibility for the Wall Street bombing is just that – a story.

What then is real and what imaginary in *The Death Instinct*? The principle I tried to follow was simple. The action of the book – the perils of its protagonists, the evildoing they uncover – is fiction. The world in which that action takes place is fact.

Thus the backdrop of events and circumstances against which *The Death Instinct* unfolds is true. At the very moment of the explosion on Wall Street, and directly opposite, almost a billion dollars in United States gold was indeed in transit from the old Sub-Treasury to the adjacent Assay Office via a wooden overhead bridge. A few miles away, a hundred working women would have been painting luminous watch dials, using their lips to point their poisonous brushes. In Washington, DC, Senator Fall was in fact machinating, nearly successfully, to bring about a war with Mexico that would have enriched himself and his powerful friends in the oil industry. Meanwhile, in war-devastated Europe, Sigmund Freud had just arrived at a new understanding of the human soul, according to which every individual is born with two fundamental instincts – one aiming at life and love, the other at death.

On the other hand, the theft of the Treasury's gold described in *The Death Instinct* is invented. The United States has always denied that any gold was lost. The accepted account is that the simultaneity of the bombing and the gold transfer was mere coincidence and that the workmen moving the precious metal happened to take their lunch break, closing up the heavy doors on either side of the bridge, moments before the explosion.

From the great occurrences like the bombing, to the *petite Curie* radiological truck driven by Colette, the world described in *The Death Instinct* is as real as I could make it, every detail based on actual historical sources. Readers who learn in these pages that thousands of soldiers were needlessly killed on November 11, 1918 – *after* their commanding officers already knew of the armistice – can be confident that this fact is documented in numerous reliable accounts. If I quote a newspaper, the quotation is verbatim or, if edited, only very slightly for style, without alteration of content. If I offer particular images from the September sixteenth explosion, every one of them is drawn from contemporaneous accounts: a taxi was in fact blown into the air; a woman's head was severed from her body; the pockmarked walls of the Morgan Bank can still be seen today. Even the outrageous forgeries I describe, purporting to show that the Mexican government had paid bribes to three anti-interventionist United States senators, are historically based, although these forgeries would not be circulated until a few years later, in another failed effort to spur an American invasion of Mexico.

To be sure, I can't vouch for the truth of the historical materials on which I rely. When I quote Toynbee describing German atrocities in France in 1914, readers can be sure the quotation is exact, but they can't know – and I don't know – whether Toynbee's account is itself correct. The ultimate validity of historical sources must be left to historians.

Nevertheless, some of the most incredible events described in *The Death Instinct* are not open to serious question. The remarkable tale of Edwin Fischer, for example, is established fact. His advance warnings, repeated to many different people, of a bombing on Wall Street after the close of business on September fifteenth or on the sixteenth are still unexplained. (All the peculiar details I mention about him – his four tennis championships, his multiple suits, his statement that he learned of the bombing 'out of the air,' his subsequent detention in an asylum, and so on – are completely factual.) If Fischer had advance knowledge of the bombing, which historians do not accept, it would suggest that there were men behind the attack belonging to a circle quite different from that of the penurious Italian anarchists usually said to be responsible.

Although it is not well known, Fischer was, as mentioned in my book, indeed in contact with federal government agents several years before the bombing. But my account of his further dealings with the Bureau of Investigation, along with the story told at the end of *The Death Instinct*, in which Littlemore figures out that the voices Fischer heard 'out of the air' came to him outside the Oyster Bar in Grand Central Terminal, is entirely fictitious. It is a fact, however, that whispers can be heard across that concourse at the spot I describe.

The Marie Curie Radium Fund, led by the indomitable Mrs William B. Meloney, eventually succeeded in purchasing a gram of radium for

Madame Curie, who traveled to the United States in 1921 to receive the gift from President Harding. In addition to being the Sorbonne's first woman professor and the first winner of two Nobel Prizes – one in Physics in 1903, the other in Chemistry in 1911 – Madame Curie remains today the only woman to have accomplished the double-Nobel feat and the only person to have won Nobel Prizes in two different scientific fields. Radiation exposure very probably caused her cataracts in 1920 and almost certainly caused her death from aplastic anemia (or perhaps leukemia) in 1934.

While my protagonists – Younger, Littlemore, Colette, and Luc – are fictional, many of those with whom they interact are not, such as Police Commissioner Enright, Treasury Secretary Houston, New York City Mayor Hylan, 'Big Bill' Flynn, and Dr Walter Prince (of the American Society for Psychical Research). There was also a real Mrs Grace Cross who apparently had an affair with Warren Harding, but the character bearing her name is not otherwise based on the actual person.

Arnold Brighton is a fictitious character. Edward Doheny was the real oilman who backed Fall's efforts to make war on Mexico and paid him at least $100,000 in bribes, for which Fall would later become the first Cabinet member ever to be imprisoned for a crime committed while in office. The real head of the US Radium Corporation in 1920, at whose New Jersey factory Quinta Maggia McDonald and her sisters worked, was Arthur Roeder. There is absolutely no reason to believe that either Doheny or Roeder had anything to do with the Wall Street bombing.

By contrast, the tragic poisoning of the radium dial painters is well established. In several respects the true facts are worse than my description. Up to one hundred twelve dial painters may have died as a result of 'pointing' their brushes with their lips – a practice not abolished until 1925. Many more suffered painful, debilitating illnesses.

The Maggia sisters – Quinta, Amelia, and Albina – were among the victims. (Although I use these three women's names in my book, my characters do not correspond to the real-life women, and the story I tell about their escape from the radium factory, their being hunted, and their efforts to communicate with Colette, is complete invention.) Amelia died in 1922, the first of the dial painters known to have perished from radium poisoning. When her body was exhumed in 1927, it was still radioactive. A handful of women, including Quinta and Albina, sued US Radium in the mid-twenties, but the law did not treat them well. In 1928, terminally ill, Quinta received a modest cash payment and an extravagant $600 annuity 'for life'; she died less than two years later. Albina lived until 1946.

The corporation apparently suppressed or even falsified a report demonstrating that its officers knew of radium's danger to the dial painters. At one point a medical specialist from Columbia University volunteered to conduct independent examinations of the complaining women and concluded that they were either in excellent health or that their symptoms were due to syphilis or other illnesses unrelated to their employment. That specialist, Frederick Flinn, neglected to mention that he was not actually a doctor – and that he was being paid by US Radium. My character Frederick Lyme engages in similar misdeeds, but his further nefarious conduct is imaginary.

Sigmund Freud first articulated his theory of the death instinct in a short book called *Beyond the Pleasure Principle*, published in 1920. Understood as a drive of pure aggression, a kind of lust for killing and destruction, the notion of a death instinct might raise questions about the goodness of human nature, but would otherwise be simple enough to comprehend. Freud insisted, however, that the instinct is fundamentally and originally directed at the self's own destruction. As a result, his death drive is regarded as a much more difficult and controversial proposition – although self-destructiveness is surely a phenomenon almost as familiar as aggression.

By and large, the psychoanalytic world since Freud has been happy to forget about the death instinct or at any rate to deemphasize it. Melanie Klein was an important exception; so was Jacques Lacan, who considered the death instinct central to psychoanalysis, although he sought to prize the instinct free from the biological foundations Freud had given it. Another exception is André Green, also a French psycho-analyst, whose excellent recent book on the death instinct – *Pourquoi les pulsions de destruction ou de mort?* (Éditions du Panama, 2007) – by contrast explicitly connects Freud's theory to apoptosis, the biological process of 'programmed' cell death or 'cell suicide.' I have Freud draw the same connection in a conversation with Colette, perhaps a little anachronistically. Although apoptosis was known to scientists by the late nineteenth century (called at that time 'chromatolysis'), its connec-tion to cancer was not established until the late twentieth.

Readers familiar with Freud's work will recognize the famous *fort-da* game that figures so prominently in *Beyond the Pleasure Principle*. The unnamed boy who plays the game in Freud's essay has been identified as Freud's grandson Ernst; his mother was the Sophie whose death Freud so deeply mourned in 1920. There is another place in my book where Luc assumes the role of one of Freud's grandsons. The anecdote I tell about Freud, Luc, and the beggar feigning epilepsy was told to me by Clement Freud – brother of the painter Lucian Freud – and appears in the late Sir Clement's auto-biography, *Freud Ego*.

The astonishing story Freud recounts to Colette and Younger demon-strating the accuracy of one of his dream interpretations – in which Freud correctly deduces that a patient witnessed an affair between the patient's nurse and a family groomsman when the patient was about four years old – is entirely true, or at any rate is attested to by the patient herself, Princess Marie Bonaparte. Princess Marie, however, did not begin her consultation with Freud until 1925, so the story is not in correct time sequence in my book. As in *The Interpretation of Murder*, many of Freud's statements in *The Death Instinct* are drawn from his actual writings. Although it is common today to refer to Freud's death drive by the name of 'Thanatos' (after a Greek god of death), Freud never did so in his writings, and accordingly that term does not appear in my pages. He does refer to the death goddess Atropos in 'The Theme of the Three Caskets,' a 1913 essay that contains the key to the symbolism of *The Death Instinct*. Freud lived in Vienna until 1938, when he narrowly escaped Nazi persecution. He died in England in 1939.

ACKNOWLEDGMENTS

I RAN UP too many debts writing this book to name them all. First and foremost, my beautiful wife, Amy, to whom I already owed nearly everything good in my life, made countless improvements, small and large, to the manuscript. My daughters, Sophia and Louisa, provided wisdom beyond their years and saved me from numerous embarrassments. Sarah Bilston, James Bundy, Alexis Contant, Anne Dailey, Susan Birke Fiedler, Paul Fiedler, Dan Knudsen, Daniel Markovits, Katherine Oberembt, Sylvia Smoller, Walter Austerer, and Lina Tetelbaum were incredibly generous, ingenious, perceptive readers. I'm grateful as well to an incomparable agent, Suzanne Gluck, my publisher at Riverhead, Geoff Kloske, and to painstaking editors, Mary-Anne Harrington and Jake Morrissey. My thanks in addition to Jennifer Barth, Diana and Leon Chua, Kathleen Brown-Dorato, Nancy Greenberg, Tony Kronman, Marina Santilli, Jordan Smoller, Anne Tofflemire, and Lucy Wang, all of whom helped more with this book than they can know.